BATTLE

SWORDS
OF THE
KING

Charlene Newcomb

BATTLE SCARS III: SWORDS OF THE KING

Published by
KindleDirect Publishing

Cover art design by ProBookCovers.com
Map ©2018 by Blue X Entertainment
Interior design by the Author

ISBN: 978-1980585848

For my family

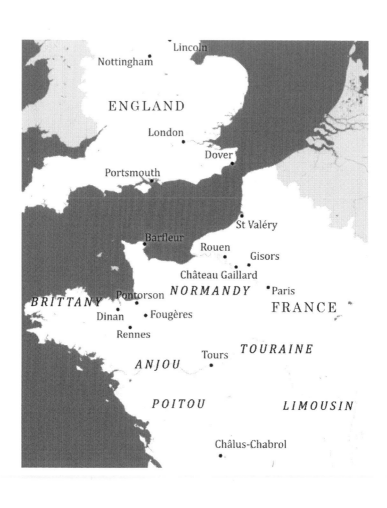

one

Count John's spy blustered into the tavern.

Henry de Grey smothered the candle flame on the trestle and leaned back into the shadows, not surprised the loyal Norman crowd acknowledged the man by name. Merchants, smith, and tanner raised their cups when the knight shouted, "God save the King!"

The drinking establishment was a popular haven for King Richard's men during the quiet winter months. Best ale and wine this side of Rouen, willing *ladies*—Henry's friends claimed—and locals eager to take the knights' coins in games of chance and brave their repeated tales of the war with the French. But no one suspected Richard's steadfast knight earned a few deniers in the pay of the Count of Mortain.

Henry clasped his mug and peered over the rim. The scent of honey and oak wafted from the brew, hiding the stale smell of ale-soaked rushes on the floor. Aimery had come alone and it was well past sunset and some four hours from the king's camp. This was a rendezvous—one Henry would not want to disrupt.

His gaze swept the smoky room as Aimery cut a path towards the hearth. There, near the fire...the other spy. Henry mustered a smile. *Hello, Robin.*

Robin du Louviers, bless his soul, was the king's man in John's camp. King Richard and his brother Count John were allies, but kept close watch on each other. Court politics and intrigue—Henry despised them. In times of war, or peace, for that matter, they were unavoidable, even among members of the same family. What had the king called it? A circle of lies and deceit, a delicate and well-established web of communications that everyone knew existed even if they did not know all the players. Madness. Pure madness.

A serving girl brought Henry another ale and, smiling suggestively, combed her fingers through his dark wind-tousled hair. She'd have been pleased to offer him more, but he waved her away without meeting her eyes. He had no time and no inclination. She was blonde and blue-eyed, but she wasn't Stephan. He stared past her, counting the hours until he would be in his lover's arms again. Hands on hips, the girl gaped at him, and walked away with a sigh.

Across the room, Aimery slipped a rolled parchment to Robin. The two knights spoke amiably, flirted with the serving girl, drank and joked. Henry wished he could hear them, but he would find out soon. Robin laughed—he played the part of John's crony better than most men. Henry studied his old friend. He was good, but even Robin knew John didn't trust him. Not when he, Henry, and Stephan foiled John's plot to usurp King Richard's throne two years past. Henry sniffed the air and scowled, the stink of John's treason as foul as rotting offal from a butcher's shop.

Aimery rose and disappeared up the stairs with the serving girl. Robin yawned and sat back in his chair, long legs stretched out towards the fire. Hay-colored hair brushed his broad shoulders and framed his face. Eyes closed, his chin fell to his chest, but a smile curled his lip as Henry drew next to him.

"A good thing we both serve the king." Robin snorted. He cracked his eyes, scrutinizing Henry's muddy boots and ruddy cheeks.

"A good thing," Henry said with a quick smile. "Does John have anyone watching you whilst you meet with his man?"

"Not on this day. Tomorrow, who knows? Join me for an ale. Aimery will be occupied the rest of the night." Robin swallowed his drink. "You've been sitting across the room for a while and not on my account, so what brings you here? Is Stephan with you?"

Henry's cheeks colored. He could reconnoiter enemy territory to track French troops, but put him in a tavern? He had let his guard down, and chose not to make excuses. "I've been on the road near a fortnight. Headed back to Rouen." He straddled the bench across from Robin and lowered his voice. "Stephan better be there when I arrive."

Chuckling, Robin's gaze flicked to the stairs. "Aimery has just come from Rouen. If Stephan is with the king, he'll be there."

"What did Aimery steal to share with John?" Henry asked.

Robin tapped his sleeve where the parchment was hidden. "Aimery claims this is one of a dozen messages to be delivered to King Richard's barons throughout the kingdom, but not one meant for John. I was hoping you might tell me what it contains. Spring campaigns against the French? The king's plan to defy the archbishop and build that castle on the Rock? I'd prefer no surprises when I hand this to John."

Henry scrubbed his close-cropped beard wearily. Robin had every reason to be wary of John. He'd warned Henry and Stephan that John had neither forgiven nor forgotten. John would seek revenge—no matter that they fought on the same side now.

"Mayhap I do know," Henry said. "I've just come from Dinan."

Robin's blue eyes narrowed. "The king sent you to the Breton court?"

Henry nodded. "With a summons for the Duchess Constance and his nephew Arthur to join him in Rouen. King Richard wants to get to know the boy, make him his ward." Everyone knew John wanted to be king should Richard die without an heir, and young Arthur could upset those plans. "He will send word to John, but not until the gathering is underway. They should arrive in Rouen near the twenty-first of March."

"Conceal a ducal train crossing from one end of Normandy to the other? Impossible." Robin poured a round of ale for himself and Henry.

Henry clenched his jaw. "John could make trouble."

The fire crackled, spitting cinders at Robin's feet. "John must stay in the king's good graces, but he won't wait for Richard's invitation. He'll ride to Rouen and be there with smiles to greet the duchess and young Arthur." Robin raised his cup. "To the king!" he shouted.

The men in the tavern echoed Robin's toast, praise for Richard's successes spilling as freely as the ale.

A burly man with arms the size of logs slapped

Robin's back good-naturedly. "Thought King Richard banished you, Carpenter."

Henry cringed for his friend, but Robin didn't take offense. "I serve Count John who faithfully bends the knee to his brother, our king. And that's *Sir* Robin to you, Smith." He was smiling and his voice slurred. He swayed slightly, but Henry knew he wasn't in his cups. Robin gently punched the big man's shoulder. "He only took my land," he added.

"That's true," someone murmured.

"A shame," another said.

Smith's eyes sparkled and he thrust his finger at Robin's chest. "You were at the king's side for years, and on crusade. He'll come round. Give you what you deserve."

"We fight on the same side now," Robin said, tipping his head at Henry. They were the only men in the room who knew Robin had never once betrayed the king. "God keep the king."

"King Richard!" the men shouted and lifted their cups in another toast.

Henry drained his ale. John *had* sworn fealty to Richard after begging his brother's forgiveness for his treason while the king had been on crusade. He had redeemed himself in the king's eyes, proven his loyalty time and again these last two years. He had little choice if he wanted to be Richard's heir. Richard may have forgiven him—something Henry would never understand—but John might never escape his brother's suspicion.

But why else would Richard invite his nine-year-old nephew to court to become his ward, if not to groom the young boy for the crown?

John would never let Arthur be king. To say John

would rejoice at this news would be to claim that pigs could fly.

"Kill the boy." Count John crumpled the parchment Robin had handed him and sent it spinning into the air. His dark eyes sliced past Robin to find the man behind him. "Captain, choose two of your best men to accompany Sir Robin. I want that boy out of my way."

Cold sweat tickled Robin's neck despite the brisk winds that rippled the canvas wall of the command tent. Serving the king's brother had built Robin's armor against the man's maliciousness, his tantrums and fists, but the pounding in Robin's chest nearly cracked that steel. He hadn't expected this. Not even from John. The man had embraced the fight against his former ally, the French king Philip Capet, with unwavering passion. Even priests admitted John had been a saint since swearing fealty to King Richard. Robin had witnessed it himself, but doubts plagued him. Now this? This was treason!

There was no mistaking John's meaning. Kill the boy. A child, nine summers, only a handful of years younger than Robin's own son. It was one thing to fight alongside John, to serve him as the king's spy, but to be a part of this treachery? This was far beyond what King Richard had asked of him.

Can I reason with him? John's order screamed of tactical foolhardiness, against everything Robin knew as a skilled commander.

"Might this start a war with the Bretons, my lord?" Robin exchanged a glance with John's captain, hoping for his agreement.

Breaths slowing, John threw his broad, stocky chest out and stiffened, eyes narrowed to slits. His grip tightened round his wine and then he flung the cup.

Robin jerked back, the wine splattering him from head to toe. Dark crimson like blood, it stained his tunic and boots, but he sucked in a breath and held his tongue.

John roared, "That is my command." He pounded the table. "Do you understand?"

Robin wiped a trail of wine from his face, his mouth set in a hard line. He kept his voice steady, diplomatic. "With troops diverted to the western front, our defenses here would be weakened. The French will rally. King Richard—"

"My brother will easily win any conflict against those Breton arses." John scoffed. "Kill the boy. Kill his mother, his guards. Make sure your actions are not tied to me."

The captain unrolled a map on the trestle, pinning it down with two jugs of wine. "There are outlaws in the marches and any number of places the ducal train might be vulnerable to attack." He traced routes stretching west to east from Brittany through Normandy. His finger was filthy, encrusted with blood from the day's encounter with a score of King Philip's men. "Easy to blame them for outrageous acts such as this. No one will be the wiser."

"Unless you blunder," John added, eyes fixed on Robin. The man would never admit he issued this heinous order.

Robin shook his head. "Outlaws would take Arthur and Duchess Constance hostage, my lord. Hold them for ransom."

John snickered. "These outlaws aren't so smart."

"Even if I succeed you might tell the king it was at my hand," Robin said, his face expressionless. "Either way I could end up dangling from a rope." *Unless Marian learns I was part of this plot and kills me first.* He wanted to smile at the thought of his wife, but knew he could not. God, how he missed her. Why had he sworn to the king he would watch John?

"You are right, Robin." John gestured the mercenary captain to leave. "I admit I do not trust you."

Nor I you, Robin thought. "I have never given you cause to doubt me, my lord. Haven't I faithfully served you?" *Just as your brother commanded me...*

John rolled his eyes. "I will have proof one day you are here at Richard's orders. He only claims you betrayed him and banned you from his sight. I have my spies. He has his." John poured another cup of wine. "Best warrior, keep him close," he muttered, and added, "At least Richard was truthful about one thing. You *are* good in a skirmish." The compliment was painful to admit and he snorted in disgust, and then spat into the rushes at Robin's feet.

"His once, ever faithful, Robin du Louviers. But wait—" John chuckled. "He took your lands and your title, didn't he? A nice touch, Robin Carpenter."

A ruse. A painful one, but a game Robin must play.

"Fail me and your life will be forfeit in any case. Succeed and I may trust you." John sipped his wine and chortled. "On second thought, I will not trust, but I can be generous. I will let you live."

Robin should know better, but he grinned broadly. "You *will* lose, my lord. Your brother will know this was ordered by your hand. Where will that leave you?"

Obscenities streamed from John's mouth, but Robin hurried away. He'd known his words would anger John, but the irony was that Richard wouldn't punish his brother. He would forgive him. Again.

Cheeks burning with anger, Robin retrieved his pack and checked long blade and dagger, bow and arrows. A squire had saddled a fresh mount for him at the stables and the two captain's men lingered in the warmth of the blacksmith's shop.

Robin exhaled deeply. Someone was going to die before this ended, and it would not be Arthur.

two

Barge captains on the river called out competing with the noisy trade from shops lining the streets of Pontorson. Henry hardly took notice of either. His attention was divided between Stephan l'Aigle and the entourage descending from the hills to the west, the ducal train accompanying Constance of Brittany and her son Arthur.

The scent of fresh bread had lured Stephan to a baker's cart. The knight stood taller than most men and had a shock of golden hair that hung to his broad shoulders. His brilliant blue eyes rivaled the spring sky. Stephan could charm most people with one look and a smile that dazzled, but the baker was not taken in and haggled with him over the cost of a loaf.

"Three livre," the baker said.

"One," Stephan argued.

Henry tried not to grin as the baker countered with two. Stephan twisted the silver filigreed band on his finger. "And that ring," the baker said.

Stephan palmed his hand, protective of the ring Henry had given him in Vienna three years past. *I have wasted so much time ignoring my heart.* The words had spilled from his lips. Pulse quickening, he thought of nights beneath the stars, being alone with his lover, a breeze rustling tree branches overhead, birdsong and the peace of the greenwood. He and Stephan might never share a home, but Henry had long since realized that home was wherever Stephan was. Friendship had come naturally for them when they'd met in Southampton before embarking for the Holy Land. There was a camaraderie among soldiers—your life was in their hands. But love? Falling in love had surprised them both.

A commotion up the road made Henry look away reluctantly. People scrambled from the street. A rider cantered into town approaching the stone bridge over the Couësnon. Henry turned his back to the dark-cloaked man as he passed, but felt the swish of his stallion's tail. His gaze drew past the rider to Duchess Constance's entourage. Was this trouble?

Henry exhaled sharply and grabbed Stephan's arm. "Pay the baker and let's be off."

Frowning, Stephan tossed the man two coins and snatched the loaf from his hands. He followed Henry's gaze and had the same thought. "Ranulf's man."

Henry scanned the crowds as they strode to the horses. He had ridden with Ranulf, the Earl of Chester, many times since returning from the Holy Land and felt no need to be alarmed. The earl's castle at St James de Beauvron was only a short distance away. Henry would have been more surprised if Ranulf had not sent his own troop. It was in his best interest to keep watch on Constance's progress. She was his wife after all. Not that Ranulf would call it a marriage, Henry thought. More like a fire pit.

At the hitching post, Henry untied his horse and rested his hand on the cantle. He spied Ranulf's man dismount on the opposite bank. Still no sign of others.

Constance despised Ranulf and had never given him any reason to be concerned for her well being. The earl might be a powerful baron and he might choke on the words, but he must cajole his wife to stay in King Richard's good graces.

"Poor Ranulf," Stephan said. He tore the bread in half and leaned across Henry's saddle. "What more could the duchess want? Chester is rich, young, a handsome figure, mayhap a little short, but taller than she."

"Oh?" Henry asked, brows rising.

Stephan brushed Henry's hand. "No need to be jealous. He likes women."

Henry laughed and Stephan leaned closer, his short-cropped beard fragrant with the lavender soap from their morning wash. "Besides, I will never stray." His voice was low, sultry. "You are the only one who will have my heart."

Henry's horse nipped at his arm reminding him of their current task. The knights slipped off their dark cloaks to reveal red surcoats emblazoned with King Richard's gold lion. Villagers pointed at them, whispering, and stepped aside as they led their horses to the bridge.

Stephan eyed Ranulf's man. "Better Chester watching rather than one of Count John's men I suppose." Even Stephan had been surprised at Robin's lack of concern, but three days' reconnoitering Pontorson gave them no indication of trouble.

Wind off the river tousled Henry's hair. He smoothed the wild dark curls and looked east. No trouble in this border town, but the ducal train might be on the road to Rouen another ten days. Henry shivered, a chill snaking through his bones, and not from the cool morning air.

The ducal train's progress seemed slower than a priest's sermon at Mass. Cart after cart came over the distant ridge and stretched to the flood plain like a serpent, an apt description when Henry remembered King Richard's words about his late brother's wife and her advisors. Covered in brown and beige tarps that looked like snakeskin when shadows fell across them, the wagons overflowed with the duchess' necessaries. Clothing and tapestries, pillows, and linens to make any room to her liking, silver and gold goblets and trenchers, pots to cook her meals, and casks of wine.

A hundred mounted riders slithered at the van- and rearguard, the procession now about half the distance between the summit of the hill and the bridge. The Breton flag, a black cross on a white field, flew above the duchess' litter. A spirited horse drew up beside it and the curtain was drawn aside. The rider was a child judging by his size—an important one, being that three guards hovered round him. *Arthur.*

"He handles his mount with the experience of someone much older," Henry said, watching the boy keep pace with the litter. The nine-year-old had likely been riding since he could walk. He pivoted in a tight circle, showing off, pulled back on the reins to have the horse take a few steps back and then sidle.

"If he can spar with a wooden stave half as good as he rides, the king will be pleased. Hard to tell if there are budding muscles beneath that dingy woolen cloak." Stephan frowned. "The men with him—none wears the ducal colors, no badges on their clothes or horses. They don't want to draw attention to the boy."

Arthur pivoted again, and then horse and rider shot away, galloping towards the rearguard with the guards at his back.

A few minutes later the procession halted and four advance scouts cantered towards town. A flurry of activity bubbled around the duchess' litter. Two large coffers from another wagon were placed inside. Four ladies carrying small chests joined the duchess and two pages delivered food and drink. It was some time before anyone reappeared, though the curtain parted once and a message was relayed to one of the mounted knights. He trotted alongside the column and disappeared in the crowd, only to return moments later leading a magnificent white stallion. Two squires quickly saddled the horse and only then did the duchess emerge from the litter.

With her knights' help, Constance was soon astride the animal. Her deep brown cloak billowed in the breeze revealing a jade and gold gown brimming with jewels that glittered in the sunlight. The knights in the vanguard lined either side of the road leading up to the bridge and Constance paraded past them. Looking intimidating, the advance scouts blocked access to the bridge, but Henry and Stephan waited at the eastern egress to greet her.

Henry caught his first glimpse of her creamy skin when she drew closer. A jade wimple hid her hair and framed her oval-shaped face. She was no beauty like his own sister Bea or the king's sister Joanna, but not unpleasant to look at. Too bad for Chester her personality was as caustic as nightshade was deadly.

"Lady Constance." Henry bowed. The duchess sat with her back straight, her nose in the air, pretending she had not met him a few weeks earlier. "Greetings from

King Richard. I am Lord Henry de Grey and this is Sir Stephan l'Aigle. The king has sent us to accompany you to Rouen."

"My lady," Stephan said with a bow.

A somber-faced advisor in a saffron robe whispered to Constance. She fought a chortle and coughed, looking past Stephan as if expecting to see a cadre of knights. "Two of you?" she asked. Disdain filled her dark eyes, cold and hard beneath dark brows.

"King Richard felt you would be uncomfortable with a host of his knights," Henry said, stepping forward. He offered her a rolled parchment with the king's seal, but her mouth pinched and she tilted her head, gesturing to her advisor.

Handing the letter to the older man, Henry said, "The king has arranged lodging a few miles north, which we should make well before dark."

The clink of mail and clatter of horses' hoofs echoed behind them in the streets. Constance paled suddenly, her face the color of freshly fallen snow. The Earl of Chester's banners rippled above his conroi.

Constance's knights drew around her, their shields raised and swords drawn. She glanced back, seeking her son atop his horse at the crest of the ridge. She realized her mistake, glared at Henry, and then turned a foul face on her estranged husband. The crowds scattered, swept back by the charge of Chester's troops.

Stephan leaned close to Henry. "Not John's men."

"What is Ranulf up to?" Henry whispered.

The earl reined in sharply. Henry and Stephan stood between his stallion and Constance's knights.

"My lady wife." Ranulf tipped his head. He was six and twenty summers like Henry, but his jewel-studded belt and scabbard spoke of wealth and station far beyond what Henry would ever know. He was a powerful baron and might choke on the words, but he sounded civil.

"My lord," Henry said with a tip of his head, "we'd not been informed—"

"That is correct, Lord de Grey."

His formal response made Henry cringe. Count John had been their common enemy in England and they'd fought side-by-side. In any other situation, Ranulf would have called Henry by his given name.

Constance hissed. "I should have been told to expect you, my lord."

"Why?" Ranulf smirked. "So you could refuse the invitation to Rouen?"

"I would rather travel in the company of the Devil than with you."

"Where is Arthur?" he asked, tossing aside the insult.

"As far from you as I might keep him."

"He was invited to meet with King Richard." Ranulf's voice was smooth as silk.

"You expect me to trust him?" Constance snarled. "You forget he holds my daughter Eleanor. I have not seen her since she was offered as marriage bait to secure his release from the emperor."

Her voice quivered, barely noticeable. Ranulf was fortunate his wife wasn't brandishing a short blade because her eyes blazed with hatred. Henry knew she spoke the truth about her daughter, who had been the king's ward since she was two. Eleanor's arranged marriage had not taken place because the groom's father, the duke of Austria, had died.

"Your daughter is fine, as you—and your son—would see in Rouen," Henry said, hoping to diffuse the nasty banter between Constance and Ranulf. "Arthur should be honored to be part of King Richard's court, my lady."

She refused to acknowledge Henry. Surely she understood the implications of Arthur being raised as the king's ward. What mother would deny her child a chance for the throne?

Ranulf rose in his stirrups to survey the ducal train. "Where is he?"

Constance stared at him, eyes ablaze. Henry glanced toward the ridge. The boy was no longer there.

Furious when she refused to produce her son, Ranulf waved a hand in the air. Two dozen crossbowmen suddenly appeared from alleyways, bolts trained on Constance's men. Ranulf's knights rushed in driving a wedge between the duchess and her men. Another troop charged up the road to join their lord.

Surrounded, Constance remained defiant. "You cannot have my son."

"For now," Ranulf conceded. "But you will come with me. We've been wed how long? Eight years?" He groaned. "You'll be my guest at St James. We shall have many days to discuss Arthur's whereabouts. Your messengers can tell the boy's protectors I will have my wife in my household until—"

"Did that bastard Richard put you up to this?" The venom in her voice sizzled hotter than a blacksmith's forge. Her glare shifted from Ranulf to Henry. "Did you know?"

"I swear I did not, my lady. I will tell the king." Henry met Ranulf's stare. "I must, my lord."

"Yes, do inform King Richard the Lady Constance had no intention of bringing Arthur to his court. He will be most displeased." He eyed his wife and said, "And your barons may pay for your stupidity."

"You cannot do this, my lord," the duchess' advisor shouted. A dozen voices joined his in protest.

Ranulf jerked the reins from Constance's hands, pivoted his mount, and led her away. His knights formed a shield behind the earl and his captive wife.

Henry stared after them. Was Ranulf under the king's orders? Had it been their intent to separate mother and child all along? Perhaps both expected the duchess had no plans to place her son in Richard's care.

The duchess' men looked stricken, arguing amongst themselves before racing back to the ducal train.

"We must find Arthur, convince him to come with us to see his uncle," Stephan said as Ranulf and his knights vanished round a bend.

Henry gestured at the ridge. "The boy will be long gone. We'll never get close to him." Breton knights were barreling their way to the rearguard and up the hill. Word of Chester's actions would spread like fire consuming thatch. Henry rubbed the ache in his temple. "Why would Ranulf do this? Surely Lady Constance is wrong. The king would not order him to intercept her."

His own doubts bled into his voice, but even if they hadn't Stephan knew Henry's mind.

"*If* he did," Stephan said as they swung astride their horses, "he knows she could be a pawn to negotiate with her Breton lords. Her hatred for the king flies like a banner in the wind. The child is lost with her influence. King Richard must isolate the boy before she aligns Brittany with the French."

Constance's stance made no sense. Her son could be King of England, lead the Normans, the Bretons, an entire empire. Philip could not offer that, except that his interest in Arthur could drive a wedge in Richard's realm. Normandy would be surrounded—France on one side, Brittany on the other. Would the king's allies turn, shift their allegiance to the French? With their support, Philip could hand the Angevin empire to Arthur with a promise of peace.

"She'll have that boy at Philip's court, raised there," Stephan added.

"To be his puppet." Henry squared his jaw. "We cannot let that happen."

Stephan pounded Henry's back. "No, we cannot."

three

MARCH 1196
Toward Fougères

Henry didn't doubt Chester would have his own version of the event, but Stephan agreed the king should hear it from Henry's hand. Within an hour, their messenger started towards Rouen. Certain Arthur's guards had been instructed to spirit him away to the French king's court, the knights laid out their plans.

"Fougères," Stephan said, swinging astride his black bay.

Henry studied the road. The direct route to Paris would lead Arthur's men through the heart of Normandy. Too dangerous. The king's troops would overtake those paths quickly once Richard learned Constance had defied his orders. By sea? Breton ports lay in easy reach, but sailing past English ships to the safety of a French-held port would be near impossible.

"Fougères," Henry repeated, remembering they'd lodged there with King Richard before Easter the previous year. Natural defenses, an impressive castle. The town wasn't small. A young boy and his traveling companions might not be noticed there.

It was a day's ride to Fougères so they pressed southward, determined to reach the first of two ferry crossings before nightfall. The wooded path along the river narrowed in places forcing them to ride single file. Naked oak and beech tree limbs creaked overhead, sunlight revealing a carpet of brown leaves on the forest floor. No heavy carts passed this way, no signs of rutted trails. Small villages with thatch-roofed cottages nestled amongst the moss-covered trees. As shadows deepened and dusk drew close, they found shelter for the night within sight of a flat-decked boat tied at the riverbank.

Crisp air and sun streaming through a crack in the timbered barn woke them at dawn. Henry languished beneath the woolen blanket tangled in Stephan's arms. Vaguely aware of voices outside their quiet place, Henry nuzzled Stephan's cheek. His lover smelled of musk and sweat, which brought him to full wakefulness. Henry sighed, wishing they could stay like this for days on end. He cherished time alone with Stephan, but that had been rare—he'd lost count of the times these last two years when they'd shared sleeping quarters with a dozen or more knights in some lord's hall or in a pavilion set up in a siege camp.

Henry forced himself to rise, brushed straw from his tunic, and pulled his leather belt round his waist while he glanced through a crack in the door.

Stephan stretched. "Anything?" he asked and then stood and rolled their bedding.

Henry's view to the opposite bank was clear. "Not a

soul." But the creak of wheels and laughter signaled someone's approach. Three men passed the barn, their breaths smoking in the air. Two of them steered an old wooden cart laden with crates. A gray-haired shorter man with powerfully-muscled arms walked alongside them kicking at leaves on the ground.

Henry held up three fingers to Stephan, gave a quick nod, and stepped outside.

"Good morrow to you," he called.

The men froze in place, eyeing the sword at Henry's waist. None had more than a short blade and dagger between them.

"I thank you for use of the barn. The nights are still cold," Henry said as a gust of wind rippled the tarp on the cart. "Who might I pay?"

The older man stepped forward. "No need." He cocked his head towards the boat while the other men lugged their goods there to load. "But a ha'penny to cross the river. I'll be off soon as these goods are loaded."

"I'll not be crossing the river, but I shall pay for a bit of information." Henry rattled the coins in the pouch at his belt.

"Aye, that will cost you." The ferryman laughed, choking when the barn door opened and Stephan led their horses out.

"He's a friend," Henry said, stepping forward and lowering his voice. "The information we need must not be spread far and wide. Do you understand?"

Brow furrowed, the old man's eyes darted to his customers on the boat. "That will cost more."

Henry fished out two coins. The ferryman reached for them smiling broadly, but Henry withdrew his hand and dangled them in the air. "We are looking for a boy of about nine summers, so tall—" He held his hand at chest height. "The last we saw him, he wore a worn brown cloak. He'll likely be in the company of one or more men."

"Seen none like that."

No surprise there, Henry thought. The Bretons would have ridden all night and hard to get this far so quickly.

Stephan glanced up river. "How many crossings from here south to the road from Rennes?"

The ferryman scratched his chin. "At least two. Beyond that I could not say," he said as Henry payed him. He rubbed a calloused thumb and forefinger across the coins. "Should you wait upriver I could send word to you if your friends pass this way."

The man was a businessman, looking for another coin to earn that the local bishop, or whoever owned the crossing, wouldn't get a part of. It was a generous offer, but Henry didn't trust him not to warn Arthur's men that others were inquiring. And surely the Bretons wouldn't choose this closest route—far too obvious, far too risky.

With a subtle head shake to Henry, Stephan said, "No need for that."

The ferryman studied them. "You look hungry. For a ha'penny my wife will feed you ere you're on your way." Still hoping to fill his pouch he smiled, tipping his head towards the cottage where a woman peered from the doorway. "I'll trust you to introduce yourselves. Give this to her if you would." He planted the deniers back in Henry's hand as one of the men by the boat shouted at him. "I'll be off now."

The ferryman's wife fed them well with eggs fresh from the fat hens pattering around the cottage. Crusty bread slathered in honey was set out and she gave them a second helping before they set off.

The road became little more than a footpath where

they dodged low-hanging tree limbs through thickets of winter-browned bramble. Two days, two crossings, and three deniers later they were no closer to discovering Arthur and turned east towards Fougères. Birdsong and creaking limbs pervaded the wood. Where the road narrowed, granite cliffs rose seeming to touch the sky. A massive stone curtain shot above the cliff wall and towered over a bustling village. Eager merchants peddled all manner of goods and shoppers inspected bright-colored cloth, pottery, leather, and steel.

After stabling the horses, they arranged for a room at an inn within a stone's throw of the drawbridge that separated town from castle. Anxious to quench their thirst and feed their growling stomachs, they crossed the muddy road to a tavern recommended by the innkeeper.

A chestnut-haired girl placed ales before them, fluttering her long lashes at Stephan. He smiled at her over the rim of the mug and then sipped his drink. When she didn't move, Henry asked, "Might we get some food?"

She scowled at him, looked coyly at Stephan and blushed before working her way to the kitchen.

Henry elbowed Stephan. "I'll bet she would offer you a warm bed tonight."

"My bed will be fiery enough, my lord."

Lust in Stephan's voice sent heat hurtling through Henry's veins. He quieted his heartbeat and brushed his leg against Stephan's beneath the trestle, content to share that small touch...for now.

The room at the inn had two beds with straw-filled mattresses and scratchy woolen blankets that smelled fresh as an early spring morning. Hauberks, tunics, and braies ended up on one bed, Stephan and Henry on the other.

Stephan traced a finger across the rippled muscles on Henry's torso. He palmed the wooden crucifix rising and falling with Henry's breaths and then kissed him deeply. "I love you."

"Forever," Henry whispered.

Stephan teased kisses along Henry's neck, across his shoulder, and down his chest, his breath warm against his skin. Henry moaned. He raised his hips, craving more…lower…and when Stephan took him in his mouth, he cried out. His hands clenched Stephan's hair and he pressed Stephan to take more, thrusting in rhythm with Stephan's ministrations.

"Stephan…" Henry murmured. His bollocks tightened and he climaxed in a rush of stars, heart raging like waves of thunder.

Stephan eased beside him, his cock rubbing Henry's hip, hard and demanding attention. When Henry found his breath he rolled Stephan on to his back and straddled him. Stephan's eyes ached with need and Henry greedily complied.

four

Stephan heard the clink of mail, but didn't move until a tunic landed on his head. He was vaguely aware of a bell pealing up the road. The shutters were cracked open and Henry stood at the window belting his hauberk. "Arthur." He checked scabbard and sword. "They must have arrived late last night."

Jerking upright, Stephan grabbed the tunic and swung his legs over the side of the bed.

"Get the horses. Meet me at the edge of town," Henry said and was gone before Stephan had pulled up his braies. Stephan dressed, watching from the window as Arthur and his two companions headed east with Henry following on foot.

Their quarry was long gone by the time Stephan retrieved their horses and two palfreys on leads. The knights set a hard pace and caught sight of them, but held back. Fougères was hours behind when they slowed their mounts to a walk.

Stephan glanced sidelong at Henry and smiled. He nudged Conqueror closer until their knees brushed. A shiver sparked up Henry's spine. The last two nights with Stephan had him craving more time alone, where there would be no need to worry about prying eyes.

"When this business with Arthur is finished I will ask the king's leave and return to Lincolnshire." Henry turned to Stephan. "We both must go."

"It's past time you gave up this knightly life."

Henry squeezed Stephan's thigh. "You wouldn't stay…at Greyton."

"How could I?" Stephan asked with dismay.

"Then I cannot stay, especially knowing you would return to the king's side."

Stephan hesitated, but placed his gloved hand on Henry's. "Mayhap your nightmares will end if you get away from this war."

Henry closed his fist tightly on the reins. The dreams had begun in Messina, months before the horrors of the Holy Land. The drums, the screams, intruded on his sleep, and came unbidden even during the day. War, the blood, the senseless acts done in God's name or the king's made him sick. Would a peaceful life at Greyton take away that burden?

"Go home," Stephan said.

Unlike Stephan, Henry wasn't retained by King Richard as a household knight. He had land and income, and he'd given the king six years of his life. From the march to Jerusalem, through snowy mountain passes in Bavaria, and at more sieges than he could count.

Stephan took his hand. "Pay your knight's fee and let the king hire another in your place."

"I will not leave you," Henry said.

Stephan closed the distance between them. He brushed his lips against Henry's forehead.

Grinning, Henry asked, "Besides, who would take care of you?"

They road in silence for a short while. Stephan's face flushed with guilt. *Take care of him.* Henry's father had spoken those words with his dying breaths. Mercenaries transporting war supplies to Lincoln had attacked them and Edward de Grey had taken a blade for Stephan. But it was his last whispered words that had racked Stephan's heart. *Let him go.* The best way to take care of Henry was to release him. *Let him go.* Stephan never told Henry his father was opposed to their love.

The lie thundered in Stephan's head like the charge of a hundred knights in battle.

"I would be lost without you," Stephan said. "But is that any reason to raise your sword day after day, kill or be killed? Why should you stay?"

"I love you." Henry's eyes softened. "I don't need any other reason."

Stephan reined in and exhaled sharply. "You avoid the question. Tell me."

Henry brought his horse round and drew next to Stephan. "I am afraid of not having you at my side."

"We survived months apart when we returned from the Holy Land." Stephan's mission for Queen Eleanor had taken him from York to Winchester and all the way to King Richard's Bavarian prison.

"I have no desire to repeat that."

Stephan reached across the space between them and touched Henry's cheek. "Nor do I." Forget the guilt. *You are wrong, Edward.* "Another night alone with you."

Henry quickly leaned in and covered Stephan's mouth with a kiss. With a sigh he broke away. "Bring on the blessed night."

Not one, but two more nights. Each day took them further from the Breton border, a good thing because they weren't ready to show themselves. Too close and their quarry could turn easily and escape to friendly territory. Arthur's men had pushed the horses forty miles yesterday. If the weather held, that would be the pace all the way to Paris. But three days out from Paris the sky opened and rain lashed them. If the sky grew any blacker, Henry would swear it was night.

Arthur took shelter in a weathered barn. The knights left their horses by a stand of trees and drew close. The barn door rattled in the March winds, but a petulant young voice wailed from inside the building.

"You must keep your voice down." The man's voice was pleading.

"Do not tell me what to do! Mama never said I would have to sleep in a cold barn that smells of cow dung. I may freeze to death if I do not die from that stench."

"You will do neither." The man was stern, but compassionate. "I will give you my blanket, as will Alain. Now come. Off with those wet clothes."

"Do not touch me!"

Henry signaled Stephan away from the barn. "If Arthur's guards were wise," Henry said, "they would sell the boy to slavers and get rid of their burden. I don't envy them."

"If we take him, that will be us soon enough." Stephan peered over Conqueror's saddle to watch the barn. "I imagine the king wouldn't be pleased if we stuffed Arthur's mouth with cloth to keep him quiet."

Henry rubbed the back of his neck and chuckled. "He'll go kicking and screaming."

"Best we grab him when they sleep tonight," Stephan said.

Henry agreed and huddled next to Stephan beneath the eaves of a storehouse, but when the rain finally stopped the barn door swung open. Arthur rode out between his guards. They were determined to spend every hour of daylight forging towards Paris.

The trees gave way now and then to reveal quiet meadows not yet budding with wildflowers. The road wound through small villages, past large manor houses with green swards stretching to the road, abandoned hovels, and dilapidated barns. When Arthur and his men finally stopped to change mounts, Henry and Stephan dismounted to do the same.

Henry quickly removed his palfrey's saddle and placed it on Greycloud. Back on the stallion, he gulped down a swig of ale from his flask. Stephan rifled through his pack for leftover bread, tossed Henry a piece, and bit into his own before saddling up.

Stephan chewed on the bread watching their quarry in the distance. "They don't appear to be in any hurry. We can catch them before they move out."

Arthur sat astride his horse. One of his guards watched as the other saddled the horses—one a soldier, the other a noble? The guard's horse munched on grass at the side of the road. Arthur pivoted his horse round and round showing off his control of the beast.

Tossing aside the lead reins of the palfrey, Henry set his jaw as Stephan mounted. "I'll take the boy."

Stephan unsheathed his sword and positioned his shield. The knights dug heels into their horses' flanks and urged them to a gallop. Wind bit into Stephan's cheeks as his stallion matched the stride of Henry's horse.

Arthur stopped his boyish display and stared at the knights pounding along the road, dust trailing in their wake. The guard was shouting, trying to secure the girth round the belly of the noble's horse. Arthur realized the danger and shot away. The noble's horse skittered and balked, but with the saddle finally secure he mounted as Henry and Stephan drew down on them.

The guard drew his sword, his loyalty to his young master. The noble took off after Arthur. Henry and Stephan barreled ahead stirrup to stirrup. Waving his sword overhead defiantly, the guard did not shrink from them. He might not get both, but he was bound to try. A brave man, Stephan thought.

The guard brought the blade down intent on ripping it across the neck of Stephan's horse. At the last possible moment, Stephan and Henry shifted to pass further to the man's right. He stepped closer and swung, but Stephan's sword met his with a harsh clang and the knights bolted past him with Arthur still in their sights.

Stephan shouted at Henry. "We can't let him follow." He slowed, pivoting to meet the guard again.

The guard must have been surprised to see Stephan turning back to fight. He had grabbed hold of his horse, but had no time to saddle him. Stephan was upon him as he seated his shield. Stephan struck the man with the flat of his blade, unbalancing him. He dropped his weapon, knees buckling, and fell to the ground.

Heart pounding, Stephan grabbed the reins of the man's horse. He would have a long walk, even to steal another horse to return to Brittany and let others know what had happened. By that time, Arthur would be firmly in King Richard's hands.

Stephan retrieved the palfreys he and Henry left

behind and then galloped on Henry's trail. The road twisted through another wooded tract. Smoke tickled Stephan's nose before a large village came in sight and he crossed a decrepit bridge over a stream. Henry's horse was tied at the far end of the street. Henry, Arthur, the noble—nowhere to be seen. Stephan cursed beneath his breath. This was exactly what they had not wanted. Arthur had found a place to hide.

five

Henry couldn't rise. His head throbbed, and the boy's screeching didn't help.

"Why shouldn't we just kill you? Who are you?" Arthur shouted. "Why are you following me?"

Henry clutched his chest. The flesh wound wasn't deadly, but the blow had been powerful enough to bruise a rib. "Thief…"

The nobleman brandished his sword and smirked. "Such a fine stallion for a thief." He wasn't a huge man, so his strength had caught Henry off guard.

Arthur laughed. "He is quite the liar, Andrew. He'll claim he stole the animal!" He circled, the dirt stirred by his boots creating a cloud drifting over Henry's face.

Coughing, Henry curled up in pain.

"And what of that fine hauberk? Stole it, too." Arthur set the tip of his small sword against Henry's throat.

"Son," Andrew said, "not so close."

Arthur snapped. "Where is my guard?"

"How should I——" Henry choked back the words, his

mouth contorted with pain. He couldn't remember the last time he'd felt helpless. Could he risk grabbing the boy's blade? Andrew had stepped closer. Henry wouldn't be fast enough to avoid his sword.

"You charged us," Arthur growled. "Two of you. You are with that bastard Richard!"

Arthur drew blood. Henry jerked away, blood dribbling down his neck, but the pain shooting across his chest made his head swim.

"Ar— Leave him, son," Andrew said. "Put your blade away. He cannot hurt us."

Arthur placed the point of the weapon on Henry's hand. "I want to gut him like a pig. That is what Richard will do to me."

"Quiet." Andrew refused to acknowledge the young duke, something a common soldier would not dare. Nose in the air, Arthur chastised the noble with a glare, but did listen.

Henry gritted his teeth. "You are wrong about King Richard. He will not harm you."

"You *are* his knight."

"Please, my lord," Andrew pleaded, "we should leave."

"I am afraid that won't be possible." The dark voice came from behind Henry, but wasn't one he recognized.

Andrew looked past Henry. Fear filled his eyes as Henry twisted painfully to get a glimpse of the newcomer. The man chuckled, dark eyes glinting with contempt. "Not so brave now, little Arthur."

"Arthur?" Andrew's voice trembled. "I don't know who you—"

"Shut up," the mercenary snarled, his armor rattling.

This was no ordinary routier, Henry thought. The man knew the young duke. The mercenary stepped towards Arthur, his massive body bathing Henry in shadows.

"Run!" Andrew cried.

Panic and fear replaced Arthur's arrogance. His path out was blocked by the would-be assassin. He could climb the ladder into the loft, but might not get halfway up before being skewered by a blade. He ran towards the stalls, ripping his clothes as he climbed over the rails. The horses weren't saddled, but he could ride bareback—if he wasn't trampled when he tried to mount.

A smile split the hired soldier's face. He raised his sword to strike.

Eyes blurred with pain, Henry rolled and grabbed the mercenary's leg. The man managed to keep his balance and fended off Andrew's charge. He twisted free and kicked Henry, blocked a second strike from Andrew and then answered it with one hack, then another, pressing Andrew closer to the stalls. He would not last long.

Henry crawled towards his sword. Cannot let him hurt the boy...cannot...

A sudden piercing howl erupted from the doorway. The mercenary glanced back as if expecting to see a companion. His eyes darkened and he swung round.

Stephan! Tension drained from Henry's body.

"Get the boy out of here!" Stephan charged towards the mercenary. His sword arced high, then down. Blocked, he threw the man off and advanced again, striking the soldier's arm, the collision of blade and mail screaming. The blow didn't pierce flesh, but his adversary grunted, twisting away.

Arthur struggled to mount, but Andrew gave him a push into the saddle. Their path to the door remained blocked. If Stephan lost, none of them would leave here alive. And the mercenary had expected help—his companions had to be in the village. Stephan had to realize this too, and kicked Henry's sword within his reach. But even if Andrew and Arthur escaped, they might fall directly into the waiting arms of their enemy.

Henry's bloodied fist curled round the hilt of his sword.

"Let us go," Andrew shouted. "I have silver."

Henry groaned. The man was more of a fool than he expected.

"Don't need your coin," the mercenary hissed and circled around Stephan. He feinted, brought his sword high and two-handed, chopped downward.

Stephan cast off the blow and countered, but the soldier ducked and spun away from the thrust. In a sudden move, he caught Stephan's blade. His arms trembled with the effort to hold their swords crossed, eyes glimmering with cold fury as he forced Stephan against the barn wall.

For one heartbeat, Stephan looked at Henry. The assassin screeched and spat in his face. He tossed off Stephan's sword and laid the blade against Stephan's neck.

"No!" Henry shouted.

The barn door swung open. Something hissed over Henry's head. He heard the thump, a gasp for breath, a cry. The arrow had driven deep into the mercenary's back. His sword fell away from Stephan and he staggered, collapsing to the ground.

Arthur leaned low over his horse's neck, trembling, tightly gripping its mane. He stared at the knight at the door. A smile lit Stephan's face. Rubbing the bloodied cut on his neck, he greeted his old friend. "Robin."

"I didn't expect to see you on Arthur's trail," Henry said and grinned, "but thank God you were here." He strained to get to his feet, and Stephan and Robin drew to his side.

"Are you all right?" Robin slung his bow over his shoulder to offer a hand.

"I should have been more careful. They surprised me," Henry muttered. He turned his anger with himself on Stephan. "And what were you thinking? You took your eyes off your enemy and nearly—"

"Do not tell me my business." Stephan huffed. "I knew what I was—" A look in Henry's eyes and a tip of his head towards the door made Stephan quiet.

"You know these two, Robin?" The newcomer held a blade at his side and looked at them warily.

Andrew's expression had frozen. Henry prayed he would keep his mouth shut. And Arthur—that mercenary would never let him get away. If Robin wasn't quick enough... *God help us all.*

Robin drew in a deep breath and laid a hand on Henry's shoulder. "Stay down," he whispered and strode towards the new arrival. He cocked his head at Henry and Stephan. "King's men."

The routier spotted the body of his companion. The arrow protruding from his back. He glared at Robin. "Bastard!"

"Josef, stop," Robin shouted, ducking the swing of the man's sword and drawing his own.

"You are dead, Robin." The mercenary advanced.

"He stepped into my shot!"

"You expect me to believe that?" Josef's sword chopped down. Robin caught the blow on his own and pressed him backwards.

"Captain told me to keep an eye on you," the mercenary growled.

Stephan retrieved his sword as Andrew came round the stall hefting his blade. Knowing he was outmanned, Josef took off at a run. Robin was first out the door with

Andrew at his back.

Stephan helped Henry to his feet.

"Go, help Robin," Henry said.

"He needs no help from me. You, on the other hand…" Stephan leaned forward as if to kiss him, stopping when he noticed Arthur watching. He slid his arm round Henry's waist and helped him outside.

Josef bolted towards the horses tied down the street. Robin followed a short way, but stopped, sheathing his sword.

"What are you doing?" Andrew shouted. "After him."

Robin swung his bow off his shoulder and grabbed a shaft from his pack. Arrow nocked, he found his target and loosed. Josef was half in the saddle when the arrow struck.

There was a sudden commotion from the barn. Arthur shot out, heels digging into his horse's flanks.

Stephan pulled Henry out of the boy's path and managed to keep them both upright.

Henry stared after Arthur and shook his head. "The boy's got spirit."

Robin started down the road for his own horse, but Andrew grabbed his arm. "You mean him no harm?"

"Not me."

"Nor us," Stephan added.

"Let us help you," Henry said. "Robin—bring him back."

"Help us by letting the boy go," Andrew said. "Let me do my duty by him, by his mother." He strode back into the barn to get his horse.

"Robin," Henry said, "go." He limped to the barn door. "Andrew, help Stephan dispose of the two dead men."

Andrew ignored him, grabbing his pack and Arthur's.

"That is your mess to clean up."

"You fool," Henry said curtly. "John will send more men after you. He will not rest."

"And you will give us over to Richard. He will lock my prince away and have his way."

Henry shook his head. "The king may be the only one who can protect Arthur. From John. From the French king."

"You cannot guarantee that."

"Mayhap you are right. But you can be assured that if Arthur falls into John's hands, he will die. Or he will be no more than a puppet when Philip gets hold of him."

Andrew stopped packing. He grunted, that as much a concession as any. When he turned to drag the mercenary's body outside Henry knew he had gotten through to the man. Leaning against the door, he held his aching ribs and watched them toss the dead men over one of the horse's backs.

Andrew retrieved his bay while Stephan tied the bodies securely and then mounted. "Rest. We'll be back soon."

As they trotted away, Henry wondered what Robin would do. He had defied John's orders. Though Robin's accomplices were dead, John would learn soon enough that Arthur was still alive. All blame would be laid at Robin's feet. Another notch against Robin in John's eyes. He wouldn't let it lie. He would have his revenge.

Six

Robin tore down the road after Arthur. God forbid the boy run into a troop of John's men. He would be done for if they recognized him.

Kill the boy. Robin couldn't scrub John's words from his mind. How like the stories he'd heard of John's father, another man with a fiery temper. Robin had been very young when Thomas Becket died, but the debate about old King Henry's exasperated plea was known throughout Christendom. *"Who will rid me of this contentious priest?"* Henry's knights had taken his words as an order and left Becket dead at Canterbury.

Marian's voice called out to him above the horse's thundering hoofs. *"What have you done, Robin?"*

"You will not be happy," he muttered to her across the miles.

The road reminded him of home near Ringsthorpe, winding and wooded, not a cottage in sight. He could imagine just ahead he'd catch sight of the village. Hear his father chipping at wood in his shop, instructing his brothers in the finer points of carpentry, and Linota—his stepmother—calling them in for the midday meal. She made the best roasted chicken, though he'd be careful not to say that in Marian's presence. What he wouldn't give to be there now. To be with Marian.

Wind stung his face and he urged his black on as if that would get him back to Marian more quickly. Get the boy. Speak with the king. *I will come home, Marian...*

His eyes narrowed. Just ahead, Arthur's palfrey, riderless. Robin reined in sharply, dust and dirt kicked up like a fog round his horse's legs. He scanned the roadside, moving forward slowly. "Arthur!"

The sun was drawing down and deep shadows blanketed the wood. Had the boy been thrown? Was he lying unconscious? He wouldn't have abandoned the animal, taken to foot. Not with darkness coming.

Arthur's horse pawed the dirt, favoring his front foot. He'd thrown a shoe. *Where are you, Arthur?*

"Come with me, my lord," Robin called, twisting in every direction.

The evergreens rustled and a small figure cloaked in brown shot away.

"Arthur, stop!" Robin jumped from his stallion and pursued Arthur into the wood. Tree branches swiped at his face. He spat leaves from his mouth, jumped a log, bushes. Arthur disappeared into a thick stand of trees, and Robin stopped to listen. Twigs snapped and leaves crunched off to his right. He chased the sounds past a rotted tree trunk.

Arthur's light hair and pale skin stood out against the browns of the early spring wood. A few more strides and he was close. The boy looked back and Robin clawed his sleeve, forcing them to a skidding halt. "You are coming with me."

Arthur bit Robin's hand.

"You little cur—" Robin grabbed a fistful of Arthur's hair. Arthur screeched, stomped on Robin's foot, but Robin wrapped his fingers tighter.

"Oww!" the boy cried, squirming to pull away.

A woman's scream suddenly echoed through the forest. Robin clamped a hand across Arthur's mouth, listening, and then dragged him towards the noise. He pressed the boy down behind a clump of evergreens and peered into the dusky gloom. Three black-leathered men-at-arms had a woman at their mercy. Her clothes were ripped, her hair mussed. Tears streaked her face as two of the men held her down and the third swived her brutally.

Arthur's dark eyes widened.

"I cannot protect you against them all," Robin whispered. "Will you keep quiet?"

The boy was trembling and shook his head yes. He had not seen a woman being raped.

Where there were three men there might be a dozen more, but when Robin saw no one else, he nocked an arrow and took aim. English knights weren't known for their skill with bow, but Robin wasn't like most knights. His first shot sliced into the neck of the man holding the girl's right arm. Consumed by the sight of his companion's cock thrusting deep, the second man didn't realize what was happening until the first fell into him. "Bloody Christ!" He released hold of the girl, but was silenced before another curse spilled from his lungs. The swiving man stared round, pushed himself off the girl, and ran. Robin's arrow struck him in the back leaving the bastard sprawled face down on the ground.

"If you see any soldiers, run," Robin said.

Arthurs's eyes were glassy. He stared at the arrows

protruding from dead bodies, blood staining their leather jerkins.

Robin shook him. "Do you understand? Find Andrew. I'll help the girl if I can, and will catch up with you and the others."

Nodding, Arthur chewed on his lip and looked at the gruesome scene. The boy had been forced to leave his home, had seen evil men killed, a woman raped—Robin wouldn't wish those experiences on anyone, let alone a nine-year old. Robin clamped a hand on his shoulder and offered a comforting squeeze.

The girl stood and tugged her torn clothing to cover her breasts. When Robin saw no sign of other mercenaries, he emerged from the wood, hands raised high, bow in hand, to show her he meant no harm. "Where are your people?" he asked.

She pointed north. "Dead. They killed them. Told them we had nothing. The French took it all." She rubbed her hand where the outlaw's nail had scratched her skin. "English are just as bad."

"I'm sorry." Robin eyed the dead. What more could he say? She was right, and he couldn't tell if the men were French soldiers or brigands—even some of Mercadier's group—out to take what they could. He retrieved a cloak from the ground where it had been tossed. He held it out, taking slow steps towards her. She swiped at the tears on her dirt-streaked cheeks and then took the cloak and wrapped it round herself. Robin could see she was not as young as he'd originally thought. She had a womanly figure—married, with children he imagined. All lost to these bastards.

She spat into the face of one of the dead men and leaned down to search his body for booty. Robin checked the other two, handing her pouches clinking with coin.

"There's a small village just west of here. You can get help there."

"Is there anywhere safe?" she asked.

Robin led the way through the underbrush, his thoughts on Marian. "I wonder that myself."

He found Arthur right where he'd left him. "This is Arthur," Robin said.

"Your boy?"

Arthur looked at the woman defiantly, his normal spirit returning. Robin interrupted him before he could say anything. "Nephew of a friend waiting for us. Let's see if we can find my horse and get back to the others."

"Arthur, like the king of Camelot," she said as they walked.

"You know that story?" Arthur asked.

"Doesn't everyone? If only all men were so gallant. It's a strong name. You must live up to it."

"I shall try." Arthur glanced at her sidelong. "Did they hurt you?"

She shivered and a tear spilled down her cheek. Arthur slid his hand into hers and held it.

There was some humanity in the boy after all, Robin thought as he helped them onto his stallion's back.

He hadn't realized how far from the village Arthur had led him. The woman drew inside herself, holding Arthur tightly, saying very little. Shock had settled in, but having the boy in her arms appeared to bring her some peace.

Darkness was descending and temperatures were falling, but they finally found the barn where the others huddled around a small fire. Andrew praised God at Arthur's return, clasping him in two strong arms and peering into his face. "Come sit by the fire."

"This is Emlyn." Robin introduced the woman whose named they had learned as he walked alongside his stallion.

She stood straight-backed, her head held high. "Water?" she asked. "That I might wash?"

Henry didn't rise. His ribs were bandaged, cuts cleaned. "Behind you, by the stall." As she turned, he met Robin's eyes. "What happened?"

Stepping up to the fire, Robin said, "I had only caught up to Arthur—"

"We heard her scream," Arthur interrupted, clenching his fists. "Ugly brutes…hurting her."

Andrew crossed himself, pulled Arthur close. "I couldn't protect you today, my lord. Forgive me. You should not have to see blood and death at so young an age."

"Mercenaries?" Stephan asked. "John's men?"

"French, we think, but they may be routiers with no master. I did not ask, but left them for the wolves and crows. We should be safe here tonight, but must move quickly on the morrow should they have friends."

"They spoke of their army east, not far." Emlyn's voice cracked. Her face was reddened from a harsh scrubbing to cleanse dirt and savage men away. She quickly turned her back to the knights and rested her foot on a wooden crate to more easily wash beneath her skirt.

"French troops," Robin said.

Henry lowered his voice. "What of the woman?"

"We cannot leave her here. They murdered her family and she would suffer the same fate if they find her."

"Enough of this talk in front of my lord Arthur," Andrew scolded.

Arthur stood abruptly. "Stop treating me like a child." He faced them, defiant yet looking small, his arrogance faded.

Children grew up too soon in times like these when

armies ravaged the land. "What are we going to do with you, my lord?" Robin asked Arthur.

Henry palmed the crucifix hanging near his heart. "We can force you to come with us, Arthur, or you come peaceably. Speak with King Richard. You must believe us—he means you no harm."

"He will keep me a prisoner," Arthur declared. "Mama says she will never see me again!"

"Take us to the French border," Andrew said. "It is less than a day's ride."

"We cannot do that, my lord," Henry said. "We helped you today, put our lives at risk. If we release you, we have committed treason against our king."

Arthur opened his mouth to speak, then thought a moment. "You could be hanged." Silence fell as he looked from Henry to Stephan and Robin.

Hanging is the least of my worries. Robin's thoughts fled to Marian, his family. "It will be dangerous for any of us," he finally said, "but mostly for you until you are in the king's camp."

"You expect us to trust your king?" Andrew asked. "He and John are cut from the same Devil."

Stephan cleared his throat. "If we tell the king your concerns, would you consider meeting with him?"

Henry gaped at Stephan, who gave a confident nod. Robin tipped his head.

"And my mother?" Arthur asked. "You will tell the king to seek her release." His words could have come off as a command, but there was genuine concern in his voice.

"I will," Henry said.

Arthur studied the knights, his eyes filled with a new maturity as Robin and Stephan repeated Henry's promise.

seven

Arthur fell asleep curled in Emlyn's arms. He was still a child, that innocence unmasked when his eyes closed and his lashes brushed his cheeks. Emlyn looked as peaceful as he did. Andrew and Robin slept to either side of the door, boots on and swords within reach.

By the last glows of the fire, the knights spoke in whispers.

"Let him return to Brittany? How did you and Robin talk me into agreeing with this plan?" Henry rubbed the ache in his temple. "Why should we help the boy? He's a spoiled brat who looks down on us."

Stephan rolled to his side, cushioning his head on his arm. "That is his mother's fault. He's only nine summers. Is he right? He'll be little better than a prisoner, caged in the king's hands?"

"And Philip is any different?" Henry asked in an annoyed voice. Arthur might only be a child, but it wasn't unusual for a noble's son to be sent away at his age and raised in another household.

"You are tired of war, fighting, and politics." Stephan brushed his thumb along Henry's brow.

"And that is why I would commit treason?" Henry asked.

Stephan rolled his eyes. "Is it right to forcibly keep a child—any person—against their will?"

"Of course not," Henry said. Had it been Stephan's compassion that had first awakened his love for the man? The fierce warrior, the one who rescued young Allan and Little John from a possible hangman's noose.

Stephan heard the concern in Henry's voice. "We were ordered to escort the boy, but the boy wasn't there to bring along," he said, trying to convince him they were in the right. "We took it upon ourselves to find him. But rather than force him to accompany us—"

"We persuade Arthur that being ward to the king is a good thing," Henry said. "Mayhap we—and the king—can convince him, assure him, of that."

Stephan nodded. "Assure him that he won't be a prisoner."

"This is a bad idea," Henry said.

Stephan rubbed the back of Henry's hand. "It may be. But we can do something good, to help us forget the awful things we've seen, the things we've done. Like Robin and Allan pilfering supplies at Nottingham Castle."

"This is not the same, Stephan."

"Treason is treason." Stephan rolled to his back and folded his hands behind his head.

The king had been a prisoner himself. His own mother had been imprisoned for fifteen years by his father. How could he keep a mother and child separated? It was one thing for a boy to leave home to become a squire, or a girl sent to be raised in the home of her betrothed. Most saw their families from time to time.

Henry sighed. "Arthur would be treated well." He couldn't imagine a vindictive Richard, no matter how much he disliked the boy's mother. "Surely the king will be generous and let him see the duchess whenever either requests it."

"We can hope the king listens to reason."

Henry stared at the weathered beams overhead. The duchess hadn't seen her daughter in years and both he and Stephan knew that. He felt a sudden chill in his bones and pulled the blanket up to his chin. "How do we explain we had the boy in our grasp and let him go?"

"I haven't figured that out yet." Stephan smiled. "We'll have several days until we face the king."

Henry lay against Stephan, his hand splayed on Stephan's chest. "Is this my fault, that you have changed so much to consider we can do good things that go against the wishes of our king?"

Stephan inched closer, his warm breath heavy with the scent of wine they'd drunk earlier. "That Stephan was always buried 'neath this skin and bones. It took you and your love to let him burst out." His lips brushed Henry's. He looked over at the sleeping bundle buried beneath the woolen blanket next to Emlyn, and then captured Henry's mouth.

Henry melted into Stephan's passion, if only for a few moments to forget treason, kings and their brothers, and war.

⚜

A rooster crowing woke Henry hours later. No one else stirred as he stretched, the hay crackling beneath his bedroll. He rubbed his face and sat up, eyes widening at Robin spooning Emlyn's body. Surely, no…

Henry was far from naive. Married men strayed. From

England to the Holy Land and back he had seen that. Priests' pockets sagged with coin from penance. *A penny and a Pater Noster.*

But Robin? After all the man had been through—leaving the woman he had planned to marry, and twelve years later winning back her trust and love. Married finally. Would he lay with another woman while Marian waited for him?

Robin jerked awake as if he'd heard the outrage in Henry's mind. His hand flopped against something soft and he took a whiff of the air, and sat up sharply. "What…how…" He stared at Emlyn, who stirred at his movement, and then jumped to his feet.

"I thought you would be warmer than the boy." She smiled. "I was right."

"But nothing…nothing…?"

Henry chuckled as Emlyn's blush could have warmed the room.

"Just sleep," she said.

"Forgive me." Robin winced. "After yesterday what could I be thinking."

Emlyn said something else in a voice so low that Henry couldn't hear. She looked close to tears.

Robin knelt beside her and stroked her forehead. "Do not worry. We will see you find a place in a good household." He noticed Henry watching. "Let's wake the others and get on our way."

"Don't return to John's camp," Henry told Robin as they saddled their horses. Even Arthur was helping, explaining to Emlyn how to check that harness and cinch were comfortable for the animal before Andrew helped her mount one of the palfreys.

Stephan swung astride, stroked his stallion's neck. "I

agree with Henry."

"I will tell John the boy was well protected," Robin said. "When we attacked, the others were killed and I barely escaped with my life." He handed his horse's reins to Henry. "You must take my horse. I'll find an old nag somewhere between here and John's camp."

Henry understood Robin's motives, but wasn't sure he liked the idea. Arthur was quiet, watching them both with eagle eyes.

"The great archer Sir Robin can take out the enemy at two hundred yards," Stephan said. "John will surely wonder how you could miss your target."

"The trees were too thick. There was no clear shot." Robin's brow furrowed and he met Arthur's hard gaze. Arthur was listening intently, mouth tight with a grimace. "I followed them and three turned back to face me, but I lost them in the wood."

Henry shook his head. Robin had no way of knowing if John would believe the story. "He will kill you. Do not go back to John."

"Then what? Come with you?" Robin asked. "The king will not have me in his sight, and even if he would, his men will never trust me."

"Not very popular, are you, Sir Robin?" Andrew said, frowning. "And we are supposed to trust you?"

Henry glared at Andrew. "The king's men *know* you," he told Robin. "A few have been fooled by this ruse, but not most. The king may be ready to give up this game with his brother. He will welcome you back."

"I have failed John. But I can return to his fold and he will have no proof that I killed his mercenaries, or that you and Stephan were involved. He will have to accept my story. But should I go with you, John *will* know I've told King Richard of this treachery." Robin's voice trembled. "We foiled his plot to overthrow the king two years ago. Now we have ruined his plans to ensure the succession. John can taste revenge. He will destroy my family. He'll destroy us all."

"Forget John and the king," Henry said. "Go to England. Take your family far from Greyton."

"Go to Castle l'Aigle," Stephan added. "My brother will find a place for all of you."

Robin chuckled. "Do you see my father willingly going along with that?"

"There is another problem, Henry." Stephan pointed to Andrew and Arthur.

Henry cursed softly. "The devil must be at work. We try to do a good deed and still, everything we work for could be destroyed. John would not leave a blade of grass standing on my land, and the house, the cottages, shops—no more than ash. He might even raze Cartholme."

"I would not put it past him," Robin agreed.

"Andrew," Henry said, "take lead. Let's be off before we change our minds."

Andrew and Emlyn started down the road, but Arthur scrutinized the knights. He might only be nine, but he seemed to grasp that his rescuers were different from most men. They were the only reason he was alive. He finally spurred his horse.

"God keep you, Robin," Henry said.

"A favor, Stephan," Robin called. "Henry, go. I promise I won't keep Stephan long."

Stephan shrugged at Henry's questioning look, and Henry dug his heels into his stallion's flanks.

"What is this favor?" Stephan asked.

"Hit me." Robin pointed to his stomach, to his face. "Hard."

"Is that blood on— Is Robin all right?" Henry asked when Stephan caught up to him.

"He has a nasty cut below the eye and a bloody nose. Ribs to match yours." Stephan grimaced, flexing his hand. "His face will be ugly by the time he shows up in John's camp."

"Can he walk? And more important, will John believe him?"

"He moves slowly, and as to the other? I cannot say." Stephan uncorked his flask to get a sip of wine. "The question is, will King Richard understand why we turned the young master back to the Breton border."

Riding a few paces ahead, Andrew glanced over his shoulder at the knights. "Have you had a change of heart?"

Stephan paused, the flask perched at his lips. He shook his head. "If Lady Constance had followed the king's order and had the boy with her—"

"So *both* would be in Ranulf's hands?" Andrew shouted.

Arthur pivoted in his saddle, eyes wary. Riding at his side, Emlyn touched him gently on the arm.

"The duchess is his vassal, my lord," Henry reminded Andrew. "One simply does not disobey your liege lord. Not without consequences."

Stephan's brows rose.

Henry realized the irony of his words. "We are not disobeying," he argued. "As soon as Earl Ranulf intercepted the duchess it was out of our hands. We protected Arthur."

"By letting him go," Stephan said.

"This is in the king's interest. To show his compassion and trust."

Stephan gestured toward the Bretons. "This will only work if they cooperate." He nudged his stallion up to Arthur. "Our friend Robin risked everything to keep you alive. It's important that Count John does not learn the truth—about him, about us." He looked hard at Arthur. "Do you understand? You must not repeat our names or tell the truth of what has passed."

"Why should I care about you?" Arthur asked indignantly.

Emlyn tapped Arthur's hand. "My lord, building alliances is the wisest thing a ruler can do. Don't make enemies of those who have helped you. These men may swear fealty to you one day."

Cheeks coloring under Emlyn's gaze, Arthur agreed. He frowned, but effortlessly said, "We knew we were being followed and set a trap. My men overpowered the assassins."

"John might believe that." Stephan tipped his head at Henry. "Richard will not."

"That will be up to you to convince them," Andrew said. "My lord Arthur cannot do more."

"Just meet us in Rennes," Henry said.

Arthur nodded, his eyes softening as he turned to Emlyn. "You should accompany me. We have a grand palace. You can live there."

Emlyn lowered her head. "It is a generous offer, my lord." Her voice grew adamant. "But I expect King Richard to pay me for my losses. I must tell him this to his face."

Arthur didn't beg Emlyn, didn't try to order her. Henry was impressed. Would that he and Stephan could get the boy to act like a reasonable human being. Must be a woman's touch. The king had always seemed less prone to anger when he was in the presence of his mother, or with his queen, or his sister. A shame none of those noble ladies would be with Richard when they brought word of Arthur's escape.

eight

Richard's voice echoed through the bishop's hall at Les Andelys, his face scarlet. "Of all the low, despicable deeds. John has out-done himself. To order a child murdered."

A chill snaked up Henry's spine despite the fire in the central hearth. Richard had confirmed he received the letter Henry sent by messenger about Chester and Duchess Constance. He listened with ever-growing blackness about the knights' tracking Arthur and the attack by John's men. The duchess' abduction was a trifling matter compared to John's transgression. Henry had tried not to look at Stephan while he spoke, but his presence was a comfort. *At least we shall hang together.*

"Thank God Robin was there," Henry said. "We'd not be standing before you now, and Duke Arthur would be dead."

Richard frowned, firelight glinting off his reddish-gold hair. "Where is he? You had the boy in your hands."

"We let our guard down." Henry swallowed hard. He didn't like to bend the truth. "The boy was grateful. We drank too—"

"You expect me to believe you were in your cups and he escaped?" Richard scoffed. He knew them too well.

"Duke Arthur wants your assurances—"

"My assur—" Outraged, Richard glared at them. "God on the Cross, you released him!" He steamed to the door, spurs clattering and spitting dust from the rushes on the rough stone floor. "Guards!"

Four men plowed into the room like charging bulls. Swords drawn, they ringed Henry and Stephan. Henry kept his hand away from the hilt of his blade. They were at Richard's mercy, and Henry prayed he would calm and see reason.

"Sire, please..." Stephan cried out and took a step forward, palms up.

One guard nicked Stephan's hand with the tip of his sword. Stephan jerked back, stared at the blood dripping on to the floor rushes and grabbed his hand to staunch it. The guards exchanged nervous glances and looked uncertainly from the king to Henry and Stephan. These men knew them well. They were friends and trusted knights of the king.

"Lock them up," Richard shouted, his chest heaving, eyes glaring.

Stripped of their swords, they were hustled from the king's sight. In the outer hall, Emlyn rose from a cushioned window seat, concern creasing her face. Henry told the king her plight before revealing John's orders. He hoped Richard's anger wouldn't shake his willingness to aid her.

The guards escorted them to a dark, cold dungeon. "I don't understand, Henry," the guard said apologetically. "What in God's name have you done?"

"It's not my place to say." Henry pulled his cloak tight. "The king is right to be upset." He let his eyes adjust to the darkness. The room was small and bare. No cot, not even scratchy straw.

Stephan made himself as comfortable as possible sitting on the dirt floor with his back against the wall. "Give him time to think. He'll calm." He sounded more confident than Henry felt.

When the guards left and bolted the door Henry sat and leaned into Stephan's embrace. They huddled together through the night, Stephan dozing on and off. Henry couldn't sleep. He wondered how Robin fared. Had John accepted his story? But if Arthur didn't keep the facts to himself, Robin would be a dead man. Henry shivered, nestled closer to Stephan. *We did right by the boy. I know we did.*

Richard sent for Henry and Stephan late the next day. He stood at the central hearth, his back to them when they entered the hall. His shoulders rose and fell, his silence unnerving. He whirled on Henry and Stephan, furious. "Arthur is in no position to negotiate! Damn his mother, his foolhardy advisors." He held his hand up before Henry could speak, and then gestured at the guards. "Leave us."

The door closed behind the guards and Richard looked pointedly at the knights. "That boy was under orders to attend me at Rouen. Where is he?" His harsh voice cracked. "Chester's scheme has driven him into hiding when you had him in your hands. I will deal with

Chester, but you. How could you let him go? What have you to say?"

Doubts pervaded Henry's thoughts, but he put himself in the boy's position. Now to place the king there. "Arthur is a frightened child, sire. Do you remember when your father locked Queen Eleanor away? The years you could not see her?"

"Think of the boy, sire," Stephan said. "Convince him you will not let that happen to him."

Richard had been fifteen when King Henry imprisoned his mother. Their time together had been rare until he was crowned king many years later.

Richard growled. "She—Emlyn—said much the same. She seemed to have a way with my nephew."

"Arthur listened to her," Henry agreed, quietly thanking Emlyn.

"I suggested she stay at Les Andelys. Arthur will see a familiar face. He doesn't need coddling."

"Emlyn will offer none, sire," Henry said.

"She'll offer that right mix of affection, insights, and common sense." Richard lifted his chin, then exhaled sharply. "What does Arthur propose?"

"His lady mother's freedom from Earl Ranulf," Henry said. "And an understanding that he may have his mother and his sister's company when any of them desires."

"Constance is a bad influence," Richard muttered.

"Yes, sire. None of us would argue with that."

Richard paced the room kicking at the floor. He stopped at the sideboard and poured himself some drink. "Tell Arthur to meet with me in Rennes in a fortnight. Let us see if we can avoid war with the Bretons." He drained the wine in one long swallow, placed the cup down, and scrubbed his eyes. "What in God's name was Chester thinking? At least I understand my brother's motives."

Henry shook his head somberly. "This is a man you might choose to be king?"

Sighing heavily, Richard said, "A nine-year old or a brutal brother—not much choice. I doubt I can change John, but I might have some influence with Arthur. The least I must do is lay the groundwork for a strong alliance with the Bretons. The empire my father built must not fall into Philip Capet's greedy hands."

Stephan cleared his throat. "Sire, your brother has little patience for men who fail him."

"Arthur can identify us all," Henry added. "If he strays from our story and word gets to John... I fear what John will do to Robin."

Richard grabbed the jug of wine and dropped into the ornately-carved chair at the trestle. "I know he is your friend. He is mine as well. I forced him to go to John's camp—"

"He does this for you, sire, but he worries for his family more than for himself. I cannot say that he serves you best by being there," Henry said. "But John doesn't trust him. He never will."

"I know that." Richard met Henry's eyes, the fire in his own melting. He looked tired, older than his eight and thirty years, the gray in his reddish-gold hair more pronounced. "A king's life, the decisions we must make, are a burden. Men die in our service all the time."

Henry exhaled. "But if there is a way to prevent an unjust death—"

"I could have you all hanged!"

Stephan chuckled. "That would not be in your best interest, sire."

"That I know," Richard conceded, a smile curling his lip. "You are fortunate that I like you two. I won't deny

Robin's work with John has been crucial in our fight against the French. I trust Robin and respect him more than any other man. I'm grateful for his watchful eye on my brother."

Henry shifted slightly. He was determined to convince the king to end Robin's service with John. "Robin doesn't believe John will make another move to usurp your throne."

"My brother would be trustworthy," Richard said, "so long as there is no other to claim my crown. But Arthur lives, and we cannot let our guard down. John plays the game well." He waved Henry and Stephan to sit. "John can be heartless," Richard said flatly. "Everything they say of him may be true, but no one should forget he is intelligent and calculating. He knows Robin helps him win battles which makes him look good in my eyes. You think he would still seek revenge?"

"If John has taken his lessons from Robin to heart, he will not need him," Stephan said.

"Robin doesn't hate your brother, sire, but if anything happens to his family he will blame John. He would regret making an enemy of Robin," Henry said, "because Robin will kill him."

Richard could hardly have been surprised, but his gaze narrowed. "You are his friends. Talk sense into him. If Robin is outlawed there is nothing I could do to save him from the noose." He sat back in his chair. "So the game is up you say? Give John the chance to prove himself without one of my best knights at his side."

"There would be no ruse involved if you recall Robin," Henry said.

"Though you would suggest I remind John he would be wise to keep Robin as a friend."

"It might help," Henry said.

Richard thought a moment, then nodded sharply. "I need wine."

Stephan poured cups brimming with the sweet-smelling berry wine. Richard called for quill and parchment and penned a message to John. "Take this to my brother. Robin will accompany you to our meeting with Arthur in Rennes. And pray your trust in the boy is not misplaced." Richard folded the letter, added his seal impressed in red wax, and handed it to Henry. "I hope this is not too late."

Robin lay curled on the rush-covered floor of the keep. He wasn't able to lift his head. Through blurred vision he discerned a pair of mud-encrusted boots of one of the two men who had held him while a third punched, kicked, and slashed him. His nose was broken and blood dribbled over his lip and into his mouth. The coppery taste made his stomach roil. His ribs and groin ached.

"Get him out of my sight." John's shrill voice would have woken the dead. "Lock him up."

Huge hands clenched his arms and lifted him. They dragged him across the rough stone of the old hall.

"Idiot," a voice spat.

"Traitor," another man growled.

The accusations registered in Robin's brain but he was in no position to respond. He had barely uttered a few words when John sicced his brutes on him. The beating was expected, but this was the worst he'd endured at John's hands. All his thoughts fled to Marian, to home. *Let me live to see my wife again...my son...*

The guards shoved Robin down a dark stairwell. Weak, his legs gave way and he rolled the last few feet to the cold dirt floor. Behind him, the hinges on the door creaked and a key clicked in the lock.

What would John do now? If he learned the true story, Robin was a dead man. Was the boy Arthur trustworthy? Would he keep the truth hidden? Robin managed a sick chuckle. *I am done for...*

Groaning, Robin spat blood pooling in his mouth. There would be no help from King Richard. He was not one to give up, but hope fled from him like stars fleeing the rising sun.

He thought of Marian as he often did when nights grew dark. He closed his eyes, his arms going round her, felt her flesh as close as two people could be, saw her smile, and his heart filled with peace.

nine

The River Seine sparkled. It snaked around the valley unfolding before Henry and Stephan as the sun slipped past midday. A church tower dominated the land, its shadow drenching the adjoining abbey like a coming storm. Pastures and farmland bore tents more numerous than Henry could count. John's camp. Troops were gathering for the spring campaign.

John had commandeered the abbot's residence, surely to the abbot's horror as John was not known to be a godly man. His banner hung by the door and two guards grew alert when Henry and Stephan drew closer.

A familiar figure emerged from the house. Mercadier. The captain waved, a hint of a smile on his battle-scarred face. Henry had met the soldier at the king's Christmas court, placing the stories he had heard about the ruthless butcher with the face. Killing the enemy was expected in battle, but harming the poor and innocent and ravaging villages were vile acts that Mercadier and his men—and John—took too far.

Mercadier tipped his head. "Lord Henry de Grey, am I

right?"

Henry acknowledged the captain and nodded towards Stephan. "Sir Stephan and I bring a message from the king." He dismounted and handed the reins to a waiting groom.

The captain jutted his chin, his hand resting on the hilt of his sword. "We'd no reports that King Richard was nearby."

Henry found a smile. "Near three days' ride, so your scouts have done their jobs well."

"They let you through. Bread and gruel for them tonight." Mercadier chuckled, pleased with his own joke. "Stand aside," he shouted at the guards, his voice a harsh contrast to the communal prayers drifting from the church. "Come. I shall see if Prince John might see you now."

Henry cringed. *Prince John.*

Boisterous voices carried from the hall. Mercadier swung the door wide. Inside, he looked to the dais, and not seeing John there, cast his gaze around the room. Forty or more knights sat at two long trestles. A fire in the hearth blazed and torches lined the bare walls. Servants refilled jugs of wine and replaced empty platters with ones overflowing with salted herring, wheaten bread, and cheeses.

"Wait here," Mercadier said and set off to a corner where a group of men huddled over a chess board.

Henry got his first good look at John. He had last seen him on his knees in Lisieux two years past, begging King Richard's forgiveness for his treason. "Don't be afraid, John, you are a child," Richard had said. It still made Henry angry. The king had brushed off John's traitorous actions.

Mercadier leaned in, whispering in John's ear. Not a

muscle in John's face twitched, but he stood, and without looking at the knights, strode to the head of the table. Conversation in the hall dwindled to nothing as he settled on the huge oaken chair. He gestured to a page, who adjusted the plush crimson cushions on the seat to his satisfaction. An invisible signal must have passed between John and his captain, because Mercadier encouraged Henry and Stephan forward.

Henry forced his hands to steady. Fear didn't make his insides quake, but rather his dread that such a dishonest man could be king. If only Richard and his queen could spend more time with each other. The king had lavished great attention on his wife during Christmastide in Poitiers, but if that had extended to intimacy in the bedchamber there was no word of an heir forthcoming.

John studied the knights over the bridge of his nose. His elbows rested on the ornate arms of chair, one he had transported with him as his army moved from one town to the next.

"My lord," Henry said as he and Stephan bowed.

John lifted a cup brimming with wine to the knights and then took a sip. "You have arrived in time to celebrate our forthcoming victories. Let's rout the French bastards, send them scurrying like wild pigs."

"To victory, my lord," Henry said.

John tapped his goblet. "Two of my dear brother's knights. What brings you here?" He drew back, suspicious. "Surely he'd have only sent a lowly messenger if this was a call to his Easter court."

Men in the room guffawed, but Henry didn't let the insult bother him. "King Richard did not tell us his plans for Easter, my lord."

John exhaled a breath, leaned forward as if expecting Henry to hand him Richard's message. Without hesitation

Henry said, "We bring a message from the king for Sir Robin."

"That man crushed my brother's heart," John cried out. "Richard wants nothing to do with him." John's eyes met a hooded monk's near the hearth and he barely tipped his head. "Let me see this message while we wait for Sir Robin."

"It is for Sir Robin's eyes only, my lord," Henry said, sensing Stephan straighten beside him.

Every breath in the room caught and men froze in place.

John lunged to his feet, wine spilling over the sides of his cup. He looked ready to split open a head or two, gulped what was left of his drink. He reddened with indignation. "I am the brother of the king. I have every right to know."

Henry didn't back down. His voice remained steady, though he wasn't certain how because his throat felt like it had been coated with glue. "The king instructed me to hand this directly to Sir Robin."

John rounded the table and bulled into Henry and Stephan. "What is this game?" He shoved Henry back, eyes livid. "What are your orders?"

"We are to accompany Sir Robin."

"Where?" John shouted.

"Sir Robin will tell us."

John laughed. "Well of course. We all do as our king commands. Sit, enjoy my generosity, while we wait for Sir Robin." He snapped his fingers at a squire who was replenishing half empty platters of cheese and fruit. "Bring food for my brother's knights. The rest of you, out! And hurry Sir Robin along if you see him."

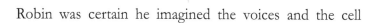

Robin was certain he imagined the voices and the cell

door swinging wide at the top of the stairs. He was too weak to look and his body would have screamed if he moved.

"Christ Jesu." The voice echoed off the stone. "You can smell the stench from here."

Boots pounded the wooden steps and then two men lifted him from the blood- and urine-soaked ground. Robin's mouth was dry, but bile rose in his throat. He was made to drink and he choked, spitting half the watered ale on the ground. He cried out when arms circled his waist to lead him up the stairs.

"Get him some clean clothes," a familiar voice ordered. Robin squinted in the dimmed light as they took him to a room with a bath.

"Want to tell me why he did this to you?" The room was dark, shuttered against late March winds, but candlelight flickered on the round gentle face.

"Brother William?" It was Tuck, the only one in John's camp that Robin trusted. They went back a long way and the former man-at-arms-turned-spy had been part of the Nottingham ring—a messenger between Robin and the king's men in the days before Richard was released from his German prison. The ginger-haired man stayed behind when the knights returned to Normandy with the king, but a few months back he appeared in John's camp with messages from Allan and Marian. Dressed in the dark robes of the Benedictine order, Tuck had been invited to stay to see to the souls of John's men.

"Sorry I couldn't get to you sooner." Tuck touched Robin's jaw, causing Robin to shrink back. "Lord John would let no one near your cell."

"How long?" Robin asked as Tuck began to strip off his clothes.

"Three days." Tuck grimaced at the bruises visible

through the dirt and blood on Robin's torso. Robin groaned stepping into the bath, glad for Tuck's help. He sank into the water and Tuck offered him the ale again. "Drink it slowly."

A page came in and set a clean tunic, braies, and hose on a coffer. "Anything else, Brother?"

"Bandages and some food—just bread. I don't think he'll manage anything more than that for another day or two."

Tuck sponged dried, crusty blood from Robin's face and chest, thanking the boy when he reappeared with linen strips and the bread. When he departed, Tuck said, "Lord Henry and Sir Stephan are in the hall with a message from the king."

Robin sat up slowly, splashing water over the side of the bath. "Has there been any word about Arthur?"

"The young Breton duke? Is that what this is about?"

"I would be surprised if it were not." Keeping his voice low, Robin told Tuck of the planned assassination and the knights' roles in it.

"Look at you—his bullies did this without knowing you foiled the attempt on Arthur's life. They could have killed you. Next time they might. And the king? He will slap John's hand and say a prayer for your soul." Tuck threw the washing cloth into the water, his wolf-green eyes narrowing and frown lines crisscrossing his forehead. "You—all of you—did the right thing by Arthur."

Robin grabbed Tuck's huge fist. "Go back to England. Carry on our good deeds. Before you return to Nottingham, take a message to Marian. Tell her my first thoughts and my last every day are of her and Robert, that I love her."

A smile washed across Tuck's face. "I will."

John drummed the arms of his plush chair, chin jutted out. Mercadier had kept council with him after the other men departed, both speaking in low voices interrupted by guffaws and sniggering.

Seated next to Stephan, Henry flicked his gaze to the two men. "What do you suppose Mercadier is telling him?"

"That it is a good thing he did not kill Robin for his failure," Stephan said, looking towards the door, anxious to see Robin.

"A pleasant thought," Henry replied sarcastically.

"I imagine Robin would think so." Stephan noticed John's hawk-like eyes on them. He smiled, raised his mug to the count, and drank down the tepid brew. "Not as awful as King Henry's," he told Henry. The old king had been notoriously miserly and purchased cheap ale and wine for his household. Stephan tipped the mug to get the last drop, smacked his lips, and then poured himself a second drink.

Henry watched Stephan douse a chunk of bread and cheese with honey. He hardly felt like eating and couldn't relax in John's presence. Murderously angry one moment, pleasant host the next, and cunning, John had been careful not to give away his knowledge of the king's summons to Constance and Arthur for the meeting in Rouen. Word of Chester's deed would have been relayed to him. Henry wanted to believe John supported his brother, but found it impossible. *Never underestimate your enemy.*

"Three more weeks," Stephan said, pushing the platter of salted herring away. "Fish pickled, fish stuffed, fish salted. I'll be glad to see meat on the table when Easter comes."

"Sacrifice is good for the soul." The voice from the

past drifted over Henry's shoulder.

Henry stood abruptly, rattling the table, breath caught in his throat. Edric Weston. Dressed in solid black, he stepped from the shadows, his pale face ghostly. Weston was three years younger than Henry, a schemer who thought nothing of destroying lives to have his own way. He'd come close to ruining Henry's. There were few men Henry despised more.

Like Count John, Weston's title had been stripped and his land taken by the king after the siege of Nottingham. And like John, the king had restored his title when his debt was paid. Henry knew Weston had left England. He shouldn't be surprised to find him here with John's household.

"But then your souls are damned," Weston added, dark eyes rippling with aversion for the men who helped destroy him.

On his feet, Stephan spat. "What would you know of souls, Weston? You do not have one."

"That is Lord Edric to you," Edric said with disdain.

Staring at the fire crackling in the hearth, Henry took a long slow breath. He finally spoke in a low voice, forcing himself to be civil. "You are fortunate to have a sister who pays your fines and a king who would rather take your coin than your head." Henry loved Elle dearly—as a friend. But her actions had shocked him, and he still struggled with her decision to help her brother after the hell he had put them both through.

Edric smirked. "I am, Henry. A pity you didn't marry Elle." He shot him an irritated look. "My sister is impetuous, marrying that landless knight when she could have had you and Greyton. Your father, rest his soul, and I would have been so pleased with that match."

"Land and wealth mean little to Elle. She and Sir John

love each other." Henry remembered his not-so-auspicious run-in with the dark-haired, scrawny camp follower. Three years later, Little John fought off men who would have usurped Richard's throne and was knighted.

Edric met Henry and Stephan with loathing in his eyes. "She saved you from the sin of adultery, leaving you free to lust after your blond lover. But what is it that you call your vile habit? Love? The priests would call it something else."

"You forget blackmail doesn't look good on you, Weston." Henry clenched his fists, his soul hotter than the dying embers in the fire. He curbed his desire to use a fist on Edric's face. Had Edric succeeded, not only would Henry be married to Elle, but Edric himself would have forced a marriage with Henry's sister Bea.

"Remaking old acquaintances, are we?" The new voice echoed from the doorway.

Henry shoved Edric aside to welcome Robin with open arms. Robin gasped when his grip tightened, but Henry eased up and studied the bruises on Robin's face. "Are you well?"

"He did not kill me," Robin said without jest. He strode over to John with a limp and bowed. "You sent for me, my lord?"

John scowled. "Pardon me for interrupting your reunion. You kept us waiting." John's eyes narrowed, his lips drawn in a hard line.

"Apologies, my lord," Robin said.

Henry bristled. It was hard to watch Robin's subservience to Count John, watch him struggle to stand upright, to keep a tremor from his voice.

Mercadier waved Henry forward, and he and Stephan stepped briskly to stand at Robin's side.

"Here's your man, Lord de Grey," John said, his tone charming.

Withdrawing the parchment, Henry turned to Robin. "From King Richard."

Robin took the letter from Henry's outstretched hand and eyed the wax seal. He slid his thumb beneath it and unrolled the message. He read it quickly, and then looked up at John. "The king would have me proceed to Rennes for his meeting with Duke Arthur and his advisors." Robin handed the letter to John.

"You?" John asked, holding the message towards the candlelight to read it. "Chester kidnapped the boy's mother? What is this!" He was incensed and seemed genuinely surprised at the news. "Good God, we shall be at war with the Bretons."

Skeptical of John's sincerity, Henry squelched a shudder. John's plot would have precipitated war, too, had it been successful, so his reaction to Duchess Constance's abduction was almost laughable. Henry imagined John would see this as another opportunity for Robin to do away with Arthur. And if Robin failed this time?

"Let me pen a message for my brother," John said, more calmly, "and then you can be on your way. Make your preparations and see me ere you leave."

"My lord, if I might ask—should we wait a day or two? Are you able to ride, Robin?" Henry asked.

"That was quite the spill you took facing those French scouts," Mercadier agreed with a lie.

Robin didn't flinch. "We can be on the road well before sunset."

"Good then, that is settled," John said and called for wine, quill, and parchment. A lute player joined the stream of men returning to the warmth of the hall. The boy sat cross-legged on the floor beside John and strummed an old tune. John even smiled at him. His men basked in the waning day and the rafters rumbled with raucous laughter and loud conversations. A few stared at Robin with pity or good riddance, Henry couldn't tell. Edric Weston didn't mask the malicious smile on his face. Henry's stomach twisted. He didn't like that Edric had overheard the king's message, and liked it less when the bastard followed them to the stables.

"Heard from your friend FitzHenry in Nottingham?" Edric asked. "I heard the king was quick to forgive his nephew. I guess it pays to be a royal bastard."

"Only when one has other skills useful to your liege lord." Pride rang through Robin's voice. "FitzHenry is good with accounts, a capable administrator for one so young." William FitzHenry was his name to the rest of the kingdom, and he was known as the bastard son of the king's late brother Hal. In truth he was Allan a Dale, an orphan taken under Robin's wing, his squire when they were on crusade. On the return to England, Allan spied for the king as a clerk to John's men at Nottingham Castle while Richard was still a captive of the Holy Roman Emperor. Richard knighted him after the siege there, ordering him to remain—one of his *observers* in England.

"Capable in many ways," Henry said. In the months prior to and since the siege, Allan's illicit supply management skills and his associates' work had been the savior of many who would have starved. Henry smiled. Robin's *merry men*—Allan, Tuck, Will, Much—brave men all. Robbing from the rich, giving to the poor.

God help them all if the king should discover their deeds.

ten

The knights let Robin set the pace straight to the stables, a timbered building that smelled of hay and dung and horse sweat. The odors were pleasant after being in Count John's presence, Henry thought. He watched Robin as two young grooms retrieved their horses and saddled Robin's gray.

"You can barely move," he said.

"That's not true. It only hurts when I lift my arms or bend...or turn." Robin grimaced as he twisted.

Stephan laughed. "Or walk?"

A groom tied down blankets and a saddle pack on Robin's horse and tried not to smile.

Robin ignored them all. "I would be happy just to crawl away from this camp."

"Now Robin, why would you say that?" Edric strode in and tossed his bag to the fair-haired squire coming up behind him. He snapped at him to saddle another mount.

"What are you doing here?" Henry snarled.

"Is that any way to speak to the man who tried to save you from possible ruin with one l'Aigle, and who would be your sister's husband were it not for another l'Aigle?" Edric's eyes bore into Stephan. "Bea was taken in by that huge castle in Yorkshire with its six stone towers and a keep the size of Nottingham's. Must be something about the de Grey's that they are attracted to men with big…" He looked suggestively at Stephan's groin.

Stephan scratched his crotch. "Envious, Weston?" he sneered.

"Get out," Henry said.

"But I cannot, Henry." Edric smacked his lips. "I'm here to accompany you."

It was to their credit that none of the knights blinked. The grooms and squire may have sensed hostility, but kept their heads low and to their work.

Edric patted his sleeve. "My orders from Count John, and greetings from him for his nephew Arthur."

Henry swung away, looking across his horse's back at Stephan. "Damn him," he whispered and then mounted.

Struggling to get astride his horse, Robin grimaced. He set heels to the animal's flanks and urged him away from camp.

"Don't wait for me," Edric waved, grunting as Henry and Stephan rode off after Robin.

"I cannot believe we must endure that bastard's company. Damn John," Henry repeated when they were out of earshot.

What should have been a pleasant journey with close friends turned into a silent and tension-filled ride. The knights could not speak freely with Weston there and even when they slowed the horses to a walk, conversation settled on the conditions of the road and the gloomy weather. Hours later, they were still dry and glad to find a barn for shelter for the night. The second day was much like the first, but longer in the saddle. The skies grew ominous as the sun set, and a cold drizzle had soaked them by the time they stopped for the night.

Edric carried on as if they were old friends. "Little Eleanor takes after her namesake," he said as he placed his saddle over a stall.

Henry thought fondly of Little John's first letter after Eleanor's birth, how touched he felt by the queen mother's gift of clothing and toys. It rankled Henry that Edric had seen the child when he had not yet laid eyes on her. He didn't want to ask if Edric had also visited Cartholme since Elle had given Little John a second child, a son, at Christmastide.

"Quite the spirited child," Edric said. He shook out his bedroll and spread it on a thin layer of hay. "Curious too, like my little sister. God, Henry—you could have married Elle."

"Shut up, Weston," Robin said, already stretched out beneath a woolen blanket.

"John must be desperate to send you along." Henry spat. "Doesn't he have his own spies in Duchess Constance's court?"

"Don't antagonize him," Stephan said, ignoring Edric's glare. "I don't want to hear his voice."

Henry exhaled sharply and not because Stephan planted himself on the other side of the barn. They certainly didn't need to give Edric proof they were more than friends. His exasperation was more with himself for letting the bastard taunt him. Edric's presence alone was enough for that.

"Why so suspicious, friends?" Edric settled himself against one of the stalls and tossed a blanket across his back. "I am here to ensure Robin completes his mission and—"

"And then kill me," Robin said, "so if I am captured I will not break under torture and tie the deed back to John."

Edric roared with laughter, even wiped tears from his eyes. "You have quite the imagination, Robin." He took a long breath. "That cannot be further from the truth. I am here to help, that is all. You underestimate your usefulness to Prince John."

"I didn't know you knew him so well," Robin said.

Henry shuddered. Edric had been a small cog in John's plot against the king in England. Had he grown that close to the count, or did he like to believe he had?

"Weston wouldn't dare kill me," Robin said. "What would John do without my sword arm and my bow?" He chuckled.

Edric started to respond but thought better of it.

"Get some sleep," Robin said.

Henry dropped his bedroll near Robin's and removed his sword belt. He took the sword from the scabbard and set it in the space between them. "Never hurts to have the blade nearby."

Robin nodded. "I think we are safe for tonight."

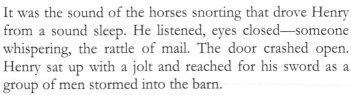

It was the sound of the horses snorting that drove Henry from a sound sleep. He listened, eyes closed—someone whispering, the rattle of mail. The door crashed open. Henry sat up with a jolt and reached for his sword as a group of men stormed into the barn.

Robin cried out as two hulking figures lifted him from the ground. Henry found himself surrounded and counted at least a dozen men. He slowly laid his weapon on the ground. Edric scrambled to hide in the horse stall but was dragged out kicking and screaming. Their captors laughed at him, quite amused by his behavior. Were they soldiers? Outlaws? The light revealed the dull beige of their tunics, their chausses black leather. Two held swords at Stephan's throat.

"We are emissaries from King Richard. Who are you and what do you want?" Henry demanded.

One of the interlopers was inspecting the knights' stallions. "Good stock. Did you steal these horses?"

An outlaw wouldn't care where they had gotten the animals. They weren't French, at least not by their accents. But mercenaries working for King Philip?

"I tell you we are knights of the king." Henry's voice sounded confident, but sharp.

"What is your business?"

"That is between us and the king. Who are you?"

"Search their—" The leader stared shrewdly at Robin as sunlight crept into the barn. "You are Robin Carpenter," he said. Henry felt a twinge of hope until he added, "The king has a price on your head."

The men holding Robin shoved him roughly to their captain. Robin groaned, bent at the waist, trying to stay on his feet. Henry stepped forward but didn't get far, stopped by a sword at his gut. "King Richard forgave that debt, just as he did for his brother the Count of Mortain," Henry said.

"We heard the king would not have Carpenter in his sight."

"That much is true," Robin said.

"Yet you are an emissary for the king."

"He is," Edric said. "I was with Prince John when Lord de Grey and Sir Stephan brought the king's message ordering Robin to—"

"Lord de Grey?" the man asked, scrutinizing Henry and Stephan. When Henry nodded, he issued orders to his second who hurried from the barn. "There may be no bounty on you, Carpenter, but my master will pay well to see you."

"Who in God's name—" Edric spluttered.

"Shut your mouth." He frowned at Edric. "Don't suppose you'll be worth more than that stallion you ride, eh?"

"I am Edric Weston, Lord of Westorby."

The mercenary appeared to have heard of Edric. "In name only, my lord," he said. "You are nothing more than Count John's lackey. Clothes on your back. That horse. And a fine leather saddle. But your lands are still in the king's hands."

Edric pouted, and though Henry was impressed with their captor's knowledge, his mind raced. Who was this man, and what of his master?

"And Sir Stephan—you've a brother who will pay a princely price for you." He tilted his head and the men guarding Stephan and Robin prodded them towards the door. "Saddle the horses," he ordered and looked from Edric to Henry. "Lord de Grey, you will also come with us."

Henry's pulse raced. Could he negotiate? "The king will be most displeased. You have disrupted a mission of great importance. Let us be on our way and we shall say nothing to him."

"You may discuss it with the one I take orders from, my lord, but I do not plan to be stripped of my rank if I do not bring you in."

"Who do you report to?" Henry asked, his voice harsh as two of the saddled horses were led outside.

"You will find out soon enough. Now, if you would, join the others."

A sword at Henry's back gave him little choice.

"What of me?" Edric asked.

The captain signaled and the burly guards grabbed Edric by the arms. Henry stepped outside as Edric's grousing rolled off his tongue. The sun was still low and the heavy wood swept ghostly shadows around them. The mercenaries had good animals, though not as fine as the ones he and Stephan rode. As they mounted, Robin gave Henry a shrug and studied their captors, accepting their current fate. He was in no condition to break away. Besides, there were fifteen of them—near four to one odds. Even their friend Allan wouldn't take that bet. Stephan held tight to the pommel of his saddle, his face grey. He hadn't said a word, which was unusual, even in this mad situation.

The captain ran his hand along the haunches of the Spanish bay. "Quite the nice beast." He grasped the reins and mounted.

"But that's my horse," Edric protested.

One of the guards shoved Edric to the ground and hurried past him to his own horse. The captain pivoted as Edric got to his feet and brushed dirt from his clothes. He started towards the one remaining mount.

"Move out," the captain ordered as a distant bell pealed Lauds and one of his men took the reins of the last horse.

"What are you doing?" Edric demanded.

"There's a village a short ways up the road. Find a horse there and go back to Count John. We'll let him tell King Richard the news that we expect to be paid well. Three hundred pounds."

"You cannot do this. The king will have your blood," Edric shouted as the mercenaries headed west. "Where will he find you?"

"Do not worry," the captain called over his shoulder.

"We'll send word to the king about the prisoner exchange within a fortnight." He kicked his horse and cantered to the head of his men.

The picture of Edric kicking at the ground was cause for a victory shout if not a laugh, but Henry and his friends were surrounded by men who might do them harm. The exhilaration of seeing Edric put in his place was fleeting.

They slowed a short while later. Henry glanced at Robin. These men, whoever they were, didn't seem to care their prize was broken and battered. Where were they taking them? "How far?" he called to the captain.

"Another day's ride."

"You've a wounded man here." Henry saw Robin wave away his concern, but Robin's face was pinched. Every jolt on the horse made him twinge.

The mercenary didn't bother to turn round.

"He can barely sit astri—" Henry's eyes caught on Stephan. His chin was pressed to his chest, that gray pallor still present. He looked worse than Robin.

"Might we stop for a piss?" Robin asked. "You'd not given us a chance after you woke us so rudely."

The captain laughed. "Would be a shame to present you with your pants soiled." He raised a hand and shouted, "Hold!"

Stephan sat like a stone on his black bay. Henry stretched, eyeing him worriedly, but jumped down from Greycloud to relieve himself on the side of the road. When he turned round, Stephan still hadn't budged. Henry strode towards him as the sun pierced the tree canopy. Stephan's mouth moved but no words formed on his lips. Suddenly, he swayed.

"Stephan!" Henry cried as Stephan toppled from the saddle. Henry caught him, staggering backwards before they both hit the ground.

Groaning, Stephan managed to sit with help from one of the guards. He leaned back into Henry's arms and closed his eyes again. Robin appeared beside them and touched Stephan's forehead. "He is burning up."

"Get him to drink," the captain said, pulling a flask from his belt, his voice revealing far more concern for his hostages than Henry expected.

"Stephan?" Robin pressed the drink to Stephan's mouth. A few drops got past his lips, the rest dribbled onto his chin.

Stephan spluttered, coughed, and tried to push the flask away, but Robin encouraged him to try another swallow.

Squeezing Stephan's hand, Henry said, "You need to drink." Another day on the road. "We'll find a healer today. Get you well," he said, imploring the captain with a look. "These men want that ransom so you'll be fine in no time." Henry met Robin's strong gaze and felt hopeful. "Let him ride with me."

Henry held Stephan tightly as the troop rode on and the sun arced across the sky. The guards gave them a wide berth, and in between prayers Henry whispered words of comfort and love. "God cannot take you like this. We must grow old and gray together, spend each day by a warm hearth." He chuckled, nuzzled Stephan's neck. "Naked. On a bear rug. Fire blazing. Your skin, hard muscles, your flesh...close as two people can be." Stephan threaded his fingers through Henry's. Resting his chin on Stephan's shoulder, Henry whispered into his ear. "I love you."

eleven

The road twisted through forest and the crags of the valley until the towers and outer massive wall of a castle loomed. Henry shifted in the saddle to keep his grip firm on Stephan. His head lolled back on Henry's shoulder, cheeks flushed and like fire. His condition had worsened as their second day on the road waned.

Guards atop the gate tower hardly gave the mercenaries a look. They had been expected. The barbican would be deadly to an enemy. Murder holes loomed overhead and arrow slits lined the thick stone walls, but their horses clattered through it and entered the bailey unchallenged. Strange. Henry still had no sense of who their captors were—they were a well disciplined troop who had spoken few words.

A clang from the blacksmith's shop sent a jolt through Henry, but Robin's emotions and physical pain remained buried behind a stoic gaze taking measure of the armored men on the wall walk. When a knight emerged from the keep and Robin spotted him, a flash of surprise swept his face.

"Do you know him?" Henry asked as the man came out of the shadows and the Templar cross on his tunic was revealed.

Before Robin could respond, the warrior monk shouted out. "Robin du Louviers!"

"Sir Guillaume! I thought you were in Anjou."

"We need a doctor," the captain interrupted, signaling his men to help Stephan.

Guillaume shouted orders, and then his eyes settled on the yellowing bruise on Robin's face and on his slow movements. "Jesu, what happened to you?"

"A story for another time," Robin said. "What are you doing here?"

"We were on route to Rouen when the king's messenger reached us with the news of the Duchess Constance and her son." Guillaume stretched his hand out to clasp Robin's arm. He acknowledged Henry with a nod as men carted Stephan into the keep. "Lord de Grey, the king said you would be traveling from Jumièges and that we should accompany you to Rennes. Come, my lady awaits you."

My lady. And a Templar courtier. Henry had his suspicions about this lady as the mercenaries dispersed and Guillaume led them inside. Two more Templars opened the heavy oaken doors into the great hall. Fire blazed in the hearth and tapestries hung from every wall to ward off the chill, but it was the lady who radiated warmth. Well into her seventies, Eleanor of Aquitaine still possessed a beauty many women were never blessed with. For all she had lived through, her face was gentle, her green eyes sparked with passion.

Henry and Robin picked up their pace to approach her. Both drew down to their knees. The ruby and emerald rings on the queen mother's slim fingers glimmered in the firelight, the sleeves of her gown brushing the floor as Henry kissed her hand. "Madam," he said and smiled up at her.

"My friends." She sighed after Robin repeated Henry's gesture. "Please rise," she said, eyes narrowing as Robin struggled to get up.

"I will be fine in a few more days, madam," Robin answered before she could ask.

Eleanor's deep blue gown rippled as she swept round to sit. "Mayhap you should ride in the litter with my ladies," she said while her attendants unfolded wooden stools to one side of her for her guests. "They would enjoy your company."

"My lady Marian would not be pleased should she hear that."

"About your injury? Or that you were surrounded by beautiful young women?" Eleanor raised a brow, grinning.

"Both, madam," Robin said with a chuckle.

"She is well, then?"

Robin's expression softened. "Her last letter came ages ago, but I oft have news of her through Henry's correspondence."

Worry must have been etched on Henry's face, because Eleanor's smile faded when she turned to him. "This picture is incomplete. My favorite blond knight is missing."

"Stephan fell ill whilst we were on the road, madam," Henry said. "Your men have taken him to the healer."

"I shall say a prayer and will look in on him if he cannot depart with us on the morrow."

Henry chewed his lower lip. It would take a miracle for Stephan to be well enough to ride in another day. He had seen him injured in the Holy Land, stayed by his side in Nottingham when he'd been wounded by a crossbow bolt—he'd suffered with fever then and recovered. It might take days, but he would be fine.

"Tell me about your sister?" Eleanor's voice broke his reverie.

"Bea and my brother-by-marriage await their second child near midsummer's day. And you may have heard that Elle delivered another babe, a boy named Geoffrey."

"I remember their wedding fondly. Sir John was such a shy young man, but the depth of his love shone like a beacon."

Her eyes met Henry's and for a moment he dreaded she might suggest he should marry. She did, but not in the way he had expected.

She laid her hand atop his. "It is rare to see that in a man's eyes. You have a special love with our dear Stephan. I once loved Henry that way. I begat many sons for him, sealing that part of the marriage bargain, and I do think he loved me. For a while." Her hand tightened on Henry's. "When love fades, it may be hard to accept. You may stop breathing, feel dead inside, but you will find your breath and move on as I did."

Henry's heart ached for her. How could old King Henry stray when he had married such a beautiful, intelligent, and vibrant wife? But Henry's love with Stephan was different. "Nothing will dim my love for Stephan. Only death will separate us, though my heart and soul will be tangled with his no matter here or in heaven."

Robin clamped a hand across his back. "I think Henry is right. I knew Stephan long before they laid eyes on each other. This man changed him. There are more men than you can count who would tempt Stephan away, but he found—they both found—something, someone to hold on to."

"Like you have found with Marian?"

"Like that, yes."

Eleanor smiled at them. Maybe she thought them both naive, and if they lived to be her age, they might look back at their lives differently. Henry imagined himself at seventy and Stephan at two and seventy and grinned. Love would still win out when their muscles sagged and gray hairs covered their balding heads and lines webbed their faces.

"Henry?" It was Eleanor again who brought him back to the present. "Why that silly face?"

Henry laughed. "It is not a picture I should share, madam, of Stephan and me as old men."

"I will keep only the thought of the dark-haired, broad-shouldered knight and his lover, the handsome blond." She chuckled. "I shall want to talk of politics—dear God, what has Chester done? I do not carry much sympathy for my former daughter-in-law, but this news weighs heavy on my mind. We shall talk later. I don't want to ruin my appetite now."

She settled at the long trestle that had been laid out with platters of cheese, dried apples, and bread. "Bring the wine from the coffer," she told Henry, and then listened intently with a smug look when Robin spoke of the early morning raid by her "mercenaries."

"I am almost sorry that Weston is not here," she said. "To see his expression as my men left him standing there without a horse must have been priceless, as when he realized his sister was about to marry Little John rather than you."

Henry agreed. He and Elle had kept that ruse for months trying to delay the marriage arranged by his father and her brother until King Richard returned from captivity. They had almost been foiled until Henry asked the queen mother to intercede.

"Weston's shock and indignation was almost as good when he betrayed Robin in Nottingham thinking the king would forgive his treason," Henry said as he poured the berry-scented wine into their goblets. Seeing Edric led away with the other traitors had been a small comfort, especially when Robin's fate hung in the air at that time.

Eleanor sighed, looked hard at Robin as he sat beside her. "Is this John's doing?"

"Your son gave me a task to do and I failed." Robin's voice cracked with emotion. "I could never kill a child."

Eleanor closed her eyes, caught her breath. Hands trembling, she gripped them as in prayer. "God forgive me for letting John become a man who would do such a horrible thing."

Henry knelt at Eleanor's side. "It is not your doing, madam."

"I was not there for him as he grew to manhood." She opened her eyes and stared at the blazing fire. John was six when she had been imprisoned by her husband. She rarely saw John before Richard was crowned.

"Through no fault of your own," Robin said.

"That is neither here nor there," Eleanor said, reaching for her wine.. "Sit, Henry, and let us cheer the failure of Robin's mission."

They raised their goblets as servants appeared with platters of roasted pike smothered in onions and garlic. Robin's aches didn't curb his appetite and he scooped a second piece of fish onto his trencher when Eleanor insisted. Between mouthfuls, Robin regaled her with the stories Gilbert l'Aigle had written of Robert's training as a squire.

Henry picked at his food as the rose-scented candles on the table burned lower. He wanted to check on Stephan and wished the meal to end. When Robin drove his eating knife into a slab of cheese, Henry was jarred by a disturbing thought about Edric. "Weston will tell John we were captured by mercenaries who expect silver for our release, but he'll soon learn we are in your company, madam. How do we explain that?"

Eleanor thought a moment. "I will send word to John that my men freed you from those routiers without one coin changing hands."

"And when Weston reappears?" Henry glanced at Robin. "You know he will. And he will recognize those *mercenaries*."

An un-queenly snort from Eleanor made both knights turn. She clapped her hands and laughed. "Another chance to see his face when he realizes he has been duped."

A grin settled on Robin's face. Even Henry smiled, but cautioned, "We must keep a close watch on Arthur at the king's meeting in Rennes."

Eleanor nodded. "Weston will see that getting close enough to follow through on John's orders will be nigh on impossible."

Mouth pursed smugly, Robin raised his goblet to the queen. Henry lifted his, and then drank. The young duke would be safe for the moment, and Robin would be away from John. And Stephan—

"Well, Henry," Eleanor said, "I can see you are of no mind for a game of chess. I shall have to play against Robin, who indulges me and makes it far too easy for me to win."

"If I might see how Stephan fares?" he asked.

She waved him away, her face filled with compassion. When the door closed behind him, she said, "Some of us bring no expectations to a marriage. It is our duty to our families, to our kingdom. If love comes, we feel blessed by God. But I wonder why He would bring two people together when they cannot have any semblance of a normal life. Is it worth the torture?" She traced her finger on the lion etched on her goblet. "Do you think Henry and Stephan ask that question of themselves?"

Robin stood and offered Eleanor his arm. "They would be less than human if they did not."

twelve

The monk leading Henry through the dim corridor held a small wooden crucifix in his hands. His leather sandals scuffed the stone floor and his robes rustled, the only sounds breaking the silence as they walked to the infirmary.

"Is the doctor with him?" Henry asked.

"He tended him when you first arrived. He has done all he can."

"What do you mean?"

"Your friend is in God's hands. Pray for him. Send for the priest if he needs—"

"No." Henry swallowed hard. "He does not need last rites." Stephan was strong. This was mere fever. And Stephan would not be happy with a priest spouting prayers over his head. He never had much use for the Church. Henry still prayed, but like Stephan, he had rejected the priests' condemnation of men who loved other men. God wouldn't banish them to the fires of Hell. He was as certain of that as he was in his love for

Stephan.

Henry's mind raced, suddenly consumed by the memory of a priest droning last rites over his servant Roger who had died on their way to the Holy Land. The sound of rain beating against the tent wall and the stench of sweat and illness lashed Henry like a whip, and he heard the monk's voice but not his words. He stopped outside Stephan's cell, his knees weak, and then stumbled to the bedside. Light from a tallow candle cast Stephan's flushed face in a sickly yellow glow. His skin was like fire, fever eating away at his body. Henry dipped a cloth in the bowl of water by the bed and sponged Stephan's forehead and cheeks. He gripped Stephan's hand with his own unaware of the time passing. Stephan's breathing was calm and he slept, but not restfully. He thrashed in the bed and called out Henry's name more than once.

"I'm here, Stephan," Henry whispered. "Tell me the story where you told Richard your tourney skills were as good as Will Marshal. Three saddles, jewel-studded bridles, two stallions. You're such a braggart... Tell me."

Stephan muttered and moaned. He settled back to sleep with Henry gently thumbing his forehead.

A hand on his shoulder shook Henry awake. "You should get to your own bed, my friend."

Henry lifted his head from Stephan's chest. "I am fine, Robin. I must stay here." He touched Stephan's brow. His fever still raged.

"We will be on the road just after daybreak."

"I cannot leave him." Henry's voice cracked. "If he should die, he must not believe I left him here alone."

Robin tightened his grip on Henry. "He cannot know—"

"He does, Robin." Henry stared at Stephan's face, stroked his temple. Nothing. Not a twitch. "I am here,

Stephan."

"Stay a day, mayhap two." Robin kissed Stephan, jarred by the heat radiating from his cheeks. He buried a kiss in Henry's hair. "We will see you in Rennes."

Henry didn't reply, but he heard Robin leave. He laid his hand atop Stephan's and felt him move. "Stephan?" With trembling fingers, he touched his face, saw his eyes flick beneath heavy lids.

Stephan groaned. "Where—" He started to cough.

"Shh. Do not try to speak." Henry reached for the cup of watered wine beside the bed. He dabbed his finger into it, pressed it to Stephan's lips.

Stephan struggled to open his eyes. Henry placed another drop of wine on his mouth and he captured it.

"I knew the wine would revive you," Henry said, smiling. "More?"

Chest rising, falling, in struggled breaths, Stephan's eyes clamped closed.

"Stephan?" Henry pressed the cloth to his cheeks again and anguish filled his voice. "Do not make me call for the priest," he cried out. Tears streamed down his face. He nuzzled Stephan's hand, cupped his chin, and then brushed his lips with a gentle kiss. "I am not ready for you to leave."

Monks chanting prayers for Lauds woke Henry and a short while later he heard the clatter of hoofs on the cobbles outside. Throat parched, he gulped down the watered wine and poured another cup. Sunlight filtering through the oil cloth on the window touched Stephan's face. Henry laid a finger on his forehead. Still warm, but not burning up. Hopeful, Henry dipped the cloth in the water basin and began his sponging routine again.

It was hours later when a monk brought him bread

and honey to break the fast. He was famished and chomped down on the warm nutty loaf. A voice at the door startled him and he almost choked on the food.

"Do I see healthy color in his face?"

Henry glanced back. He didn't recognize the stout gray-haired man. "Are you the doctor?"

"That is what they call me. I am but a servant of God here, but I treat the sick amongst us." He slogged into the room and looked down at Stephan. "He looks better. You have been with him all night?"

Henry nodded, refusing to meet the man's eyes. He wasn't certain he could mask the depth of his feelings after his restless sleep at Stephan's side.

The monk felt Stephan's head, pressed his hand on his chest. "The dying often sense the presence of others. Mayhap it strengthens their will to live, though they are in God's hands."

"He is not dying," Henry insisted.

"I would not have said that when he was first brought to me. But I do not understand our Heavenly Father's ways."

Henry dabbed Stephan's forehead with the dampened cloth. "He heard my prayers."

"God works in mysterious ways." The monk's body blocked the sun and cast a shadow across Stephan's face. His voice grew low and dark. "Did you ask forgiveness for your sins? He does see and know all."

The words made Henry's gut twist and he had to still his trembling hands. He dipped one corner of the cloth into the water bowl again and then touched it to Stephan's lips. "My sins?"

"Your concern for this knight goes beyond friendship, doesn't it? You have given this man more than your heart."

How can loving another person be a sin? Stephan's words.

"God knows my heart," Henry said quietly. "I do not need a lecture from you. He will be my judge."

With a muttered Latin oath, the monk crossed himself and stalked towards the door. He hovered there a moment and called back, "*If* he wakes, send for me."

Henry refused to acknowledge him, but his hands shook violently. When, not if, he mouthed, threading his fingers through Stephan's. "You must fight. You would not be happy passing because of a mere fever. You are a warrior, Stephan. Fight this like you are on a field of battle. Slash, thrust—drive this illness into the ground. Fight, Stephan, fight."

Henry began his ministrations, repeating the cool cloth to forehead, cheeks, temple, and neck. The bell was ringing Sext and he realized he had dozed off again, his head resting on Stephan's chest. Stiff, he stood and stretched, and then wandered to the window. Robin and Queen Eleanor would arrive in Rennes by sunset on the morrow. He could ride at twice their pace, but to meet them he must leave in the morning.

He pulled the oil cloth on the window aside and stared at the arched columns of the cloisters and the monks walking in silence there. Please, he prayed, let me see that Stephan is well before then.

"Do you give up?"

The voice was scratchy and weak, but sounded like birdsong to Henry's ear.

"Stephan!" Henry flew to his side.

"A drink, please."

Henry's fingers wouldn't work and he fumbled, nearly tipping the watered wine to the floor. As he lifted Stephan's head to bring the cup to his mouth he knew the fever had broken. "Just a sip," he said, quietly thanking God and watching the dullness in Stephan's eyes turn to a familiar glint.

Swallowing the wine, Stephan's lips curled in a crooked smile. "Did I dream you were cursing a priest?"

Henry laughed. "Not a curse. I told him to mind his own business."

He offered Stephan another taste of the drink, but Stephan clutched his wrist with a feeble grip, his touch powerful with unspoken words. Henry leaned close and kissed him.

Stephan cupped Henry's chin and stroked the dark fuzz of his beard. There could be a hundred knights charging him atop magnificent white stallions, but Henry would see nothing but the love in his knight's tender gaze. His heart beat wildly and he smiled down at Stephan. "Let's get you well, sir knight."

The afternoon wore on and Stephan ate a few morsels of bread and then slept until the monks' chants echoed through the corridors.

"Help me up," Stephan said as bells pealed the call to Vespers.

"You aren't going anywhere." Henry plumped the thin pillow. "Lie down."

Stephan shifted slightly, tossing off the woolen blanket and struggling to get his legs off the bed. "The chamber pot? And hurry, before I piss myself." He burst out laughing.

thirteen

Queen Eleanor's entourage settled in at the palace in Rennes. Robin was exhausted, his body aching after two more days on the road. On the ramparts, he watched dark clouds scudding across the sky and wondered if the king's troop would arrive before rain set in. He ignored the scuff of boots on the stairs, too tired to turn until the intruder gasped.

"Sir Robert? Robert du Louviers?" Though he wore the fleur-de-lis on his surcoat, it was Jean de Charny's smile that filled Robin's vision. Jean was one of the few men who called Robin by his given name.

"It is Robin Carpenter now."

"Like the penniless knight I first met, newly arrived from England and taken under Richard's wing. We were allies then, standing up to King Henry." Jean's smile faded. Deep lines furrowed his brow and his hair was the color of snow. "So it's true? King Richard took the lands he had given you?"

Robin chuckled ruefully. "I would say your king took them first, and that whilst my king suffered in the hands of the Holy Roman Emperor."

"An unfortunate event."

"More than thirteen months, Jean." Bitterness crept into Robin's voice. "And it would have been longer if King Philip and Count John had had their way."

Jean extended his hand and Robin took it vigorously noting the strength in the elderly knight's grip. Not just strong, he was lean and looking like a prince in his dark blue surcoat and jewel-studded belt.

"I am glad to see you well," Robin said, "though as we had feared in Acre, we no longer sit on the same side. I wonder if you're there when we meet your king on the battlefield." Robin looked at the cottages and shops outside the city walls. Farmland stretched beyond the town and he wondered whether war would mar the landscape here as he'd seen in far too many places. "Why are you here and not with Philip?"

"I could ask the same of you and your liege lord." The wind rippled the flag above the keep and whipped Jean's hair. Smoothing it away from his face he followed Robin's gaze. "It is a peaceful place, no?"

Distant thunder sounded, but it was calming rather than threatening. It wouldn't last. Like the peace here—the specter of war was too close.

Weariness plagued Robin. "Jean, we are old friends and need not play games with each other."

Jean spread his hands. "I am here to bring Arthur to Paris," he said. "Did Richard send you to take the boy?"

"The king knows I have met the young duke, and believes he will trust me."

"Let me guess. You showed him your recurve bow, let him loose a few arrows, and captured his heart." Jean was amused. "You do not play fair, Robin."

Robin would have laughed, but the threats against Arthur were too great. "It is John that I worry about."

"I'm not surprised." Jean leaned on the ramparts and stared at the distant horizon.

Robin hesitated before he spoke. "Let us face facts. Neither your king nor mine have the boy's best interests at heart. Both will use him. Philip because he hates King Richard, and Richard because he will dangle Arthur to keep John in line, and because he *does* want to see if the young duke has what it takes to be named his successor. You and I both know Philip would never name Arthur heir to the kingdom of France. Why would the boy—or his mother—see Philip or France as a better choice?"

"Richard is a sodomite," Jean said flatly.

"Then call your king one as well!" Robin protested. "He was the one who invited Richard to share his bed when he pledged himself to Philip against old King Henry."

"That was nothing more than a gesture of solidarity and you know it."

"Then why do you think Richard takes pleasure with boys, because that is the furthest from the truth. If you mean he is an adulterer, then yes, I won't deny that."

"He would be a bad influence."

"And Philip Capet is pure and holy? Good God, I find that hard to believe. King Richard is no threat to Arthur. I trust him, Jean. If you have any influence over his mother, please speak with her. But let me tell you it is John we must watch." Robin checked that no one might overhear him and spread his palms against the rough stone of the embrasures. He leaned towards Jean and whispered. "He wants Arthur dead."

Jean's mouth twitched. "How do you know this?"

"Because I am supposed to kill him." Robin told Jean the sordid story, and how he, Stephan and Henry had prevented the assassination. He chose not to reveal their role in Arthur's escape. "You can trust me, Jean. I would never harm Arthur. Let us keep the boy safe."

"I should warn the Bretons about John's orders, though honestly, I doubt Richard will have any luck in his negotiations. Watch your step here, Robert, else you'll end up in chains." Jean vigorously shook his head. "You are but one man standing between Arthur and the Count of Mortain, and if you do not carry out John's orders, someone else will. Arthur must come back to Paris with me."

"Jean—"

"He is not in Rennes you know."

"My God, they would not dare defy the king a second time." Robin clenched his fist. "Fools. Of course they would. Where is he? Wait—you are here, so you do not know, do you?"

Jean chuckled. "My spies report he has been seen at Brest, St Malo, Dinan, Nantes, and a score of other places. We both leave Rennes empty-handed."

Giving the roads one last glance, Robin was already dreading the king's arrival. Still no sign of him. Wind from the north made him shiver. Thunder echoed in the distance again and a soft drizzle began to fall. Richard would be cold, wet and tired, and angry when he learned his orders had been tossed onto a burning pyre. Perhaps the presence of the queen mother would soothe the Lionheart's Angevin temper.

Robin rubbed his hands together. "Empty-handed?" He tapped the leather coin purse strapped to his belt. "What say you—a round of chess?"

"Like old times." Jean waved his hand towards the

stairs.

In the great hall a young page poured wine for the knights before Jean shooed him from the room. The shutters on the windows rattled from the approaching storm and by the time Robin made his second move rain was beating on the walls.

King Richard's long legs took him from one side of the chamber to the other like a whirlwind. "Not here?" His voice rattled the glass on the windows, recent additions to the upper room of the keep that had been set aside for his visit.

Robin stood at Queen Eleanor's side. He had warned her that Arthur would not be joining them. By the time King Richard had ridden through the gates the skies were unleashing their fury—not that the storm matched the thunder in the king's eyes.

Warming herself by the brazier Eleanor looked into the courtyard. "Well, that ruins the idea of a nice family gathering for Easter court." Her voice dripped with sarcasm. Still, she was pragmatic, and wholly unsurprised by the Bretons' actions.

"War will do that," Richard muttered impatiently. "Damn John. Damn Chester and the Bretons." He sat heavily and reached for a goblet of wine. War aged him. He was more gray, his brow furrowed, and his once youthful body sagged.

Swallowing back his drink, he watched Robin, studying the bruises on his face. "It appears that Lord de Grey and Sir Stephan arrived just before John killed you."

Robin lowered his head. "Thank you for sending them, sire."

"Where is your merry little band?"

Eleanor crossed herself, brought her gold and

bejeweled crucifix to her lips. Richard looked from her to Robin. "Has something happened?"

"Sir Stephan took ill, sire, and is in the care of monks at the monastery at Alençon. Henry refused to leave his side. The physician did not expect Stephan to live."

A trace of sadness flickered in Richard's eyes. "Ten years. Barely a pup when he arrived in Poitou. You did not know Stephan then, Maman, but he was like me at eighteen summers. Strong, fearless. Had skills that rivaled Will Marshal's in the tournaments. Robin introduced us, and from that day forward, he had his sword at my back more times than you would want to know. His loss grieves me greatly. May God keep him."

"He is not dead yet." Eleanor tsked.

"You are right, Maman. Prayers, not mourning." Richard smacked his thigh. "Now what are we to do with Johnny?"

The king rarely used John's nickname, except with other family. The name fit a child, which is how Richard often felt about his brother's behavior.

"Prayers will do little good where your brother is concerned. John feels threatened." Eleanor smoothed her thumb across the raised design on the wine goblet. "He expects to inherit your crown. Your wife—have you seen her of late?"

"You know I have not. Joanna would have told you."

"Berengaria is your queen and should provide you heirs, Richard. Get you to her—"

"I have no time to idle away in bed, Maman."

"It does not take long as you well know. If you can find time to bed your whores—" She held her hand up before a word of protest escaped his mouth. "Yes, Berengaria knows, as does your sister Joanna. I would wager the entire kingdom knows. And God certainly does."

Robin shifted uncomfortably. He was not an innocent himself, but that was in days before he married Marian.

"It is not their business." Richard was indignant, but he did not deny the truth. "If the negotiations go well with the Bretons, I will make my way to my wife. It is true we have not been together for months, but the fact remains that God has not blessed us—"

"Mayhap because you swive anything with breasts?"

"Enough, Maman."

Eleanor traced the deep groove in the arms of her chair. "I know Henry and Stephan do not stray."

Robin agreed, nodding. "And Stephan was not always that way, madam."

"A shame you picked up that trait from your father." Eleanor dug her nails into the chair and studied her son.

A good thing old King Henry is in his grave, bless his soul, Robin thought. The queen looked like she would scratch out his eyes if he were here.

The room descended into uneasy silence. Richard jutted his chin defiantly, the muscles of his jaw bulging.

Eleanor turned to Robin. "Do you find pleasure with the camp whores?"

"Madame, I—" Robin searched for words that would not sound critical of the king. Before he had married Robin enjoyed the ladies, but now he wouldn't dream of being with another woman. His body ached on many a night, but he desperately wanted Marian only.

Richard scoffed. "We did not come to Rennes to discuss Robin's whoring or my own physical needs. I'll take that up with my confessor. Mayhap the good Lord will see it is an act of charity." He looked at Robin, charm and innocence glowing on his ruddy complexion. "Isn't that so, Robin?"

Robin stiffened under the queen's gaze, but conceded with a nod, "The ladies need coin so they will not starve."

"Exactly!" Richard cried, lifting his empty goblet to Robin.

"Oh you two." Eleanor blew out a disgusted breath.

"And the Church will not starve either. You can wager my penance will be more than in *Pater Nosters* alone." Richard chuckled, tipping his head at Robin. "Have Allan take bets on that one."

Eleanor's face softened at the mention of Allan. Like Robin, she hadn't seen the former squire since the king had knighted him after the siege in Nottingham.

Richard strode to the side table and poured a round of wine. "John must be dealt with."

"Let me speak with John." Eleanor tapped her fingers together. "I will convince him you have no intention of naming Arthur your heir."

"Is that true?" Robin looked from Richard to Eleanor. "Will John believe you?"

"He will listen to Maman. But we must be prepared should anything happen to either John or me. We cannot have Arthur under Philip's wing." Richard handed Robin a cup overflowing with a smoky oak-scented drink.

"I will keep you out of this as best I can," Eleanor said, "and not indicate that Richard knows of John's orders for you to take my grandson from this earth."

"He has his suspicions." Robin rubbed his sore ribs. "And likely has more now that the king ordered me to Rennes."

"Are you tiring of service to my brother, Robin?" Richard asked with a dry smile. "I recognize the difficulty of your position, but who else can I trust?"

John held his family at sword point no matter which camp Robin served. He didn't trust John not to harm them, but he wouldn't forsake his king. Not yet. Not after fifteen years at his side. He must trust his instincts. "You asked me to stay at John's side for as long as you lived, sire, which God willing, will be for a very long time."

"You found Arthur once," Richard said. "I want you to find him again before his men steal him away to France."

"And what of Chester and Constance?" Eleanor asked. "Have you received word from the earl?"

"Ranulf is as stubborn as she is. He hasn't locked her in the dungeon, but with that mouth of hers I could not blame him if he did. I must sweeten the pot to convince him to release her."

"Sweeten it?" Eleanor snarled. "He needs no silver, no more land from you. He is already the wealthiest baron in your kingdom. He is defying you, Richard. You are the king. Demand—"

Richard held his hand up. "For the moment it serves a purpose."

"You did not…" Eleanor shook her head.

"I had nothing to do with Ranulf's plot to abduct Constance, and never would have approved of it had I known. But she and her barons have ill-treated him, given him none of the rights as duke that are his by his marriage to the woman." Richard looked shrewdly at his mother. "I did agree he might keep her under house arrest until such time as I say. This might just bring Arthur and his advisors to their knees without a drop of blood spilled."

A bolt of lightning struck nearby and showered them in light. Thunder rumbled, echoing off the stone façade of the keep. The tall oaken doors of the chamber quaked and tapestries hung to either side rippled. Lightning crackled and the wind howled, but it was a knock on the door that made them all jump.

"Come," Richard shouted.

Thoroughly soaked, Henry strode up to the king and knelt. His dark hair was plastered to his head, his boots splattered with mud. He looked weary but confident, which gave Robin hope.

"Tell us you have good news of our friend," Richard said, dispensing with the usual formal greetings and gesturing for Henry to rise.

Eleanor clasped her hands in her lap, fingers clenching the fabric of her gown.

"Stephan will recover." Henry smiled as Eleanor reached for him and rested her palm against his cheek. He took her hand, kissing her ruby-bejeweled finger.

Richard looked at the servant. "Draw a warm bath for Lord de Grey," he said and turned back to Henry. "We cannot have you catch a chill. There is work ahead for you and Robin. While we are here, listen for talk of Arthur's whereabouts. But for now," he looked between the two knights, "get some sleep. We shall talk on the morrow. And Maman, I will have you accompany me when I meet with the Bretons. You might help curb my desire to strangle someone."

fourteen

Fine gold-plated trenchers and platters of roasted salmon in a saffron and wine sauce, fruit, and wheaten bread were spread on the table, the bread so warm that Henry could see steam rising from it. He reached for the pot of lavender-infused honey, mouth watering at the thought of the bread dripping with it, when King Richard stormed into the hall.

"Fools!" Richard shouted.

The young page pouring wine startled, sending cups crashing into each other. Henry and Robin rose and stepped back from the table, their heads bowed as Queen Eleanor followed the king into the room. Her deep crimson gown nearly matched the color in his face.

"Eat and enjoy ere we pack and leave on the morrow." Richard's voice was hoarse from hours negotiating Arthur's future.

A failure then. Henry was hardly surprised.

As the page hustled to wipe the spill, the king grabbed

a goblet overflowing with wine and sent more sloshing over its rim. He took a long drink, paced to the window and stared outside. "Tell me you discovered Arthur's whereabouts." His grip tightened on the cup like it was someone's neck. "I've a mind to plunder everything between here and there and pull the boy to my bosom, into my saddle, and whisk him to Rouen on my own." He twisted round, hurling the goblet across the room.

Henry looked apprehensively from Robin to the king. "He has been placed at St Malo, Dinan, and in Paris." He swallowed hard. If only they had taken Arthur to the king when they'd had the chance. It was a miracle the king even allowed them in his presence.

"Get me another drink," Richard shouted at the trembling servant. Calming a moment, he helped his mother sit and then took his place at the head of the table. He piled his plate with fish and fiercely ripped a chunk of bread from the loaf. "Sit down."

Henry and Robin took their places opposite Eleanor. Robin waited until the page served the queen and then filled his own plate. Henry's stomach churned, his appetite gone. Their betrayal meant war. What had he been thinking, him, so opposed to war.

"You will find Arthur," Richard said.

A disturbance outside the hall had Henry and Robin on their feet. A sharp voice warned, "You cannot interrupt—"

The door flew open. Three paces in Edric Weston stopped abruptly and bowed, the king's clerk nearly plowing into him.

"My king," Edric said.

"I am sorry, sire," the clerk said. "I tried to stop Lord Weston but he insisted he must see you."

"Weston? Do I know you?" Richard glared at Edric,

his eating knife poised and ready to strike.

Weaponless like Richard, their swords left at the gate, Henry and Robin stood between Edric and the king and queen mother. Henry had prayed they were rid of the man and struggled to keep his anger in check.

Edric bowed deeply. "Your brother, the Count of Mortain, sent me to accompany Sir Robin, sire." He chose his words carefully with no intention of reminding the king of their last meeting after the siege of Nottingham. "Surely these good knights told you of our encounter with the outlaws and the ransom. Prince John was relieved to hear the queen's men—"

Two burly knights flew into the room, weapons at Edric's back. "Shall we escort Lord Weston out, sire?" one asked.

Edric spun around, the voice familiar to him. "You?" he cried, recognizing the leader of the mercenaries who had left him stranded a few days earlier with nothing but the clothes on his back.

Sir Guillaume smirked, tipping his head at the baffled baron.

"Who are you? What are you doing here?" Edric whirled back on Robin. "You bastards—you knew?"

Sir Guillaume butted Edric's shoulder with the pommel of his sword. Edric stumbled forward, but caught himself.

"Watch your tongue in the presence of the queen mother," the guard hissed.

"Do you mean there was no ransom, and never would be? The queen's message about your rescue—just a ruse?" Heat colored Edric's cheeks. "You are not mercenaries at all. You are king's men."

"Queen's men," Henry corrected. "And no, we did not know until we were escorted before Queen Eleanor."

Eleanor was trying hard not to laugh. "I knew this would be entertaining." She winked at Henry who had to admit Edric's expression reminded him of someone who had fallen into pig slop.

"My queen," Edric bowed. "You are magnificent as ever, madam."

"And you, Lord Weston, appear to be as perturbed as on your sister's wedding day." Eleanor dug the proverbial blade deeper, and Henry struggled to keep a straight face. "Elle and Sir John make such a handsome couple. And I understand they have made you an uncle!"

Fists clenched at his side, Edric drew a long breath but managed a tight smile.

The king was in no mood for pleasantries. "My brother's orders give you no right to barge into my hall."

Eleanor stiffened in her chair. "This is the one who betrayed Robin to you. Surely you remember, Richard. He is one of the Nottingham fourteen."

"And you have *him* at your table." Edric sneered at Robin.

"I choose who sits with me, Weston," Richard said, his voice menacingly low. "Robin does not need a caretaker. You may leave."

"I am only here to help, sire." The guard prodded Weston, but he ignored him. "Your brother, the prince, ordered me to accompany Sir Robin. I must do—"

"Tomorrow, if you must. Not tonight. Now get out of my sight."

Sir Guillaume clamped a hand on Edric. Edric ripped his arm from the knight's grasp. Flushed with anger, he sent a scathing look to Henry and Robin, and then marched from the room with a huff.

Richard stabbed his fish with his knife. "That was satisfying," he said and snarled as he crammed the food into his mouth. "Eat, eat up." He looked from his mother to the knights. "You look worried."

Robin rubbed the back of his neck. "Your brother still expects me to get rid of Arthur. I swear…I'll keep that boy from harm if I can, but Weston will be there, close enough to pounce and ensure I don't fail a second time."

"Do what you must," Richard said.

"I do not mean to kill Weston either." Robin exchanged a glance with Henry.

Henry agreed with a nod, though the thought had crossed his mind. Edric had only caused pain to the people closest to him. *God forgive me. I only want him dead.*

"Weston is a man who shifts loyalties at the slightest provocation." Eleanor smiled mischievously. "Remind Lord Weston that John will deny all involvement. Rather than finding John will reward him—should he become king—Weston might find himself as John's whipping boy."

"He wants his lands back," Henry said. "Likely seeks a marriage that will bring him that and more."

"And I am not inclined to give him either," Richard said. "I would sooner give your hand in marriage to an heiress than his any day."

Henry coughed. "Sire, please, you know how I—"

"Another time, Henry. Let us enjoy this meal in peace. On the morrow we depart under a flag of truce. But by Holy Week my troops will be gathered to put these Bretons in their place."

The fire had been banked and it was only the snores, coughs, and whispering voices that told Henry the hall had been transformed into sleeping quarters for two score knights and their retainers. Navigating the maze, Robin stepped on someone's hand and earned a curse as he made his way to pallets the queen's servants had set out for them. Robin plunked down on his mat and set his belt aside. He unrolled the woolen blanket, shook it vigorously, and pulled it over himself.

"Goodnight," Henry whispered. He leaned down to straighten his own bedding. "God's bones. This cannot be."

Robin rolled over. "What's amiss?"

"Edric," Henry said, pointing to the sleeping body next to his pallet. He stood, frantically seeking another spot in the hall where he might lay. If there was one, he couldn't see it in the darkened room.

Exhaling sharply, he moved Robin's belt and placed it with his own at their heads. He shoved his pallet to butt up against Robin's, fell onto it and tossed and turned beneath his blanket, shivering at the thought of being so near Edric Weston. Trying to remove all traces of that from his mind, he said a silent prayer for Stephan. He saw him standing in a field of lavender. Naked. The muscles on his torso shone with moisture, his golden hair windswept. With that thought, he finally dozed off.

The room was still dark when Henry woke to the rustle of clothing and the moans of heated sex. The court whores were servicing knights, a few minutes' pleasure for a coin or two. Beside him, Edric moaned. His breaths were swift, loud from exertion. Too close. Henry threw his arm across his ear to mask the noise. He buried his chin against his chest, but his movement attracted attention. A small hand crept over his hip and slid to his groin. Henry gasped, feeling his cock swell from the swift strokes against his braies.

Edric slapped the girl. "Hands off," he sputtered between thrusts. "Feisty bitch." She didn't even whimper as he pressed her back to the bedding and viciously pounded his manhood into her. "He doesn't swive women anyway."

"Then he must be ready for you, my lord." She cried out as Edric claimed her body, hard and deep.

Henry wanted to pummel the bastard, but that would've woken the whole room. He lay unmoving, shocked that another's touch had sent that familiar ache to his groin. When Stephan was at his side, beautiful young women might turn his head but didn't cause a rise. But Stephan wasn't here. Henry missed him so. His laugh. The way his hair fell across his face, his eyelashes brushing his cheeks when he slept.

Edric's grunts and the smell of sex broke his thoughts. Edric drew in a sharp breath and froze, spent his seed, and collapsed atop the girl. Her fingers drifted to Henry's back.

"Leave me be." Henry threw off her hand.

"Girl just trying to feed herself," she whispered. Edric started to snore and she pushed him off, tugging her kirtle down. "Don't mean anything. Don't mean you love your honey less."

"But it does."

"Must be a special kind of love. Lucky you." She stood, brushed herself off, and carefully stepped over Edric to ply her trade to another willing taker.

"Lucky me," Henry said and closed his eyes, letting sleep take him back to Stephan.

fifteen

"The king would not truly marry me off to an heiress," Henry said, watching Queen Eleanor's retinue starting towards the gate, cart wheels creaking and horse hoofs clacking on the stone cobbles. With war looming, there would be no Easter court and she was returning to Fontevrault.

"Wouldn't that be better than turning a poor girl over to Edric Weston?" Robin checked the cinch on his saddle as a squire led Henry's horse from the stable. "Do you think you will avoid marriage forever? The king is distracted by this business with Arthur and by the war against France. You had better hope this never ends, ere he has time to consider your station."

Henry scowled, took the reins from the squire and stroked his horse's neck. "At least he will think of the alliances his sister might bring before he thinks of me. Joanna tells me she hears rumors more than anything from the king's own mouth. She only dreams of having a loving husband, but knows she must do the *right* thing for her family." Right as defined by her brother, Henry thought. Most widows could choose whether to remarry, but a sister of the king had little choice.

"You forget she flatly refused to marry Al-Adil when the king suggested that as part of a truce with Saladin."

Henry had never been certain if Richard meant that offer as a serious proposal, or merely a ploy during negotiations rather than meeting Saladin on the battlefield. Surely the latter. A Christian marrying a Muslim? It would have required Joanna's conversion or Al-Adil's, and approval from the Pope.

Laughter caused Henry to spin round. Edric sauntered from the hall sharing a joke with group of king's men.

God help me. Another day in that bastard's company.

The door to a bakeshop swung wide filling the courtyard with divine aromas of wheaten bread and meat pies. A pretty young woman with an infectious smile offered loaves to the knights. Edric drew up beside her pretending to inspect her wares, his hand resting in the small of her back and moving lower to caress her buttocks as he placed a penny in her pouch. "You will have all my coin, woman," he said.

Edric's night visitor?

She scowled at Edric, but did not pull away. Her basket emptied quickly under the watchful eye of a thin child. He approached the knights as if he belonged amongst them. In his brown woolen tunic and handsomely stitched belt, he looked too well dressed for a thief, though he reminded Henry of his introduction to Little John in the king's camp at Tours. He'd been about the boy's size, had the same dark wavy hair, stealing what he and Allan needed to survive.

The boy held his palms up for a handout from the knights. "Away, boy," one shouted.

Edric shoved the child. He lost his footing and plowed into Henry's horse, which skittered and sidled. The bread woman cried out, jerking away from Edric.

"Careful," Henry said, grabbing the boy before he fell beneath the animal's hoofs.

"Thank you, my lord," the woman said.

Henry looked from her to the boy—her son? Both had the same blue eyes, and a few strands of hair the color of his had escaped from her wimple.

"Are you hungry?" Henry asked.

"I help my ma," he said.

Henry nodded and gave him a penny. The woman curtsied, poking the boy when he failed to give thanks. He tipped his head, a shock of that dark hair covering his face, and then darted past the horses being trooped from the stables for the king's men.

"My God," Edric said as she wandered back to the shop, "not only pleasing in bed, but she's pretty in daylight. We *could* bring her along to keep us warm." He leaned across Henry's saddle and smirked. "What am I thinking? Less to share I suppose. But the boy? A bit young, though mayhap you are like the ancient Romans?"

Henry grasped Edric wrists. The bastard was lucky Henry didn't have a dagger in his hand. "You vile, despicable—"

"Henry, leave him." Robin's voice was cool, but his glare at Edric would cut through mail.

Edric resisted Henry's grip, but Henry held tight.

"I haven't seen Sir Stephan in Rennes." Edric lean closer, whispering, "Last night...no wonder you are lonely. For one moment did you think of me fucking you? Is that why you grew hard?"

A storm crashed through Henry, his insides ripped by powerful waves like surf slamming a rocky beach. His hands flew to Edric's neck and he practically dragged Edric across the horse's back.

"Henry, let him go." Robin sounded distant, his voice buried beneath deafening roils of disgust in Henry's mind. Others had stopped their own business to watch, but rage blurred Henry's vision. He couldn't see them and did not care.

"This piece of shite is not worth your head," Robin said.

Feet kicking, Edric gurgled, trying to draw air into his lungs. He struggled to pry Henry's fingers away, his face purpling. Henry gripped him tighter, his own breaths ragged.

"Robin is right, Lord de Grey."

The king's voice calmed the storm in Henry's mind.

"My father would be alive if not for this bastard." Henry loosed his grip and shoved Edric.

Edric coughed as he sucked in air and his feet slammed the ground. He rubbed his neck, his eyes on King Richard.

"Your business is to bring my nephew to me. You may plot and plan with these men to that end, Lord Weston. You will keep all other thoughts to yourself." Richard's tone left no doubt this was an order that should be taken seriously. If Edric ever expected to have his lands restored he had better pay heed.

With a stiff nod, Edric said, "As you command, sire."

The sun was high overhead when the three knights broke from the king's troop and turned to the north and west. They had not traveled far when Robin reined in.

"We shall cover more territory if we split apart. You two take the road to St. Malo and then Dinan."

"I will not ride with Weston." Henry's disgust could

light a bonfire.

Edric's eyes sparked suspiciously. "Go alone, Robin? Even with help you failed once. We don't know who guards the boy, or how many. It may take all of us to secret him away. Besides, Prince John ordered me to stay with you."

Robin ignored Edric. "If you find Arthur, stay close to him. In six days time we meet in Fougères. If one of us has not appeared by the morning of day seven, the others will know to join the third. When we know what we're up against we'll work out our plan, together, and at the proper moment, grab Arthur." Robin could see the two men mulling over the plan.

"I would rather be burned alive than ride alongside Weston. I will not, Robin," Henry said.

Robin gave an exasperated sigh. "All right. Henry to Dinan, Edric to St Malo. I will go to Saint-Brieuc."

"The prince will not like this," Edric said, his jaw tight. "What do I tell him?"

"He doesn't need to know. First we find Arthur. Until he is in our hands, my whereabouts will not matter." *And I pray that I find him before you.*

They rode another hour where the road forked. "Fougères." Robin nodded confidently. He waited for Henry and Weston to nudge their horses, one brow raised as neither man made to move. The same trail would start towards Dinan and St Malo before it split again. Edric finally frowned, and growling, he kicked his horse's flanks and cantered off.

Henry clasped Robin's arm. "I will not see you in Fougères, will I?" When Robin shook his head, he said, "I suppose I should not ask."

"The king will know. It was his idea."

Henry chuckled, but turned serious. "Is there any

reason I should go to Dinan?"

"No. King Richard will be expecting you in Fougères. The campaign against the Bretons is at our doorstep, days away. He's already sent word to his men."

"What of John?"

"When Edric arrives in Fougères the king will send him back to his brother with the news and a sturdy warning from both himself and the queen mother that he should well consider any actions against us, our families, or Arthur."

Henry nodded. "Let us pray the king outlives us both. As long as he reigns, our families should be safe."

"God speed, Henry."

"And to you, my friend."

sixteen

King Richard's siege camp, on the Breton border

Rumors of the king's failed mission to Rennes had reached the monastery, and after eight days in the sickbed, Stephan took to the road. Two days in the saddle led him to Fougères where he heard rumors that the king's troops had engaged the Bretons less than thirty miles to the west. Another day's ride if the gossips were right.

Stephan left Fougères just after dawn. The gossips were wrong. By midday he heard distant booms and smelled smoke in the air. He nudged his stallion ahead cautiously until the wooded road gave way to a valley painted white with the tents of King Richard's siege camp.

Beyond the camp, mangonels targeted the castle, concentrating on the northeast tower. Crossbowmen stood idle behind a barricade of carts weighed down with boulders. Three more wagons rumbled past as Stephan tossed his reins to a squire and instructed him to have the smith check the animal's hoofs. He had ridden him harder than he liked, but seeing Henry had been foremost on his mind. He was disappointed Henry's face wasn't the first he spied in the camp.

There were washerwomen scrubbing clothes by the creek, their laughter ringing out over the sounds of war. Up the road two mounted knights inspected the men-at-arms' positions along a ditch. Shields planted in the muddy ground, the soldiers sat on crates sharpening their lances and swords and keeping watch.

"Two of the traitors crossed the ditch during the night," a squire said noting Stephan's interest in the activity there. "One got away and the knights are on the hunt." The young man sighed. "A pity it's not for boar." He cocked his head toward the fires where large cauldrons bubbled with broth. "We could do with a hearty bowl of pottage."

Stephan's stomach grumbled. The bread he'd eaten to break his fast had hardly satisfied him. His appetite had come back strong as he recovered from his illness, not necessarily a good thing during Lent or when your caretakers were frugal monks. He'd gotten plenty of broth and bread, but not much more.

He grabbed his saddle pack and approached a cook tossing chopped onions and leeks into a stew. The clang of the smith's hammer muffled the shouts from someone near the ditch. Stephan turned, spotting a knight trotting towards him and calling his name.

"Stephan l'Aigle!" The knight waved his arms with an exaggerated flourish. "My God, I did not think I might ever see you again." He swept down from his chestnut palfrey and strode up to Stephan.

"Geoffrey!" Stephan grasped the knight's arm.

Geoffrey of Leicester pulled Stephan into a bear of an embrace. Stephan felt the breath leave his lungs. Years past, the blond knight had left him breathless on numerous nights when they served the young Duke Richard. Age had not taken a toll on Geoffrey's handsome face. His shoulders were broad, his grip as strong as Stephan remembered when their flesh had been closer than most men ever knew.

Geoffrey pulled away, the dimples in his cheeks accentuated by his smile. "Look at you! What is this I see in those blue eyes?"

Stephan fingered the ring Henry had given him. Geoffrey placed an arm across his shoulders and dragged him to a bench by the fires.

"Tell me my eyes deceive me. You?" Geoffrey looked at him incredulous, his voice just above a whisper. "You are in love? How did you let that happen? What became of that playful knight I swived."

Stephan chuckled. Eighteen summers, recently knighted, those lust-filled nights and frolicsome trysts were memorable, but sent an ache through him for Henry. Geoffrey had been the first lover he took in Richard's mesnie. Or had the older, wiser Geoffrey taken him? God, how different he had been back then.

"You will find none more playful. But Christ help me, I love him." Stephan touched the ring again. "Henry and I have been lovers more than three years."

"Henry? Is that the dark knight you met in Southampton? That was six years past. Have you lost your touch?"

"Of course not! It has been different for me and Henry."

"Are you telling me you haven't fallen into another's bed in more than three years?"

"Closer to six."

"My God, man," Geoffrey shouted, "are you well?"

Stephan laughed, looking round the camp to ensure he'd not be overheard after Geoffrey's outburst caught the ear of the nearby washerwomen and at least one cook. They turned back to their tasks, but Stephan kept his voice low. "Sick in love, Geoffrey."

Geoffrey's hand slid down Stephan's back and round to his thigh. Stephan drew in a sharp breath. He wasn't immune to the touch. "I see a swelling," Geoffrey said, leaning close and firmly resting his hand over Stephan's hardening cock. "I think you should let me check it. Henry need not know."

"Geoffrey," Stephan tried to push the hand away, but the knight held him tighter. Heat crawled up his neck. "Please...don't."

Releasing him, Geoffrey sighed. "I think you've forgotten playful. Man was not made for one woman—or man—alone." He pulled a leather wineskin from his belt and gulped down a mouthful. Offering the skin to Stephan he said, "I married Hawise after my father died. She has given me two sons and a daughter and is quite delighted to know I'll have no bastards at our doorstep."

"She knows you like men? And not jealous?" Stephan took a swig of the smoky-flavored wine.

"She finds the act dirty and smelly and encourages me to take my pleasures elsewhere." He sighed again and breathed in Stephan. "Oh that sweet perfume. And I do not speak of the wine." Grabbing the skin from Stephan, he took another drink and walked towards the cook's fires.

Stephan cleared his throat and decided to turn the conversation to the current campaign. "When did you arrive from England?"

Geoffrey could have paid his knights' fees and left the king's fighting to hired soldiers, but he had tired of listening to his reeve, of inspecting repaired hedges and bridges—the man ran his estates efficiently. He felt useless, even at the manor court. Loose pigs, arguments over payments—boring. He had nothing good to say about the repeated tax notices from the king's clerks. "Give me sword and lance where I might make a difference for my king."

"And it's a good thing, Sir Geoffrey," the cook said as he set two trenchers of wheaten bread on the trestle behind the knights. "These hired routiers—they have no loyalty."

"You don't trust them, Martin?" Geoffrey asked. "They are good warriors."

The cook eyed the soldiers cleaning their weapons along the ditch. "Pay them, feed them, and you've no worries." Two young servants hanging at his side shifted uncomfortably. "Just like these boys." He laughed and winked. "Gather more wood for the fires. The king will return from the hunt soon."

Stephan smiled after the boys as they hustled away. Henry would be with the king. It felt like a year since he had seen him, held him, though he knew it had been little more than a week.

Geoffrey must have seen a look of longing on his face and clamped a hand on his shoulder. "We should eat ere the king arrives. There may be little time for food when you see him." He winked again and Stephan knew Geoffrey spoke of Henry, not King Richard.

Martin stirred the pottage and gestured towards the trenchers. The knights grabbed them from the trestle and held them out like two young beggars. Martin ladled the stew, thick with beans and chunks of bread, into their bowls. They ate heartily and drank more wine, brooding with the cook over the present and laughing over the past.

seventeen

Henry knew warriors who claimed every battle was the same. Details were lost in the charge, in the flight of arrows overhead. The noise. Siege machines ripping large boulders through the air. Rocks smashing into a stone curtain wall. The clink of armor, the clank of swords. The screams and the sounds of men dying. The smell… Oh God. Henry shuddered. The smell of blood stung his nostrils and bile rose in his throat.

He had been riding towards the siege camp with King Richard and thirty of his company when they'd intercepted twice that number of Breton knights headed to the aid of the besieged castle. Dust and dirt flew into the air and settled fog-like on the road. Sweat burned Henry's eyes, but he blinked it back and gripped his horse's reins tightly. As his sword arced down, he thought of drums. So prominent a sound in the Holy Land. "We are coming," the enemy said. There were no drums beating here, and after the initial rallying cries, there were only grunts and curses.

Henry's sword met mail and sparked. The blow screamed through the aches in his arm, but the Breton knight wobbled in his saddle. Henry brought his blade down again to glance off a battered shield. Guiding his horse with his knees, he pivoted the gray and swung, catching the Breton across the back and sending him reeling to the ground.

Just ahead the king swung a mace in one hand, his sword in the other. Richard barreled towards three Bretons pouncing on one of his knights. The king was like a bull, all muscle in every move, graceful, yet sweat-drenched and splattered with blood from sword tip to his boots. His mace shattered one man's shield; his sword caught another's helm. The distraction let Richard's knight land a punishing strike.

Richard didn't slow and urged his destrier forward. Suddenly he was surrounded, but his sword was true. He found shields, helms, and mail with every blow, his blade glimmering when the sun broke through the tree canopy. One adversary grabbed Richard to pull him from the saddle. Heart pounding, Henry spurred his horse and sliced through the Breton circle. His sword rammed the attacker's shoulder. The blow rippled up Henry's arm, but bone cracked and the knight screamed in pain and released the king. The wounded man spun away as Richard's sword arced wide and found another victim.

"Behind you," the king bellowed.

Henry twisted, adjusting his shield. It shook from a heavy blow, but he shoved his attacker and brought his blade down once, twice, until the man retreated. Sweat dripping into his eyes, Henry looked round—all the Bretons were withdrawing or surrendering.

"Round up our prisoners," the king shouted, surveying the prone bodies and the men on foot. "Leave their dead for the Bretons to bury."

Two of their own had lost mounts and one knight was dead. Others were covered in blood—their own or the enemies', it was impossible to tell.

Heartbeat slowing, Henry removed his helm and swiped a bloodied glove across his forehead. Their serious wounded were tended and the dead wrapped in blankets and laid across the backs of hearty pack horses before they started towards the camp.

King Richard trotted past his command tent, his stallion prancing up and down the line as he inspected the mangonels. A captain shouted orders when he realized the king and his men were battered and bruised. A lanky squire wove through the mass of horse flesh and hastened to the king's side as others gathered to help. Richard reined in and took the flask from the boy's outstretched hands. Blood dribbled from a cut on his cheek. He licked his lips getting a taste of it and then swallowed back the wine. He tossed the skin back to the squire and gestured towards his captain. "Bring the prisoners. Let the garrison see they should not expect any help."

"Shall we hang one of the traitors, sire?" the captain asked. The tactic had been used in Nottingham two years past to show the men defending the castle that this would be their fate. "Or tie one to a boulder and fling him at the wall?" He sounded intrigued by the thought.

"You wouldn't dare," one of the Breton knights growled. Others crossed themselves, mouthing pleas to the good Lord.

Henry pressed his eyes closed, hoping he never again witnessed the gruesome act of flinging body parts from stone throwers. God forbid should the king order such grisly punishment.

Richard offered a guttural laugh. "You do not know me, does he, Lord de Grey?"

Henry's eyes flew open, but before he could respond the captain ordered the siege machines to pause. The sudden quiet caught the attention of the men on the battlements. The captain paraded the captives up and down the line. Some stumbled, some limped. Like Henry, they were coated in blood. From the wall walk their compatriots looked on somberly. It was hard to watch the prisoners' humiliation and Henry was glad when the king ordered them taken away. God, what he wouldn't give for a hot bath. Perhaps those fools in the castle would surrender and they might get that and a warm hall tonight.

The prisoners were prodded away from the line and Henry started towards the corral. His gaze drifted past the fire to a man scanning the faces of the returning knights. *Stephan!* He might not have that bath—though one with Stephan sounded like heaven—but warmth rushed through him.

"Do you see him?" Geoffrey's voice sounded distant.

Stephan searched the faces of the returning men. *Christ!* The battle must have been vicious. So much blood. *Henry, where are you?* Grimacing, his gaze fell on the bodies flung across the backs of two horses. He felt the color drain from his face.

"I'm sure he is fine," Geoffrey added. "Baldwin, there," he pointed, recognizing a familiar face. "Let's ask him about Henry."

Heart crashing in his chest, Stephan's gaze ricocheted. He scoured one face, then another. With their helms on and cheeks blood-streaked, layered with sweat, dust and dirt, it was hard to tell them apart, but he *would* know Henry. *He is with them.*

He started towards the knights. His feet felt leaden and his legs trembled, and suddenly gave out beneath him. Thank God Geoffrey grasped his arms and kept him from falling flat to the ground.

Stephan looked towards the king and then back at Geoffrey. "He must be here."

The knight wrapped him in another bear hug. "We shall find him." He twisted him round until he faced the mounted riders just to the king's left.

Henry!

Only days had passed since their eyes last met, since words passed between them. It only took a subtle look, but the strength of Henry's love thundered between them and Stephan felt his heart would explode. Behind closed doors his greeting would make the saints blush, but there were no doors in the siege camp, not even a tree to hide behind. Surrounded by the king's men there could be little more than a brotherly hug, and while that came natural to them after three years, it was never easy.

A fleeting smile curled the edges of Henry's mouth. Geoffrey saw it, too, and he released his hold on Stephan and nudged him forward.

Stephan hurried through the maze of horses and men, slapping backs along the way. Friends welcomed him with open arms, teased him for his late arrival.

"We could have used your help today, Stephan," one of the knights said.

"Still looks sickly," said another, joking.

From the corner of his eye Stephan caught Henry watching him to see he was steady on his feet. Stephan shouldered his way to the king's side.

"Your sword sharp?" Richard asked as he dismounted.

"Always for you, sire." Stephan bowed deeply.

"Good. I want to show these bastards that I've little time for them." He tossed his helm and sword belt to another squire. "I'd rather send Philip to the Devil, but if we must take a few Bretons with him I shall not weep."

The knights around them sounded with cheers and grunts and approbation.

Stephan clamped a hand across Henry's shoulders as they trod in Richard's footsteps towards the command pavilion. "You are a bloody sight."

"We'd chased one man and ran into a troop headed to reinforce the castle."

Stephan caught a whiff of blood, sweat and musk. Christ! How he wanted to hold the man, cleanse every sign of the gore. Henry's boots scuffed dirt and pebbles into the air. Ahead of them Richard issued orders, his words lost to Stephan's ears.

Henry tugged the stained leather gloves from his hands and glanced back towards the cooks' fires. "Who were you talking to? He looks familiar."

"An old friend, Geoffrey of Leicester." Stephan wondered if Henry recalled their meeting on the streets in Southampton. He felt heat redden his cheeks when he remembered he'd met the fair-headed knight at the baths and afterwards for a heart-pumping tumble in bed. "My old gambling companion."

"Your old lover. I saw the way he held you." Mischievousness filled Henry's voice. "Should I be jealous?"

Stephan's fingers slid across Henry's hand. "Geoffrey knows where my heart lies."

"Good," Henry said, smiling.

Behind them, the mangonels groaned back to life.

Henry's smile vanished and he rubbed his temple. At the king's pavilion, a squire handed him a warm damp cloth to wipe his face. He helped him remove hauberk and gambeson. Henry tossed his linen shirt on his pallet and wandered wearily to the water barrel where the men wiped the day's battle from their flesh.

Dirt had hidden a cut on his forehead and the rough scrubbing sent a thin trail of blood from the wound. The water was cool, but shivers racked his body at the sight of the washing cloth now streaked red and black with blood and grime. Stephan wanted to tend to the blood trailing towards Henry's dark brow, but he set his jaw knowing he could not and then joined the men hovering near the king.

Richard's squires hustled to shed his mail—not an easy task when the king would not stand still. One of his knights urged him to warm himself by the brazier. It would not do for the king to take ill with the Bretons hounding him on one side and the French on the other.

"They won't hold out much longer, sire," the king's captain insisted.

"You see the future, do you, Aimery?" Richard chuckled as someone handed him a cup of wine.

Stephan laughed along with the others, but his gaze drifted across the room. Worriedly, he watched Henry mechanically cleanse the sweat from his chest and arms before he stumbled back to his pallet and sank to the ground. Unfurling his blanket, Henry twisted restlessly and finally, with his back to the jests of the king and his men, he lay still.

eighteen

JUNE 1196
St James de Beuvron

One Breton village after another had fallen in a month of fighting, and messages flew between the warring parties. There would be a meeting soon, and the king sent Henry and Stephan to talk sense into the Earl of Chester regarding the Duchess Constance's imprisonment. Henry found it hard to muster more than dread.

It was early June and though days were warmed by the late spring sun, the great hall at St James de Beuvron felt damp and cool. Lights from the rush torches flickered off the gray stone and servants' shadows seemed to slither across the tapestry on one wall as they laid out food and drink for Ranulf's guests. Voices wafted from the next room and Henry wanted to think one of the feminine ones belonged to the duchess, that, though a prisoner, she was able to move about freely.

The highly polished doors swung wide and Ranulf swaggered in, thumbs tucked into his belt. "Did I miss the herald announcing your visit, Henry?"

"No herald was sent ahead, my lord," Henry said. "King Richard sent us straight away."

"Were you hoping to find my wife chained to the wall?"

"Of course not, my lord," Henry exclaimed.

Stephan couldn't hide a smirk. "It is good to see you again, my lord."

"Sit," Ranulf said, smiling, waving his arm towards the trestle, the gold embroidery on his wide sleeve catching the light. "You've come from the front just to confirm what the king's spies already know." He shooed a servant from the room and poured drinks. His dark eyes showed no hint of malice, his expression pleasant.

"He thought you might listen to an appeal from friends." Henry had a sick feeling—nothing would change and more bloodshed and heartache lay ahead.

"Rather than a direct order from him," Ranulf said.

Henry shrugged. "I suppose you'd say it's implied," he said. "The king expects to meet us—and you—in Les Andelys five days hence. He would like to know you have released the duchess."

Ranulf refused to talk of his wife. "So Richard proceeds with the plan to build a fortress there despite the threat of interdict from Archbishop Walter?" He drank down his wine and refilled his goblet. "Have you seen the drawings?"

"Remarkable," Stephan said. "The king claims he'll see it built in less than three years."

Ranulf nodded. "He has ordered masons, carpenters, and engineers from every village, even as far north as Northumbria in England. The rest of us will have no one to hire for our own needs for the time it takes to build his castle."

Building on the rock above Les Andelys violated the treaty signed by King Philip and Richard in January, but Henry understood the king's reasons. The location could control the Seine and would be a staging point for troops and materials in the struggle for him to take back the Norman Vexin, territory the French had captured while he was imprisoned.

"Castle Gaillard," Henry said.

Ranulf shook his head and chuckled. "Not a stone turned and he's already given it a name. *If* the archbishop lets him have his way." He speared a piece of cheese and gestured for Henry and Stephan to help themselves. "Though when would Richard let that stop him?"

Henry dangled a slice of dried apple between thumb and forefingers. "The king will find as good a prize to cajole Archbishop Walter." He bit into the fruit, savoring its sweet taste and the king's coming victory, one *not* on the field of battle. "Negotiation is one of his strong points."

"Breaking treaties is another," Ranulf said.

Henry swallowed hard. "King Philip has done more than break treaties." He wrapped two hands round his cup like he was squeezing Philip's neck. Red wine spilled over the rim. "Whilst Richard led us towards Jerusalem, Philip violated the Pope's edict by invading the king's Norman lands. He supported the imprisonment of a fellow crusader. King Richard has every right to take back what is his. He has been wronged."

"I don't disagree, Henry."

Stephan nodded. "The French will be up in arms whether over Andelys or another strategic location," he said.

Raising his mug, Ranulf toasted the king. Stephan and Henry joined him and Henry slugged the wine. He smacked his empty cup on the table. The flame of the candle there flickered from the quake, reminding him of the purpose of their visit.

Henry looked at the empty cup. Another round of wine wouldn't make a conversation about Lady Constance any easier. "May we see the duchess?" he asked.

"On the morrow." Ranulf saw the frown cross Henry's face. "Be assured she is well treated. And she'll be glad of company from the world beyond these walls, even from servants of the king." He rubbed the ruby jewel on his ring finger. "I'll arrange an audience and let you meet her without me. She might speak more openly."

"King Richard met the Bretons in Rennes and agreed to secure her release by the fifteenth day of August. Will you consider releasing her?"

"No," Ranulf snapped. The muscles in his neck tightened. "Not yet."

Henry started to protest, but Stephan's light touch on his hand stayed his thoughts.

Stephan drummed his fingers on the table. "You intend to prove to her you can defy the king with little impunity."

Ranulf smiled, his eyes brightening. "It sends a message, do you agree? Constance has overestimated her barons' loyalty. Their refusal to turn Arthur over shows how little they care for her. My dear wife is nothing to them. Knowing they do not support her will drive her mad." He snorted. "I would do anything to see her drown in her own ego."

Henry doubted Richard would disagree, but saying it aloud would do nothing to help matters. "The king cannot wage war on two fronts, Ranulf. Her barons place the blame for your actions on him. You do him no favor by holding the duchess."

"The king's army already has the Bretons on their knees, and with little effort. He can shift his focus back to the Capetian bastard quickly. I am sick of my wife and her barons. I want her to feel what it is liked to be deprived of power. Show her that in the end, the king will side with me. Her barons can stand down now, or they—she—will be bowing to my wishes when Richard is done with them."

Henry knew the earl was one of the king's wealthiest and most powerful barons, but could he hold sway over Richard? God, how he hated these political games.

Ranulf had enough talk of his wife and spent the remainder of the afternoon at the chess board opposite Stephan first, and then Henry, with conversation settling on hunting and horses. Ranulf's chamberlain appeared as candles sputtered and shadows deepened. The servants had prepared a bedchamber for the knights.

"I imagine it's been a while since you slept on anything other than a pallet on the ground," Ranulf said.

"You learn to close your eyes anywhere, but a bed? A room with a door?" Stephan sighed. "It's been months."

Surely Ranulf heard the mischievousness in Stephan's voice, but Henry tried not to look at Stephan and thanked Ranulf. There might be *some* sleep tonight…

A servant led them upstairs by way of a narrow stone circular stairway. Henry pitied the lord's retainers hauling baggage from bottom to top, but it made the tower easier to defend. Men couldn't advance side by side and the door into the bedchamber wasn't wide. Attackers could storm the room one man at a time—right into the lord's sword.

The servant placed their packs on an old oak chest. The brazier hadn't been lit, but a thick layer of blankets covered the bed that would easily sleep four adults. Candlelight illuminated the chamber in a golden glow.

"I hope you will be comfortable, my lord," the servant said.

Henry studied the well-appointed room. A small desk and chair occupied space near the arrow-slit window. A coffer held a silver jug and two goblets, each one engraved with Ranulf's crest.

"Thank you," Henry said. "That will be all."

It seemed forever until the door closed and the servant's steps faded on the stairs. Stephan found the wash basin opposite the bed and splashed his face with the tepid water. Candlelight flickered on the water droplets on his face. Henry felt a rush of heat in his groin, his heart pounded in rhythm with the tapestry rippling from the breeze through the window.

Stephan turned, approached Henry like a fox, slow and stealthily, prolonging that moment where one touch would set blood afire. Fingers caressed Henry's temple, his cheek. Breath rasping, his eyes locked on Henry's face, he marked the curve of his lips as if to hold a memory that would never fade.

Henry shivered beneath his fingers. Stephan cupped his chin and smiled softly, tipping Henry's head to bring their mouths together. Moaning, Henry pressed Stephan's lips apart with his tongue and kissed him deeply. Stephan's hand roamed, tugging at the edges of his tunic, at the drawstrings on his chausses. Henry began to remove Stephan's clothing, but Stephan pressed him backwards stirring the dried flowers on the rush mats. The scent of lavender filled the air.

Trapped against the wall, Henry pretended to resist, but Stephan pressed closer and covered his mouth with a kiss. Henry clung to his lover, the ache in his groin fiery.

Stephan twined their fingers together. He dragged their hands above Henry's head, kissed him again, and thrust slowly against him.

Desperate to rid himself of clothes, Henry uttered a low growl and struggled to get free.

"Henry," Stephan whispered, hot breath brushing his ear. "We have all night." He gripped Henry's tunic, pulled it slowly over his head. His eyes drank in Henry. The light from the candles revealed the passion and love on his boyishly handsome face.

"We can make love twice," Henry moaned, arching against Stephan.

"Only twice?" Stephan teased.

The stone was cool and rough on Henry's back, but he hardly noticed. Their mouths collided as Stephan's hand found bare flesh. They found release within minutes.

Henry lay cradled in Stephan's arms. He nuzzled Stephan's chest, resting his head there, reveling in his lover's musky scent. Could there ever be anything greater than being with the one you loved? He craved nothing more—not land, wealth, or titles. Knowing he was loved by this man was enough.

His calloused palms explored every battle-hardened muscle on Stephan's torso. Lower, he found soft curls of hair and felt Stephan shudder. Stephan's breathing quickened, but his eyes were closed, his lashes brushing his cheeks.

Henry flicked his tongue across Stephan's nipple.

"Good Christ!" Stephan gasped.

Henry nipped at the nub. He pressed one kiss then another down Stephan's chest. Stephan thrust his hips, his flaccid cock coming back to life. But Henry took his time, teasing with slow kisses and skillful fondling, peering up and content to see the anticipation simmering on Stephan's face.

Another kiss, lower.

The night was still young.

Footsteps outside the bedchamber woke them though the sun was barely up. Henry sat up as voices drifted from the room at the top of the tower, but Stephan pulled him back into his embrace.

"If we ignore them, no one should bother us," Stephan said.

Henry nestled against Stephan's shoulder and yawned. "Ranulf may expect us at morning prayers." He didn't sound very convincing even to his own ears and he had little desire to climb out of the bed.

"He knows me better than that." Stephan kissed Henry's forehead. "We could give them something to pray about." In a sudden move that rattled the bed, Stephan flipped Henry on to his back and straddled him.

"You rogue!" Henry cried out louder than he had intended.

The voices upstairs went quiet. Henry looked up into Stephan's face. Even in the early morning light, he looked ravenous. But his touches on Henry's throat, his shoulders, and chest, were light, sensual. Maddening. Henry stifled pleasurable sighs through gritted teeth.

There was laughter from upstairs, but suddenly Henry didn't care. His arms enveloped Stephan and he rolled them over. Rather than submit, Stephan wriggled beneath him. He twisted, pitching them both to the ground with a thud. Wrestling, laughing, they tumbled across the room like children. The noise above them died.

Still chuckling, Henry ended their escapade on top of Stephan, their sweat-slick bodies pressed together. Henry ran his hands up Stephan's muscular arms, traced the puckered skin from his encounter with a sword in Lincoln. His fingers trailed into Stephan's hair and lingered there. Their eyes met.

Sunlight crept through the window and Stephan's sky-blue eyes sparked with intimacy and fire. Breath rasping, he said, "Take me. Now."

nineteen

An hour later the knights dressed, listening to the bustle of people returning after Lauds. Upstairs, they were admitted to the Duchess Constance's rooms for the meeting Ranulf had arranged. He had spared no expense for her comfort. The outer room where her maids slept was decorated with the same care as her chamber. Embroidered tapestries in Breton blue and gold veiled every wall. Carved in oak, the Breton crest hung over her curtained bed.

Constance sat in a cushioned high-backed chair—more throne-like than sitting room chair. "You have news of my son?" she asked curtly. Seated on the window bench, two of her ladies set their embroidery aside, their faces as stern as hers.

Still demanding, Henry thought. Her present situation hadn't tempered her manner. "We are here to inquire after your well-being, nothing more," he said, hearing Stephan shift behind him.

"Wait... I know you." Eyes narrowed, hands clenched

in her lap, she grew more agitated. "You were with Chester in Pontorson when he brutally forced me to leave with him."

"We were not with him," Henry said. "Our arrival was coincidental to his."

"Ah, yes. Escorts from the king." She huffed angrily, exchanged a glance with her ladies, one scowling and rolling her eyes.

"And I would not say my lord Chester was brutal."

"He threatened my men! He would have taken my son…" She softened and suddenly looked vulnerable. "My son, Arthur. Truly, Lord de Grey, have you no word?"

"The young duke failed to meet King Richard in Rennes. We assume he is in the care of one of your barons."

She stared out the window, sunlight painting her face in pale hues the color of the bed curtains. "I have heard nothing."

"Have you asked your husband to send a letter to your men?"

She turned abruptly to face Henry. "He would destroy anything I write."

Henry frowned. "You do not know that. And if you suspect, send for quill and parchment and prepare a note we might see delivered."

"No doubt by way of your king," she spat.

Henry felt her venom inching through his veins and clenched his fingers. "Your choice, my lady."

"You believe Chester will let you leave here with my words scribbled on vellum?" She scoffed. "He has no children. He does not understand. He and your king are cut from the same cold mold." She exhaled sharply. "What of you? Do you have sons?" Studying the two knights she added, "I see," when they shook their heads.

Stephan let out an unintentional groan.

"What?" Constance asked.

"You assume we cannot understand a mother's love," Stephan said, a hint of anger in his voice.

Henry glanced sidelong at his lover and quickly interrupted before he said something they both might regret. "Queen Joanna looked forward to spending time with you and Arthur. She writes that your daughter—"

"Whom the king ransomed off to marry that Austrian."

Henry ignored the nods of her ladies. "Your daughter would have ruled at her husband's side as duchess of Austria. Your son could be Richard's heir with titles far grander than duke of Brittany." It felt odd to argue for an arranged marriage when Henry could fall victim to one himself.

Constance scoffed. "John will see my son dead before he sees him on the throne." She closed her eyes and turned away. When she finally looked at them her dark orbs shone with bitterness. "Chester keeps me from Arthur, hoping my barons lack vigilance and will let him fall into John's hands. You think Chester—or John— serves Richard? Think again, Lord de Grey. Both serve themselves."

Henry felt his skin crawl. He would not trust John, no matter the man's proclaimed loyalty to his brother. But Ranulf? Henry struggled to see any reason the earl would throw in with the Count of Mortain.

"My Lord Chester has everything to benefit if your son is heir," he said. "Should anything befall King Richard, Chester would be regent of England, Normandy, and more until Arthur comes of age. The king will do everything in his power to protect Arthur. The boy is his nephew, his brother Geoffrey's only son."

Her eyes flashed with pain at the mention of her late husband. But then it only fueled her resentment. "He only cares to keep French influence at bay."

"If not for King Richard, Philip will swallow every acre of land west of Paris. Your son and his heirs will have nothing, my lady. Brittany would fast fall under French domination."

Constance's dark brows rose.

Henry cleared his throat. "It would be in your best interest and your son's to tell your barons to deliver Arthur to King Richard. Sir Stephan and I leave on the morrow. Have your maid bring us your messages."

Constance sniffled, caught somewhere between anger and tears. There was no justice in her current predicament. Her husband's prisoner. Her son a pawn.

She stiffened in the chair. "You may go."

The knights bowed and took their leave. Henry's mind swirled around the duchess' accusations. Should he confront Ranulf? Political positioning was so common, why should it surprise him. If he was involved in this mess, Ranulf's favor for John now could be advantageous later.

The great hall was empty, but a side table had been spread with bread, fruit, and wine to break the fast. The scent of garlic, onion and sage wafted from the kitchen and made Henry's mouth water, but the warm bread slathered with butter satisfied his hunger. Ranulf's voice drifted from the bailey and the door into the hall swung wide as the earl, his steward, the captain of his guards, and a clerk strode in. Ranulf was issuing orders, his imminent departure for Les Andelys on his mind.

"No baggage cart. If I'm to stay for any extended—" Ranulf interrupted his orders when he saw Henry and

Stephan. "Finally crawled out from beneath the blankets?" He chuckled. "I thought we'd need to send someone up to rouse you. It's a fine morning for a hunt."

"The horses will be saddled before Sir Ralph thanks the good Lord for breakfast," his captain said, glancing at Ranulf's long-time clerk, a man who had served his father.

Sir Ralph frowned at the knights, the lines around his eyes deepening. "You should have been at Mass to thank God for your comfort."

"God hears my thanks and prayers whether at Mass or not," Henry said.

"God heard us this morning indeed," Stephan added to Sir Ralph's scrutiny.

Henry withheld a guilty grin. "And we've already spoken with the Lady Constance."

Ranulf's smile was less than genuine. "I'm sure that was enlightening." He turned to his clerk. "Come, bless this food, Ralph, so we can eat and be off."

***

Ranulf led a charge scattering chickens and dogs in the lane leading to the west gate. On the cart track beyond St James' walls they rode two abreast. The hunting party galloped through open rolling hills where cows grazed on a green carpet under the late spring sun. Ranulf pressed ahead until the thick birch and oak of the forest forced a slower gait.

Henry couldn't remember the last time he felt so carefree, like a young lad with only the hunt and his friends on his mind. Trotting behind Stephan, he watched the knight's graceful handling of his black bay. The sun lit the gold in Stephan's hair, the breeze sweeping it off his broad straight shoulders. None of the men but the captain wore hauberks so Stephan's tunic clung to his skin. His thighs and calves gripped the horse's girth tight sending waves of tantalizing thoughts through Henry's mind.

The pad of hoofs made him glance sidelong. Sir Ralph scrutinized him, but finally turned his gaze to Ranulf and the road ahead. Henry wondered if the clerk-turned-priest could read minds, but he didn't let it trouble him. Other thoughts were more troublesome. Ranulf. Count John. Was there a connection between the two?

He spurred his horse to come alongside Ranulf ready to plunge into the abyss. "Ranulf, what would you have done if Arthur had been with your wife at Pontorson?"

"Do you think I would harm the boy?"

"There are rumors you collude with John."

Ranulf wasn't put off by the speculation. "I can see how others would assume I play both sides. How many of us do it to survive? Even John himself." He stroked his palfrey's neck and looked directly at Henry. "Arthur is a brat, but I wouldn't harm him. I understand the king's reasons for making the boy his ward."

Henry could argue he would never straddle the fence to gain favor in the future, but this wasn't the time to travel that road. "You would support Arthur as heir to the throne?" he asked.

Ranulf was quiet, but finally gathered his thoughts. "Richard needs to see what the boy is made of. Without his mother's influence he might make a king who recognizes the French threat. He might have the support of barons who have not forgotten John's treason. We should give him that chance."

"The king..." Henry wanted to believe the king had not put Ranulf up to imprisoning his wife. He had to ask. "Did he ask you to seize the duchess?"

Again Ranulf met Henry's eyes. "I took that upon

myself. If Arthur had been with her, I would see him escorted to Richard's hands."

Henry nodded. There was no hint of a lie in Ranulf's voice or manner. Speculation would do nothing but make Henry mad. He had to accept Ranulf's answer.

Ranulf suddenly yelled, "Get that beast!"

Henry jerked in the saddle, but as Ranulf tore into the woods he scrambled after him with the hunting party at their backs. Henry caught a glimpse of the large black boar zigzagging through a stand of brambles and bushes. Ranulf spurred forward, brought his crossbow to hand. The boar shot into a clearing and raced across the dew-covered field. Ranulf slowed, took aim, and fired. The animal stumbled, dropped, and with a shudder, died.

The hunting party returned to the castle and were joined in the hall by Ranulf's knights and the village chaplain, a lively group who insisted on tales from the hunt. They drank to Ranulf's prowess with the crossbow. Curses of the French flowed as freely as the wine.

Henry took Stephan's cup and dumped it into the floor rushes. "I want you sober tonight." He picked up a strawberry from the silver-gilt tray on the table and offered it to his lover. Stephan bit into it greedily, eyes sparking. He nudged Henry, leaned close and whispered in his ear. Henry laughed.

Ranulf stood and swayed at the head of the table after one too many cups of wine. "Share your joke, Stephan," he said and fell back into his chair.

"Go on," Stephan told Henry. "Tell them."

Henry stood. "The king claims the French will shite in their braies when they see his new castle high on the rocks above the Seine." The men roared with laughter, but he pounded the table to quiet them. "There's no other like it. Impregnable. King Richard could hold it against Philip even if its walls were made of butter."

"To the king," the men chorused and drank to Richard.

Ranulf beat the table and the men joined in. The noise grew to a deafening roar, sounding like hundreds of knights charging an enemy.

twenty

JUNE 1196
Les Andelys, Normandy

Early morning light grazed the large pavilion in Petit
Andely, but it was the clink of armor that induced a
chorus of groans from men trying to sleep. Stephan and
Ranulf had stayed up drinking late into the night and were
less than enthusiastic when they'd been roused to meet
with the king. Stephan stood with his eyes closed and
arms outstretched while a squire laced his gambeson.
Ranulf looked the worst of the two and Henry had to
stifle a laugh when the man swayed and fell into his
squire's arms cursing.

Since arriving with Ranulf four days past, Henry had
gotten a lay of the land. Emlyn accompanied him to the
clifftop where work on Richard's grand castle was about
to begin. "This won't fail to impress young Arthur," she
had said. "Rich—the king has so much to offer his
nephew. The boy could learn so much from him."

Richard?   Henry   wondered   what—beyond

conversation—the king had offered her. He shook off the thought. It was none of his business.

The king's pavilion sat amidst the growing town, a maze of shops and cottages that hadn't existed on Henry's visit a few weeks earlier. Masons, carpenters, and engineers, their apprentices, and hundreds of others called Petit Andely home.

Henry sighed, wishing himself in a broad green meadow listening to the rustle of the trees and the ripple of water in the river.

"Is everything all right, my lord?" The squire looked at him worriedly. When Henry nodded, the young man gestured for him to lean forward. A second squire helped heft the mail over Henry's head.

Stephan cracked his eyes open. "What is on your mind?"

"Breaking treaties, interdict, the war," Henry said as he righted himself and the squires adjusted his hauberk.

Stephan chuckled, but compassion lit his eyes.

Henry frowned at him. "I would take the archbishop's threat seriously if I were king."

"You worry too much, Henry." Ranulf looked between the two knights. "Especially at this hour."

A shadow fell across the room. "I do not take the good archbishop's threat of interdict lightly."

The knights and earl turned abruptly to the door. Richard's massive frame blocked the light.

"Sire," Henry said, his head lowered, "I did not mean to—"

"Yes, you did, but it is my worry, not yours. I've just returned from Rouen where I offered concessions to our dear Archbishop Walter, but the man is stubborn. He tells me he will personally appeal to the Pope, but then so shall I." Richard's hand dropped to his sword hilt. "We have work to do," he said and strode outside where the horses were saddled.

"Lady Constance is well?" Richard asked when Ranulf swung astride his Spanish gray. He glanced at Henry who agreed with a nod.

"Why would anyone assume otherwise, my lord king?" Ranulf asked. "Do I have the reputation of an ogre?"

"A message to Philip said as much. Deplorable conditions, locked in a dark dungeon. French lies of course, but it does nothing to further my desire to bring Arthur under my wing. This is nasty business, Ranulf. I want her released."

The cords in Ranulf's neck pulsed. "I cannot, sire. Not yet. She has humiliated me." Color rose in his face. "She ignores me and openly disregards your orders."

"And you have let this happen!" Richard's patience was thinning.

"Tell me how I should control such a bitch." Ranulf clenched his jaw, and then dug his heels to his horse's flanks.

As Ranulf cantered away, Stephan tried to break the tension. "Flowers? Jewels?" he said. "A charity or chapel established in her name?"

Henry risked a look at the king. He wasn't angry, but to be spoken to in that manner—what would he do? Ranulf could turn against the king, and with him, hundreds of his loyal knights. The king must choose his battles, play the political games.

"The woman needs a good swiving." Richard scowled.

Henry's eyes widened. "Sire, you wouldn't suggest Ranulf force himself on his wife."

"Of course not. Even Constance doesn't deserve that. I never understood what my brother saw in the woman. What did he do to tame her?" Richard grabbed a wineskin from his saddle hook, took a swig. "I do not know what my father was thinking when he threw that inexperienced cub into her lair."

"Mayhap your brother didn't tame her," Stephan said. "They merely saw eye to eye."

"Ranulf must figure out how to do both! I do not know. I never learned to properly woo a woman." Richard looked from Stephan to Henry and shook his head. "I doubt I should seek advice from you two about women."

Henry laughed. "Stephan charms them with his good looks alone."

"Through no fault of my own, Lord de Grey," Stephan teased. "I do not encourage them."

"Some of us are cursed." Richard's lip curled. Being king was a draw for many wenches to fill his physical needs, but love was a different matter. "I shall speak with Ranulf alone. If he will not see reason I may call in the Marshal."

Will Marshal's marriage seemed loving despite the ages that set he and his young wife apart. He must have secrets to share.

Richard spurred his stallion, Henry and Stephan rallying behind him. The horses splashed through a deep stream. As they got to the opposite bank a bent figure emerged from the trees and blocked their way.

Richard reined in sharply, his horse sawing his head and tamping the ground. "Jesu, brother."

Henry drove his horse forward. "Out of our way," he said, putting himself between the old man and the king.

Dressed in a ragged brown robe, carrying a sack, and wearing well worn shoes, the man looked like a monk or a pilgrim trekking towards a holy shrine. He looked harmless, though Henry felt a chill under his scrutiny.

"You will be cursed." The man met Henry's eyes, and then he turned his gaze on the king.

Stephan drew his sword as Richard's stallion sidled. "Back away, old man."

The man stepped back, arms raised. "You will be cursed." Dark eyes bulging, he pointed at Richard.

Henry said, "You fool. This is your k—"

"Your liege lord has nothing to fear from me." He gestured towards the heavens. "Only from God," he said and crossed himself.

Sweat beaded on Richard's brow. "We all answer to God, old man."

"And I have seen you, lord king." His eyes bored into Richard. "Be thou mindful of the destruction of Sodom, and abstain from what is unlawful, for if thou dost not, a vengeance worthy of God shall overtake thee."

"Leave, old man," Henry commanded.

Eyes narrowed, the man stared at Henry. "I am no false prophet."

Henry shifted uneasily as the old man shuffled into the wood, his voice in prayer. Could he know? Henry looked at Stephan. The man's judgement hit close to their hearts though it was meant to remind the king that his adultery was as much a sin as theirs—at least in the eyes of the Church. Perhaps it was worse that Richard was married and fornicated with other women. Henry and Stephan had no wives. They loved each other. Like Stephan, Henry would place his faith in God and not the mortal men of the Church.

Frowning, Richard put heels to his horse to catch up to Ranulf. The drum of hoofs faded, and it wasn't long after that shouts echoed through the trees.

"The king!" Stephan shouted.

Spurs to horses' flanks, the knights galloped through

the greenwood. The road twisted through tall birch and oak, past downed limbs, and over a rickety wooden bridge. Two riderless stallions nibbled at the grassy bank of the creek, looking up at their frantic approach.

"There!" Henry shouted when sunlight streaking through the trees glinted off mail.

Ranulf hovered over Richard on the ground.

Dear God…

But as Henry tore closer, he realized Ranulf was embracing the king. Both men were laughing. A foot away, a wild boar writhed, struck through the neck by a crossbow bolt. Henry and Stephan flew off their horses as the animal shuddered and took its last breath.

Ranulf sat back on his haunches, hands resting on his thighs, red-faced and still laughing. Henry checked the king from head to foot and felt relief flood him. No sign of injury.

"A good hunt?" Stephan asked and brushed leaves from Ranulf's tunic.

"None better," Ranulf said.

Henry helped the king to his feet. "Are you both well?" he asked.

"We are fine," Richard said and slapped Ranulf's back. "The men shall dine on good meat tonight."

And so they did.

Knights crammed the pavilion and the king's table was draped in white cloths with crimson runners and laden with silver goblets and platters. Squires hustled to keep cups filled around the room. Trenchers overflowed with the day's kill, fragrant from hours roasting on the spit. The noise swelled as night came and drinking loosed loud tongues.

Henry sopped the gravy on his plate with a chunk of

bread and glanced over his shoulder. King Richard sat beside Ranulf deep in conversation, serious one moment, light the next. Henry chewed on the bread and leaned close to Stephan relishing the feel of their thighs rubbing. "I do not think the king has convinced him yet."

"Ranulf must show strength and weigh a heavy hand against his wife and her barons. I cannot say I blame him." Stephan shrugged. "Don't let his youth or impetuousness fool you. He is powerful, but King Richard will bend only so far. He'll give Ranulf time to make his point and they will reach a resolution before one raises a sword against the other."

A dark-clad knight hurried towards the dais. The king recognized the hooded man and brightened.

"Lady Constance will be freed eventually," Stephan added. "She was well. You saw that with your own eyes. Ranulf is within his rights whether we approve or not." He rested his hand on Henry's leg, his gaze caught on the mounting ferocity on the king's face.

"God's nails! Damn them." King Richard's curses smothered the yammering in the room. He flew from his seat, his chair slamming into the ground.

Startled, Henry pulled away from Stephan. His heart battered his chest like waves pummeling a rocky shore. Stephan brushed his leg, which calmed him, but Richard raged past them, the look on his face leaving Henry uneasy.

Speculation suddenly buzzed around them, like hens cackling. A hand gripped Henry's shoulder and he jumped again. Stephan turned, face alighting on the knight in the dark cloak. "Robin."

"Come with me," Robin said. "Both of you."

A wrinkled map covered the table in the king's tent and tallow candles made the air stale with smoke.

Richard's advisors hovered over it like a pack of wolves. Snarling, Richard whisked out his dagger and stabbed Paris. "Philip consorts with Flanders, Ponthieu, and Boulogne. Where will they strike?"

Robin pressed his palms to the table, his eyes focused on the map. "Your brother has his hands full against the French army north of Rouen, sire. Philip knows this and will press his advantages there, especially with support from the count of Flanders and the others."

Richard scowled. "Back to Dieppe?" There had been a fierce battle there the previous year and Philip had devastated the port city with Greek fire. Richard had taken it back—for now.

Dragging his finger southeast of the port, Robin pointed out other strategic towns, some in Philip's hands, others held by King Richard. "He has ordered his scouts to explore weaknesses along this line. If Aumâle surrenders, you would lose a base of operations within striking distance of Dieppe. Philip's cousin, the Bishop of Beauvais, holds Milly-sur-Thérain."

From the far side of the command tent Henry could see the sour expression on the king's face. He whispered to Stephan. "I would wager the king counts the days until he can force the bishop to his knees."

Stephan nodded. Richard hated Beauvais, who had been one of Philip's messengers to the Holy Roman Emperor during his imprisonment.

The French king's determination to secure all land east of the Seine could not have been more apparent. Philip would be a few miles from Rouen's doorstep, Richard's ducal capital. If that city fell, the French would control the river north to the Narrow Sea and, with his new allies, a wide swath of the coast. A huge threat to shipping to and from England.

"I can deal with the counts' betrayals." Richard's eyes grew dark, his anger hidden behind cold, calculated reasoning. "English ships continue to frequent Flanders' ports. That must stop. Now. Any trade with them, to Ponthieu and Boulogne, will be severely punished."

"That will hurt," Stephan said under his breath.

"Grey's used to ship more wool to Flanders than to all of England. That fed my villeins," Henry said.

Stephan rubbed his hand across Henry's back. "Greyton will be fine. Surely this won't last long. The counts will come to their senses and the king will remove the embargoes."

Stephan's words gave little hope to Henry. He thought of his last letter from Little John describing increasing hardships as the king's war demanded more resources. Richard's tax collectors would have to be satisfied with wool in lieu of coin. When would this end?

There was nothing on Richard's face to indicate he had considered the impact of this dogged determination to undermine his adversary. He was resolute, unshakable. "Aumâle's defenses are strong and should withstand an assault." He turned to Robin. "But take a message to John. He must reinforce Dieppe. Philip insists on breaking the peace so I will show him that I can do the same just as easily. January's treaty left many of my Norman castles in his hands." He pointed to a line from Nonancourt to Neufmarché. "We will take them back. I will not rest until every piece of land Philip has taken is secure in my arms."

twenty-one

JULY-AUGUST 1196

The summer campaign began in early July. Aumâle, not Dieppe as they'd suspected, was under attack by Philip's army. Rather than marching to Aumâle's aid immediately the king had turned his sights south. Nonancourt surrendered with hardly a shot fired. But no sooner had it fallen when Robin returned with bad news.

He had delivered the king's message to Count John, turned east to track the French to report on their movements, and nearly galloped headlong into them. "Six hundred men," he told the king. "More than a hundred wagons with wood, iron, and rope for their siege engines." When the supply train turned towards Aumâle rather than Dieppe, Robin had raced ahead to warn the castle garrison. Sneaking past the small detachment had not been difficult, but he barely managed to escape as the larger French force moved in.

Strong as its defenses were, the French attack had grown from a small force to an elite troop. Without reinforcements, Philip's banners would fly over Aumâle.

In two days time, Richard's knights stormed near eighty miles and bedded down in a forest within five miles of the castle. Their supply train and foot soldiers followed a day behind.

It was well past dusk when the king sent Henry and Stephan with Robin to reconnoiter the French camp. Fires illuminated a score of siege machines. Their crews loaded and re-loaded an endless supply of boulders. Wheels groaned as slings were drawn back and aims adjusted. Henry shivered. He would never get used to the incessant crash of boulders, but imagined Robin could be lulled to sleep by the noise.

"I heard them whinging about sleeping another night on the hard ground. Some wondered if they'd be home in time for the harvest," Robin said from their position along a tree line. Lying flat on the ground they were a stone's throw from the French tents.

Henry looked at him, incredulous. "You heard—you were inside their camp?"

"Many times. I followed them for three days," Robin said without bragging. "Slipped in after dark."

"Six hundred men?" Stephan asked. Beside him on the ground, Henry whistled quietly.

Robin nodded. "And we have—will have—half that number when the others arrive. Philip has one hundred fifty cavalry to our seventy."

"We have defeated enemies with greater numbers," Henry said.

"We have indeed," Richard said, slipping in between them.

"Sire, you should not be here."

"The question is, why didn't you hear me approach?" Richard sighed. "When will you learn, Robin?" The boom of boulders against the stone curtain wall could be heard from the camp and the lure had been too great for him. "The perimeter guards are set, the men quieted. I am here. I trust your report, but I had to see this for myself."

The castle garrison might hold out a month, but a brilliant full moon revealed extensive damage to the battlements and a tower on the southeast wall. Effective strikes could bring down that wall at any time. King Philip had already razed a number of Norman castles. He seemed determined to add Aumâle to that list rather than keep it intact for defensive purposes.

"The sappers are quiet now," Richard said. "But come daybreak…" Undermining to hasten the collapse of the stone wall would commence after morning prayers.

Robin pointed towards a large tent where a banner with a fleur-de-lys whipped in the wind. Philip's pavilion. "We could take the French king. A nighttime raid. Surprise them whilst they sleep."

Stephan nodded. "Set fire to their siege machines, destroy supplies."

"The four of us," Richard said. "Now."

Henry's brows rose, but Richard was smiling. "Sixty knights and their mounts will not stay hidden. Philip's scouts will find us before the rest of our men arrive. We cannot wait."

"I will take care of his scouts long before they discover our camp, sire."

"I am certain you could, Robin, and as much as I would relish dragging Philip from his bed tonight, we would do nothing but draw attention to ourselves and lose the surprise. The odds are against us, but three score of us will inflict more pain than we four."

Henry stared into the darkness. They would kill or be killed, but the garrison would not be freed unless by some miracle. Even King Richard knew this, and when it was a matter of honor to make an attempt, he would never back down. Henry pressed his palm to his chest where his crucifix lay. *God keep us.*

Richard drew to his feet. "We attack before dawn."

"The men will be ready," Robin said.

There was a gleam in Richard's eyes. "They fight for me."

"For the king," Henry said, remembering times too numerous to count that men from Outremer to England had rallied behind the Lionheart.

"For the king," Robin and Stephan repeated.

They were as stealthy as wolves. Metal on the horses' harnesses were muffled, wrapped in whatever pieces of cloth the men could find. Shields and axes lay against blankets draped across the pommels of their saddles. Scabbards held still so as not to rub chausses.

Henry warily eyed the wood skirting the dirt track. Clouds concealed the moon and it was black as pitch. Sweat dampened his chest and back, but dread of what was to come and the horrors that came in his dreams now fled to the deepest corners of his mind. He glanced at Stephan and Robin beside him drawing on their strength, reminding himself that over-confidence could be as deadly as fear in battle.

Less than two miles from the besieged castle they took to the cover of the trees. Lookouts were silently taken out before they could wake the French camp, and the knights took their positions along the tree line.

Robin hovered over a small smoking stack of twigs and leaves. An orange glow grew, spitting and crackling and the light flared. At the king's signal, Robin lit the oil-soaked cloth tied to his arrow. He gave a nod and the knights sidled their horses to give him clear aim. One arrow loosed. A second. A squire handed him three more in quick succession. The French king's pavilion and two supply tents burst into flames.

Curses and shouts rang. French horses, set loose by Richard's men, stampeded through the camp. Richard shouted the charge and Henry dug his spurs into his mount's flanks and plunged through the darkness. To either side of him, horses' hoofs struck the ground like a wave of beating drums. Clods of dirt flew, filling the air with the smell of fresh-turned soil.

Roused from sleep by the commotion, the French stumbled from their tents nearly trampled by their own horses. Within seconds, the soldiers spied Richard and his knights clearing the edge of the camp. Richard swept towards Philip's pavilion like a mad bull, his sword reflecting light from the fires and blazing like a beacon.

A bolt swished past Henry's head. Another bounced off Stephan's shield. Brandishing swords, crossbows, axes and lances, the French soldiers stood their ground. Most had slept in their armor, and the light from the fires glinted off their hauberks.

Henry gripped his shield tightly and raised his sword, spurring alongside Stephan. The French swarmed like bees towards King Richard. Angry, resolute, but exhilarated, Henry slashed left, right, pivoting his horse with knees and heels only. Stephan left a path of injured and dead men in his wake. The echo of shield and blade clashing pierced the early morning air. Henry's heart hammered. He cut down with his sword, finding flesh, but his horse pressed past the French soldier and he didn't look back to see if the man had fallen. Another knight swinging a mace confronted him. Henry's blade came down, missed. His adversary ducked and swung round. The mace glanced off Henry's leg, the blow so powerful he could hear the clang against his mail chausses. Pain shot down his calf, but he didn't stop, lifting his blade again and again, fending off lances, blocking the swing of weapons one after the other. Aches burned his shoulders, yet still he fought on.

Blood-drenched swords crossed around him. The smell of blood and smoke filled his nostrils, and then he heard the screams, the cries and curses of dying men. Above the cries, he heard the king, his voice hoarse but strong. He had lost sight of Stephan, but knew he fought on. It was as if he felt his touch.

More French bastards joined the fray, and Henry hacked his way through them. *Too many, too many.* He urged his horse over and around prone bodies. The ground was slick with blood. And not just French blood. A knight from Sussex lay dead, dragged from his horse, his eyes vacant and staring towards the fiery sun as it peeked its head above the horizon.

Robin had others stopping in their tracks. None had seen a knight loose arrows from atop a charging horse. In the Holy Land, Saracen warriors had perfected the maneuver, and Robin was one of few English knights whose skills rivaled theirs. Before he drew his sword, he had set a dozen more tents aflame.

Through the chaos of battle, Henry spotted an unorganized rally of soldiers beneath Flanders' banner, a black lion on gold. "Flemish curs," he shouted at Stephan.

"Too many," Stephan heaved between blows.

With Richard's small force against one several times larger, the only hope of breaking the siege would have been the capture of King Philip. The initial charge sliced a path as far as the king's flaming pavilion, but he had slipped through their fingers. Richard recognized the recklessness of prolonging the inevitable outcome. His face contorted in helpless rage, but he roared the retreat. "Fall back!"

The French and Flemish taunted them and gave chase as they fled to the wood. Glancing back, Henry saw Thomas of Hereford thrown from his horse when it was struck by a lance. Henry shuddered, powerless to help as men-at-arms overwhelmed Thomas and stabbed him repeatedly. Henry swallowed back the bile in his throat. As the battle scene faded behind him, his stomach curled and he slowed his horse and wretched. *Dear God, why?* He wiped the grit from his mouth trying to justify the king's actions. Richard had to show good faith to the defenders behind the castle wall. They tried, failed. Lost good men. Would their sacrifice have been worth more had Philip Capet been captured?

The bellows of war cries grew faint, not even a whisper when they returned to the camp. The French had not pursued them, but might once they retrieved their horses. The king sent a messenger south to turn the supply train back. The knights did not pause to cleanse the blood and grime from their mail, but hurriedly gathered what they needed while the tents were torn down. With fresh mounts saddled, they set out to join the larger troop.

Richard's expression sparked daggers, and no one approached him even after they camped for the night. Henry wandered to the riverside to wash himself. The water felt cool and refreshing on his face. It revived his spirits until Stephan and another knight settled beside him and made count of their friends who had died at Aumâle. Suddenly Henry's arms felt leaden. Wringing out his washing cloth was a chore. Weariness settled into his bones and he sat unmoving staring at the water rippling across moss-covered stones.

Stephan's voice broke Henry's reverie. "Will you sit here 'til the sun rises?" Standing, he took the cloth from Henry and extended his hand.

Fresh cuts crisscrossed Stephan's hand. Throat tight, Henry finally grasped it and let himself be pulled upright. Off balance, Stephan gripped him round the waist and caught his eyes. They were so close their breaths warmed the other's cheeks. Henry could smell leather, musk, and sweat, could almost feel the stubble on Stephan's jaw. He relished those few moments.

Back at the camp they rolled out their pallets in a secluded spot beneath an old oak.

"We've abandoned the garrison at Aumâle." Henry knew only two options existed for the men, women and children holed up there. If they did not give themselves up, the French would overrun them and would kill many who had chosen to fight. Surrender, and they might be ransomed. But for how much? And how would the king find the coin for that when so much was being spent on his new castle at Les Andelys and on his mercenaries. "What will the king do now?"

Stephan drew up on one elbow. "Wait for terms for Aumâle and move on." He tipped his head towards a small group gathered by the fire with Richard. "I will wager they are planning our next actions."

The idea of bets turned Henry's thoughts to their friend Allan and he managed a smile.

Stephan touched the corner of Henry's mouth. "What's this?" he asked, but quickly placed his hand down. He fell back on to the ground with a sigh.

"Thinking of Allan. We've not heard from him in an age. I should pen a message to him." Henry closed his eyes. "On the morrow."

Stephan's fingers locked with his and Henry exhaled deeply, letting his imagination take them to a place where they could live and love with no worries of others' expectations. Stephan caressed his hand in the darkness and the two lovers drifted off to sleep.

twenty-two

AUGUST 1196
Gaillon, Normandy

King Richard threw himself into physical labor at Gaillon after the disappointing attempt to free Aumâle. He worked side by side the carpenters and engineers and it seemed to improve his mood. Sweat poured off his body which glistened in the August sun. Lifting a hammer, he drove nails into the roof of the siege machine. Closer to the castle mangonels ripped one boulder after another. The barbican had taken extensive damage and this siege tower, with a huge log suspended beneath its roof, would soon be rolled within striking distance of the gate.

Robin arrived, vaulting down from his horse. Henry strode over to meet his weary-looking friend. He looked like he'd being riding through the night.

"Sire," Robin called. "I've news from Aumâle."

Richard waved the hammer to acknowledge Robin, but seemed in no hurry to climb down for what would be bad tidings. The castle had been severely damaged by

French siege engines. The garrison there must be low on supplies.

Robin took the king's reticence in stride and waited patiently at the foot of the tower. He'd been away five days and studied the progress of the siege as the king finally started down. Men shoveled dirt, downed trees, and parts of dismantled cottages and barns into the ditch. Whatever could be scavenged had been taken to create a bridge passable for the siege tower. Crossbowmen on the castle battlements loosed bolts at the workers that harmlessly bounced off the cover protecting them.

"It will be done ere the sun sets," Henry said, noting Robin's interest in the siege tower.

"And a good thing." Richard noticed the rolled parchment in Robin's hand and grimaced as he took it. It bore the French king's seal. He swiped his arm across his damp forehead. With a vicious tug, he cracked the red wax.

Richard stared at the message, the veins in his neck pulsing. "Three thousand marks! God's nails, I will show Philip Capet no mercy." Richard tossed the message to the ground and stomped on it. He bellowed like a wounded animal. "Get this siege machine ready," he shouted and turned to the defenders on the wall walk. "Gaillon will fall tonight. Do you hear me? Surrender now, else you will have nothing left to defend, and your lives will be forfeit!" He stormed towards the command tent, his boots demolishing everything in his path. "Find my clerk."

Robin looked at Henry somberly. "The garrison at Aumâle surrendered," he said.

"Three thousand marks?" Henry asked.

Robin nodded. "To secure the garrison's release."

"Come on, you pups, you look like you're pushing a dead horse in your grubby little hands. Push! Heave," the captain shouted. It had been two hours since the king warned the defenders on the battlements and now his siege tower was moving into place. "Push!"

Henry's leather-gloved hands were soaked with sweat. Astride his horse, he felt every vibration of the wheels, of the setting of the mangonels, of boulders smashing the curtain wall.

Nearby, Richard observed the action, anxious for the machine to do its damage to the portcullis and thick oak doors. His white stallion tamped the ground, itched at the bit, feeling the king's anticipation to charge through the gate and into the castle bailey.

The siege tower gained another foot, then faltered when one wheel struck loose soil and dipped into a hole. "Together, fools," the captain shouted. "Ready, and push…push…push."

Horns blared from the castle to drown out the rhythmic beat of orders to Richard's men-at-arms. But the captain's voice grew stronger to defy them. Bolts ricocheted off the shielded roof and sides of the tower. As it lurched closer, angry curses and spears, lances, and rocks rained down on them. Hot oil would follow, oil that might seep through cracks in the shield and find flesh. If the defenders had Greek fire—

"Sire!"

Henry jerked at Robin's shout. Richard was running towards the tower. Robin bolted from his horse after the king.

"Christ," Stephan cried. The knights around them shuffled nervously, crossed themselves, and cursed.

Henry rested his palm on his heart, urging the king on, praying he reached cover before being struck. Richard bellowed a war cry and the knights joined in. Bolts slammed the ground around him. His shield took a hit that jostled his arm, but hardly slowed him. He tossed the shield aside and elbowed his way beneath the cover of the tower, making room when Robin ducked in beside him. Thundering the battle cry, the men worked harder and the wooden monster lurched forward, its wheels groaning with each step gained.

Arrows flew from Richard's archers positioned in front of the knights. Screams told Henry more than one found its mark on the wall walk, but the defenders weren't ready to quit. Three large boulders dropped between the siege tower and the portcullis. The tower ground to a halt, but the battering ram sprang to life, the men forcing it to swing back and forth. The swings grew longer, building power until the tree-sized log bashed one boulder, knocking a second to one side. Another landed in its place and the men grunted and cursed, levering their bodies to throw more weight behind the swinging ram. It connected with the boulder and shards of rock splattered the air. But one still impeded their path to the gate. The angle of the tower made it impossible to strike.

King Richard and a giant of a man muscled their way from beneath the tower. Richard used his shield to cover their heads, but it wasn't enough and he needed his hands free.

"More shields," Robin cried as he joined them, bolts striking the ground round their feet.

Henry, Stephan, and a half dozen others had already sprung from their mounts.

"Target those men on the wall!" Henry ordered and sprinted towards the king.

They were too late to help the giant. A bolt struck him in the neck. Collapsing to the ground, blood spilled from his mouth, a harsh gurgle emanated from his throat, and then he grew still.

"Henry, cover me," Stephan shouted. Henry hefted Stephan's shield over their heads, lifting his own to protect himself and Robin. Stephan tossed his muscle in with the king's. He and Richard shoved the boulder like two bulls ramming a wall. The seconds seemed like minutes. Henry's arms began to burn. Bolts hissed around them, ricocheted off the shields.

The boulder budged, gave way, finally dislodged. Richard stepped back from the path of the tower as the men propelled it forward. Robin tried desperately to keep up with him.

"Bloody Christ!" Richard roared.

Henry paled, saw the bolt protruding from Richard's knee. The wheels of the siege tower groaned and the knights shielded Richard as he limped back to the line of his mounted men.

"The surgeon claims I won't be sparring for at least a month." Richard tapped the poultice wrapped round his knee, frowning at the little man sitting on the stool beside him.

The doctor stood and retrieved a bowl stinking of bloodied linens, animal guts, burnt mushrooms and other herbs. "Stay off the leg, sire. I shall be back in the morning to change the wrapping and check that infection has not set in."

"Hurts like hell," Richard growled as the man slipped out of the tent. He looked at Robin. "Pour me some wine."

A handful of Richard's advisors had gathered in the command tent and laughed, a sound more of relief than mirth. Henry would have chided the king for his recklessness and couldn't find it in himself to laugh. God forbid, but one day the king might not be so lucky. His men knew this and he recognized their concern, but chose to ignore them.

Robin handed the king a cup of wine, poured one for himself, and took a long draught.

"A month." Richard grunted. The sounds of the siege penetrated the tent, the ground rumbling beneath the men's boots. "Have we broken through the gate?"

Robin had been with the men at the siege tower until the surgeon's first report had filtered down to them. "The gate has cracked. It won't be long."

"All of you, get out of here. They shall need your swords."

Henry and Stephan were nearly out the door with Robin when the king called out. "Robin, when this is done I must send you back to John."

Shock rippled through Henry's bones. "Sire," he said, "your brother nearly killed Robin."

Robin closed his eyes and drew in a long breath, disappointment on his face.

"This sends a message to John, does it not? He will know I haven't forgiven Robin for his *treason*, but I have faith that he serves a purpose at John's side."

"Captain Mercadier is with John," Stephan said. "He could do your spying as well as Robin."

Richard smacked the cot. "Tell me how to run my wars, will you?"

The knights shifted uncomfortably. "Of course not, sire," Stephan said.

"My friends only worry for my life," Robin said. "As we worry for yours."

"Stop with the sweet words. Bribery will not work." Richard smiled. "I will remind John—again—that he's not to touch a hair on your head."

That leaves plenty of other body parts, Henry thought. Stephan covered his mouth, turned away. Henry could hear the same words going through his mind.

"Last time, I swear to you, Robin. We shall all be in Rouen in October. I'll bring you back into my fold at that time." Richard's gaze found Henry, who suddenly felt his innards twist under that look. "Negotiations with various parties will be settled by then, and I will have new orders for you."

Henry swallowed hard. "For all of us?"

Nodding, Richard tried to rise, but grimaced when he set his foot on the ground. "In the meantime," he said, tugging his leg back up on the cot, "get these bastards to surrender."

twenty-three

Henry accompanied King Richard to Vaudreil after his injury. The doctors insisted he would require rest, something Richard despised. His advisors encouraged him to send word to his wife and mother and he had rolled his eyes at them. "I am not dying. I've had worse wounds!" In truth, he hated to be coddled by meddling women, but he finally gave in and sent Henry to Le Mans to deliver a message to the queen and his sister.

Henry had seen Lady Joanna and the queen at Christmas court the previous year. Fragrant holly and pine and scented candles had decorated the great hall then, but today the smell of roses and lavender wafted on the air. Bright linen tapestries hung from the old stone walls and dazzling sunlight lit the room from the open shutters.

"Henry!" Lady Joanna glided into the hall like a breeze.

"My lady." Henry bowed deeply.

Joanna raised him up and swept him into her arms. "When the clerk announced you had arrived I scolded him for not retrieving me from the gardens immediately." She wore late summer's blush like the cherubs painted on the walls at the cathedral in Rouen and smelled of roses and sunshine. Henry remembered their first meeting in Messina and his visits to the palace in Acre during the war. She looked as lovely as ever, her green eyes vivid, her skin more pale than during their time in the Holy Land.

"Come, sit with me." Joanna led him to the ornate chairs by the south-facing windows.

"I have letters from King Richard for you and the queen. Is she here?"

A servant poured drinks and set a platter of fruit and bread before them. Joanna thanked the young man and gestured for him to leave.

"Letters?" She blew out a disgusted breath. "When will my brother visit his wife? I had hoped he would find time to romance her."

Henry's feelings about Richard's attitude towards his marriage matched Joanna's, but he certainly wouldn't agree with her out loud. "Mayhap the letter asks his wife to attend him in Vaudreil."

"He is at— Why?" Joanna grasped Henry's hand. "What has happened?" She was an astute woman, as brilliant and perceptive as her mother Queen Eleanor.

Henry placed his free hand atop Joanna's and gave it a squeeze. Anyone could have delivered the news to her. Henry had been surprised Richard thought to ease the ladies' concern by sending a friend. "He was struck in the leg by a crossbow bolt at Gaillon, but he will be fine. The wound was clean and there is no sign of infection. His mood is foul and he limps about, pouting like a child who cannot have his way."

Joanna laughed. "That would be Richard. Keep him from what he loves most and he will make life miserable for everyone around him."

"The injury has given him pause." Henry didn't feel it was his place to tell Joanna about the hermit's prediction that God would seek vengeance for Richard's adultery. The failure to break the siege at Aumâle, the Flemish and others climbing into bed with King Philip, and Richard's arguments with Archbishop Walter about Les Andelys— even those of little faith might see these setbacks as signs of God's displeasure.

Joanna crossed herself and took the letter from Henry's hand. "You must tell me how Sir Stephan fares, and Robin." She looked towards the door. "Are they with you?"

"Robin is off to share the king's news with your brother John, but Stephan should be along any moment."

Joanna broke the seal on Richard's message. "Berengaria is at chapel now. She prays all hours of the day. Such a sad little thing," she said and unfolded the letter, smoothing the creases with her finger.

Poor Berengaria. Henry wondered if the queen wondered if the king might set her aside. The king had seemed so close to her in Acre. They had laughed together, enjoyed each other's company. Henry assumed that had extended to the bedchamber. But the times they'd been together the last two years could be counted on one hand. Even his mother chided him. Had his time as a prisoner of the Holy Roman Emperor and this war against Philip Capet changed him so much?

"Richard says we should not worry." Joanna smiled and read on with rapt attention. Her breathing grew rapid, fingers clutching the parchment. She rested it in her lap and stared out the window for a long moment. With a shake of her head, she said, "I am to be married."

Henry watched her, unable to decide whether she was happy or was going to cry.

"Richard has made a deal with the enemy," she added.

Flanders, Boulogne, Ponthieu—might it be one of them? Henry didn't know if the counts were married. *God in heaven, could it be Philip himself?* He couldn't read Joanna's face. She would know that Philip had asked Pope Celestine to annul his marriage to Ingeborg of Denmark, but that had been denied. Henry swore he'd heard rumor that Philip had defied the Pope and married another anyway.

Henry wanted to grasp her hand, but would not be so bold. "Who are you marry, my lady?"

"Raymond, the count of Toulouse."

Henry's eyes widened. What a coup for Richard! Toulouse and his predecessors had been burrs in the Angevin's side for forty years.

"Richard has conceded all claims to Toulouse to secure this alliance." Joanna spoke without emotion, but Henry heard her voice quiver. "Our southern borders will be safe. Richard will be able to divert his troops there to reinforce the Norman frontier against Philip."

An end to constant warfare and threats in the south bordering Aquitaine was a tremendous gift, Henry wouldn't deny that. But knowing Joanna's hand was being forced with an arranged marriage still made him sick at heart. He remembered their conversation in Acre. Finding love was something she desired, though she knew it was little more than a dream.

Joanna did know Count Raymond, but had never spoken more than a few words about him. Despite the enmity between the families, Toulouse had seen Joanna and Berengaria safely escorted home from Rome after they returned from the Holy Land.

"How do you feel about this?" he asked. "About Toulouse?"

"I am…pleased that Richard has found an ally against Philip Capet."

"That is not what I meant."

Joanna held her head steady. "I will go to this marriage with an open mind and an open heart, and pray God bless us with love and children. We all have duties—to God, to our king." She looked down at the letter and then met Henry's gaze, her deep green eyes intense. "You have a duty, Henry."

The tone of her words made Henry swallow hard. What else had King Richard written?

"You will accompany me to Rouen. You, and Stephan."

Henry didn't realize he'd been holding his breath and released it loudly, but he watched her uneasily. She crumpled the bottom edge of the letter. "Richard repeats duty and honor three times! He writes that you and I must speak on this though he knows we may not be happy."

"We?" Henry asked, confused. Was there more to the king's meaning? *Duty and honor.* He had pledged himself to his king, but the words seemed harsh now.

"The vows will be spoken in October," Joanna added. Henry barely heard the business details she repeated. "Archbishop Walter is angry about the construction at Les Andelys, but Richard is confident he will preside over the ceremony. Maman should be here in a week's time, and then we will make our way to Rouen. Richard will meet us there."

The door of the great hall swung wide and Richard's

queen was announced. Berengaria entered the room on Stephan's arm.

"Look who I found wandering," Berengaria said.

Joanna beamed, clapping. Stephan managed no more than a nod to Joanna because Berengaria did not slow. She was small next to him, but took forceful strides, the folds of her deep crimson gown rippling as if caught on a breeze. Her golden wimple heightened her dark eyes and pale face.

"My queen," Henry said and kissed the solitary jewel on her finger.

"Lord de Grey." The slightest smile curved her lips. "My lord husband has not sent his regular messenger, so your news must have some import? Good news, I pray." She noticed the letter in Joanna's hand, but chose to sit before she took the one Henry proffered.

He watched as Berengaria read the king's message. She pinched her eyes shut and crossed herself at one point, and when she continued she seemed less than enthusiastic.

Joanna tried to lighten her mood. "We have much to be joyful for."

"Yes, sister, my lord husband's wound is not so serious." Berengaria's voice had a bitter edge. She scrutinized the knights to see if there was more that the king had not said. "He sees no reason for me to come to his side."

She seemed so small, vulnerable. Almost like a child.

Joanna squeezed Berengaria's hand. "Richard doesn't want you to feel sorry for him, or see him in this weakened state. He is too proud for his own good."

"Is it not a wife's duty to care for her husband? When he was sick with the Arnaldia in Acre I sat at his bedside, cooled his brow."

"He knows your caring and your compassion," Joanna said.

"But wants none of it," Berengaria snapped, whipping her hand from Joanna's. She straightened her back, and smoothed her gown, suddenly regal and calm. "He suggests I would be happier helping you prepare for your wedding."

"Yes, please, you must! Help me decide which dress I should wear." Joanna beamed. "Having you, Maman, and Richard at my side will be so different from my wedding to William." She had been eleven then, sent off with great fanfare to Sicily but with only a few members of her household retinue.

"The queen mother?" Berengaria asked.

"Richard has sent a messenger to Maman at the abbey. We shall await her arrival and then journey to Rouen."

Berengaria snorted. That little detail must have been missing in her letter from Richard. "I think she would bypass us and trek straight to Richard's side."

Joanna pursed her lips, staring at her sister-in-law. Henry and Stephan held their breaths.

"Forgive me," Berengaria said. "Lord de Grey, Sir Stephan, I must speak with Joanna alone."

The knights bowed to both queens, but as the door closed, they heard Berengaria. "The Count of Toulouse? Are you pleased…"

Stephan brushed Henry's hand, exchanged a glance. Richard would give Joanna's hand to Toulouse to strengthen his cause against Philip Capet. A cunning move. And Joanna was pleased. What more could the king ask?

twenty-four

SEPTEMBER 1196
Rouen, Normandy

Queen Eleanor's arrival from Fontevrault sent the castle into a frenzied pace and it was almost a relief when the royal train departed for Rouen four days later. Henry was no stranger to baggage trains transporting army supplies. But escorting three queens more than one hundred miles was an extravaganza like he had never seen. One royal household would be a show, but three? A hundred knights, twice that number of soldiers and squires, two smiths, a cooper, plus ladies' maids, pages, cooks, attendants, and more. Wagons were laden with the ladies' clothing, with bedding, scented candles, silver goblets and platters, and food. They even carried dried flowers to spread on the rushes at manors and castles where they stopped each night.

King Richard joined the entourage at Vaudreuil and seemed pleased to see his wife. All the women doted on him, which he tried to accept with humor and graciousness. On the final leg of the journey to Rouen, Berengaria rode with him atop his white stallion. A woolen cloak trimmed with ermine was wrapped round them both to ward off the cool October breeze.

It was easy to forget the archbishop's interdict hanging over Normandy. Signs of the people's suffering had been hidden. At midday in Rouen, thousands had gathered to see the king. There was an air of hope despite the war with France, despite the interdict. Hundreds of torches blazed along the path to the castle gate. The streets were immaculate, lined with bowers of flowers and fragrant greenery that masked the rot of unburied corpses.

A great banquet was spread the first night. Fires in two massive hearths warmed the hall. Henry wasn't close enough to hear the animated conversation on the dais where the king sat between his mother and his wife. Their gazes fell on Henry more times than he could count. The queen mother looked stoic, Berengaria righteous. Richard was impatient, the bulk of the discussion between him and Joanna, seated at Berengaria's side. Something Richard said upset Joanna greatly. When he dismissed her with a wave of his hand, she grew angry and came round the dais. She headed straight for Henry.

"I must speak with you," she said as Henry drew to his feet. Everyone stared at Joanna but she glared right back and threw hot darts at her brother, whose face heated. Queen Eleanor was shaking her head.

Joanna stalked from the hall with Henry and Stephan in her wake. She led them outside to a secluded spot in the garden, ignoring the ominous clouds rolling across the sky.

"All his talk of duty and honor." Joanna's voice seemed caught between outrage and tears. "My duty. Your duty. There are times I think Richard has a heart, but he has proven his compassion is about the size of a pea."

Your duty—the same words Joanna had spoken when she first learned she would marry the Count of Toulouse. Henry shivered. He stepped closer to Stephan, who exchanged a look with him and shrugged.

"And his brain as well," Joanna added.

Henry placed his hand on hers when he saw how she trembled. "What did the king tell you? Is it about your future husband? Has he had a change of heart?" he asked. "I apologize, my lady, but I know there are many who accuse Toulouse of heresy."

"No, it is not about Raymond, and I do not believe those gossips. He is tolerant of the Cathars and their beliefs, but nothing more. His enemies will use anything against him." Joanna sat down hard on the garden bench. Her face had gone as gray as the stone. "Richard could not tell you himself. The man would fight when he is outnumbered five times over. But he asked me to tell you. Oh, Henry…" She met Stephan's gaze. "I am sorry," she said, turning back to Henry. "He has arranged your betrothal to the daughter of the castellan at Lincoln."

"What!" Stephan shouted, his fists clenched.

Henry's head spun. "That is not possible!" His voice trembled and he grabbed hold of Stephan. "He knows how I…that Stephan and I…"

"Bastard," Stephan said. "What is he thinking?"

Henry held Stephan's gaze—no one else in the world mattered. He wanted to spend his days and his nights with this man. There were tears in Henry's eyes, but he didn't care. Losing him… *I might as well be dead.*

Married… *I could not be with him.* It was a sin. But loving Stephan was not a sin. It was not! But if he had a wife…that was adultery. God's blood. *Why…why must I feel this way?*

Stephan's face was the color of the ruby on Joanna's hand. "Does he explain?"

"He is the king," Joanna muttered. "He need explain his actions to no one."

Stephan kicked at the ground spraying pebbles in the yard.

Henry's mind whirled. He had sworn he would never marry. He knew love with Stephan, a love he would never find with another. The thought of marriage, of bedding a woman while he loved Stephan—his stomach churned and sent a hammer of drums to his head.

Joanna's voice brought him back. "You are to be in Lincoln before Lent."

Henry shook his head. There was no sense to this arranged marriage. Nichola de la Haye and her husband had supported John. But they'd paid their fines and pledged loyalty to King Richard to secure her hereditary right as castellan. Why would they agree to this marriage when any daughter of theirs would have eyes set on a prize much larger than Henry could offer?

"This cannot be." Henry pulled Stephan closer, his voice a whisper. "We must speak with the king."

"King Richard seems to have his mind set." Stephan's breaths came hard. "What choice do you have?"

"Choice?" Henry cried. "I said I would go to the greenwood with you to live out our lives."

Stephan shook his head. "I will not let you give up your birthright."

"Don't be so chivalrous!" Henry glowered at him. "A moment ago you were angry."

"It is the king's command," Stephan shouted, his voice caught somewhere between anger and misery.

Hands clasped in her lap, Joanna's knuckles whitened.

"I would like to thrash my brother."

"I could be talked into holding him down for you, my lady," Stephan said, trying to break his foul mood.

Henry scrubbed his hand through his hair and gaped. *How can they talk like this?*

"Oh, Henry, I am sorry. If I could talk sense into Richard, I would." Joanna took his hand and made him sit. "Instead, I will bend your ear on the good points of arranged marriages, and we shall find gifts for you to take to your bride. You will go to England and wed as your king has commanded." She rubbed the back of his hand. "She probably likes dolls. I still did when I was eleven."

Stephan's eyes widened. "How old is she?"

Henry's back went rigid. He had attended the wedding of Gerard de Camville and Nichola. He was thirteen then, just two years before the earthquake rent Lincoln Cathedral in two. He couldn't remember how many children they had, but knew their son was oldest, only ten or eleven summers. Which meant...

"Henry?" Stephan repeated.

Should he laugh or cry? "She is a child."

"What, four, six? How old?"

"Not more than nine or ten."

Stephan's eyes flicked from Joanna to Henry. "That is a good thing. You cannot marry for several years. Anything might happen between now and then." He realized that might mean death for Henry or his bride-to-be and he grabbed Henry's hand. "God forbid..."

"But betrothal..." Henry rubbed the ache in his temple. The marriage ceremony sealed the contract, but he would be tied to the girl until she came of age and they both consented to wed. "How can the king ask this of me?" He looked morosely at the ground, his heart cold.

Stephan slid a hand across his back. "Nothing need

change between us."

Henry wanted to hold Stephan in his arms. He wanted to believe he could live like that, but his faith hounded him. He let out a long breath. "You know how I felt when Alys was alive."

"You have changed, our love changed you," Stephan said. "If Alys had lived, would things be different between us? We love each other."

"Love is one thing. But adultery is still a sin, Stephan."

"You are not married!" Stephan waved his hand to cut Henry's next words. He shook his head and barreled away.

Henry had watched the king with his whores and chastised him for his betrayal of his marriage vows. *If I marry, I will be true to my wife. Adultery is a sin. God help me...*

Joanna watched Stephan tear back into the castle. "Surely you knew Richard would expect you to marry."

"I thought you of all people understood," Henry said.

"I do, but you must be practical."

Henry scoffed. "Get married and live my life in torment? Have children. Pretend that this is how all things should be?"

"I did not say that," Joanna said quietly.

"What then?"

"Henry, in the eyes of the Church you are already damned." Like her mother, Joanna did not mince words. "Marry the girl, but do not forsake the love you have with Stephan."

He wanted to embrace her words, but he could hardly believe Joanna would feel this way. "You saw your own mother suffer when your father took up with other women. What if I was to be *your* husband?"

"But I know you and Stephan."

"Just answer."

Joanna drew a long breath. "I would do everything in my power to keep you happy, to keep you in my bed. To hope I could turn your eyes to me, and me only. But in the end, that might not be enough. In the end, I may be wife and mother, but never lover." She touched his cheek. "Now go after Stephan."

Stephan pounded up the circular stairwell of the keep, spurs sparking on the stone. The tower was deserted, which suited him just fine. He wasn't certain he even wanted to talk to Henry, didn't know what else he could say. Years earlier, Henry's faith had been shaken when he realized he was falling in love with another man. If Alys hadn't died—if Henry *had* married—would they have remained friends only? It was futile to think what might have been when he knew he and Henry shared a great love.

Guards stood on the wall walk below him, more intent on watching storm clouds roll in rather than worrying about the French. When Henry came up beside him thunder rumbled in the distance like an omen.

"My feelings for you have not changed," Henry said quietly.

The cool wind tousled Henry's hair and burnished his cheeks. That dark wavy mass had been one of the things Stephan had remembered about their first meeting. That, and his incredible blue eyes and his Lincoln green cloak. Six years. Three years later friendship had finally become love. He should have known… Sorrow and loss suddenly overwhelmed him.

"I love you, Stephan. You fill every part of my soul."

Stephan wished he could hide in the gray mist creeping over the town. He couldn't look at Henry. "I was a fool to think—" He scoffed. "Why did we have to fall in love?

It was never hard to walk away from another man's bed. Never. Until I met you."

"We will always have love." Henry tipped Stephan's chin to meet his eyes, but Stephan ripped it away and stared at the trees swaying in the distance.

"And that memory will be all you need as you go off to England," Stephan said.

Henry buried his head in his hands. "I do not think I can give you more. Why did King Rich—"

"Stop blaming him. You can do as he orders but still choose to be with me. The choice is yours."

"Give me time." Henry's voice cracked. "Let me think."

Stephan felt the words like a blow. He struggled to find a breath, and then scowled, all patience deserting him. "You have had more than three years to think. Fuck me and it's fine as long as you are not married. But the sin is a hundred times greater after you marry? You are a hypocrite."

Henry's eyes were filling with tears, but Stephan couldn't see past his own hurt. He pried the ring off his trembling finger. "This means nothing to you?" He shoved it into Henry's hand.

"Keep it," Henry cried, thrusting the silver filigreed ring back into Stephan's palm. "That was my gift to you."

"I should have taken your father's dying words to heart and run."

"My father accepted our love." He grasped Stephan's arm. "He told you to take care of me."

"That wasn't all he said." Anger and hurt filled Stephan's soul. *I should not say it...*

"What have you been keeping from me?" When Stephan didn't answer, he said, "Tell me."

"'Let him go.' That's what he said," Stephan said flatly.

"'Take care of him. Let him go.' Your father did not want us together."

Henry choked. "I don't believe you. You are just saying that."

"Have a long and happy life, Henry."

Without another word Stephan shot back down the stairs.

twenty-five

Henry pounded the stone merlon, scraping his knuckles, too numb to feel the pain.

God's bones, what did it matter that his father had not approved? The man was dead, in his grave three years. Still, it hurt to hear those words—*let him go*. It hurt more to hear the anger in Stephan's voice. God, he loved Stephan. He told him that. But if he had to marry...

I must speak to the king.

Henry started for the stairwell, but shouts from the battlements drew him back to the wall. A retinue of knights and mounted men-at-arms with Count John at its head approached the gates. There'd be no chance to meet privately with the king now. Cursing beneath his breath, he hurried downstairs.

John had made his way to the dais by the time Henry took a seat at the far end of the hall. Stephan's laughter carried above the buzz in the room. Maybe he was still angry, but it was impossible to tell from the way he bantered with the other knights around him. Henry brought wine to his lips, looking towards the king because it hurt too much to look at his lover. *His friend.* Would Stephan even call him that?

Henry took several deep gulps of wine, nearly choking when someone smacked his back. Heart thudding, Henry whirled, the sweet drink soaking his trencher and the man next to him. "God's nails!"

"And good day to you, Henry."

"Weston?" Henry jumped to his feet. "What are you doing here?"

"Why, the same as you, my lord." Edric chuckled, tipped his head toward Stephan. "Have you been banned to the back of the hall?"

"Be gone, Weston," a familiar voice growled.

"Robin!" Henry shoved Edric away and grabbed Robin in bear hug. "It is good to see you."

Robin pounded Henry's back, and then steered him away from Edric.

On the dais, Count John had Joanna's attention, his spirits high. He held his sister's hand, but waved his free one animatedly in the air as he spoke. Joanna laughed, enjoying his company. Berengaria was amused, but she paled abruptly, her eyes on some commotion near the door. Captain Mercadier blustered into the room. The storm of voices ebbed as he passed on his way to the dais.

"He loves to make an entrance," Robin said. He grabbed a jug of wine from the trestle and dragged Henry to an empty bench. He swallowed back a long draught.

Stephan's voice rang out above the raucous chatter.

Henry rolled his eyes and tapped the jug. "Save some for me."

Robin looked from Henry to Stephan and back. He leaned close to Henry. "Why *are* you back here?" As

Henry explained his betrothal, adultery, the argument with Stephan, Robin took another slug of wine. He wiped his mouth on his sleeve. "I am sorry, Henry, but I agree with Stephan. You are not married, and only God above knows what the future holds."

"Lady Joanna said the same," Henry said.

"Then why aren't you with Stephan? Why do you waste time arguing about something that may not happen?" Robin stood. "Come with me."

Henry started after Robin, but curses suddenly flew at the front of the room. Stephan scrambled atop a trestle and the curses weren't the only thing in flight. He landed on Edric Weston and both men disappeared from sight.

Chairs toppled, wine and food sailed through the air, and men clambered to get out of the way. Stephan and Edric rolled across the floor and the crowd cheered, definitely more in Stephan's favor than Edric's from the shouts Henry heard. King Richard was on his feet spurring them on, but one quick glance at his wife and at Queen Eleanor, and he immediately ordered them to stop.

Stephan had pinned Edric down, his hands wrapped round Edric's throat. He didn't heed the king's command, but someone tore him away. Edric rose and charged Stephan, kneeing him in the gut. Stephan crumpled to the floor.

Robin reached the scrape before Henry, clutched a handful of Edric's hair and jerked his head back sharply. He threw Edric into the crowd. Edric glowered, swiping at blood on his cheek, and spat at Stephan.

Henry pressed Stephan upright. Sweat mingled with blood seeping from a cut on Stephan's head and his face was smudged with dirt. He struggled out of Henry's arms, angry, and bolted forward, his fist swinging and connecting with Edric's nose.

"Stop this now!" Richard's voice rang out.

Edric reeled from the blow, but two men steadied him. Stephan glared at him, hands clenched ready to throw another punch, but Robin held him fast. "It's done, Stephan." He grabbed his arm and guided him past Henry. Stephan refused to look at him.

"The cut isn't too bad," Robin said, holding a cloth to Stephan's head after they'd seated him on a barrel in the buttery. The place smelled of oak and wine.

"What started this, or need I ask?" Robin asked.

Henry started to wipe the dirt from Stephan's cheek, but he wouldn't let him and brusquely grabbed the damp cloth. He saw the anguish on Henry's face. "Sorry," he said half-heartedly.

Robin knocked Stephan gently on the head.

"Ouch!" Stephan cried and stared at the cloth in his hands. "I will forever defend your honor, Henry."

"And I yours, Stephan. I love you."

Stephan grimaced and finally met his gaze. "Just not the same way."

"No, I mean…I just need to—"

"To hear your friends tell you that you are being a fool?" Robin asked. He clamped a hand on Henry's back. "Just kiss him. Put this behind you." His gaze flicked between the two men. "Did anyone overhear Edric's accusations?"

"They are too drunk to care, or would just ignore him." Stephan wiped his brow, looked tentatively at Henry.

Henry reached for Stephan, palming his cheek, running his thumb along a dark spot beneath his eye. Robin urged him on with a nod and then bid them good-bye.

Henry slid his hand behind Stephan's neck. He kissed him fiercely, pressing his body between Stephan's legs. Stephan responded with a strangled moan and tugged at his tunic. Heat snaked from Henry's head to his toes, but he shivered and pulled away.

A plaintive cry broke from Stephan's throat. "What do you want, Henry?"

"I want you with me forever," Henry said. "Greyton will never be home without you. Come with me."

"As your friend. A fellow soldier." Stephan shook his head. "I know myself. I will not watch you marry, see you at another's side. Being that close would be far too painful. I couldn't do it." He pressed his palm to Henry's chest. "My heart will always belong to you, Henry. Remember that. Without you, I would never have known love. When you accept you are like any other man who can have a wife and a lover, come back to me."

Henry stared at the cracks in the wall. *Why can't I be any man? How can I give up my only love?* Just marry. Get the wife with child, and come back to Stephan. He wouldn't have to think about her if he was here across the Narrow Sea.

Wouldn't have to...but he would.

Henry's heart felt like it would burst. *I cannot live like that.*

What about the truth? Was the answer right before his eyes?

Breaths quickening, he said, "Let me talk to de Camville. I'll tell him the truth. Surely he'll throw me out on my heels. There will be no marriage."

"And what about the next time, and the next?" Stephan said, his voice breaking with raw emotion. "What if de Camville says he doesn't care? Daughters and sons are just pawns in their fathers'—and kings'—eyes. Politics and power. You would let this game keep us apart." He rubbed his eyes. "I don't know what else I can do to convince you to be with me."

"Don't give up on me." Henry reached for Stephan, but Stephan shouldered past him, his pain-filled eyes striking Henry like the tip of a dagger.

twenty-six

OCTOBER 1196
Rouen, Normandy

Raymond, Count of Toulouse, arrived with a large entourage and all the trappings of royalty. Five days later he and Joanna spoke their vows at the doors of Notre-Dame. After the wedding mass, a litter draped in white and lined with flowers carried them back to the celebration at the castle.

"You look radiant, my lady," Henry said as he danced with Joanna.

Her dress was the color of gold, with wide sleeves that nearly swept the floor. It was trimmed in scarlet and white, with pearls and rubies stitched in circlets from her neck down to a sunburst at her waist.

"I haven't seen you with Stephan today," Joanna said, her palm brushing his as they turned from side to side.

Today, the last seven... Henry had lost count. The days were long, nights longer. But Joanna didn't need to know.

"This is your wedding day," he said. "You only need to have one man on your mind."

Joanna glanced at her husband across the dance floor and blushed. To Henry's chagrin, Raymond and his partner did a twirl directly in front of Stephan. Joanna recognized Henry's desire to steer the conversation away from the state of his relationship, and her green eyes narrowed. "Stephan has managed a smile from Chester. The earl must despise weddings."

Of course Joanna would know of Ranulf's disastrous marriage and the abduction of his wife. "Has the king convinced him to release the duchess?" Henry asked.

She shook her head. "Richard has been in such a foul mood. He received an envoy from the Bretons once more demanding that Ranulf be punished and his castle attacked to free Constance. They decried Richard's request that Arthur come to the wedding."

Henry understood the king's frustration. He drew a deep breath thinking of his own part in Arthur's life. It was too late for regrets.

"Arthur was in hiding the last I heard," he said. "Have the king's spies discovered his whereabouts?"

"In Brittany, in France." She twirled, her sleeves brushing Henry's dark blue tunic. "It is anyone's guess," she said as their hands met left to right.

They stepped back to back, bowed to the dancers facing them, and then turned. Joanna placed her palm on Henry's arm.

"Freeing Constance would help the king's argument," Henry said.

Joanna nodded. "Richard asks me to cajole Ranulf, not that it will do any good." She noticed the frown on his face. "What is it?"

"Didn't you just tell me no one questions orders from

the king? 'He is the king'."

"The king has not *commanded* Ranulf to release her."

Henry glanced towards the king at the candlelit dais. "No need to make an enemy of one of the richest men in the kingdom."

"Ranulf will be with Richard at Les Andelys until Christmastide. My brother will bend the poor man's ear, and not just about building his Castle Gaillard." She stepped to the left, back to center and when they circled round she was smiling. "You might take a lesson from Ranulf."

Henry chuckled as they circled back to back. "Lock Stephan up?"

"It is an idea," she said, clapping her hands with the music as the vielle, drum, and pipe accelerated.

When the clapping stopped and the music slowed, Henry said, "I asked Stephan to come with me to England."

Joanna frowned. The final dance steps brought them close. "Is that fair to him? To watch you face your future bride."

Henry bowed as the dance ended. "There will be no marriage. In fact, my lord de Camville will end the betrothal."

She nodded, understanding. "You plan to tell him you are a sodomite."

Henry cringed at the word. It sounded so ugly. Love was not ugly. It never could be.

"It's the only way," he said and led Joanna towards her husband. They skirted near Stephan and Henry imagined his musky scent, warm breath against his skin. His face suddenly felt warm.

Joanna was watching. "You are thinking about him." She stopped and leaned close. "Thinking of him in your bed?"

Henry blushed a deeper shade of crimson. "My lady!"

"I have a good imagination." She smiled wickedly. "I hope I will please Raymond and find the kind of love you and Stephan have."

"He would be a fool not to love you, my lady."

A rosy color spread across her cheeks. She was looking at her husband, and he at her. Raymond's dark eyes sparkled. He seemed as happy for this marriage as Joanna.

"Do you remember the last time we danced?" Henry asked. "You opened my eyes to my heart. You saved me, my lady."

"In Acre, and only moments before I realized you were torn over your love for Stephan." She laughed gently. "I never told you I was jealous." She kissed Henry on the cheek, the pearls in her reddish-gold hair shimmering beneath the rush torchlights. "I told you to be true to yourself."

"I kept your words close, thought hard on them."

She laughed again. "You mean you stubbornly resisted."

"Poor Stephan had to wait months before I came to my senses."

"You are blessed he is such a patient man." Joanna looked at Stephan. "But will he wait this time?"

Stephan turned towards them as Joanna spoke, his eyes on Henry. Henry's breath caught. Stephan's pain had vanished, replaced by a stone mask.

Joanna touched Henry's hand lightly and he let himself breathe. He led her towards the dais, but Edric intercepted them by the long coffers set with golden bowls of wine. "Lord de Grey has little experience with the dance, my lady." He bowed and offered his hand. "Might I have the pleasure?"

Joanna scrutinized Edric. "You've danced with Henry, have you?" she asked, taking pleasure in the blush that colored his cheeks. "I believe he has much improved since we danced at the palace in Acre. And he had some practice, did he not? With your sister when she wed my dear friend Sir John."

Pinching his mouth, Edric pressed his shoulders back.

"We would have been pleased to see you at Greyton, Joanna," Henry said, adding to Edric's resentment. He knew of Henry's friendship with Queen Eleanor, but hadn't realized the extent of his relationship with the Lady Joanna. Henry couldn't be more pleased when Edric's smug expression disappeared.

Raymond strode up to them and rescued Edric from further embarrassment. "My dear lady wife, I beg a dance with you ere we leave this festive celebration."

Joanna gave a subtle nod to Edric, but kissed Henry on the cheek. "My lords," she said, and slid her hand into Raymond's.

The king's laugh from the dais echoed above the music. A half dozen men, including Robin and Count John, stood with rapt attention by his table. Henry joined them and noticed Edric elbowing his way to the front of the crowd near John. Queen Eleanor's story had men slapping Robin's back.

"You are too generous with your praise, madam," Robin said.

"And you are usually so brash, Robin," John said and smirked. "Why so humble today?"

"It is not my place to shine when we are here to celebrate your sister's wedding to the Count of Toulouse. A glorious day for the wedded couple, and for King Richard," Robin declared.

John raised his golden goblet to his brother, and then

looked for his sister on the dance floor. "Indeed it is." He swallowed back his drink. "More wine," he called, and a young page appeared immediately to refill his cup.

Eleanor smiled at Henry. "When will you leave for England?" she asked.

Henry hesitated. He shouldn't have been surprised the queen mother knew about his betrothal, but wished the news could have been kept quiet a while longer, especially from the likes of Edric Weston, who was intent on hearing every word.

"In the next few weeks, madam," Henry said, "before winter storms churn the sea."

Eleanor nodded, frowned Edric's way, and then turned to Henry with a smile. "After you meet your intended bride, you must convince Sir John and his wife to visit us here. And Allan." Her fondness for the two former squires shone through her words.

"I will extend your invitation to them," Henry said.

A malevolent smile crossed Edric's face. A question formed on his lips as the men congratulated Henry, but John was more interested in his mother's invitation. "Allan?" he asked.

"The castellan's man at Nottingham Castle. You know him as William FitzHenry," Richard said.

"Hal's bastard?" John's brows pinched and he turned to his mother.

With a shrewd smile, Eleanor said, "He is a loyal and devoted young man." She eyed John. "*He* can be trusted."

John started to protest, but Robin piped in. "I should like to accompany Lord de Grey, sire."

Richard tapped on the table. "The campaign season is near at end. We shall speak of your place when you return. Go see your wi—family."

Robin ignored the slip, hoping John hadn't noticed.

John looked curiously between him and Richard. His mouth opened, but Queen Eleanor was the quicker of the two.

"Mayhap by spring we shall have peace with Philip Capet," she offered.

"Maman," Richard chided her, "you know Philip better than that." He stared into his goblet. "He will not rest until he drives us all across the Narrow Sea." He tossed back his wine, nodded to Robin. "Check in on FitzHenry in Nottingham. At least this time you won't need to prowl in like a thief through the caves."

"I'll go through the gate proudly in your name, sire," Robin said.

Henry shifted uneasily. The caves, the pilfered stores. Treason stuck in his gut and he swallowed hard. Robin's brave merry men. A band of thieves, most would say.

The king laughed, breaking Henry's thoughts. "FitzHenry's luck at the games still holds, so I hear. He may be the wealthiest man in the shire." Richard frowned, thinking. "I might need to take a loan from him!"

Everyone laughed, Henry included, though his smile faded as Count John pulled Edric aside. What were those two plotting?

twenty-seven

NOVEMBER 1196
On the Narrow Sea

Choppy seas battered the galley. Ominous clouds blanketed the skies. Dark, like Henry's mood. There'd been no goodbyes with Stephan before he sailed from Barfleur. Only one thing was worse. Seeing Edric Weston prance up the quay and board the *Goldfinch*. He would never be rid of the man.

Robin drew up beside him at the rail. He glanced at Edric talking with the captain at the wheel. "Tell me about Boneil. You said he transported Grey's wool to Flanders?"

"He worked for my father, and moved goods for anyone who paid, including Count John. Boneil would claim he never inspected the cargo and didn't know he was transporting Greek fire that John planned to use against King Richard. A businessman who didn't take sides, except—" Henry's mouth twitched. "He is good in a fight. Saved Stephan's head from a nasty blow." No need to mention the man had lusted after Stephan when they'd first met in Boston.

"A friend, then. And with a boat. Never know when that might be of use." Robin leaned against the rail and stared at the dark waters lashing the galley. "Weston has a letter from King Richard for his sister. The king has restored Westorby to him." Scowling, Robin scrubbed his hands through his hair as if to rid himself of the traitor. "He also carries orders from Count John and plans to meet with the castellan in Lincoln."

Henry groaned. "So Weston and John *were* plotting some mischief the night of Lady Joanna's wedding. And John's orders? Watch your back, Robin."

"Marian and I will be discreet. But what if Weston gets to de Camville before you and tells him—"

"Let him." Henry stood stiff-backed, his clenched fist pounding the rail. "I plan to tell de Camville myself. Either way, he'll break the marriage contract between me and his daughter."

The king would express his displeasure, and though Henry's troubles would be over for a while, Stephan was right. The king would find him another bride. *I'll have to go through this nightmare again.* Henry's head pounded like the waves rocking the boat.

Robin sidled closer. "What if Edric proposes himself as husband to the child?"

"God's blood—the bastard would, wouldn't he?" That had been furthest from Henry's mind, but the truth would out Weston for the bastard he was. "De Camville will get an earful from me, and Bea and Elle can appeal to Lady Nichola and attest to the man's nature. De Camville will never let his child marry a monster like Weston by the time we've told him what we have witnessed."

"Why not deny Weston's accusations?" Robin asked.

Henry looked out over the water. "That would keep Weston away from the girl, and keep me safe from some other heiress for a few years. *If* de Camville believes me." The wind rose, tossing his hair into his eyes. He raked it back, and then rubbed the back of his neck. In good conscience, did he have a choice? "I hate to lie to de Camville. I do not know if I could do this."

"Think on it," Robin said.

"Cannot do what, Henry?" Edric had come up skulking behind them. He sounded far too confident and condescending. "Deceive that poor child and her parents? What in the name of God is King Richard thinking?"

Henry gripped the rail until his knuckles turned white. "The king knows better than to give her to a wife-beating bastard like you."

Edric scoffed. "Is it true that men like you cannot swive a woman? That your cock stays as limp as a blade of grass in the snow?"

Henry started for Edric's throat. Without warning a wave crashed over the rail. The boat slid into a trough and Edric careened off Henry's shoulder. He slammed into Robin, sending him to the deck. Edric scrambled to get hold of something to avoid going overboard. For a heartbeat, Henry pictured tossing the cur into the sea. But as the vessel slammed into another trough Henry caught him with one free hand. He wrenched him backwards onto the deck and fell atop him.

"Are you all right?" Robin had dragged himself upright and gripped the rail.

Breathless, Henry could only nod.

Why did I save the bastard? Guilt flashed through him. How could he even think such a thing?

Suddenly Captain Boneil was there, seizing Henry's

arms. He dragged Henry off Edric and planted him firmly at the rail. "Hold tight—here comes another one!" Boneil shouted.

Boneil had a rope tied at his waist. He sprawled atop Edric to keep him pinned down. The boat crested a wave and plunged downward, the sea soaking them again. Boneil shouted orders above the howling wind. Two of the crew helped him and Edric to their feet and Boneil steadied the man as waves broke over the rail.

"Thank you," Edric said.

"Thank Lord de Grey," Boneil said as his crew members led Edric beneath the canvas near the stern.

Henry turned his back to Edric wanting no thanks. He wiped the sea spray from his face. Blinking, he spotted the horizon, a ribbon of blue sky behind the storm. Robin clamped a hand across his back and laughed. "Almost as bad as the storms we faced near Ragusa after we left the Holy Land."

"Almost?" Henry asked.

"I don't think the boat will crash ashore this time," Robin said.

"Not under my command," Boneil said. The wind tore at the canvas tent, and through the opening he eyed Edric sitting, head buried in his hands. "Looks like your friend will live."

"He is no friend of ours," Henry spat. "It's good you came along when you did. I might have let the sea take him."

"I see," Boneil said, pursing his lips. He was soaked to the skin, his golden hair matted to his face. The gray of the sky tinted his eyes a smoky blue. "And where is Sir Stephan these days?"

Boneil's interest in Stephan hit a jealous bone heightening the empty feeling plaguing Henry, though

Stephan had never given Boneil a second glance.

"Stephan is on the king's business," Henry said flatly.

Boneil nodded, lips curled in a tight smile. "None of mine then." His eyes flicked between Robin and Henry. "I would suggest you rest under the tent to escape this rain and dry out, my lords, but apparently the company there is not to your liking. I have some good wine in the hold. Join me?" He saw Henry's hesitation. "Just for drinks, my lord."

Crates stacked with goods lined the hold and served as a wall for the captain's chamber. Inside, a rope bed hung between two beams. A bench and small table were tied to hooks on the wall to keep them from thrashing about in rough seas.

The men hung their rain drenched cloaks and sat. The wine warmed Henry's belly. Robin had downed a cup and promptly fell asleep at the table to the creaks and groans of the boat. Boneil retrieved a woolen blanket from his bed and tossed it to Henry. Waves battered the gunwale one after another, but Boneil refilled Henry's mug without spilling one drop while Henry settled the blanket over Robin.

"Stephan did not tell you, did he?" Boneil asked.

Henry had to fight the sudden roiling in his stomach. When had Boneil seen Stephan?

"You are a lucky man," Boneil said. "I misjudged Stephan. It is rare, no, unheard of, that I find myself receiving a 'no'."

Stephan rejected him? "When had you seen him?"

Boneil didn't even have to think. "Around midsummer's day three summers past, near Boston." He shook his head, perhaps recovered but still disbelieving. "He had no interest in sharing anything more than a drink with me. He loves you. That's a rare find."

Henry felt himself breathe. Stephan hadn't told him about Boneil's offer. "With all these men on board, why would you want Stephan?"

"I have rules for myself. I will not bed the men who serve me. Jealousy on board a small ship can be deadly."

"You know this from experience," Henry said.

Boneil raised his mug and drank down the sweet wine. "How goes this war, my lord? Mayhap you hear more than we lowly seamen."

"The Count of Flanders provided aid to the French at Aumâle. Pity any English who continue to do business with Flanders," Henry said, knowing the wool trade out of Boston that had been Boneil's livelihood had disintegrated with the first embargoes in 1194. It had impacted Greyton's income as well, though some of the wool processed at Grey's Mill shipped south to Dover and was sold to local weavers. Other wool went via Ermine Street to points north and south. But shipping overland was slow and expensive.

"King Richard won't forget that," Henry added.

"That is one reason I left Boston." Boneil sat back rubbing his thumb on his cup. "I like to think of myself as a smart man. I've no desire to face a noose. I won't turn pirate."

Henry tugged at the neck of his tunic. At home in Greyton he'd be that much closer to Nottingham and to hanging should Allan and Robin's band of men be caught. "A wise choice, captain," he said. "What other reason made you choose Portsmouth as home for the *Goldfinch*?"

"Ha! Why, more men, of course," he said mischievously.

Henry laughed, and then they drank in silence. Henry thought of asking Boneil if he sought love, but he knew the answer. Stephan had once been the same way. Finding fleeting comfort in another man's arms that vanished as soon as the heart calmed. So alone. Their love had changed that. Warmth flooded Henry's soul and he smiled. Neither he nor Stephan had been seeking love, yet they had found it.

"You are thinking about him," Boneil said.

Touching his hand to his forehead and then resting it over his heart, Henry said, "That is love."

twenty-eight

NOVEMBER 1196
Greyton, Lincolnshire

Henry reined in his horse at the stone bridge crossing the Witham at Greyton. He was weary from five days on the road, anxious to see home, but heartsick Stephan was not at his side.

Steadying his chestnut, Robin eyed the stonework. "Well kept."

Henry remembered his shock when he returned from the Holy Land. His father had let repairs slide. Coin had been scarce, and Edward had chosen to use what he had to keep their villeins fed and clothed. The three years Henry had been gone were difficult ones. Henry's mother had died and Edward had taken to drink heavily, found himself torn between loyalty to the king and threats from Count John's supporters.

Henry trembled. His father was dead three years now, killed while fighting for the honor of the king. Saving Stephan. *Take care of him. Let him go.* His father's last words to Stephan cut deep. Henry stroked his horse's mane to steady his hands.

"Shall we go?" Robin asked.

Henry shook the sad thoughts from his mind. "Anxious to see Marian?" he asked.

"What a beautiful word—Marian." Robin grinned. It was the first time since they'd left Portsmouth that they'd spoken of Marian. Edric had been their annoying companion the entire journey and Robin was determined John's spy would not learn about his marriage. Five miles back at the Nottingham crossroads the bastard had cantered off east to his manor at Westorby.

Robin spurred his horse and whooped like a young boy who'd had his first kiss. Henry set heels to his bay. His cloak billowed out behind him. Bare trees and evergreens thinned as they galloped along the leaf-covered road away from the river. The land gave way to pastures and beyond that barren fields where grain would be sown come spring.

Greyton Manor came into view, gray stone and weathered oak in the shadows of the forested hillside. The crisp air smelled of smoke curling above the rooftop. Henry slowed, listening to the clang of metal from the blacksmith's shop. His gaze swept from the mill at the south end of the village to cottages and workshops stretching north.

Henry half expected to see Robin's son run to greet them from the stables, but Robert was miles away in Yorkshire. One good would come from this—Robin would take Marian to see their son. She could make a new home at Castle l'Aigle with Bea and Stephan's brother. Robin still had doubts he could convince his father to leave, but he was certain Lincolnshire would not be safe for them.

The door to the manor flew open and Mary stepped outside. Cook and housekeeper since Henry was a babe, the round woman squinted, accentuating the deepening lines round her eyes. A wide smile settled on her face. "Master Henry! Praise God, you're home!" She took the steps slower than he remembered.

Henry jumped down from his horse. Smith and Tanner had appeared from their shops and come to greet him. Leda Tanner joined her husband, a little baby in her arms and a second child peering out from behind her skirts. Robin studied the windows of the manor house looking for Marian. To Henry's knowledge, none of the villagers save for his house staff knew his two friends had taken vows. It would be quite eye-raising if Marian rushed outside and into Robin's arms.

"Mary, what's happened to you?" Henry asked.

"Just a small spill," she said, pressing her wind-blown wimple away from her face. "Hurt my knee."

"Small?" The smith laughed. "I don't think Hugh would think so."

"Hush now," Mary scolded the man. "I'm fine. Come inside, the two of you. This wind is biting."

The hall had barely warmed from the sun and no fire had been set in the hearth. Mary hurried to remove canvas covering the chairs and trestle, stirring the dried lavender scenting the floor rushes as she worked. Henry missed the familiar smells from the kitchen. Mary had always made the best wheaten bread and stew laced with garlic and other herbs. His stomach growled.

"I don't know how to do the cooking so much as when your father, bless his soul, was still alive." Mary filled two cups with wine from the coffer and offered them to Robin and Henry. "Sir John and Lady le Grand make a weekly visit and I always have a meal ready for them."

"It's fine, Mary," Henry said, lifting the mug to her in thanks. "Mayhap some bread and cheese? That's all we'll need for tonight."

"Should have sent word ahead," Mary muttered. "Forgive me for speaking out, my lord. Mayhap you did and the messenger got attacked—"

"No, no messenger. I did not want you to go to any trouble. I am a soldier after all. I'm used to dried meat and stale biscuits in the camps. Whatever you find will be delicious compared to that."

"Where is Marian?" Robin asked.

Mary smiled mischievously. "So you want to see your lady wife?"

"Shh—no one else must hear."

She pressed her hands on her hips and scowled. "Robin Carpenter, don't you think I know that?"

"Where is she?"

Pointing round the hall Mary said, "There's little work for Marian here with Master Henry being away. Not to say she doesn't come each day and tidy up, sweeps the rooms, and lays fresh linens for Sir John and Lady Elle. She and Hugh went up to Ringsthorpe before Terce this morn. Mercy heavens, mayhap you don't know."

"Is something wrong?" Robin asked. "Why are they in Ringsthorpe?" It was well past midday so they'd been gone for hours.

"Linota, your father's wife—she's having a babe. Lost one last year and she's been mighty ill with this one. Her ma used to help birth little ones, but she passed. Marian wanted to help where she could."

"I must go." Robin bolted for the door.

Henry nodded as Robin flew outside, but startled when Mary laid a hand on his arm. "You should go, master. Robin may not be so close to Linota or his da, but those young brothers of his will need him. And he may need you."

Pulling the older woman into his arms, Henry said, "Was it that bad last time?"

"Was a miracle Linota lived." Mary's voice trembled. "I fear for her."

Henry pulled back, planted a kiss on Mary's forehead and then hurried to follow Robin. This was not the reunion anyone would wish for.

As they approached the cottages at Ringsthorpe Henry saw William Carpenter busy with chisel and mallet at his workbench. Robin's brother Thomas was no where in sight, but dark-haired David imitated the carpenter, his face intent on the work. Henry admired William for taking the boy as his own after his parents passed.

Moans from the house grabbed David's attention. Linota was his cousin and he had grown as close to her as a son would. He straightened at the work table, his twelve year old body tall and gangly, his weight not yet caught up. Despair contorted his face before he noticed Robin and Henry's arrival. He rushed to greet them.

"Sir Henry," David said with a bow.

"Lord de Grey," Robin reminded the boy. He slapped his hand across David's back. "You'll be as tall as me in no time."

"My lord," David said shyly and then embraced Robin.

William acknowledged them with a nod but kept working.

"Let me speak with Da. Find Thomas," Robin said and pressed towards his father.

William didn't look up. "What is there to say?" He chipped away at a design, mallet gently tapping the chisel. "Just leave me be. Let me work."

Robin forced his father to turn and wrapped him in his arms. He held on tightly, eyes closed. "Linota is a stubborn woman."

"That she is. Has told me off a time or two. And I right deserved it." William's voice cracked. "She is a good wife, a good mother." He squirmed free of Robin's hold. "As is your Marian. She has kept your secret, hard as it was. Seeing you off to the king and young Robert up to York."

"He must not be so young now." Robin's eyes misted.

William smiled, and then his eyes grew sad. "Mayhap as big as you, but I suppose I won't know that, aye?"

"There is something I must speak with you about, da. But later."

"Tell me you're here to stay. For your wife's sake. She shouldn't have to send you back to King Richard. He's had enough of your time." William looked at Henry. "Am I right, my lord?"

"Robin has served the king well and long," Henry agreed with a nod.

"But how would I support Marian?" Robin asked. "The king has not restored my land or my title. I am on a knight's pay, no more."

William's mouth curled, but before the man suggested he take up carpentry, Robin said, "I am not you, da."

Henry chuckled, but he felt the anguish in Robin's voice. He knew what it meant to love someone and not have them at your side. He thanked God for the time he and Stephan had had together and wondered if he was too bold to ask the Lord to let this be the last time they must be apart. What life was this without his lover? *No life at all.* His heart clenched.

Twigs snapped behind the shop and David reappeared from the wood with Thomas. Rabbits hung from his belt and a bow was slung over his shoulder. His blue eyes flicked from Robin and his father to the cottage and back. Like Henry, he knew it was far too quiet for a birthing, making the breeze rustling the trees far too loud.

Thomas stopped in his tracks, looking for comfort from William, but the carpenter offered none. "Where are your manners, Thomas?"

"Lord de Grey." Thomas tipped his head.

Henry smiled at the boy. He was still the spitting image of Robin, his hay-colored hair flopping in his eyes as he bowed.

"Come here," Robin said.

Thomas was chest-high to Robin, already growing broad through the chest and shoulders, so unlike David. Child-like features had deserted him these last two years and he looked more man than young boy even at twelve summers.

Robin gripped Thomas' hand just as a feeble cry came from the house. William's mouth fell open. He'd been preparing for the worst, but what was this? A baby's cry. Shock became surprise, hope, and he tossed his tools aside and hurried to the door.

Robin clasped Thomas close. The door creaked open and a somber Marian appeared. The babe in her arms was swaddled in linens. "A girl," Marian said, handing the tiny infant to William.

"And Linota?" he asked, watching his daughter struggle for breaths.

"Not well." Marian rested her hand on William's arm. "Best we send for the priest."

"I'll get him," Henry said, stepping forward. "Hello, Marian."

"Master Henry!" she cried out, surprised, and then gasped when Robin came into her sight. She would have run to him, but the babe whimpered and she saw the uncertainty on William's face. "William, boys, come inside."

She stepped aside to let them pass. Robin was last and he kissed her on the lips, on her forehead. Tears spilled down her cheeks. "Oh Robin, Robin."

twenty-nine

Henry didn't return to Ringsthorpe with the priest. He felt useless despite Mary's insistence he should be there. He grieved for Robin, for William Carpenter and the younger boys, but Marian was with them.

The sky should not be such a brilliant blue, he thought as he walked up the hill behind the manor. His mind raced to the autumn three years past when his father died. He had only wanted Stephan's comfort then. Dealing with wave after wave of mourning peasants and minor nobles had made his stomach twist and his head pound.

Kneeling at his parents' graves he said a prayer for their souls more out of habit then belief in God's help, and then sat in the feathery tall grass next to his father's gravestone. "Stephan told me your last words, father. He ignored you." *Let him go?* Never! "I'm sorry you couldn't understand the love we share."

Henry's thoughts quickly turned to his betrothal to Gerard de Camville's daughter. He could hear his father's arguments about marriage and heirs, just as clear as in those last months before he died. "I will not marry, father. I cannot." Henry plucked a long blade of grass and used the stem like a sword, batting away the golden dried ones around him.

Laying back on the grass he watched the clouds scud past, wrapping his cloak tightly round himself when a fierce gust of cold wind sent the crows complaining. The crescent moon began to rise and Henry closed his eyes wanting only to drift off to sleep. He remembered summer times here when the crickets chirred and birdsong filled the air. But suddenly he was jostled back to the Holy Land and the sounds of Saracen war cries. The smith's hammer pounded incessantly like drums and children's playful shouts were like death screams. Hoofs clattered—a cavalry charge. He struggled to forget the battles, but his mind raged with the clang of swords and the smell of blood.

Henry sat up with a start, trembling. He blinked blood from his eyes, swiped a hand across his face. Sweat, not blood. Would he have no peace?

Shouts from the yard drew his eye. The priest cantered in from Ringsthorpe, reining in by the Tanner's cottage. Leda came outside and took a bundle from him. Linota's babe. She was alive. With her own child still at breast, Leda could suckle the Carpenter's daughter.

Linota's body was brought to Greyton the following day for burial in the church yard. By some miracle, her tiny daughter Elizabeth, the name William gave the child, held on to life and slept quietly while the priest spoke. After the funeral, the manor hall overflowed with people. Marian cradled Elizabeth in her arms, but gave her to Leda when she cried to be fed.

William looked waxen, except for the dark circles

beneath his eyes. He didn't touch the food Mary had spread on the table, and only stayed long enough to thank Henry for his kindness. He waved David and Thomas to his side, but Henry said, "We've room here for all of you. Stay tonight."

"I'd rather be home with my memories and not surrounded by so many. The boys and I have work—"

"Not before the morrow, William." Henry's voice was understanding, but insistent.

"Thank you, my lord, but I must go."

"I'll ride back to Ringsthorpe with you," Robin said.

"I can find my way."

"Father, please…" Robin couldn't help the anguish in his voice.

Resigned, William nodded.

"And the boys?" Robin asked. He hated to think of them alone in the cottage so soon after watching Linota suffer. The smell of death would linger there though Marian and two other villagers had placed fresh rushes laced with dried roses on the floor and replaced the sweat soaked linens.

William looked from his sons to Henry. "Send them home when the sun rises."

The two-wheeled cart that William used to bring Linota to her final resting place was still hitched to the mule. He climbed on to the seat and slapped the reins while Robin hurried to saddle his horse. Just as he mounted, Mary appeared with a basket of food. "Stay the night with your da. I know you've not had a moment alone with Marian, but you can both wait another day, if you don't mind my saying so, Robin." She tapped the basket. "Have him eat 'fore he faints away. I packed two skins with the master's best wine."

"You're a gem, Mary," Robin said and set spurs to his

horse.

The shadows deepened and spread like a cloak billowing in the wind. Light flickered through the trees, the cottages of Ringsthorpe not too far ahead. William kept his eyes on the road, but finally spoke. "You and Marian should take the child, raise her as your own."

Robin's mouth dropped open. He fumbled for words, wishing he could see his father's face. "Elizabeth…she's your daughter."

"What do I know of girls? She needs a mother, and Marian loves the babe." William exhaled sharply. "Do right by your wife. She should not have to be alone with you off fighting the king's wars."

William wouldn't listen to arguments that a king simply could not ignore men who would take his land, so Robin chose not to explain King Richard's political machinations that would eventually bring Philip Capet to his knees. "Marian and I will be together soon. Just not here. We cannot stay here."

"We've kept your secret," William said, glancing sidelong at Robin.

"That is not enough." Robin was silent a moment, steeling himself for a conversation he knew his father would reject. "We—*you* cannot remain in Ringsthorpe. Count John knows you are here. I do not trust him."

"You've been serving the man for near three years."

"And I know him that much better. I must take you all far from here."

William scoffed. "You are mad. I will not leave. My work is here." He slapped the mule harder and the animal trotted ahead, surefooted on the wooded path even in the dark. Ringsthorpe lay hushed beneath the black-as-pitch sky when they arrived, but candlelight flickered from one neighbor's cottage. William stopped at the village barn and jumped from the cart, groaning as his feet struck the ground.

Robin dismounted by the water trough to let his horse drink. *How will I convince him to leave?* Staying anywhere near Greyton—even in Lincolnshire—would be dangerous.

"Da, when John finishes with me, there will be no Ringsthorpe." He grabbed the bridle while William unhitched the mule from the cart. "I destroyed his plans to take King Richard's crown. He is a vengeful man. You and the boys, and Elizabeth, must leave this place and make a new life."

William paused, blue eyes scrutinizing Robin. "Have you told Marian? What does she think of this plan?"

"We've hardly had a chance to speak."

"Open the barn door," William said, grabbing the mule's harness. "You tell Marian about Elizabeth."

"You'll consider my words?" Robin asked.

William settled the beast in a stall. He exhaled impatiently and walked towards his empty cottage.

Robin caught up to him. "John will burn this place to the ground. He may kill everyone in his path."

"What is he waiting for? Wouldn't he have tried something if he meant to harm us?" William asked sharply.

"The king has kept him in line, but that may not last. God willing, Richard will live for years to come. But John is unpredictable. The sooner we get you settled away from here, the better. My heart will rest easier."

William stopped outside the cottage. His gaze swept the darkened village. "And what of the others here?"

Only two other families remained in Ringsthorpe. It should not be hard to resettle them all. "I will speak with Henry," Robin said. "They can settle in Greyton."

William grunted. "Safer there? A mile down the road?"

"Other barons would not look lightly on John if he attacks one of their own. He may find other ways to destroy Henry." Stephan. The de Grey wool trade. And use Edric Weston for the dirty work. Robin had not forgotten the fire at Cartholme. The devastating blaze at the estate of Henry's sister had destroyed stables and shops and nearly killed Bea and Little John's wife. They'd not proven Edric was behind it, but it had been a warning to Henry.

"John's true grudge is against me," Robin added. "He intends to see me suffer."

William pressed the cottage door open and struck a flint to light a candle on the table. "Go see your wife."

"I will be here a few days—"

"Off again?" William growled.

"I must see Allan at Nottingham Castle. King's business, and my own." Allan had been putting aside Robin's share—the men only split one-tenth of what they took to give to the poor. It would not be much, but Robin hoped it would be enough to settle his family in York.

"Please think about what I've said." Robin studied the empty cottage, heart clenching at the touches Linota had added to make her home comfortable for William and the boys. The embroidered tapestry on the wall—she'd done the work herself. "Will you be all right? I will stay if you like."

"Your wife is waiting for you." William shooed him out the door.

The hall of the manor house was still brightly lit when Robin returned. Light flickered through the window of Marian's cottage. He remembered the young girl he had courted so long ago, his heart pounding. Long hair that fell to her waist, round cheeks, dark eyes that saw through him. The kindest spirit, but stubborn. He thought she was lost to him when he'd left Ringsthorpe. When he returned, he was as cocksure at one and thirty as he'd been at eighteen summers except where Marian was concerned. Oh, he loved her, but he wasn't sure how she would feel seeing him back from the dead. That's what she had assumed when he had not reached out to her in all those years. *What a lucky man I am.* He offered her his heart and she had taken him back. When they had married at Clipstone almost three years past, he had not promised her a normal life, but God, how he had missed being at her side. He loved the woman she had become. His wife, the mother of his son.

He took a deep breath before rapping on her door. "Marian?"

A cock crowed outside and Robin cracked his eyelids open. It was still dark in the cottage and he reached for Marian, the thought of her sending a fiery spark to his groin. "Marian?" He sat up and shivered. She wasn't in bed, but bent near the central hearth to stoke life into the fire.

"We don't need that. Come back to bed."

"You do have a way of warming me up," she said, glancing at him. Her shift shimmered in the fire's glow and outlined her bosom and slender waist.

"Do you know how much I have missed you?"

She smiled. "After last night, I think I do."

Marian crawled beneath the woolen blanket and rested her head on Robin's chest. He tilted her chin up and kissed her deep and long. He wanted to make love to her again, but he thought of all the times he had only wanted her in his arms, so holding her, being here, was heaven.

"I want to take you to York," he said.

Marian looked him in the eye. "To see Robert? Yes, yes, when can we leave?"

"Soon. And there's more." When she looked at him, curious, he said, "My father wants us to raise Elizabeth as our own."

"Us? Does that mean…"

"That I will stay? Not yet." He kissed her forehead.

"Robin," she hesitated and he could hear the quiver in her voice. "I would be glad to help your father with Elizabeth, but I am young and strong. I want *your* child."

His arms trembled, but he pulled her close. "I want that too, but if I lost you… I cannot bear that thought."

"We are all in God's hands. Think what I must live with every day knowing you fight for the king."

"It's what is yet to come that worries me, Marian." He ran his hand up and down her back not wanting to tell her how deep his fear ran for her, for his father and brothers.

"Count John," she said quietly.

She knew of course. But she didn't know how many times John had nearly killed him.

"Will we ever be able to tell others that we are married?" she asked.

"Not as long as you live here," he said. He drew her hand to her belly. If her womb were to quicken with his seed, she could not stay in Greyton without bringing shame on herself as an unmarried woman.

"Leave Greyton? I did that once when I carried Robert. I hate the lies I spoke, the secrets. I do not want to do that again."

"You won't have to keep us secret."

"You just said you worried about John."

He couldn't put this off any longer. "I want to take you far from here."

"Louviers? Has the king given you your lands and title? That is even closer to John than we are here."

"Richard has not restored them, but I was thinking of York. Stephan l'Aigle's brother, Lady Bea—they will take you in. I would ask them when we visit Robert. Henry has little need for you at the manor, so it would not seem unusual for you to leave. You were Bea's maid when she was a girl here. She would love to have you. And I might ask to join l'Aigle's mesnie."

Marian smiled. She would be with Robin and Robert. But a frown followed and he wondered if she was realizing that she would leave behind this home and the people closest to her since childhood.

"But Elizabeth?" she asked. "She needs a wet nurse."

"I doubt I'd convince Tanner to let his wife accompany us."

"It will be near a year until we could take Elizabeth."

Linota's passing and the newborn added more complications that he'd never considered when thinking how to convince his father to move.

"There are women in York," he reminded Marian.

"But the journey there will take days. We cannot starve the child."

Robin was determined to get Marian away from here as soon as possible. And if she was with child she could not stay here a year. Suddenly, he remembered that Edric Weston mentioned visiting his new nephew, a child born before Easter. "Elle?"

Marian's eyes grew wide. Little John and Elle's son would still be at the breast. "Do you think they'd accompany us north?"

"Little John manages Bea's affairs at Cartholme. Their visit to Castle l'Aigle would be business." Robin kissed her and then sat up, planting his feet on the floor. He shook his head. "Now we must convince my father to go with us."

thirty

"Welcome home, Lord de Grey. Henry," Nichola de la Haye, the Lady de Camville, added informally. She had been castellan of Lincoln Castle since before Henry's birth. In her forties now, she was still an attractive woman. She sat near the brazier, the hot coals the color of her wine-colored gown.

Henry bowed. "Lady de Camville."

"We'd not expected you so soon, but I will have Adela fetched to meet you."

She gestured to one of the servants, but Henry held up his hand. "There will be time enough for that later, my lady. I saw her in the bailey. Don't disturb her play."

Waving the guard off, Nichola eyed him shrewdly with her deep blue calculating eyes. A smile settled on her face. "She is young, but she'll blossom in a few short years."

"Yes, my lady." Henry shifted uneasily, glancing at the young pages by the sweets-laden side table and the guards by the stairwell. Noise drifted from the hall downstairs. "I want to spare her from me and seek to—"

"Spare her?" Nichola snapped her fingers and the pages and guards left them alone.

As steps faded on the stone stairs, Henry said, "You will not want Adela to marry a man like me. I may be a baron with a small bit of land and a good wool trade, but surely a daughter of Nichola de la Haye deserves more?"

Nichola looked at him, surprised. "Men have been vying for my daughter's hand since the day I brought her into this world, Henry. I have known your family well before you were born. Your father spoke highly of you, even after you'd left on crusade against his wishes. You may not be wealthy in lands stretching from the Welsh marches across the sea to Normandy, but you have the support of King Richard. Why would he suggest you as a suitable husband for my daughter if it were not so?"

"I asked him that myself, my lady. Begged him to reconsider."

She frowned. "Do you detest my daughter? You've not even met her. You have years to get to know her."

The veins in Henry's neck pulsed and he swallowed hard. "I could never love Adela."

"Love has nothing to do with marriage." Nichola sat back in her chair. "She is a loving girl and you will grow fond of her. Treat her kindly and she may come to love you, a rare gift in these arrangements."

Henry forced himself to meet her eyes. "I could not be with her…the way a husband should be with a wife."

Nichola studied him up and down. Henry blushed as her gaze settled on his groin. "You are impotent?"

"No, hardly," Henry said. Her bluntness and straightforward manner reminded him of Queen Eleanor. She deserved the truth. "I love another and have no intention of breaking my vows."

"Secretly married? You did this without the king's permission."

"I am not married."

"Then what is the problem?"

Sweat tickled Henry's neck, but he straightened, prepared for her scorn. He loved Stephan. Didn't care what others thought. "I have given my heart to another knight. We are lovers. Do you want your daughter to marry someone the Church condemns to Hell?"

Nichola grasped the arms of her chair so tightly Henry feared they would crack. She avoided his eyes and stared at the wine on the side table. She didn't call guards to drag him out, but Henry waited for the curses, stood stiffly expecting to be doused with the drink.

"A sodomite." Nichola pursed her lips, her shoulders tensed. "Richard knows this?"

"He does, my lady."

Her breaths lengthened and slowed, but she straightened, her grip loosening on the chair. She met Henry's eyes. "Who else?"

Henry stood stiff as the saints carved in the stone at Notre-Dame. "A few close friends and family," he said. Muffled voices wafted from the hall downstairs. Henry shivered—he swore he heard Edric Weston. "Others suspect...including an enemy far too close to home." He looked towards the open stairwell. "I could deny any who accuse me and pretend to be the good, loving husband." He met Nichola's probing eyes. "I could have lied to you, my lady, but I don't want to hurt your daughter. I do not believe my love for another man is sinful, but if I marry..."

"You commit adultery, another sin that will send you to the fires of Hell." Nichola chuckled, surprising Henry.

"An interesting take on sin. And a refreshing view of marriage, Henry, mayhap an unrealistic one. Men are weak, so easily enticed by women. With your service to the king, I imagine you have seen long lines at the confessional, priests growing rich on sinners' fines. Even the threat of Hell cannot keep men from their lust."

"I am not so worried about Hell, but rather the vow spoken in God's presence. I believe in God and the sanctity of marriage." *I believe, but it hurts so.* "My friends tell me to be with Stephan, and then seek forgiveness, but I cannot see myself breaking the marriage vows. This will make me a miserable being and an awful husband. Would I do my duty? Would I resent the poor woman who was forced into a marriage with me? I cannot deny my love for Stephan, my desire to be with him. Your daughter should not have to live with that."

Boots pounded the stairs. "Lady de Camville. My lady, let me—"

"Stop!" two guards' voices echoed in the stairwell.

Henry stepped in front of Nichola, ready to defend her with his bare hands. The guards were not quick enough and suddenly Edric Weston stormed in. "My lady…" Edric gasped for breath, and then slowed to cross the room. The guards grabbed him.

"Sorry, my lady," the sergeant said. "I told Lord Weston you were meeting with Lord de Grey, but he insisted that he could not wait."

Edric bowed. "Apologies."

"You have no right to barge into my chamber, Weston. Please wa—"

"I know, my lady, but it concerns this man." Edric sneered at Henry. "You must know the truth about his vile, unnatural vice. You would not want your daughter to marry a man like him."

Nichola sat up as if intrigued by Edric's accusation. "How is he vile?"

"I wanted to spare using crude language," Edric said.

"Oh, please do not, Lord Weston," Nichola said, not stemming her desire to encourage him. "What are you saying?"

"Weston—" Henry pleaded, playing along with Nichola.

"You filthy, loathsome pig," Edric spat. "He is a sodomite, my lady. He lays with other men."

Nichola nodded. "Henry and I were just talking about this. How is this different from married men who sleep with women who are not their wives?"

"It is two men! It is against the laws of God."

"And you have never broken God's laws yourself, my lord?"

"This is different. Unnatural." Edric shook his head vehemently, shocked by her reaction. "Think of your daughter."

"I believe *you* are thinking of my daughter, Lord Weston. She would be quite the prize. And that is how you would think of her."

"Me? I had not considered—"

"Spare me, Weston." Nichola glared at Edric. "Lord de Grey is betrothed to my daughter. I would sooner marry her to a man who is honest with her rather than one whose reputation for beating his wife is known round Lincolnshire. Would you like to confess you had a hand in her death?"

"What?" Incensed, Edric's gaze flicked from Nichola to Henry and back again. Henry was shocked she knew, or had heard rumors about the bastard.

"Amicia died after giving birth to my poor son," Edric cried, "may God rest their souls."

Nichola jumped to her feet, pointing an accusatory finger at him like a judge. "A man like you calling on God? You will never marry any of my daughters, nor any daughter from King Richard's realms. Now leave this place, Lord Weston. Get out."

Edric sucked in a deep breath, eyes blazing with hatred. He bowed curtly to Nichola and departed without looking at Henry.

"You would still allow Adela to marry me?" Henry asked as the guards' footsteps faded behind Edric's.

"No, I did not say that." Nichola swallowed back her wine and sat. "I said you are betrothed. This helps us both, Henry. I will have time to seek out a suitable husband for my daughter and remind the king he proposed to give Adela to a sodomite. He will see that the fine to break this contract with you should be little to nothing."

"And I will be tied to Adela until that time." Henry thought of his nephew David as a possible match, but he would save that discussion for another day. His heart felt lighter knowing the king wouldn't be compelled to find a wife for him any time too soon. "What of Lord de Camville? Weston may go to him."

"I will soothe my lord husband. And we need not tell Adela what the future holds. You must meet her. Nothing should look amiss."

"The guards?"

"Are well paid and will remain silent." Nichola fingered a biscuit from the tray and crumbled it in her hand. "If anyone hurts my family they will pay." Brushing the crumbs away, she said, "I'll send for Adela to introduce you before the midday meal. For now, tell me of the king's war with the French. You'll return there for the spring campaigns?"

The hours passed as they spoke, and not just of the war, but of Count John, of Henry's plans to see Bea in Yorkshire, and of Stephan.

"The Lady Adela," a servant announced and a young girl with chestnut-colored hair appeared at the top of the stairwell.

Henry stood as Adela curtsied deeply. Her hair was laced with ribbons and pearls, her gown an imitation of the gold and crimson her mother wore. Her eyes were a deep blue—like Stephan's, Henry thought and bowed. A shy smile lit her round face and she looked tentatively from Henry to her mother. Nichola waved her forward.

"My lord," she said, holding out a small bouquet of dried flowers, "welcome to Lincoln." Her voice rang stronger than Henry expected.

"Thank you, Lady Adela." He accepted the flowers and retrieved a small brooch from his pouch.

She studied it, running her finger across the sapphire and gold set into the smooth pin. "It is beautiful, my lord."

"I did not know it would match your eyes," he said. "It belonged to my mother."

"I will treasure it."

She sounded so much older than eight and Henry was impressed with her comfort in this situation. He suddenly wished he had asked Nichola what Adela understood of arranged marriages. The last thing he wanted was a conversation on wedding plans, and he feared the child might grow too close. As much as he had always loved Greyton, he would be glad to be far away come spring.

When they gathered in the hall for the midday meal, her sisters and brothers joined them. "I thought that other man was Adela's betrothed," ten-year-old Maud said. "But he wasn't happy when he left."

Weston?

Nichola exchanged a glance with Henry, and he watched her suppress a frown. "Why did you think that?" she asked.

Adela's hands slid to her lap. After a moment she showed off a hand-sown doll with life-like hair. "He gave me this."

"It's so lovely," said Nichole, the youngest of the children.

"And with real hair," Maud said.

Thomas was unimpressed, not surprising for a boy of eleven. "You are jealous."

"If he'd given a long blade or a sword, I would be jealous," Richard said.

Maud rolled her eyes. "Why would he give a gift like that?"

Shaking his head, Richard said, "Girls."

Henry smiled. He would have done the same at that age.

"Maman, Thomas and I have practice in the courtyard. May we go now?"

"Be off," Nichola told the boys.

They made a gentlemanly retreat from the table, but as soon as the old oak door closed behind them, Thomas shouted, "Race you!" and their boots struck the stone stairs like wild horses.

"Nichole, Maud—upstairs for your embroidery lessons."

"Oh Maman, can't we stay down here by the brazier where it's warmer?" Nichole pleaded.

"So you can listen to your sister and Lord de Grey." Nichola wasn't asking a question. She knew the young girls' minds. "Upstairs. Tell Joseph to stir the fire."

Nichole huffed, but followed her sister in a curtsey

and then off they went.

Adela watched them. "I could give the doll to Nichole."

"Why would you do that?" Henry asked.

"You do not mind if I keep it?"

Henry wanted to rip the toy from her hands, strangle it, and then toss it off the battlements. It would be a good fate for Edric Weston. But he could see Adela's longing look at the doll and it tugged at his heart. "You will receive many gifts."

Adela touched the pin her mother had placed on the collar beneath her throat. "I do so like the brooch, my lord," she said hastily, her face coloring with embarrassment.

"I am glad," Henry said with a smile. He wondered what other gifts Weston would bring. Thank God Nichola saw the bastard for what he was worth.

"Keep the doll for now," Nichola said. "You'll quickly outgrow it and can pass it on to your sister."

Adela nodded, but Henry could see the little girl in her was skeptical of her mother's words. She stayed a while longer discussing her Latin and mathematics lessons and how she preferred to watch her brothers at the quintain in the bailey.

"Your mother may not want to hear it," Henry said, "but my sister Bea used to practice with me when I was your brother Richard's age."

Adela's eyes widened with delight, but Nichola sent him a stern look. "Do not put ideas in her head, Henry." The look also seemed to imply that Adela would grow fond of him if he indulged her. Growing fond in a sisterly way was one matter, but if she grew too close then breaking the betrothal in the future might break her heart.

"Listen to your lady mother," Henry said.

Nichola tipped her head and smiled at her daughter. "And I say you may join your sisters upstairs."

"When will you visit again, my lord?" Adela asked as she stood.

"Join us on Sundays, Henry," Nichola suggested. As she'd mentioned, everything must appear normal, and avoiding his betrothed would cause a stir. "Bishop Hugh sups with us and would be pleased to see you. I hope you will not find his bending your ear too boring. He speaks endlessly about rebuilding the Cathedral and progress on the Bishop's Palace. Work has begun on the West Hall, and I must admit it will be magnificent."

"Sundays, yes," Henry said. "I will be here, at least until I travel to Yorkshire."

Adela beamed and curtsied and then scurried up the stairs.

"Do not bring gifts every week," Nichola admonished, "unless you have some fine wine Lord de Camville might appreciate."

Henry nodded. He was still betrothed, but this solution would keep him from the marriage bed and safeguard young Adela. And Edric Weston? Nichola would see him ruined if he dared speak ill of Henry.

Stephan... It wasn't a perfect solution, but hopefully they would have years before Richard chose another bride for him.

thirty-one

Lincolnshire

Henry spent the next morning surveying his land with the reeve. With harvest well past and no sowing until spring, the villeins toiled nonetheless. Fences needed mending, ditches needed digging, the barn would get new thatch, and the stables a new roof. A messenger arrived midday from Cartholme. Little John suggested Henry wait to visit until the day after next as Edric had arrived just before noon. Henry took the news well—he had no desire to run into Weston again.

Robin and Marian joined him for the midday meal. Hugh served them cups filled with warmed wine and then set the fire to blazing in the hearth before shuffling off to help Mary.

"I'll accompany you to Cartholme," Robin said when Henry informed them of his plans.

"You don't want another day alone with your wife?" Henry winked at Marian.

She hid a smile behind her hand. "Mary will be glad to see Robin gone and me back to my regular chores."

"I heard that," Mary said as she appeared from the kitchen, arms laden with two baskets of bread and honey that she set down on the trestle table. Hugh came in behind her with a pot of lamb stew. "And Hugh and me are doing fine with the chores. It's a wonderful thing to see Marian as happy as she's been in an age."

"Well good, then," Henry said, breathing in the scent of meat simmering with garlic and onions. "Smells almost as good as your pork, Mary. I am famished!"

Mary placed her hands on her round hips. "Almost?" she teased.

He laughed as she ladled the stew. The rich brown gravy nearly spilled over the rim of his trencher. He dunked a chunk of bread in the gravy and took a bite, savoring the taste even more than the smell. Mary grinned to see his response and happily retired with Hugh to the kitchen.

"Why don't you both come with me?" Henry asked.

Robin told Henry about his father's wishes for Elizabeth. "Do you think we might convince Elle and Little John to accompany us to Yorkshire?" Robin asked.

"Elle has a wet-nurse for the little babe John," Marian explained.

Henry couldn't imagine Elle would be unwilling to help. "I'll write Bea after we visit with Elle and Little John. Christmastide in Yorkshire." He chomped on a piece of lamb dripping with gravy and then wiped his mouth on his sleeve.

Robin squeezed Marian's hand. Henry nodded to them, hoping this would keep Marian far from Count John's reach.

"How did the de Camvilles take your news?" Robin

asked. "Are you still betrothed?"

"Lord de Camville was away, but the Lady Nichola sees advantage in leaving the betrothal in place for the moment."

Robin laughed when Henry described Edric's arrival and abrupt departure, quickly silenced by Marian's frown. "That poor child is just a pawn. No one thinks of her feelings."

"Of course we do, Marian," Henry said. "But Adela is Nichola de la Haye's daughter. Made of strong stuff. Her mother will guide her through this and ensure men like Edric Weston cannot hurt her."

"My lord Henry!" Little John raced into the bailey and embraced Henry. "Sir Robin, Lady Marian. By the saints it is good to see you. Come in, come in."

If it was possible, Henry was sure Little John had grown taller and broader. He clamped an arm across the younger man's back and they strode into the manor. Elle greeted them, more bright and lovely than ever. She and Marian had grown close and she quickly teased her about having Robin back. Henry smiled, imagining Elle would be much more forthright when she was alone with Marian.

Motherhood suited Elle. Her face was slightly rounder, her curves more accentuated by her deep blue linen gown. She defied common practice and refused to wear a wimple in her home. Her golden hair was plaited and tied back with silk ribbons. Still girlish as ever at eighteen, she grabbed Marian's hand and they hurried up the stairs.

Little John poured drinks and a servant left fruit and wafers on the trestle where the men settled in. "You'll want a report on Cartholme?"

"It looks as fine as when Bea ran the place and I know

you keep her informed. I saw copies of your letters to her at Greyton," Henry said. "If there's more to tell that couldn't be written in a message, then we've all night and the morrow to listen."

Little John took Henry's meaning. There was always information too sensitive, too political, to share in writing.

"We were shocked to have Edric at our doorstep with no warning." Little John recounted that unexpected visit, the man laden with gifts for his niece and nephew. He'd even brought a pearl necklace for Elle and complimented her on her management of Westorby in his absence. She had seen right through him, for he had changed little. Still a braggart, exaggerating his service to Count John and his plans for the future. "He said you sailed from Normandy together." Little John looked at Henry. "Is it true you're betrothed to Gerard de Camville's daughter?"

Henry nodded. "Let me guess—Edric didn't tell you he went straight to Lady Nichola, ready to defend Adela and save her from me. Odd that he had no such worries about his own sister when he and my father plotted to marry me to Elle," Henry said sarcastically.

"Edric only looks out for himself, and I'm glad that scheme failed." Little John gave a swift nod, closing his fingers over his wedding band. "What of Sir Stephan? He didn't come to England with you?"

Henry swallowed back his wine. Despite his lingering hope that all would turn out well, it was hard to talk about Stephan's decision to stay behind. Little John listened intently, eyes widening when Henry spoke of Lady Nichola's plan.

"It's a lot to ask of a man," Little John said, never one to mince words when it came to matters of the heart. "The scheme is a good one and may keep you from marriage, but what of the next one hanging over your head. Where does that leave you with the man you love?"

Henry shook his head impatiently, thoughts churning over the struggle of being with Stephan, but not *with* him. "What I feel for Stephan will never change."

Little John started to speak, but Henry was in no mood for a lecture from another friend and quickly changed the subject. "Robin and I will go to Nottingham within the fortnight to visit with Allan."

"I've not seen him in an age, my lord."

"No need for formalities amongst old friends," Henry said.

"Yes…Henry." Little John still hesitated, remembering his humble roots. "I've not heard from Allan directly, but I have had word *of* him."

"Has he been strung up?" Robin asked, only half joking.

"Thank the good Lord, no," Little John said and crossed himself. "Messages come by way of Tuck. He worries about Allan. Most days he does his job, but he missed a run or two. Drunk—angry drunk—and not the first time. Some wonder if he's not Hal's bastard but John's. His gambling is worse. He still wins, but he flaunts it and makes no friends. He looks to blame others."

"For his winning?" Robin asked, incredulous.

"For everything." Little John chewed on his lip, shook his head. "If the food is not hot, the ale or wine sour, if a man is sloppy, or a thread hangs from his tunic."

"That doesn't sound like Allan," Henry said. "Is it not a ruse? Best not to have so-called friends who get too close and discover Robin's band of merry men."

Robin blew out a breath. "We shall be there soon enough and see it for ourselves."

A little child squealed and laughter echoed down the stone stairwell. Henry glanced overhead where the wood creaked beneath the ladies' footfalls and a child's steps.

"Marian is enjoying the babies," Little John said.

Robin placed his elbows on the table and raised his brows. "We've a proposition for you and Elle. Marian may be telling Elle as we speak," he said. "We want you and the children to go to Yorkshire."

Little John studied his two friends. "Has something happened?"

"Linota died."

"God have mercy." Little John crossed himself again. "She lost the babe?"

"No, and that is why we need you. My da wants Marian and me to raise Elizabeth, and I want Marian away from Greyton. But Elizabeth needs a wet-nurse, and your son has one who could also feed her, at least until we get to Castle l'Aigle where we can find another."

"What about your da and brothers?" Little John asked.

"I pray I can get them to leave."

Elle had slipped down the stairs. "You must," she said and walked across the hall with a dark-haired child on her hip. "Henry, Sir Robin, meet Eleanor."

The two knights stood and bowed as Elle set the child down.

"Lady Eleanor," Henry said, drawing to his knee. The two-year old held her hand out and touched his close-cropped beard. Her father's was fuller, and she looked back and forth, smiling when Little John winked at her.

Marian came up behind them. "And this is Geoffrey."

The baby turned shy and rested his head on Marian's shoulder. "He's taken to you," Henry said. "Eleanor, will you sit with me?" He offered her a hand and she enthusiastically climbed into his lap and reached for a wafer, but not before getting the nod from her mother.

"Did you sew this pretty dress, Eleanor?" Henry asked.

Her dark eyes widened and she noticed crumbs had fallen into her lap. She brushed them from the soft blue wool. "Mama did," she said and laughed.

Henry planted a kiss on the back of her head. "Mama will have to make you other clothes to wear when she teaches you to loose arrows."

Eleanor looked at Elle and agreed, clapping loudly. Little John seemed to recognize he would have no say in the matter, not that Henry thought he would mind.

They passed the afternoon planning for Yorkshire and laughing over Edric's encounter with the Lady de Camville.

Elle remained concerned. "You are right not to trust my brother," she said. "If we are to go to York, we should travel separately to avoid bringing on his suspicion. Marian can accompany us. You should go by way of Nottingham."

"You've it all planned out, Elle," Henry said.

She looked at them, embarrassed and surprised, until she saw Henry's wide grin.

"It's perfect," Henry added. He watched his friends, how Little John swept glances at his wife, would lay his palm on her hand. Henry tickled Eleanor, planted kisses on her nose and cheeks, and when the nurse took the baby away for feeding and a nap, Little John fixed his gaze on them as they left the hall. Eleanor wanted her father's attention and slid from Henry's lap and into his arms. Little John's eyes sparkled.

Robin had hardly moved from Marian's side. How was the man going to leave her behind again?

An ache coursed through Henry. He shivered, thinking

of catching Stephan watching him across a crowded room, knowing their thoughts aligned like the stars. *Stephan...I miss you.*

Elle noticed Henry's melancholy and moved to sit by him. "Why didn't Stephan come with you?"

"And give Edric more room to talk?"

"I cannot imagine being without John for more than a day or two."

Henry squeezed her hand. She was a kindred spirit. "Your children are beautiful. I am so pleased for you and Little John."

Staring at her daughter and husband, Elle set her mouth in a hard line. "Do you think my family will be spared Count John's wrath?"

When Henry had returned to Greyton after his pilgrimage to the Holy Land and met Elle Weston, he had been impressed with her strength and resilience. It was rare to hear a tremble in her voice.

"Will the Count be the problem, or your brother?" he asked. "I will repeat what you said to me—you should not trust him. He would be the one to benefit if, God forbid, something happens to you and your children."

thirty-two

DECEMBER 1196
Nottingham, Nottinghamshire

Henry brushed snowflakes from his mantle and gazed at
the keep perched high on the cliffside over Nottingham.
Robin's horse sidled restlessly beside his as if the animal
could smell the war. The siege engines had been quiet for
more than two years, but Henry's mind filled with the
sounds of boulders slamming the stone walls of the
castle's middle bailey. The coppery scent of blood struck
his nostrils and he shuddered, closing his eyes, breaths
short.

Robin's voice drifted into his consciousness and
Henry fought to push away the memories.

"Tuck will find us, but Much will be at his father's mill
until the sun goes down," Robin said.

They nudged their horses towards Castle Gate Road
and the wooden palisade of the outer bailey came into
view. Workers were repairing one section and the
pounding of hammers echoed through the streets. Burnt

out shells and rubble from the siege were gone, replaced by new buildings in the outer bailey. Henry swallowed hard remembering how they crossed the bailey and stormed the barbican, crossbow bolts raining down from the battlements.

Though it was cold, sweat trickled down Henry's neck. Stephan had been injured that day. He could have lost him here.

Henry exhaled sharply. The sooner he could leave England and be at Stephan's side the better.

He glanced down the road. "Shall we wait for Allan at The Trip?" Tuck's messages to Little John claimed Allan was there every day. It seemed like a good bet.

Bells from St. Nicholas rang out None. "That'll be hours yet." Robin patted the empty flask hanging from his saddle hook. "I could do with an ale. A hot meal would settle the gnaw in my belly, not that I'll deny Mary's cheese and bread were fine for the road. But we don't want to be in our cups by the time Allan arrives."

Henry laughed. "But after?"

"I'll make no promises," Robin said.

"I do have a letter from the king," Henry said. "We can go to the castle, get an audience with Allan, if not with the Sheriff himself. He might be inclined to offer us a meal in the hall. Save us a penny or two at The Trip."

Robin agreed and they joined the procession of people through the gate. The crowds thinned as they approached the middle bailey and guards inspected the seal on the king's letter closely before waving them forward. Maneuvering along the muddied road, they found the stables along the western wall and left their horses to be tended. From there it was a short walk to the bridge into the upper bailey. The guard there was not so quick to let them pass and made them leave their swords. Another sergeant led them to the hall, despite Robin's argument that they'd been at the castle before and could easily find their way. "We are personal friends of Sir William FitzHenry, clerk of the castellan, nephew of King Richard."

Henry hid a grin. The sergeant wasn't impressed.

A fire warmed the long chamber connecting what would be the king and queen's apartments on official visits. The sergeant issued instructions to two servants who spread the trestle with herb-crusted meats, fruit, and bread.

"They let all kinds in here."

Chuckling, Henry stood of his own accord, something he hadn't been able to do the first time Allan had spoken those words.

Robin jumped up and met Allan as he strode into the room.

"My God, it is good to see you." Allan's eyes sparkled with a boyish hint of mischievousness. He looked past Robin and bowed to Henry. "My lord."

Robin clamped a hand on his arm and then wrapped him in a brotherly hug.

"What has taken you so long to visit?" Allan asked. He lowered his voice. "Leaving me here amongst these curs to run your *business*."

"Curs?" Robin shook his head. "The man I remember gets all the pleasure conning people, especially those who most deserve it."

Allan pounded Robin's back, and suddenly the boy was gone, the nineteen-year-old all business. "The Sheriff is not here. He has many estates to inspect and business beyond Nottinghamshire, but I will relay the king's greetings on his return."

"The king knows you provide a thorough report to

him," Henry said, "but asks if there are any personal observations that you would share."

Allan's gaze flicked to the servants and back to Henry. "King Richard has placed trustworthy men in his offices."

"He'll be pleased to hear that," Robin said.

Allan waved the servants from the room. He picked at the bread, ripped a chunk off and flung it across the table. He sat in the sturdy oak chair at the head of the trestle and gestured for the knights to sit. "This is not how I intended to spend my life. I'm not meant for this."

"Others pay huge sums to have a job like this." Henry looked towards the doors at either end of the hall, kept his voice down to ensure no one overheard. "And you do important work for the poor."

"Tuck can manage that without me."

"Not the goods from the castle stores," Robin said quietly.

Allan smacked the table. "Tuck knows the way in and out. He can adjust the barrels and crates just as I do."

"But you know the guards' schedules. You *set* them! God's nails, Allan. You could have a normal life, settle down and marry—just an extra bit of night duty in the undercroft now and then." Robin groaned. "Why would you want to follow the king from one battlefield to the next?"

"Henry could do the same!" Allan shouted. "Stay safe and sound at Greyton."

"You know why I don't, Allan." Henry cleared his throat. "We should not be discussing any of this here."

Allan nodded. "Sorry. I do have news for the king." He planted his elbows on the table and leaned closer. "Voices near and far speak out about the rise of taxes and fees supporting the war against the French. The barons, the merchants, peasants—everyone suffers. They tire of the king fighting across the Narrow Sea. They see no need or reason for it. If Hubert Walter invents one more tax, King Richard will have a rebellion here, in England, to put down. He can add that to his fight with the French, with Aquitaine's rebellious barons, and Toulouse, Flanders—I don't need to name the others."

"Surely not all the barons would side against him." Henry and Robin exchanged glances. Many barons had lands across the sea, some still in King Philip's hands. "Many have King Richard to thank for recovering their castles. And Toulouse has married the king's sister. Surely you heard about the Lady Joanna."

"Bless her." Allan smiled, but his expression changed quickly. "But all pay scuttage to keep Richard's army fed and clothed, and more taxes on top of that. Even the bishops are grumbling." Allan stood abruptly. "I must attend to the king's business now. Off to inspect a delivery, meet with two bickering merchants, prepare invoices and see to the feast being prepared for the Archbishop's visit."

"We'll meet with you later," Henry said. "At the Trip?"

Allan nodded and walked out, picking up his pace and straightening his shoulders as if all was right in the world.

The brown-robed monk drew back his cowl, his wolf-green eyes sizing up Henry and Robin. "What have we here?"

"New sinners for your preaching, Tuck," one round-faced merchant cried. "God has answered our prayers."

His companions at The Trip laughed because for once they wouldn't have to hear the monk's lecture. They clinked their mugs and drank their ale.

"Lord Henry. Sir Robin." Tuck bowed and then

crossed himself.

"Is this how you spend your days?" Robin asked. He gestured to the boy serving drinks to bring one for Tuck.

"In prayer with these drinking fools, or at St. Mary's. The priest there is a friend," he said, tipping his head in a knowing manner. His robe didn't disguise his broad shoulders, but wide sleeves concealed the thick muscles of his arms. His leather boots were scuffed and caked with mud and likely concealed a long blade.

"I can tell you've been out of John's reach for a while," Tuck said as he sat.

Henry looked between the two men, confused.

Robin laughed. "I cannot say I miss the king's brother." He rubbed his jaw. "When did you leave Normandy?"

"Shortly after you departed for Rennes with Lord Henry."

Henry nodded, not surprised Tuck might come and go to Robin with information from Nottingham. Their talk quickly turned to the knights' business in England and of old friends, including Allan.

"I'm glad you're back to give Allan a hand," Robin said.

"Don't say his name too loudly, else every sore loser in the tavern might have your hide," Tuck said. "I have tried to talk to him."

Henry would have laughed, but Allan's behavior brought unwanted attention. It could compromise their work here, if not get him killed by a disgruntled gambling competitor. Perhaps Robin could make him see sense.

Tuck glanced up and frowned at someone coming up behind Robin and Henry.

"I thought I recognized you," the man said and whipped a short blade from his belt.

"Put that away before you hurt someone, Peter," Tuck said.

"This man is a traitor to the crown. He was put in chains by King Richard." Peter's harsh voice sent a jolt like lightning through The Trip and quiet suddenly pervaded the room.

Henry stood slowly, his hand on his sword. "Sir Robin was pardoned by the king. He is in Nottingham with a message for the Sheriff."

"Where? Where's his message?"

"We delivered it to William FitzHenry only an hour ago."

Grumbles and curses sounded from the men gathered. "Who the hell are you?" Peter asked.

"Lord Henry de Grey of Lincolnshire. A king's man. Now, Peter, do as our good brother here suggests." Henry scanned the room. Allan didn't have any friends here that he could see.

"How do we know *Sir Robin* is not an outlaw? Your word only?"

"De Grey was here too," another gruff voice shouted. "A friend of the outlaw."

"Lord de Grey is no outlaw." Tuck tried to reason with the increasingly clamorous crowd.

"Let the Sheriff decide," a familiar voice shouted. A cold draft swept the room as the door shut behind the newcomer.

Parting the crowd, Edric Weston drew his sword. Robin remained perfectly still.

"Weston, tell them," Henry said, his heart pounding. "You know as well as I do that Robin faithfully serves King Richard and his brother Count John now."

"Let's take him to the Castle," Edric said.

Henry's brows rose.

"To the dungeons," a cry rang out.

They could fight their way from the tavern, Henry thought. It wouldn't have been the first time.

Tuck leaned across the table and whispered something to Robin, who nodded and held his hands up in surrender. Henry realized that getting Robin outside—even to the Castle—would be the best way to protect him.

"What have you done now?" Allan scowled at Robin, then turned eyes on Edric Weston.

"It was for his own safety," Edric said. "That crowd was unruly."

Robin frowned at Edric through pinched eyes. "For once I would say Weston is right."

"You finally admit that I—"

"Do not push me, Weston. You are in this for your own gain, nothing more." Robin scrubbed a hand through his hair and looked at Allan. "You've a bad reputation in town. Gloating about your winnings I hear."

"That's my business," Allan said bluntly. "Nothing for you to worry about."

Henry strode into the hall. "I thanked Brother Tuck for his help."

"Tuck?" Edric's lids narrowed. "He was here during the siege—an old friend of yours? Another king's man?"

"He is no longer in the king's service, not that it should matter to you," Henry said, immediately regretting speaking of Tuck.

Edric scoffed. Henry wondered if he would recognize him from John's camp. Or would remember that Tuck ran Greek fire from Boston to Nottingham before the king's return to England. But Edric had been so full of himself, he hardly noticed the wagon drivers.

"What are you doing here, Edric? Following us?" Henry asked him.

"Staying with Robin, as Count John ordered."

"There is nothing to be gained by that," Robin said. "What does John expect to learn? He knows I am here on his brother's business. King Richard trusts me once again, and I will prove his faith in me is warranted. I am done with John. Go home, Lord Weston. Or go back to your master in Normandy."

"I don't take orders from you, Robin."

"But I can have you thrown out of the castle," Allan said. Robin snickered and Allan's mouth became a hard line. "As for you, stay here for now. You'd best not venture out before dark. Let me deal with this rabble, and get to the king's work."

"You're a busy man," Robin said wryly.

"Yes, I am, and now I must waste time settling—"

"What devil is up your arse, Allan?" Henry asked, surprised by the anger in his own voice. "Do not take your frustrations out on Robin."

Allan scowled and turned on his heels.

"After all you have done for him," Edric said, shaking his head.

Henry smacked the table with his fist. "Shut up, Weston." He wished he could lock Edric away.

"Well it's true, isn't it? William FitzHenry...or Allan? Whoever he is. He's no bastard of the king's late brother," Edric sneered. "Where did you find him?"

"He is whoever King Richard says he is." Henry drew himself up to his full height. "And he is a powerful young man. John best remember that." Oh, to have a sword in hand. Perhaps a good thing he did not. Henry wasn't sure he could restrain his desire to be rid of the scum once and for all. "Now, was there anything else you wanted?"

The fire in the hearth spat. Robin wandered over to it, pulled up a stool and sat, his back to both men. Edric glared at Henry and stomped from the room.

Henry poured two goblets of wine at the sideboard. "We must speak with Allan."

"You heard the man. He's got work to do." Robin poked the fire to stir the flames.

"I'm sure he must, but was that a ruse? I haven't heard him so angry since Sarah was killed." Allan's affection for a servant girl at Greyton had run deep. "He is not the Allan I remember." Henry swallowed back the wine.

Robin nodded and smacked the rod on the fire. "He needs to understand that we cannot let our emotions keep us from tasks. That there are things we must do that we may not like." He blew out a sharp breath. "I don't want Marian anywhere near Edric Weston."

"She'll be leaving with Little John and Elle for Yorkshire soon."

"I want to be with her. I need her, like you need Stephan." Robin took the cup Henry proffered. He swirled the dark liquid, stared into it as it settled. "I should have Allan lock me in the dungeons, and then I would escape."

"Confirm to the rabble you *are* a traitor and an outlaw? That will not make being with Marian any easier."

"I will live in the greenwood. Visit her in the dark of night. Quietly make love to her."

Henry gazed into the fire, the flames warming him as much as his thoughts of Stephan. "It is a good thing we do not let our feelings get in the way."

Robin glanced up at him and chuckled with a shake of his head. They clanked their mugs and drank to their loves.

thirty-three

When Allan returned after the sun had set he didn't throw Robin in the dungeons, but led the knights deep into the undercroft. Allan sat atop a crate of goods awaiting removal through the tunnels. He slugged down wine from a leather costrel. The torch he'd lit at the entryway cast a dim golden light, but Henry could barely make out his face.

"We've nearly completed new tunnels from both the king and queen's apartments, connecting to the existing ones," Allan said. "'Course, that work is done during the day with king's men. I convinced Hubert Walter that it was coin well spent. The route through the kitchens is too far should there be a need for the king's hasty escape. Everyone assumes the castle is impregnable, but he'd have to fight his way across the bailey to get here. With an entry through his chambers, we've a faster way to depart." Allan took another swig and offered the skin to Robin and Henry who both waved off the offer. "I suggested we replace the timber gate and palisade with stone, too, but that must wait until this war with France ends and the coffers are refilled."

Allan sounded his normal self—normal given the responsibilities he'd been saddled with. In the old days, he was good at mimicking anyone, including those above his station. He wasn't pretending now. Henry thought his administrative skills would soon rival Walter's, the king's trusted justiciar. Allan managed the castellan's finances and still found ways to keep food and coin funneled to Nottingham's poor.

"You make me proud, Allan," Robin said, echoing Henry's thoughts.

That should have drawn a smile from Allan. Instead, he finished off his wine and got to his feet. He paced a few steps, opened and rummaged through another crate. Pulling the stashed flask stored there, he brought it to his lips and gulped down the drink.

Henry exchanged a worried glance with Robin. Allan turned back to them, his face somber. Tuck had been right. Allan was turning to drink to rid himself of his troubles.

Allan stared at the flask then looked up. "I am alone here. Even when I lived on the streets of London and begged and stole for my daily bread I was not so alone. I oft had a place to sleep. It might not have been warm, but the boys there looked after each other. And once I met Little John—" He choked back a breath. "We were together every day. To the Holy Land and back. Until Henry took Little John with him to Boston and beyond. I understood that, and took trust I'd be at your side, Robin. But you left, told me to stay at Greyton, which broke my heart. Sarah helped me through those days, but she was taken from me, and then you and Queen Eleanor decided I should be a royal bastard and sent me here."

"This work keeps you from getting close to anyone," Henry said, nodding. "I understand, and I'm sorry, but we all make sacrifices."

"Keeping people at arm's length doesn't mean you should make enemies," Robin added. Allan started to lift the wine to his lips, but Robin grabbed it from his hands. He ignored Allan's frown. "If they drag you off and hang you from a tree because you treat them like scum—something Count John would do—you won't do the poor any good."

Allan heaved a heavy sigh. "There's little more I can do here in the castle. Goods move from the undercroft one time a month now." He rubbed his neck, his gaze jumping from one stack of crates to another. "Supplies are limited, the harvest poor. Even the cooks complain they hardly have enough grain to keep the guards fed."

"Do you still work with Much Miller?" Robin asked. The miller's son had been Robin's way into the castle when it was held by the king's enemies.

"Aye, he diverts sacks directly to Tuck before his deliveries are made to the castle."

A curl tickled Robin's lip. "I wonder how he gets that round his da'." Elias Miller nearly caught him and Much in a compromising situation—a meeting in a candlelit storeroom that began this little operation. "I miss that man. Wish I'd seen him at The Trip. Does he still lose at the dice games?"

"Leena won't let him play," Allan said.

Robin slapped his thigh. "Did he marry that girl, the one from the kitchens? Good for him. You tell Tuck to tell him that."

"Next time Tuck comes to listen to my sins I'll do that." Allan noticed the confusion on Henry's face. "He's not a priest. We just talk."

Robin held up the flask. "He says you need to put the wine away. I tend to agree with him."

Before Allan protested Henry chimed in. "Too much and you risk slipping information to enemies."

"I know when to stop."

"When you get one of us killed?" Robin muttered.

Allan gave him an angry look. "God in heaven, no. No! I swear."

Henry clamped Allan's arm. "Good. Do not forget that. Now, let's to the greenwood. We talk to Will tonight."

They trod through the tunnel single file. It angled downhill, and side passages cut away at sharp angles with nothing to mark which path would lead them out. A man could get lost here, so Henry was glad to have Allan as a guide. He wondered if Robin remembered the way from his days as the king's spy.

Ahead, Allan slowed. The golden glow of his torch faintly lit the cave entrance. He whispered a warning and extinguished the light. Plunged into darkness, Henry felt along the wall, his hand sliding over the uneven pockmarked sandstone. He heard Robin's boots scuff the ground behind him.

Allan stopped, peering outside where the bright moon illuminated the wood on the opposite bank of the Leen. It wouldn't be easy to explain their business here this time of night if anyone spotted them, but a pristine blanket of snow covered the ground, a good sign no one lurked near the caves.

The air was crisp and boisterous voices hung on the night from The Trip and Brewhouse yard just round the bend. Allan crossed the short distance from the cave to riverside like a stealthy wolf. Robin and Henry followed him on to the rope-pulled ferry. Allan untied the tether and pushed off the river bottom with a long oak pole. "Give me a hand here," he said.

Standing behind Allan, Robin and Henry hauled on the rope to drag the flat boat across the narrow stretch of water. The craft creaked in the shimmering moonlight, but the river was calm and there was little drag so the crossing wouldn't take long.

Allan studied the battlements of the castle far above them on the cliffside. The stone curtain was dark and gray against the sky. He glanced towards the Brewhouse yard, and seeing no one in sight looked over his shoulder at Robin. "Will you return to Greyton to be with Marian?"

When Robin told him the plan to place his family at Castle l'Aigle, of baby Elizabeth, and getting Marian there as a maid to Elle, Allan nodded sullenly. "Little John and Elle will be there?" There was hurt in his voice. "I suppose Sir Stephan will arrive from Normandy too. A great Christmastide celebration with your families."

"I don't know when I'll see Stephan," Henry said, "but Little John does have business of Cartholme for Bea." He felt sorry for his young friend. Allan had no one to love. No one to go back to. Henry only wanted Christmas done with so he could return to Normandy to be with Stephan.

Robin hissed beneath his breath. "Bea is your sister, so spending Christmas there is reasonable. But me?" He sounded more agitated than apprehensive.

For the first time all evening Allan's spirits rose. "You could stay in Nottingham, help distribute goods to the poor," he suggested.

It wasn't a bad idea Henry thought, though Edric and his spies might wonder why the knight would stay in Nottingham. "That might draw more attention to this operation. Edric already keeps a close eye on you. The king only ordered you to check Allan's work, which is done. Nothing more. So it is set," Henry said. "You accompany me."

"Will Edric wonder why Marian doesn't return with Elle and Little John?" Allan asked. "Marian is part of Greyton's household after all."

"I've no need for a maid at Greyton, and Marian used to be Bea's maid. Why wouldn't she stay? Besides, Edric won't think twice of Marian. And if he does, he might learn her son is there, even more reason Bea and I came to this agreement. There is still no tie to Robin, or any reason for her to be hiding."

"Edric could put the pieces together," Robin said.

"You worry too much, Robin. I do not think he will. After Christmas, we return to Greyton. I will visit my betrothed at Lincoln. You will talk your father into leaving for York in the spring. Then you and I sail back to Normandy."

"With Edric right behind," Robin said.

Henry groaned. "Mayhap Allan could lock him in the dungeon for a while." He stopped in his tracks. His gaze drifted back across the river where shadows hid the entrance to the tunnels.

"Who needs the dungeon?" Allan chuckled, following Henry's gaze. "A man could get lost in the caves."

Robin clapped a hand on Allan's shoulder. "That would be too good for him."

Was it? Henry laughed uneasily. After everything Edric Weston had done to him, his family, to Robin—the threats, the treason—was any end too good for him?

thirty-four

DECEMBER 1196
Nottinghamshire

They secured the boat and Allan led the way into
Sherwood, turning on to paths Henry wouldn't have seen
even in daylight. In the dark he could barely see Allan
three paces ahead. Deep shadows from the canopy of
evergreens enveloped them. Their fragrant smell caressed
the winter air. Snow crunched beneath their boots. That,
and the rustle of tree branches, the only sounds.

They had walked near a mile when Allan parted a thick
stand of bushes revealing a cave. A torch flickered just
inside the entrance, shedding enough light to reveal
footprints in the snow.

"Tuck," Allan said, and gestured towards a second set
of prints half-covered by drifting snow. Will Scaflock was
supposed to be meeting them.

Henry scanned the wood. "I'd forgotten how far this
is from the river." He shifted uncomfortably,
remembering his participation in nightly raids to procure

food and coin from the castle stores. *Rob from the rich, give to the poor.* Treason. He rubbed his neck.

"Still using the miller's wagons?" Robin asked.

"Wagon," Allan corrected. "We bought one of our own, and Much provided a draught horse until last year when Will got us an old mule."

"My friends," Tuck called as he stepped from the cave. "We have a new accomplice."

"Tuck," Robin greeted him.

Henry was struck by the dark tone in Tuck's voice. His gut wrenched. A shadowy figure came up behind their stocky accomplice. Henry's jaw dropped and his hand went to his sword. *Edric Weston.*

"Why did you bring him here?" Henry asked.

"Two of our men stopped him on the North Road," Tuck said, "He told them he had a message for our leader from the king."

"God's blood," Robin muttered.

"Fools," Henry said. Now the bastard knew all of them but Much and Will, and knew where the stores were kept.

"I've had a chat with them. It will not happen again." Tuck held up a black hood. "At least they covered his eyes."

Edric lifted his arms, his wrists pressed together. "And tied my hands." He gestured, hoping someone would remove the rope, and gave them a lopsided smile. "You can trust me. I want in on this."

Robin scowled, his eyes guarded. "In? Do you think we keep this for ourselves?"

"Well, there's always a first time."

"How much do you want for your silence, Weston?" Henry asked.

"If only I had waited another day I could have

included this incredible operation of yours in my message to Count John. Robbing the rich—"

"To help the poor and suffering," Tuck added.

Edric ignored him. "Robbing the rich who pay the king's taxes to support the war against the French. And what good fortune that FitzHenry, er Allan whoever-you-are, is the castellan's clerk. Does he let you know when important guests will be at the castle? The king has seen the reports of the victims of your road robberies, as has his brother." Edric shook his head, eyes narrowed and focused on Allan. "How did you ever convince King Richard that this man is his nephew?"

Robin stood stiff-backed, hand poised on the hilt of his sword, his stare glacial. *We are done for,* Henry thought. Bile rose in his throat.

No one spoke and Edric realized he would get no information from the knights.

"Keep that to yourself then," Edric said, "but do not think you are so easily rid of me. The note I sent to Prince John indicates that should he not hear from me, he should assume the worst and have FitzHenry arrested." Edric sneered at Allan. "Shall we see how quickly you break on the rack? Or perhaps we arrest Robin's father, or Henry—what about your lover? You would speak before seeing either of them harmed, wouldn't you?"

Henry felt the veins in his neck pulse. How could they have underestimated the bastard? Henry's anger was tinged with regret. *Stephan, have I let you down?*

"Speaking of your dear Sir Stephan—Prince John will be sure to send him news that you are still betrothed to the de Camville girl. That letter you wrote telling Stephan your little plan with Nichola de la Haye? The poor messenger was thrown from his horse just south of Grantham. Broke the man's neck."

"Bastard!" Henry lunged at Edric and grabbed him by the throat.

Robin signaled Tuck to leave them alone until Edric fell to his knees, his face turning blue. "Henry—enough!" Robin grasped Henry, separating him from Edric. "You heard what he said. You cannot kill him."

Henry drew his sword and made to lunge again. Robin blocked the blade. "Think, my friend. Write another letter to Stephan."

Seething, Henry stepped back. "How can we trust him? He threatens Allan, your family, and mine. He is no man of honor."

Robin looked icily at Edric. "A shilling for every one hundred we take."

"One?" Edric laughed.

Robin laid his arms across his chest. "That is what Brother Tuck gets and he is in harm's way."

"And the rest of you?"

"I take nothing," Henry said.

"Who else is involved?" Edric asked. "Do not tell me it is only those two buffoons who tried to rob me, Tuck here, and FitzHenry alone."

"That is not for you to know, Weston," Robin said. "Trust, my friends."

How could they do this, Henry thought.

Robin turned to Tuck. "Get the rope."

Edric started to back away, but Robin caught hold of him and nearly dragged him to the ground. "You cannot hang me." He whimpered. "The prince will—"

"Quiet! I've no plan to let you dangle." Robin regarded Edric as if questioning his decision, but then said, "You want us to trust you? You'll have to show us that we can."

Robin strode back towards the river. Henry stood with

his mouth open. What was Robin thinking? Showing Weston the tunnel, the supplies they pilfered from the undercroft? Even Allan and Tuck looked agape.

"We've work to do," Robin said, waving them to follow. "Do you think we just came here to visit?"

Allan stared after him. "The wagon is—"

"I know it will be here soon as we have wasted time talking and not working." For a moment Robin's eyes bored into Henry and their friends. There was no scheduled pick-up tonight and they all knew it. He rubbed his hands together and met Edric's scrutiny with one brow raised. "Ready for a climb?"

Tuck untied Edric. He hurried after Robin with Henry and Allan bringing up the rear and remained suspicious and guarded on the river crossing. Robin jumped off the boat when they docked and disappeared into the tunnel while Allan secured it.

Henry hurried after Robin. "Weston only knew of the highwaymen. He had no clue that we were stealing from the undercroft. Why are you doing this?"

Robin moved steadily up the path despite the utter darkness. The others' footfalls indicated they weren't far behind. "I only said we would not hang him."

Allan's torch threw ragged shadows on the walls and illuminated Edric's face. He already appeared to be breathless.

"Surely he cannot be so stupid?" Henry whispered, imagining the dozens of little-used tunnels carved into the sandstone and a number of ways that rope might come in handy. "We outnumber him."

"He is confident. Believes his threats of turning over our families to Count John will keep him safe. But he is such a greedy bastard. So we show him around." Robin's voice lacked all emotion. "Then we kill him."

The tunnels were eerily quiet except for their footsteps and the sounds of small creatures that inhabited the caves.

"Could you slow down," Edric called from the back of the line, his voice spilling from the darkness. "I cannot see my feet."

"Watch out for the rats," Allan said, sidestepping as one skittered across his path.

"Give him the torch," Henry said. "The path is uneven, and I for one don't want to carry Weston if his foot catches in a hole."

"Or slips in the pigeon shite," Allan added, turning to hand the rush light to Edric.

"Is that what smells like an overripe privy?" Edric slowed and groaned, lowering the flame to inspect the sandstone.

"I thought that was you, Weston," Robin said and increased his pace uphill.

Allan gave a low throaty laugh and the others joined in, even Edric. The noise disturbed the nesting birds and there was a telling flutter of wings and fitful squawks. Hundreds, maybe a thousand birds roosted in the caves. A moment later Edric's boot struck a slippery spot. Stumbling, he cursed and landed on his arse, the torch sailing from his hands. It struck Allan, sending sparks down the back of his cloak.

"God's nails!" Allan smacked the cloak with his palm and chucked it over his head, dislodging dirt and stone from the cave ceiling.

Henry brushed himself off and retrieved the flickering torch. "Little good this did you." He didn't bother to extend a hand to help Edric back to his feet.

Still swearing, his face twisted in disgust, Edric wiped his hands on his cloak. Henry covered his nose and handed the torch back.

Allan took the lead, he and Robin just silhouettes on the wall. Allan could maneuver through the passages with a blindfold. Edric's torch illuminated dozens of recesses in the sandstone walls, but the light didn't extend deep enough to show whether they marked paths or small alcoves.

"You with us?" Allan had stopped where the passage forked.

"Is it much farther?" Edric paused to catch his breath and wiped the sweat beaded on his brow.

"Pigeons only roost to the halfway point," Allan said.

"What welcome news," Edric growled sarcastically. The others were moving again and he sucked in a deep breath and strode after them.

It had been more than two years since Henry had climbed from the riverside to the castle undercroft. When Allan took the left fork, Henry followed as blindly as Edric. The path opened into a huge cavern with ceilings so high they were lost in the blackness. But Allan didn't stop, only led them through more twists and turns. The path rose at a less steep angle for a short time, and then leveled out. Henry thought they must be nearing the gate, but this part of the tunnel was significantly narrower and not as tall as he remembered.

No mules had been this way. And perhaps few men but for Allan.

"Watch your head," Allan called.

Henry had to duck. They were definitely not headed to the undercroft.

thirty-five

Allan's torch lit the room from one end to the other illuminating barrels of wine and crates stacked along one wall. If they contained dried meat, a man could live here for months. Henry rested his hand atop one—it shifted. Empty. His eyes flicked from Allan to Edric. Weston hadn't heard it. A man could die here in a matter of days...

"Is this it?" Edric asked.

"Our monthly take," Allan said.

Henry wondered if Allan had realized early on he might need a place like this. Off the usual path, squirreled away in a remote section of the extensive tunnel system.

"It's a very precise operation, Weston." Robin rested the rope on a wine barrel. "Our men cannot simply empty the castellan's undercroft. That would end our work for good."

Edric snorted. "I suppose so." He looked back

towards the way they'd come. "Where is the entry into the castle?"

"Robin, no," Henry started.

"If I'm to be part of this I want to see it all."

"I'm sure you do," Henry snapped.

"Trust, Henry," Edric taunted. His steady gaze turned on Robin.

Robin shrugged indifference. "What could it hurt? We can't take too much time. Tuck might worry."

Robin wasn't asking for opinions. Edric would never be able to find his way on his own. An escape route would serve little purpose when he realized Henry and his friends had no intention of letting him leave this place alive.

"Allan, lead the way," Robin said. "Henry, you could start down with a load."

Robin tossed him the rope, offering him a chance to not be a witness to whatever he had planned. Would it be a slow death, leaving Weston tied up, alone, letting him starve? Henry had seen too many men die and those memories haunted him. This one might too, but Weston had hurt him, his family, his friends. And he would do so until he took his last breath.

"No, let's to the undercroft," Henry said, slinging the rope over his shoulder. "You might need an extra hand to keep Weston from being a greedy bastard."

Edric rolled his dark eyes, but he followed Allan back into the tunnel. After a series of twists and turns and double backs, Allan signaled the men to wait. He padded ahead, careful to place each foot without making a sound. He was back moments later and led them into a large cavernous area. Edric prowled around the towers of supplies, touching one crate after another like a ravenous wolf.

The center of the cavern stood empty. "This whole place spilled over with goods two years past," Allan said. "We could hardly make our way through." He opened a chest and held the torch close. Edric's eyes glinted from the reflection of light striking golden plates and goblets, coins and jewels. He nabbed a ruby necklace and held it to the light.

"Your future wife might appreciate a gift like this, Henry," he said and then gasped.

Robin held his sword at Edric's throat. Henry unsheathed his own.

Edric swallowed hard, dropped the necklace, and twisted round. "So this is trust."

"You are a man with nothing but evil and greed in your heart," Robin said.

"He does not have a heart," Henry added.

Robin dug the tip of his blade into Edric's neck. Edric used his forearm to shove the sword away and cursed them loudly. He swiped at the blood trickling down his neck.

"No one will hear you," Allan said.

Stepping back, Robin said, "No heart, but he does bleed." His sword remained leveled at Edric's head.

"You cowards," Edric spat.

"Fool," Allan shot back. "Any one of us could take you down."

Edric and Allan drew their swords at the same time. Edric thrust at him, but Allan brushed his blade away. Edric lunged and Allan stepped aside letting Robin tease the bastard into the open space.

Henry swallowed hard, shuddering at the clank of steel on steel. But his anger grew, hatred simmering like a cauldron on a flame. *God forgive us.* Luring a man to his death, but giving him a chance to die like a man rather than the coward he was—it wasn't something Edric would do for any of them. Still, a mortal sin. Murder. No matter the bastard was the Devil. *God forgive us.*

Edric bolted straight for Henry, blade arced over his head. An eerie quiet gripped the night, broken only by Edric's harsh breaths and the pounding of Henry's heart. This was little different from fighting a horde of Saracens or French enemies. After the initial strike it became personal—one man against one man. Focused. Eyes and ears tuned to nothing but the immediate threat and little awareness of anything else.

Henry ripped the air with his sword, starting low, cutting up as Edric's came down. Edric had a powerful swing and a tremor slid from Henry's hand to his shoulder. He was ready when Edric swung again. Edric roared, their blades tangled. Henry grasped Edric's wrist, pressing him backwards, every muscle in his arms burning. They turned in a mad dance, Robin side-stepping out of their way.

"Bastard," Edric cursed again, driving Henry's blade towards the ground. Breaking Henry's grip, Edric swiped his arm, pulled back to thrust again.

Robin shouted, catching Edric's sword and blocking the blow aimed at Henry's throat. He locked blades with Edric, holding fast. Henry cradled his arm, that sickly smell of copper striking his nose. Anger tempered his pain. He'd had much worse.

"Your turn?" Edric snarled at Robin.

Twisting, Robin threw Edric off-balance. "With pleasure." Robin growled, but he backed away, giving Edric time to recover.

Edric charged, and every parry, every thrust, and their harsh grunts echoed in the room. Lunging, Robin pressed Edric back, one step, then another. Edric breathed hard and then suddenly, his eyes widened. He whimpered, glanced down at the sword thrust through his chest from behind. Henry dug the blade into him up to the hilt. Blood spilled from Edric's mouth. He collapsed face first into the dirt and the sword slid from his body.

Henry held the blade so tightly his hands ached. He stared at the ground mushrooming deep red around Edric. His arms shook violently, his stomach roiled. He blinked sweat from his eyes, found his breath, and felt relief flood through him.

Within moments Allan retrieved blankets to wrap the body. He stayed behind to erase evidence of Edric's demise. Henry and Robin lugged the body down the tunnel without a word between them, but Henry's mind whirled. Voices in his head cried out. Had Edric been lying about the letter to Count John, the intercepted messenger? Travel across the Narrow Sea was always uncertain. He prayed he could get word to Stephan before John passed on only half-truths.

Robin slowed and they shifted grips on their bundled burden, which seemed to get heavier the further they trudged. Both men were grunting and Henry's arms felt like fire by the time they emerged from the cave. Tuck had not been idle. A wagon sat nestled amongst the trees on the far bank. The forester Will Scaflock walked into the clearing, their signal to ferry their load.

"Sorry we had to bother you at this hour, my friend," Robin said when he stepped off the boat. He and Will shook hands.

"It is good to see you again." Bowing to Henry, he said, "Lord de Grey. I didn't realize we'd have cargo tonight."

Henry acknowledged him and they quickly placed Edric's corpse in the hollowed out compartment of the wagon beneath sweet smelling hay.

"Our good work will be for naught if we are labeled as murderers, Will," Robin said. "It's best Weston and his horse just disappear."

"Sherwood is a big place," Will said. "There are places so remote that chances are by the time he is discovered there will be little left of him but dirt and dust."

"Tuck says there's no worry the men will reveal they've seen Weston, but the Sheriff will eventually be asking questions. A reward may be tempting, so you two must be even more cautious than usual." Robin scratched his beard. "And the stores—we'll need to find another place in Sherwood."

Will nodded. "I know just the one. Meet me at the caves tomorrow night."

Henry didn't hear Robin's response. His hand slid to the pouch dangling from his sword belt. He fingered two rings pulled from the body. He should give them to Edric's sister. God...dear Elle. Should he tell her the truth? He clenched his fist to stop trembling. Why did this make him ill?

He startled when Robin placed a hand on his arm. "Shall we go?" Robin asked.

Will had slapped the reins and the wagon lurched away deep into Sherwood's shadows.

"He needs no help?" Henry asked, head tipped towards Will.

"Best no one know where he buries the body," Tuck said. "I offered to go with him, but he claims he can manage on his own." He studied Henry. "And you, my lord? Can I help you?"

"You don't do confessions," Henry said.

Tuck shook his head. "Sorry, but I can pray for you."

"I'll have Allan send a contribution to St. Mary's for

our penance," Robin said and cocked his head back to the boat. "Let's be off."

The night sky brimmed with stars. Henry stared at the distant points of light, asked God's forgiveness for his sins. He knew ten *Pater Nosters*, even a hundred, might never be enough when his soul lay tarnished by the hatred in his heart. He had murdered Edric Weston and could not bring himself to regret it.

thirty-six

DECEMBER 1196
Barfleur, Normandy

A raging downpour could do little to make Stephan more miserable. His hair was plastered to his cheeks and hung limp to his shoulders, his clothes soaked to the skin. He could hardly see with cold rain stinging his face, but his horse cantered on to the quay without hesitation. The docks were deserted, boats buffeted in the water like toys. He knew galleys wouldn't depart in these rough seas, but logic wouldn't stop him from trying to find passage. He had to get to Henry.

Edric Weston's letter lay crumbled in his saddle bag. Surely it was false. Henry—still betrothed? He promised he would see the contract ended. *Why, Henry, why?*

The wind howled and masts swayed against the dark skies. One boat dipped savagely. Stephan knew that one—the *Goldfinch*. Albin Boneil's.

Stephan swiped the rain from his eyes and headed into town. He left his horse at the livery and sloshed through the muddied street to the nearest tavern. Ale would warm his body and numb his mind. He wouldn't have to think about that letter for a short while.

The plan might have worked if Albin Boneil hadn't been there.

"God, man, sit here by the fire and warm yourself."

"Ale," Stephan mumbled.

Boneil gestured to the gap-toothed serving girl to bring food and drink.

"What are you doing here?" Boneil asked.

"I have lost him," Stephan said quietly.

"Who?"

"Henry. I must go talk some sense into him." Stephan told Boneil of Henry's betrothal and Edric's letter, of Henry and marriage and sin.

"It's odd how some men's minds work. One of my acquaintances confessed to the priest and was told to fast for two years. So he fasts, but we meet every time I'm in Portsmouth." Boneil shook his head. "If Henry must marry, will seeing him do any good?"

"You must take me to England," Stephan insisted.

"You won't change his mind."

"You must—"

"I will. In three days time, if the weather clears."

"I cannot wait that long."

"I doubt you'll find a boat leaving before then. Drink a bit and eat. We'll warm you up, put you to bed. Get a good sleep. You'll see things differently on the morrow and put this behind you."

Not true, Stephan thought. He raked his hands through his hair, stared at the cracks in the grain of the trestle. Before he loved Henry he didn't think twice about the men he bedded, who bedded him. They met, they fucked, they left. They would drink together, fight side-by-side. He might think of their tumble. Might even have another round or two to bury the day's woes. But Henry...

Stephan thumbed the ring Henry had given him. "I have been on the road two days and doubt sleep will keep my mind—my heart, my soul—from thinking of him."

He remembered Henry's stubborn righteousness, his naivety. That gentle smile and the love in his eyes. Every breath. The way his skin heated when they touched. The taste of him. The way he shivered. That voice, low, urgent, when he repeated his name.

"Why in God's name did you let yourself fall in love?" Boneil's tone wasn't harsh, but the concept of men in love was too foreign to his thinking, as it was to most people. Stephan swore he saw pity in the man's eyes.

"I've been with many a man I would not mind swiving time and again," Boneil said. "But love? You should have known this would never end well."

Stephan smacked the mug off the table. Heads turned when it shattered against the wall, but Stephan's snarl sent everyone back to their own business.

Boneil laid a hand across his shoulder. Stephan didn't want a lecture and started to rise.

"Forgive me," Boneil said. "I shouldn't be so unkind." He handed Stephan his own ale and urged him to stay.

Stephan drank it down, refilled the cup. "Six, almost seven years. From the first day we met I wanted him, loved him. And when he finally admitted he felt the same way..." He lowered his head, hiding his eyes with his hands. "We survived his father's wrath. His sister came to understand. My brother..."

Boneil said nothing, just watched him as he mindlessly began picking at the salted fish on the trencher and then guzzled more ale. Perhaps he was trying to understand.

The fish settled heavy in Stephan's stomach. Though the ale warmed his insides, he was exhausted and his wet clothes chilled his skin. "I must get a bed for tonight," he said and got to his feet.

Boneil laid a finger on his hand. "I've a room here."

The gentle touch combined with the low voice crashed Stephan's senses like two swords tangling. He stared at Boneil's hand until he removed it. He should say no, but with the storm he would be hard-pressed to find a room. Meeting Boneil's eyes, he inhaled the scent of ale and sweat and the sea. He nodded, and then trudged after him up the creaking wooden stairs.

Lightning flashed through gaps in the window shutters as Stephan closed the world behind them. He leaned on the door and watched Boneil strip to his braies despite the chill in the Spartan room. The sea captain was well-built, but not broad of shoulder like the soldiers Stephan knew. *Like Henry.*

Stephan swallowed hard. He looked at the rope bed. One bed. Men slept together all the time, even men who had never met.

I cannot be here. He turned round to open the door.

Boneil was behind him in two long strides. "Where are you going?" he asked, leaning into the door so Stephan couldn't get out.

"Let me go."

"You are wet and exhausted. You are upset, angry with Edric Weston. Mayhap with Henry."

"You don't know that." A sob caught in Stephan's throat. Sweat beaded on his forehead. Hadn't he rid himself of the anger and hurt? Weston's letter had stirred them. *Christ, Henry, I am not angry, I am not—*

"I can hear it in your voice." Boneil leaned closer, his breath hot on Stephan's neck. "Henry is going to marry that woman."

Stephan stroked the ring Henry had given him. "She is just a child!"

"Who will be of marriageable age in a few short years." Boneil slid his arms around Stephan and just held him, resting his chin on Stephan's shoulder. "If not her, there will be another."

Stephan shoved Boneil back roughly. Punching the door he exhaled, then turned and charged. Lightning flashed revealing surprise on Boneil's face. He brought his hands up to defend himself. Stephan slapped them away and pressed Boneil against the wall. Boneil grabbed his head and brought their mouths together. Teeth and tongues clashed, rough and hard.

Outside, thunder reverberated across the water.

Boneil pulled Stephan's tunic over his head and tossed it on the floor. He maneuvered so Stephan suddenly felt his own back against the wall and Boneil's hands on his buttocks. He pressed his groin to Stephan's and even through their clothes Stephan could feel his erection. Fire snaked from his groin, his heart pounding as another crash of thunder sounded. Boneil kissed him, thrust against him, and before he could think, the captain was on his knees tugging Stephan's hose down, hands sliding into his braies. Stephan moaned as Boneil's warm fist wrapped around his cock. He felt his braies slip from his hips and Boneil took him.

Stephan couldn't breathe. He kept his eyes pinched shut. He didn't want to see Boneil, could only think of Henry. His knees grew weak and he gripped Boneil's shoulders. "Henry!" he cried out.

Boneil pulled away, but didn't stop exploring Stephan's body with kisses and bites. "I will be Henry," he said softly, their hard cocks sliding against each other.

Stephan groaned and twisted Boneil around. He did not make love to the captain. The sex was angry, hard, and lustful. Boneil's voice was gravelly, begging for more, harder. When Stephan climaxed, he felt nothing but contempt for himself.

What have I done?

His heart was still thundering when Boneil dragged him to the bed and took him. It didn't take long for him to spill his seed, and Stephan was left numb and sore. Trapped on the straw-filled mattress beneath Boneil's dead weight, a sour taste filled his mouth. He struggled and finally shoved Boneil off his back. Sitting on the edge of the bed he cleaned himself with the captain's tunic.

Boneil glanced up at him when he stood. "What are you doing?"

Stephan didn't answer, tormented by guilt. Had there been one word of truth in Weston's message? Henry would explain. He would...

Rain and wind beat relentlessly against the window. Stephen dressed, wishing the lightning and thunder drowned out his thoughts. He found his cloak and headed out the door. Boneil called after him, but Stephan prayed he wouldn't follow.

Outside, he threw his damp cloak over his head and ran towards the stables. His horse nudged him playfully as he changed into dry clothing. He wrapped himself in a smelly horse blanket and curled up in an empty stall to bed down for the night. Guilt and regrets hammered his brain until a crowing rooster roused him from a fitful sleep. The cock crowed again, and he realized the storm had passed.

"I will not let you go, Henry," he said.

Gathering his belongings and his horse, he hurried towards the quay. One of those boats would slip its ties this morn, and he would be headed to England. To Henry.

Stephan tried to remember the last time he prayed. A time or two he had asked God to keep Henry safe, but those weren't really prayers. He prayed when he was twelve before his mother died. God hadn't listened to him. Then he discovered his appetite for men and the priests said that was a mortal sin. He hadn't seen it that way, and refused to ask forgiveness. He faced death on the field of battle, heard the men around him call upon the Good Lord.

"Save us, O Lord." The prayerful man beside him retched into a chamber pot.

The boat pitched and rolled in the swells and the others in the dark cabin cried out and pleaded with God.

Stephan's stomach roiled, his guts churning like the wild sea. Waves crashed over the gunwale. A crewman was swept overboard and others held tight to ropes, tried to right themselves as the boat plunged again. "Watch over us, Lord. Forgive us," someone shouted.

"The rocks!"

"Too close!"

We are going to die…

NO! Not this way, not now!

His stomach heaved, and he realized that the storm made no difference. He was sick at heart, his mind filled with the thoughts that the last person who held him was Boneil. Not his love, his Henry.

A tearing, crashing noise tore out above the thunder. The boat smashed against the rocky shore, shuddering as it splintered. Water inundated the deck. Timbers were stripped away like blades of grain beneath a scythe. Screams rippled through the air.

Henry, my heart will always belong to you. Stephan's eyes blurred whether from the rain and seawater or tears.

The sea seized him. There was nothing he could do. The ship broke up around him and the last thing he saw was a huge blackish-gray boulder as the waves tossed him like a twig.

thirty-seven

JANUARY 1197
Yorkshire

Blustery January winds stung Henry's face, but he welcomed them. He had escaped the mass of people in the hall. The gossip, raucous voices, the clink of cups, and boots—even the crackle of the fire had grated. His sister Bea braved the weather and stood beside him atop the keep of Castle l'Aigle. The l'Aigle blue and white standards whipped in the gale.

"My maids and ladies tell me you come here often," Bea said.

"Spying on me?"

Bea smiled. "Who wouldn't be watching a handsome young baron?" She glanced from Henry to the village outside the castle walls, and off to the distant horizon. "It's a peaceful place, especially like this, at night with the moon and a thousand stars." She hadn't expected a response. "You are leaving."

Henry's mind was far away. "I have heard nothing

from Stephan." Within a day of his arrival in Yorkshire, he'd told Bea of his betrothal and how just speaking of it or of Stephan was too hard to bear. Bea had been mindful of his feelings and Stephan's name only came up when they'd spoken of the campaigns in Normandy.

Bea pulled her cloak tighter to ward off the cold and nestled herself against his shoulder. Though she was three years younger they had always been close. She knew his impatience was not with her. "A message will surely greet you at Greyton when you return," she said. "But why must you go back to Normandy? You've been at the king's side longer than every baron I know. Pay his knight's fee. Stay in England and tell Stephan to join you at Greyton."

"It is not so simple as that." Henry scrubbed a hand across his eyes. "Stephan living in my home would raise many a brow. I don't have a mesnie of knights like your husband."

"Let him have a cottage at Greyton."

"Lady de Camville has agreed to let my betrothal to Adela stand, but she would know that was just for show. And gossip would flow like a river through the shire."

"Stephan could offer his sword to the castellan in Lincoln. That would keep him close by."

"If I live at Greyton, I will be obligated to attend my betrothed in Lincoln with some frequency. Stephan doesn't want to hear about her, see her, or see us together."

Bea's face clouded with disbelief. "Henry, you say this betrothal means nothing to you or the de Camville's. There will be no wedding. Get on with your life."

Trees swayed in the distance and smoke curled into the sky from cottages and shops in the village. It was time to go. He had stayed longer in Yorkshire than he'd intended. Little John and Elle had departed a few days after Christmas. *Their* messages had arrived. Of course, Stephan's would have had to come across the Narrow Sea in winter.

Bea distracted him with questions about Richard's Castle Gaillard. Every aspect of the building project fascinated her—from the baileys, the keep, to the king's ambitious plans to have the fortress completed within two years.

The sounds of swordplay drifted from the bailey far below them. A crowd paraded from the hall, setting torches alight to enjoy a contest. Bea watched with bright eyes. Henry was surprised she didn't suggest they join the practice, but turned the conversation back to Stephan.

"Would he join Gil's mesnie?"

Three years past Stephan would have laughed at the idea, but he and Gil had not been on good terms then. Now?

"He could live here and you would visit often to see me." Bea added, "To be with him."

That was not the life Henry wanted. Two hard days ride from the man he wanted to spend every waking moment with? He shook his head. Serving together in the king's mesnie in Normandy was best, even if it meant facing war for days on end until King Philip was finally defeated.

Bea's voice brought him back. "I only wish you did not have to leave. I miss the days when we raced along the road."

"You frightened Maman with your wild ways." Henry finally found something to smile about. "Sword play, loosing arrows."

"And I beat you at the tiltyard!" She laughed lightly.

"Does Gil know your plans for your children yet?"

Bea poked him in the side. Her cheeks were rosy, whether from the brisk air or her latest pregnancy. On the Epiphany, he had learned he would be an uncle again. Bea slid her arm through Henry's and he felt her shiver. He was about to suggest they get themselves to the hall when she pointed to Robin and Robert loosing arrows in another corner of the yard.

Marian was watching her husband and son across the brightly lit snow-covered sward. Henry remembered Robert's skill with the horses when he had worked in the stables at Greyton. Now fifteen, the boy—the young man—stood head-to-head with Robin. His shoulders had broadened, his muscles no where near Robin's yet, but daily training with sword and in the tiltyard would endow him soon enough. Archery contests had become a ritual between the two, begun right before Christmas. Robert quickly proved he had his father's gift with bow.

"I have never seen Marian so happy," Bea said.

"And Robin." Henry rubbed Bea's arm for warmth and smiled down at his friends. "Marian is with child."

"She told me." Bea beamed. "What wonderful news."

He felt Bea shiver again and guided her down the stairs. Surrounded by his family and friends Henry never felt more alone. Bea and her children cheered him, but made him realize how much he longed to be with Stephan. Cradling baby Reynaud by the blazing hearth was a comfort. His nephew David was near five years old, an inquisitive child with Bea's dark hair and cornflower blue eyes. Gil l'Aigle doted on his wife and their children and had made David his own. Henry was happy for Bea. For Robin and Marian.

"I will settle my business at Greyton and plan to be on a boat bound for Barfleur by the end of February."

"Winter seas..." She shook her head.

"It cannot be any worse than November." He settled her near the hearth and retrieved two goblets with wine from the coffer.

"I hope you plan to let Robin stay here," she said when he sat.

"It is his decision," Henry said, suddenly distracted when Robin's laughter drifted from the doorway. The knight swept into the hall with one arm hooked across his son's shoulders, and the other wrapped at Marian's waist. "If he even suggests returning to Normandy before this child is delivered, I will tie him down."

Bea grinned. "I will help you."

thirty-eight

JANUARY 1197
St Malo, Brittany

Stephan turned his head and wanted to scream. Pain shot through his body. His throat was dry, his mouth gummy, and no words escaped. His head felt like it had been split with a broadsword, or that a smith's hammer struck one nail after another into it. He groaned, remembered being thrown onto the rocks. Then...nothing.

Stephan jerked awake. *Where am I?*

"Do you understand me?" The man at his bedside spoke in Latin. He was average height, wore a black robe, and had a tonsured head. A Benedictine. "Do you remember what happened?"

"A storm. The boat smashed into rocks."

The monk watched him, his look encouraging. "You speak Latin. Good. I am Brother Martis. What is your name?"

"Stephan l'Aigle," he said. "How long...?"

"Five days."

Over the next two weeks Stephan remembered pieces of conversation. Brother Martis told him how scavengers had come upon the wreckage of the boat and found him unconscious. The crew, other passengers—no one else had been found. "Our flock has heard us preach of being kind to those in need. You were fortunate they chose to carry you here to the abbey," Martis had said. His face twisted in a cynical frown. "Or mayhap they were hopeful our Heavenly Father would forgive them for taking the barrels of grain and goods washed up on the shore if they helped the one survivor."

Each night Stephan dreamed of the storm, the boat lashed by rain, his body tossed on the rocks. He also remembered Boneil. The crash of his body into Boneil. Being sheathed by Boneil. The smell of his sweat and the sex.

Stephan tossed violently in bed. *Why did I let that happen? God, Henry, I am sorry.* He woke in a sweat, struggling to breathe.

"Another bad dream?" Martis stood at the door. "Good morrow, Stephan."

Stephan flinched from the strong smell of the poultice wrapped round his head. He tried to sit up and cried out, his shoulder stiff, his arm splinted.

"Rest, my son. Your body is battered, your arm broken. Healing takes time." Martis' voice was kind, but he spoke in a slow chant-like rhythm. "Brother Elyas will be round shortly to bring you broth. Mayhap you're stronger now. We shall get you on your feet."

Candlelight flickered against the bare stone walls of the room. A bed, a stool, and coffer took up the small space. Martis saw Stephan's eyes catch on his ragged tunic and hose, which hung from a peg near the door. "I fear they left you with little," he said.

Boots, cloak, sword. All gone. What had Robin said? Take from the rich, give to the poor. Stephan thought of his friends, but mostly Henry. He started to smile, his hand snaking beneath the woolen blanket for the comfort of the ring Henry had given him.

No! My ring—gone! His eyes grew glassy.

"Do not weep, Stephan. We come into this world with nothing and will leave with nothing."

The last thing Stephan wanted was a homily on the Faith, which had served him little in his years on this earth. He clenched his jaw, swallowed back the hurt of losing the precious gift from Henry.

"I must get word to King Richard," he told Martis.

The monk nodded. "My brothers wondered where you had sailed from. I suppose that answers our question and leads to more." He rubbed his jaw. "We are not a wealthy order."

"I have nothing to give you now, but the king will be glad to pay your messenger on my behalf." Stephan could hear the wind rattling the oil cloth on the small window and distant voices sounded from the corridor.

"How much will the king pay?" Martis asked.

The voices drew closer. That was not the Latin of the Church, or the Norman-French of the nobility. The dialect—he had heard it before, but where?

"I am sure the king will give enough to pay for a night's sleep at an inn, and food for—"

"Will he pay to ransom you?"

The voices... Stephan's eyes widened. That was a Breton dialect. He was in enemy hands.

⸸

Brother Martis let him think on his predicament for two days before anyone returned to question him. Stephan explained he was a poor, lowly knight in the king's service. King Richard might offer a few marks, his brother Gil would contribute some shillings, but he laughed when Martis' superior suggested they would only exchange Stephan for the Duchess Constance. The abbot did not find Stephan's reaction amusing. He set parchment and quill in front of him. "If you are so sure of the king's response, then you will write to the earl," the abbot said. "Beg if you must, but appeal to his Christian soul."

Stephan knew Ranulf's pride and stubbornness. "The king has ordered the earl to release his wife and he has not listened. You expect him to respond favorably to a message from me?"

The abbot twirled his thumbs. "Then you will be with us for a long time, Stephan."

Within days, Stephan could walk the halls of the abbey without help. The pain was tolerable, but he grew dizzy if he rose too quickly. Brother Martis visited him daily, answering Stephan's questions. The messenger had departed for St James de Beuvron. It was a three day ride and back to Chester's castle, but now, two more weeks had passed and there was still no news.

"He would not harm Brother Guilliame, would he?" Martis asked, concerned about the messenger.

"I'm certain he would not."

Stephan began to attend daily mass, and not because of some new-found faith in God. If he was going to leave this place he must know every room, every corner. He explored the abbey and its cloisters, the church, the chapels, always moving much slower than he could to disguise his returning strength. He began to horde bread and cheese from his meals. He complained of being cold and Martis provided a second woolen blanket.

Every night he curled beneath the cover thinking of Henry. Christ, how he loved him. Was there ever a more honest and devoted man? Shamed by the anger he'd felt, Stephan's face heated. Henry's marriage was years away. They must cherish every moment until then...if there ever was a marriage. He shunned the turmoil in his mind and remembered the peace in the comfort of Henry's arms.

thirty-nine

Henry had left Yorkshire with mixed feelings—that peaceful life was such a contrast to what Normandy held for him. But Stephan would be there, and that would make it all worthwhile. In Greyton, he concluded his business. The manor and wool trade were in good hands. He visited his villeins, assuring them that Little John would see to their concerns. Receipt of the reeve's reports and Little John's visits to Greyton would proceed as usual, his role unchanged, just as he'd done all the while Henry had been serving the king across the Narrow Sea.

By mid-February he stood on the quay in Portsmouth and watched gentle swells brush the *Goldfinch*. Four muscled men carted supplies up the gangway and the crew hustled to prepare to sail. Henry was about to shout out to inquire about the captain, when a familiar voice rang behind him.

"Lord Henry! I thought that was you."

"Captain Boneil, are you slipping anchor soon? Have you room for one more?"

Boneil looked past Henry, and back towards the town. Confused, he asked, "Just one? Where is Sir Stephan? I thought he would be with you."

"With me? I haven't seen him in months."

"He was in Barfleur near Christmastide looking for passage here. He was desperate to see you. He wasn't willing to wait three days for the *Goldfinch*. I assumed..." He left the rest unsaid.

Stephan had departed for England *to see me*. But weeks had passed. "I've had no word from him," Henry said.

Was Stephan in England? Hurt or ill?

"Someone would remember if he'd come through. I'll check with the other boats," Boneil said. "Sir Stephan is hard to forget."

Henry heard the wistfulness in Boneil's voice. Was he holding something back? Not wanting to come right out and say the worst? *Where are you, Stephan?*

He rubbed his neck worriedly. "I'll ask at the taverns. When do you depart?"

"Tonight."

Henry thanked Boneil and made his way into town. The captain was right. Stephan left an impression wherever he went. Someone would remember him.

Henry stopped mid-stride, frowning. And if they did not?

He turned back to the sea, struggling to breathe, as if each breath were his last. *Dear God, no, not the sea.*

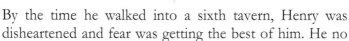

By the time he walked into a sixth tavern, Henry was disheartened and fear was getting the best of him. He no longer described Stephan or gave his name. "Have any boats from Normandy been lost at sea in recent months?" he asked.

"*Black Moon* sailed there in November. Haven't seen her since," the tavern keeper said.

Henry swore and pounded the bar top. He looked at the barkeeper apologetically, but his heart sank. He might never see Stephan again. "Could she have set anchor in another port?"

"Captain Black's sailed from Southampton for years, but only from Portsmouth of late. Think he would have said if he was movin' on," the man replied and a dozen others agreed with nods and ayes.

Barreling back to the *Goldfinch* Henry steeled himself for a conversation with Boneil. He stormed up the gangplank. He elbowed past crewmen and tore into the captain's quarters in the hold. "You knew about the *Black Moon*, didn't you?" Henry raged. "Why didn't you say anything?"

"I suspected." Compassion and sadness mixed with hope burned in Boneil's eyes. "I wanted to see what information others might have. It may give you peace, or a place to start looking."

Henry sat down hard on the chest by Boneil's small trestle table. *Christ in heaven!* He buried his head in his hands. "Dead? This cannot be."

"If locals found wreckage or bodies, they wouldn't tell. They scavenge what is left, keeping any goods and coin for themselves." Boneil was sympathetic to their plight. The people weren't pirates, just poor, trying to keep bread on their tables. "If bodies washed ashore, they might bury them. Or not."

"I must try to find him."

"The boat left Barfleur after a storm passed, but must have run into another." Boneil unrolled a map. "I've been caught in these rough waters and watched the rocks loom.

Been thrown off course as far west as the Breton coast. The seas are the master. Man is small, oft times powerless."

Not Stephan. He survived. Henry was sure of that and would ride from one coastal town to the next, steal into Brittany to find someone to tell him of the fate of the *Black Moon's* passengers. To find Stephan.

"I must send a message to Sir Robin," he said, his voice catching in his throat.

Boneil found something for him to scribble on and left. With shaking hands, Henry asked Robin to make enquiries from Portsmouth and north. Scour England for news. Had Stephan been on another boat, made it to England, and then got waylaid?

Tears stung his eyes. Despair tried to grasp his heart. He refused to believe Stephan was lost to him.

At the abbey in St Malo the messenger Guilliame finally returned, but empty-handed. The Earl of Chester's clerk at St James couldn't authorize the exchange of Stephan for the duchess. The clerk had sent word to the earl, but that would take time as he was last known to be in Rouen.

"Do you think the Duchess Constance would be allowed to receive a letter from her son?" Brother Martis had joined Stephan for an evening meal and spoke openly. What harm was there? Their invalid captive was not going anywhere. "Duke Arthur is worried for her."

Stephan paused mid-chew. "You've seen the young duke?"

Boots scraped on the stone behind Stephan and he turned. Arthur paraded into the room with a huge hound at his heels. He was dressed for his rank with a blue surcoat that fit him well, much richer than the ragged brown wool he'd been wearing when they had last met. A jeweled clasp held his cloak in place, and his dark neatly-combed hair fell in waves to his shoulders. His chausses and black boots were of the finest leather. He had grown, but his face was boyish-round, his body still that of a child.

Stephan rose slowly, gripping the edge of the trestle to steady himself. "My lord," he said and bowed. He wanted to berate Arthur for foregoing the king's meeting in Rennes, but held his tongue in respect for the boy's rank. It would do little good anyway, and he was certain that had been a decision out of Arthur's hands. His advisors had made a stupid choice, given the destruction it had wrought.

Studying Stephan, Arthur scratched the dog's ear. "Please, sit."

Brother Martis offered Arthur the seat at the head of the table. He gestured a servant to pour wine.

"The abbot tells me you nearly died."

What's this? Compassion from the boy?

"I am mending in their generous care," Stephan said.

Arthur tossed his cloak back and sat, ordering the servant from the room. He called the hound to his side.

"Shall I—" Martis started.

"Stay," Arthur said.

Stephan lowered himself into his chair. "I saw your lady mother last summer," he said. "She worries for you, my lord."

Arthur sat stiff-backed, revealing nothing in his face. "What good is being a king when your barons ignore your orders, Sir Stephan?" He sounded incredibly mature for his age. "King Richard delivered a command to Ranulf, yet my mother remains his prisoner."

"She is well treated, my lord."

"She is being held against her will!" Arthur huffed, a hint of the petulant child emerging. The dog raised its head.

Stephan couldn't argue the point, but he could mention the king's efforts—even when he wasn't sure if Richard was complicit with Ranulf. "Lord de Grey and I were sent on the king's orders to speak with the earl. You see we failed miserably and your lady mother remains at St James. I cannot condone what Chester has done, but put yourself in his position. By virtue of his marriage to your mother he is duke of Brittany, but the duchess gives him little due," he said. "He is bitter. Mayhap if your Breton barons were more generous towards him…?"

"Ranulf is the king's puppet." Arthur's eyes flicked past Stephan scanning the hall. "My barons—*we*—want no interference from Richard." The hound nudged his hand and Arthur calmed, stroking its head.

Annoyed, Stephan wondered if he should waste one breath attempting reason when Arthur merely mouthed his mother's and his barons' words. He staunched his desire to speak, drowning the foul taste on his tongue with wine. In the flickering candlelight he saw the frown on Brother Martis' face.

Arthur noticed it too. "This is best for Brittany, don't you agree, Brother?"

Martis stepped closer to the table, hands clasped at his waist. He should have addressed Arthur, but looked at Stephan. "Do you believe the king might name Duke Arthur his successor?"

"If the boy is raised in King Philip's court? Never." Stephan's eyes locked on Arthur. "Who would be the puppet then, my lord? A French puppet. Don't you and your barons realize that England and all the king's domains stretch five times the size of Brittany? Think of the land and the power that would answer to King Arthur."

Arthur withheld a smile, a glint of determination and political shrewdness spreading across his face. "What of Count John?"

The question Stephan, his friends, even the king, wondered, especially knowing that John wanted Arthur dead.

"With the right support behind your succession, John might stay in line," Stephan said. A fine line indeed.

A messenger departed at first light. Stephan wasn't privy to the contents of Arthur's letter to his mother or a second one he penned to King Richard, but he hoped for the best. When he escaped from this place, he would talk to Ranulf again, convince him he'd proven his point. Release the duchess. Secure Arthur's succession. If only the boy's advisors would open their eyes to the possibilities of Camelot.

Stephan observed carts from the village arriving with great regularity. It was just a matter of choosing one that had room for a stowaway and delivered supplies when the majority of the monks were at prayer or in the refectory where they gathered for their daily meal.

On a snowy day one week later, Stephan found his chance. The monks were in the chapel and the hall was empty but for two servants in the kitchen. Stephan hurried out the door where a wagon had emptied its crates. He crawled beneath the seat, tugging the empty crates close to hide himself. He squirreled the tarp over his body, not an easy thing with his arm still in a sling.

"Bless you, brother," a voice coming from the kitchen

said. The cart driver's footsteps scattered pebbles near the door. He grunted with some effort and suddenly, a bag of goods landed on the wagon bed. Stephan flinched, but kept quiet. The cart tipped as the man pulled himself into the seat. Settled, he clucked at the mule and smacked the reins. They were moving! He would soon be free.

"Pascal, Pascal! Stop!" someone cried out.

The cart jerked to a halt and wobbled when the driver shifted in his seat. Stephan stiffened, held his breath, and drew his head to his chest. His feet felt cold with the flimsy shoes provided by Brother Martis. He was hunched in an odd position, too tall for the cramped space beneath the seat, and the toes of one shoe stuck out from the tarp. Had he been seen?

Footsteps grew closer. "You forgot this."

The driver chuckled. "Bless you, Arnauld, my wife would not forgive me if I'd left the monk's fine cheese behind."

Arnauld laid a small basket in the back of the wagon and Stephan quietly released his breath. Pascal imitated his wife, his voice high and filled with scorn. "You are trying to kill me, husband. Turn this cart around now. I will die without my blessed cheese." The two men laughed, and within moments the cart began its bumpy passage back to the village. The driver hummed a tune Stephan didn't recognize, the soft notes like a melody over the rush of wind through the narrow streets. Stephan peeked out from beneath the tarp and spied the gibbous moon rising gloriously like a beacon in the sky.

forty

Rocks and massive boulders studded the coastline west of Barfleur. Henry rode north and west and then south along the coast, inquiring at every village. Boneil had not exaggerated about men's willingness to speak out, for he saw fear in the peasants' eyes. None would admit seeing remnants of a boat washed ashore. The booty might see them through until summer.

He'd lost track of the days and the number of people he had spoken with, the churches where he stopped to pray. He remembered hearing knights speak of the monastery at Mont St Michel that could be reached on foot at low tide and watched for it as he traveled south. Beyond that was Brittany's coast. Boneil claimed the cliffs there shadowed the sea and safe inlets were few. Would the boat have been tossed this far off course?

Henry tugged his cloak tight against the biting wind and huddled on the cliffside in the crevice of a boulder.

With each stop he had become more dispirited. Night would be upon him too soon. His horse needed food, they both needed shelter, but he couldn't move. Frozen with grief, he dropped his head to his knees and cried. He didn't want to go on, couldn't face another person regaling tales of the cold winter waters. None could survive they said. He wanted to hold out hope that Stephan was in England, but he knew how unlikely that might be. Robin's search would be for naught. Boneil's queries had turned up nothing about the *Black Moon*, so why did he think Robin might find something?

The truth strangled Henry. The *Black Moon* had been taken by the sea with Stephan on board, drowned in its black depths.

Henry's hand found the old wooden cross hanging round his neck. He pressed his gloved palm to it. *God's will?* His breath rattled in his throat. "It was not his time!" Henry shouted to the wind.

You let me love him, and now you have taken him from me.

Henry curled up, drawing his knees to his chest. *Stephan, are you gone from me?* His heart felt broken, pierced through with a blade. The loneliness slammed into him, so different than other times when they'd been apart. He could see Stephan's face, blue eyes bright with love and wonder, blonde hair brushing his shoulders, his short-cropped beard scratchy against Henry's cheek. Breath so warm on Henry's skin. *I will never see him again.* Their bodies close, joined as one. He trembled at the memories of their love-making. *I will never hold him again.*

Henry sobbed, his cries rivaling the squawks of the gulls. Perched on the rocks, the sea crashed and roiled around them and Henry could hear nothing else but the howling of the wind. He imagined the December cold.

He pictured Stephan on the quay, on the boat, wind tousling his hair, sunlight highlighting its golden hue.

Shivering, Henry drew his arms tight round himself. He brushed the hilt of his sword, felt the dagger in his belt. He unsheathed the blade, eyes riveted on it.

It would be quick, easy. He could be with Stephan. He rubbed his sleeve across his eyes to wipe the tears. With Stephan. In heaven. Because loving another person—a man—was *not* a sin. "It is not a sin! Dear God…" He pressed the tip of the dagger against his throat. It was a mortal sin to take your own life. Damn! He could not be buried on Christian ground.

Suddenly Henry laughed. He drank in the rocks, the grass and sand, the sea. Stephan would laugh. A Christian burial? His body would rot here on the shore, which Stephan would prefer to having a priest pray over him. But here—who would find him and even think to bury him? Henry glanced across the water again and up at the sky. Fog enshrouded the coastline, heavy and gray. Had the day been bright and clear he might see for miles, but truly, he would only see emptiness. His life was nothing without Stephan.

"Forgive me, oh Lord. But I cannot live without my love." He whispered the *Pater Noster* and laid the blade to his neck.

A burst of neighing made him look up the path where he'd left his horse to graze. Someone would find the animal, sell him or keep him. What did it matter? Henry dug the tip of the dagger into his throat.

Live, Henry, live!

His mind filled with Stephan's voice. Stephan wouldn't want him to take his own life. *We will be together someday, just not today.*

The horse protested loudly and curiosity drove Henry

to stand. A thin peasant mounted the bay, thwacked the reins, and man and beast shot away. Henry barreled up the hill, panting when he reached the top, and watched his horse disappear from sight. Not another person within view, not a village. Henry kicked at the grass. He could follow the thief, but the man needed the animal more than he did.

Henry walked south for hours determined to find shelter in the next village. He would ask more questions, even if there would be no answers. He could buy a horse, a mule if that was all he could find. And then? He stole a ragged breath. He would try to find the strength to say good-bye and turn east to join the king's men.

He heard the hammers before he saw the villeins. Some repaired a wattle fence while children played games around them. A parade of women carrying bundles walked towards the large village in the distance past fields that would be readied soon for planting. Henry turned away from the seaside trail to meet them. By the time he drew close, the men were packing their tools on a mule-drawn cart.

"Papa!" one of the children shouted, pointing at Henry.

He must look dirty and wind-blown—he certainly felt that way.

"Come here." The man calling the boy looked to be Henry's age.

Henry waved, smiling, being careful not to place his hand near his sword. Several women hurried to gather their little ones.

A man with dark hair streaked with gray approached Henry cautiously. "Who are you?"

When Henry introduced himself, Rollo, the reeve

overseeing the day's work on the fence, straightened in his presence. He listened to Henry's story with a skeptical eye. "We've little time to look out at the sea, my lord. We know the sand flats are dangerous, and the tides swirl and shift. We stay away." He pointed towards the village. "The steward might help you track your horse. We are done here for the day so I'll take you to him."

Henry pitched in to pack the last of the tools, aware of the curious eyes on him.

A young boy touched his scabbard. "Master has a sword like that. Are you a knight?"

"I serve King Richard," Henry said.

"Guy, leave the lord alone," Rollo said. "Run ahead."

Henry waved off Rollo's concern, but the child heeded the reeve's words.

"The king will want to know the boat's fate since he had men on board."

"If none have seen it, the sea has claimed it." Rollo shrugged and started towards the village.

Walking beside Rollo, Henry asked, "Do you know the story of the White Ship?" That shipwreck had been near Barfleur, a hundred miles away and about the time Henry's grand-pere had been born.

Rollo nodded. "The king's son died, along with many from noble families."

"But one man survived by clinging to a rock," Henry said.

"I told you we've found no one, nor heard if others have." Rollo pointed to the southwest across the sand flats. "You could go to the monastery. They might have word."

Fog hid the towers of Mont St Michel, but now Henry knew how far he'd come from Barfleur. A days' ride south would take him to St James de Beuvron. The Earl of Chester might not be there, but Ranulf's men would surely offer him a place to rest. And, it wouldn't hurt if he visited with the Duchess Constance, if he could convince the earl's men that he asked in the name of the king.

Henry heard the groan of the cart wheels. Rollo had left him standing there like a lost sheep. Visiting the monastery would serve little purpose. Stephan was gone.

forty-one

The chamberlain Hugo waved and hustled across the courtyard at St James to greet Henry. "Welcome, Lord de Grey."

Henry handed the reins of his horse to a groom. He remembered the wiry servant from his last visit to Earl Ranulf's castle and returned his warm greeting. Smoke curled above the rooftops and the smell of baking bread and roasting meat meant there might be nobles and knights in residence. "Is my lord Chester here?" he asked, rubbing his gloved hands for warmth.

"No, my lord, but what a surprise to see you." He led Henry towards the hall. "Our other guests have gone out for a hunt this morning, but we imagine the aromas of a hot meal will bring them back soon."

Both men knew that scent wouldn't travel far. The hunters would be driven back by their stomachs. The hall was empty but for the trestle that two pages were setting with cups and jugs. The chamberlain snapped his fingers and one boy took Henry's gloves, cloak, and sword belt. "Please come in. A drink perhaps, whilst you wait?"

Henry nodded. "I've been on the road more than seven days."

"Of course, my lord. Let us draw a bath for you."

"Just water and soap, Hugo."

"I assure you it is not a bother, my lord. The others will expect a hot soak when they return from the forest and we had already begun preparing the baths." He gestured smartly at the second page, and turned back to Henry. "Ralph will show you the way. He'll bring some wine and retrieve your pack—"

"I fear I've nothing but what you see. My clothes and horse were stolen."

Shock and outrage fired in Hugo's eyes, but Henry continued, "I had coin to buy an old palfrey—a long story I will not dwell on now."

Within minutes Henry sank into the steaming bath in an upstairs room. Servants delivered two more rounds of water to fill the tub. Ralph left him a cup of wine and a soap cake on the small trestle by the tub and hung a large linen cloth near the brazier to use for drying. He had barely whisked away Henry's dirty clothes when he returned with clean tunic, braies, and hose and laid them on one of the cots.

The small room was masculine, Spartan, and occupied by two other men if the clothes set out on the beds was evidence. A tallow candle on a chest cast a faint yellow light and dimly lit the room, the arrow-slit window covered to keep out the cold.

Dismissing Ralph, Henry slipped below the water and scrubbed his hands through his hair. Surfacing, he reached for the soap. It slipped to the bottom of the bath and when he finally had a hold on it, the scent of lavender struck his nose. Images of Stephan overwhelmed him. Stephan spooning his body, feeling the beat of his heart. Holding each other close. Henry rubbed the soap on his face, tears forming in his eyes. *I miss you.* He stared at his hands remembering the strength in Stephan's, feeling his lover's fingers enfolding his. He could smell him, closed his eyes as tears streamed down his cheeks. Voices from the hall echoed up the stone stairwell, but Henry could hear Stephan's whispered "I love you" above them.

Laughter from downstairs made Henry sit up, a sound so familiar he was certain he imagined it. "Stephan?"

The laughter died, replaced by conversation muffled by wood, walls, and stone. "Here?" a voice cried out.

"Stephan?" Henry shouted. He stood abruptly sending a wave of water over the side of the bath. "Stephan!"

Boots rang on the steps. "Henry?"

The door flew open.

"You're alive! Dear God, you're alive," Henry cried.

"You are naked." Stephan rushed into Henry's arms. "Don't weep, my love," he said and kissed him fiercely.

Henry was lost to Stephan for a moment, but pulled back to look at him. "How long have you been here? Did you leave for England on the *Black Moon*? Boneil thinks you were lost at sea. I have been searching the coastline from Barfleur to near Mont St Michel, thinking you were dead."

Stephan paled. "Boneil?"

"I thought I had lost you forever, and you've been here? Hunting with Ranulf's friends?"

"Wait—are you angry with me?" Stephan asked.

"I had no word, not one word from you," Henry cried.

"And I had none from you." Stephan's voice was near a shout. He exhaled sharply. "You said you would tell de

Camville about us, and then Edric Weston wrote that you intended to marry that child. I didn't know what to think." Clenching and unclenching his fists, Stephan looked away, caught somewhere between anger and anguish. "I felt betrayed. But I had to see you. I had to hear it from you."

Henry tipped Stephan's chin up, intent on gazing into his lover's blue eyes. "I feared his message would get to you before I could explain. I did send word, Stephan, I swear. I sailed to Normandy as soon as I was able. Edric spoke only half-truths. And no, I'm not angry. Not with you. Just upset... I thought you were dead." Henry suddenly noticed the gash healing on Stephan's head. He touched it. "You're hurt."

"The *Black Moon* was dashed against the rocks. Peasants found me, but took my sword, my boots." He rubbed his finger, held it up, and choked. "My ring."

Henry kissed his hand, his lips. "I will get you another. You're alive. Nothing else matters."

"The peasants left me with the monks of St Malo." He took a deep breath. "They wanted a ransom—me in exchange for the duchess."

Henry brushed his lips against the tip of Stephan's nose. He couldn't help but chuckle. "Ranulf would never agree to that."

"Exactly," Stephan said, a half-hearted smile washing across his face. "So I planned my escape as soon as my strength returned and my arm healed. I dragged in here seven days past. There is little else to tell, but—" He shivered, holding Henry's gaze, choosing not to finish his last thought. Thumbing water droplets from Henry's chest, he asked, "Is the water still warm?"

"It will be if you join me," Henry teased.

Stephan pulled Henry close and they kissed slowly,

savoring the taste of each other. Noise from the hall ended the kiss and Stephan glanced over his shoulder. "They know you are here, and they'll want their own baths soon enough."

Dripping wet, Henry stepped from the tub. Pressing Stephan across the room he kissed him, separating only to remove Stephan's tunic. Stephan nuzzled the scruff on Henry's face as Henry bolted the door.

"They shall have to wait," Henry said. His hands slid into Stephan's braies, the feel so familiar, the memories of the love they shared sending aches through his body.

Stephan grew hard at his touch and moaned, arms tight around Henry's back. He gripped his buttocks, willing Henry closer. Henry's breaths quickened, pleasurable groans escaping from his throat. They thrust against each other. Want and desire rushed through Henry. "I love you. You," he repeated. "Forever." Like a wave crashing on the shore, he climaxed with Stephan, flesh to flesh, hearts and souls afire.

While the others bathed, servants provided drinks by the blazing fire in the great hall. Henry and Stephan slipped into quiet conversation. "There will be no wedding," Henry said, explaining his agreement with Lady Nichola.

"This time," Stephan replied. Before Henry could respond, Stephan placed a finger on his lips, and then planted a kiss on his forehead. "I love you. We'll take each day as it comes, and if we face another plot to marry you off, we'll find our way."

They spoke of Robin and Marian and the new life they would bring into the world. "And then Marian loses him again," Henry said, seeing Stephan disliked the idea as much as he did.

Henry said nothing of Edric and only spoke of Allan

and Nottingham, of Elle and Little John. Stephan avoided questions about Edric, much to Henry's relief. Duchess Constance, Arthur's letter—Stephan's eyes flicked round the hall and he lowered his voice. The duchess remained secluded in the north tower, but he had seen her a few days earlier.

"She lacks for nothing but her freedom," Stephan said, "and acknowledged Arthur's letter. I cautioned her that Arthur could be his own man, his own king, answerable to no one, if he heeded King Richard's summons. She could be assured Philip would be much more than an observer if she and Arthur ignore Richard. I promised I would beseech the king and Ranulf to release her."

"Will one more request make a difference?" Henry asked.

The sounds of laughter drifted down the stairs and footsteps followed as the hunting party congregated in the hall. The evening filled with stories and song, fine Lenten fare, far too much wine, and politics. Still recuperating after his escape from St Malo, Stephan was exhausted and laid down by the fire. Henry threw a thick woolen blanket over him and he drifted off to sleep. The fire died down, and when the other knights dispersed in the wee hours, Henry stretched out beside him.

Stealthy footsteps signaled morning. Henry waved away a youth preparing to place logs on the fire. It was worth being chilly just to watch Stephan sleeping soundly. Memories of their first morning together echoed vividly in his mind. The smell of musk and roses, his arm across Stephan's chest, the heat of his skin, Stephan's heart beating beneath his palm.

Stephan stirred, reached for Henry's hand.

"Good morning," Henry whispered. He tickled Stephan's neck with his nose.

Stephan rolled onto his side and smiled. "I like waking up next to you."

"Every day I pray." Henry kissed him lightly on the cheek.

forty-two

MARCH - APRIL 1197

Ten days later the knights rendezvoused with the king at Les Andelys. Richard was pleased to see them, but disheartened when he learned of Arthur's letter—it had never arrived. He refused to speak of Duchess Constance, only to say messages intercepted from the French court and her own brimmed with vitriol. Henry wouldn't accuse Ranulf of being delighted by the exchanges, but he was smug. He had no need to worry the king would force him to release her, at least until Arthur appeared at Richard's court.

As March ended, they realized that would not happen. The king's spies had spotted Arthur in Paris. "I am not surprised," Stephan had said, though Henry decided Stephan was more disappointed than the king, since he had been the last to see the boy at St Malo.

The king's negotiations with Arthur's advisors would continue, but he had thrown one more carrot to the rabbit. He sent Emlyn to cajole the Duchess Constance at

St James. Since his return to Les Andelys, Henry had seen Emlyn come from the king's chambers twice. The rapport between them went beyond the physical. Empathy, friendship, trust. She had made an impression on King Richard, just as she had with Arthur. Perhaps Constance would listen to another woman, a mother like herself who had lost her husband and her children.

A ferocious spring storm forced a halt to construction on Castle Gaillard. Richard had spent hours some days working alongside the carpenters and stone masons, but now he sulked, unable to use physical labor to release his pent-up frustration with the French and Arthur. He had added a little weight round his gut, had webbed lines at his eyes, and more gray dimmed his once striking reddish-gold hair. But he was a soldier's soldier and had changed little, Henry thought, remembering how he labored with his men to rebuild Jaffa after the crusaders took it.

In early April, the spring campaigns began. With Toulouse married to his sister and firmly in his camp, the king's southern borders were calm. Richard marched his forces north, where they camped near Rouen and reconnoitered points north and east. Negotiations with the Count of Flanders had not been successful, but trade embargoes were effective. Spies reported unrest in Flemish ports, and Richard set his sights on winning the Flemish over, with a heavy hand if necessary.

A day ahead of the army, Henry and Stephan forayed deep into Ponthieu, Count Baldwin's territory. The sun slid behind clouds lending gloom to the encroaching dusk, but torchlights from the port of St Valéry flickered through the trees. The River Somme lapped the riverbank, as soothing a sound as their horses' steady hoofbeats. Henry wouldn't complain that they'd seen nothing except one barge on the river more than an hour past.

Emerging from the trees, Stephan drew rein. St Valéry lay before them. A prominent abbey towered above buildings lining narrow streets, the town surrounded by stone ramparts. The waterfront was busy.

"Those are English ships," Stephan said as they watched cargo from boats being loaded on to wagons.

Just as the king suspected, English merchants had defied the embargo. Caught in English ports, they'd be slapped with fines for attempting to do business with the Flemish. But here?

Henry scoffed. "Fools. There will be more than fines for the captains of these vessels." He tried not to imagine the king's response.

White caps crested on the waves where the sea hurtled towards the mouth of the river.

"Christ!" Stephan pointed at a boat docking at the quay. "That's the *Goldfinch*."

Henry shifted in his saddle. "Why is Boneil here? He swore he'd stay away from illicit trade." On the deck men secured the ropes and set out the plank under the captain's watchful eye. "We must warn him, Stephan."

Stephan turned away, covered his mouth.

"You don't think we should?" Henry asked when Stephan didn't reply.

"Risk our lives for someone who breaks the king's edicts?" Stephan shook his head.

"We do it for Allan and Tuck and the others in Nottingham." It would take little to tie Henry and Stephan to that operation, especially with Allan's fondness for the drink and the enemies he'd made. Henry prayed he and Robin had curbed their young friend's downward spiral.

"That's for a good cause—feeding the poor," Stephan

said. "But warning Boneil is different."

Was that fear in Stephan's voice? That wasn't like him. But he *had* nearly died. In battle would be one thing, but at the hands of the sea? Or by the noose or a sword across the neck if they were caught spying here in St Valéry?

Henry swiped his brow. "He saved our necks a time or two." His gaze slid from the boat to Stephan. "You go, report to the king. I'll be a few hours behind you."

"No! If anyone is to warn Boneil, it should be me," Stephan said a bit too quickly, and then exhaled impatiently. "He thinks I'm dead."

"I can tell him what happened. You aren't as strong as—"

"I am fine." Stephan's voice was terse. He wouldn't admit the slow recovery from his ordeal had been surprising. He refused to look at Henry and tipped his head towards the quay. "He'll head to the taverns. I have more experience—"

"With men like him?"

Stephan looked up abruptly, eyes narrowed. "I know where to find them." Sliding his hand along Henry's jaw, Stephan pulled him close and kissed him.

"What was that for?" Henry asked.

"Just remember, I am yours." *And I will never stray again...*

Had this been Southampton or Barfleur Stephan could point to establishments where a man might find the physical companionship of other men. But he knew nothing of St Valéry. He hoped to follow Boneil from the *Goldfinch*, but the captain had wasted no time and had already made his way into town. The roads leading away from the quay had emptied, but drink fueled boisterous conversations pouring from a dozen taverns. Stephan took a quick look inside a few and moved on. Boneil liked fine things. He had good taste, and if given a choice, he would be sitting in one of the nicer establishments. But most of the taverns looked the same—the customers, too, young and old, missing teeth, broken noses, stale breath, sailors or tradesmen, all dirty after a hard day's work and lending odious odors to the air. That, and the smell of stale rushes and spilled ale on creaking wooden floors filled Stephan's nostrils.

"*Goldfinch*?" The barkeeper at Stephan's sixth stop set an ale in front of him, his first of the night. The old-timer studied him. "What business have you with the captain?"

"My own." Stephan took a swig of the brew.

The barkeeper looked past Stephan's shoulder, dark eyes sweeping the tavern. "I want no trouble."

A young boy who had the same bulging eyes and straight dark hair as the barkeeper stepped up and signaled for three drinks, which were poured without a word between the two. When the boy went about his work, Stephan laid two silver pennies on the grimy bar top.

"I just want to speak with him," Stephan said. Trouble might come tomorrow under the king's banner, but he wouldn't say that aloud in a room full of enemies.

The barkeeper coughed, spittle flying but missing Stephan by a nose. "He's already *speaking* with someone, upstairs, the room at the end of the hall."

Stephan didn't relish the idea of seeing Boneil dressed or undressed so he nursed his ale, hoping Boneil would make an appearance. He kept his back to the braggarts and increasingly drunken men in the tavern, not out of fear of being recognized, but for the dread of remembering their faces. In the chaos of battle, a knight might see his enemies' eyes for one brief moment. There was no time to think, no time to see the shock on a face when swords pierced flesh. But if he looked too closely at the men here, he might remember them when the king pillaged the town.

The barkeeper's laughter made him catch a breath. Stephan glanced sidelong, saw the man tousle his son's hair. Smiling, he sent him off past the linen curtain and into the private quarters where his family lived.

A sour taste bubbled in Stephan's mouth. He downed the last of his ale to douse the vile bite. Reaching into his pouch he retrieved two shillings. He wouldn't need the coin and waved the barkeeper over.

"Another ale?" the man asked.

Shaking his head, Stephan opened his fist to show the coins. The man would have to pour many mugs of ale to make two shillings. "If I gave you this," Stephan said, "would you close shop and take your family north early on the morrow?"

"Why would I…" He paused, nervously rubbing a thumb to his forefingers. "Not east? We've family a day away."

"Far north." Stephan realized the man could tell his friends to pack up and leave. Allan would be taking bets if he were here, the chances increased significantly the king would learn who warned them away.

Stephan sighed. He might be joining his friends in Sherwood sooner than expected.

Stephan did have that second drink, and got tired of waiting for Boneil. Wandering up the stairs and past the sounds of pleasure-seekers, he paused at the far end of the black-as-pitch hallway. Quiet as an empty church. He knocked on the door, heard the creak of the bed and footsteps.

Light from an oil lamp in the room silhouetted Boneil's form. He had wrapped a blanket round himself. "God's bones," Boneil said when the light struck Stephan's face. "You're alive and come back to the Devil? Does Henry know…" He left the rest unspoken.

"We saw the *Goldfinch* in the harbor. Henry left when the bells tolled Vespers to return to King Richard's camp. He doesn't know our transgressions, and I must thank you for that."

Boneil opened the door and tugged Stephan into the room. Boneil's companion snored softly, oblivious to the living. "What are you doing here?" he asked.

"You must set sail on the morning tide, Boneil. The king is in a foul mood, and by sunrise he will know that four English ships have ignored his embargo."

"Four?" Boneil frowned. "Ah, four if the *Goldfinch* sails. Did Henry approve this warning?"

"He did. But there will be nothing we can do for you if the king storms St Valéry."

"My cargo won't be unloaded before sunrise, meaning I've not a denier to pay my crew. Why the worry? The king will lay a fine, nothing more."

"This isn't an English port. He may seize your ship or worse. Please, Boneil, leave. The camp is a half day's march. A hundred knights or more, and twice that number of men-at-arms. They'll not leave here empty-handed. The king will raze this town, and only God knows—"

"Enough, Stephan." Boneil let the blanket slip to the floor, not bothering to hide his erection. Talk of big strong knights or perhaps just the sight of Stephan had stirred his blood. "Morning, you say?" He ran his hands seductively through his shoulder-length blonde hair and tossed his head towards the bed. "I can throw this fellow out if you'd like to stay."

Stephan laughed at his boldness. "I've delivered my message and must go."

Boneil bowed. "I'm teasing you. It was a mistake, and I will never tell Henry. I think you are both mad, but I respect you. I don't understand you. Truly, I am surprised you were ever attracted to someone like him. What was it?"

"Friendship firstly." Stephan's heart began to pound. "He was so naive when we first met. Innocent. I wanted to protect him."

"And have you? Honestly?"

"I have been there for him."

"But you cannot always be at his side. You *chose* to let him return to England on his own. And look at the hurt your loving has caused both of you. Making each other miserable over something you can never have. Was it ever that way with other lovers before you met Henry? No, I think not. You are a bit selfish, Stephan, but I'll say no more."

"Selfishness be damned. We love each other." Stephan pressed the door latch to leave, but turned back. "I was ready to give myself to some *one* and to be true to that man. Mayhap you will never be able to do that. Mayhap you are too frightened and for that I pity you, because you will never know joy."

Stephan drew close to Henry. The pavilion was dark and a dozen men slept, their snorts and snores and steady breathing hiding the chirp of crickets outside. A sentinel walked past, his boots scuffling the ground.

Smoothing Henry's hair back, Stephan kissed his neck and drank in the salt and musky taste of his lover. This is where he wanted to wake every morning. The face he wanted to see. His smile, those eyes. His voice.

Henry stirred and reached for Stephan, pressed back into him. Their fingers entwined.

"It is done," Stephan said.

He felt Henry nod against him, closed his eyes, and drifted off to sleep.

forty-three

APRIL 1197

St Valéry

Dew sparkled on new blades of grass touched by a fiery morning sun. The road to St Valéry lay quiet except along pastureland where bleating lambs chased their mothers' teats. Distant farm houses and villages stood shuttered even at mid-morning. Word had spread. King Richard's army marched. Flemish and French troops had fled.

By late morning the smell of the sea drifted to Henry's nose. He quelled the pounding in his head. It was one thing to besiege an enemy castle. But to storm a town, fire buildings, kill innocents…

"Lord de Grey!"

The shout settled his eyes on the rider approaching from the front of the column. He slowed and pivoted beside Henry. "Lord de Grey, Sir Stephan, the king commands your presence."

Henry shot Stephan a questioning look and both men spurred their horses to the van. Sitting atop a Spanish bay, King Richard had reined in and was issuing orders.

"You have deceived me, Lord de Grey," Richard cried. The knights around him sidled their mounts to let Henry and Stephan through.

Henry's heart felt like a boulder colliding with his gut. "Sire, I would do no such—"

"Four English ships?" Richard snapped, but then smiled and pivoted to face the harbor. "No, my friends, we shall have booty from five."

The sun beat down more like a midsummer day rather than early spring. Sweat glistened on Henry's forehead. He gaped at the *Goldfinch* bobbing lazily on the water. If he looked shocked, no one seemed to notice.

Richard growled. "Let's make an example of all of them for English who would be traitors."

Drawing himself up in the saddle, Henry swiped his brow. "A lucky day for the men, sire."

Henry met Stephan's stone face for only a moment, hardly hearing the king's orders. Stephan had warned Boneil. Richard would show no mercy. His three hundred men had marched relentlessly for days. Show regard for the town, its people, or the English traitors? God have mercy on them.

Richard signaled and deafening war cries rose through the ranks. Henry's horse tossed his head, snorting, black coat gleaming in the sunlight. The sounds of a hundred horsemen blurred in the charge and time seemed to slow. The knights' bellows sounded distant and muffled, but hoofbeats struck Henry's ears like drums. For a moment he remembered the Saracen cavalry in the desert, arrows whooshing past his head or thudding against his shield. His stomach churned, those memories a deep ache, but he positioned his shield close to his body and gripped his sword.

Dirt kicked up by the horses turned the air a hazy brown. The knights weren't challenged at the city walls and thundered through the gate at the Guillaume Towers. The garrison at St Valéry was small, no match for King Richard's men. Bells rang out a warning, too late for many. Sword, mace, and ax found flesh. Women screamed and cries of children punctuated the air. Everywhere, people were fleeing, shouting, "God have mercy."

"This way," Stephan roared, avoiding a blow from a man with a club. He struck aside a lance with his shield. Beside him, a horse screamed, impaled in the neck, and horse and rider spilled to the ground. Henry and Stephan beat off townsfolk intent on killing or capturing the knight. On his feet, he acknowledged their help and shot after the king.

Rancid smoke curled in the air. Dozens of buildings spewed flames and thatched roofs collapsed in a great roar and whoosh. A villager pulled a little girl from the conflagration, but stumbled head on into a soldier who ran him through and left the child weeping at his side. Behind them men-at-arms looted shops. Innocents were dragged into alleyways. No mercy, no mercy...

Curses spilled from a feminine voice to Henry's right. Two men had ripped a young woman's clothes and pinned her down in a cart. She kicked one hard, shouting words Henry rarely heard from soldiers. But she was no match for them.

Henry maneuvered his horse towards the cart, reining in sharply. His stallion reared, catching the shoulder of one attacker. The man screamed, loosed his hold on the girl, and landed on his ass.

Henry bellowed at sword point, "Leave her be!"

Both men scrambled away and the girl covered herself

as best she could and hurried up the alleyway. In sight of the quay and up the street another horrific scene caught Henry's eye. His shoulders sagged and he pounded the pommel of his saddle with his fist. One of the English boats in the harbor was aflame. Richard's men stormed the others, slashing and hacking anyone in their way. Sailors who hadn't been caught were jumping into the river. And there, at the bow of the *Goldfinch*, Henry saw Boneil.

Swallowing hard, Henry looked away to find Stephan in the chaos. He had reined in, controlling his horse with a tight grip, stroking the animal's dark mane and gaping at the boats. Henry spurred his stallion to Stephan's side. Their knees brushed, but Henry desperately wished he could grasp Stephan's hand. Boneil held his palms out to the attackers. Shoved to the deck, he was teased with sword and kicked. Not by one man, but by four.

Henry shuddered. "Why did he stay?"

Boneil lay motionless while the soldiers carted away anything of value from his boat. An explosion on another galley rocked the quay. Flames shot into the air and lashed the *Goldfinch*. Her mainmast caught fire, sparks dancing, its sail devoured as the wind fed the flames.

Henry pressed his shaking hand to Stephan's knee, eyes closed. His home at Greyton flashed in his mind— fire engulfing the hall and consuming the thatched roof. The stable, chapel, mill and smith's, every cottage—in flames. "No!"

His cry frightened his horse and it flinched, jerking him back to the present. The smell of blood and burnt flesh made him gag. Stephan squeezed his hand, and looked anywhere but the docks. His face was streaked with grime. Blood coated his mail, his sword, his stallion. The animal pawed the dirt where early spring grass had perished beneath the army's pounding. Painted in browns and reds, the ground was littered with the dead and wounded.

On the *Goldfinch*, soldiers dragged Boneil to his feet. A rope was slid round his neck.

Henry drew in a deep breath. "We must stop this."

"We cannot do—" Stephan started.

But Henry pressed his heels to his horse and shot towards the quay. Sweat blurred his vision, but he knew Stephan was not far behind.

The soldiers had tied Boneil's hands, stripped the black silk tunic from his back and taken his boots. The rope was tossed over the foremast and four men tugged it, lifting Boneil off the deck slowly. He kicked and flailed, and cried out when someone held a torch to his hose.

"Stop!" Shouting for others to get out of the way, Henry twisted through the crowds. His throat was parched and he could barely hear himself over the crackle of fire, the groan of roofs caving in and walls collapsing. Somewhere behind him, Stephan's voice called his name, but the closer he drew to the ship, the louder the sounds of the rape of St Valéry assaulted his senses. It was not so much the clink of swords and bash of shields now. It was the curses of doomed men, the harsh laughter of victors scavenging dead bodies and goods tossed on the streets, the cries of little ones, and the screams of women and young girls being ravished.

Bile rose in Henry's throat. He couldn't save them all. He could do nothing to stop this.

Near the *Goldfinch*, he leaped from the saddle. Boneil dangled from the yard arm and the mast was engulfed in flames. His arms were limp at his side, his body buffeted by wind.

Henry didn't remember Stephan dragging him away from the quay. From a distance they silently watched the *Goldfinch* swallowed up by fire. Stephan had removed his helm, shoved back his mail hood. He gaped at Boneil's body, now blackened and burnt, swaying in the breeze until the mast cracked and collapsed to the deck. Moisture tinged his eyes. He wanted to say something, but no words came.

Henry closed his fist on the pommel of his saddle and ground his teeth. Rage and horror clawed at him. The riverfront smoldered and smoke choked the air. Wagons overflowing with booty rumbled along the road, and knights trotted past without a care. Near dusk, the pale sun slid through an orange and gray mist eerily enfolding St Valéry and the last of the retreating king's men. There was nothing left to pillage.

"We should leave," Stephan said.

It was more a command than a suggestion, and Henry had little left in him to argue. He rode in silence next to Stephan, not questioning his decision to leave the main road. No one would miss them tonight. The men would be celebrating their victory, telling stories of their prowess, and drinking too much wine. Henry wanted none of it, and when they came upon a barn in small village, both men knew they could have a few hours of peace. At the water trough they cleaned the blood from their mail and their faces, wiped down their swords, and paid a young boy to brush down and feed the horses.

In the barn loft, they ate sparingly from the dried beef and day old bread in Stephan's pack. Henry drained his wineskin. He held it upside down and grimaced. Managing a smile, Stephan offered him the last of his own and then set about spreading their blankets. They laid down and, wrapped in each other's arms against the ugly world outside, sleep finally came to them.

forty-four

JUNE - DECEMBER 1197

Henry wasn't certain if the assault at St Valéry was a turning point in the king's struggle against Philip Capet, but the tide seemed to shift in his favor. A month later, the castle at Milli fell, and while Richard and Will Marshal led that assault, Count John and Captain Mercadier scored a coup and captured the French king's cousin. Philip of Beauvais, an envoy to the Holy Roman Emperor during Richard's captivity, would have seen him kept in chains in the darkest and coldest dungeon and on a diet of bread and water. Richard detested the man and his stories about the warrior bishop sent chills down Henry's spine.

In the months that followed, the king spurned one message after another about Bishop Philip's circumstances from French liaisons and Pope Celestine III. Richard had no intention of releasing the man for any sum. The interdict of Normandy over the construction of

Castle Gaillard had been lifted. What was one new check on his soul?

Baldwin, Count of Flanders, had come to the negotiating table in late June. Richard had summoned his chancellor, Archbishop Hubert Walter, to bargain with Flanders. The archbishop, a skilled diplomat, convinced the Count to break with King Philip. Richard ended the trade embargo, and with Baldwin firmly in his camp, other Norman Marcher barons fell in line. Even the Bretons came back into the fold on condition that the Duchess Constance was released. The king must have offered Ranulf an impressive deal, though Henry found it hard to imagine Richard's most wealthy earl wanted for anything. Except perhaps an annulment.

It was a glorious summer. Castles lost to Philip while Richard was on crusade or in captivity were recaptured. Count Baldwin invaded Artois, had taken Douai and other castles, and was besieging Arras. Though forced to retreat from Arras with Philip at his back, Baldwin's maneuvers left the French trapped. Philip agreed to meet with Richard in mid-September and a truce to last for fifteen months was signed.

With peace at hand for the time being, political maneuvering consumed King Richard's days.

"You have great trust in us, sire," Henry had said when he and Stephan were ordered to St James de Beuvron to escort the Duchess Constance to Rouen.

"The Earl will not interfere this time," Richard had said. "The French know their best chance of hurting us is to disrupt the river trade so Ranulf will remain at Les Andelys to oversee troops there and secure our supply lines from Rouen."

The knights' journey and the king's subsequent meeting with his former sister-in-law had gone well.

Emlyn had accompanied Constance from St James, stood by her when she met with King Richard. Very few knew her humble origins. She looked and acted no differently than any of the duchess' ladies and appeared to have as much influence as the others. The king focused on Constance, but his eyes flicked to Emlyn throughout the day.

Constance worried about her son, still at the French court. "She truly hates you, sire," Emlyn said after Constance's audience ended. Her ladies had given Richard the eye when he asked Emlyn to stay behind. "But I told her you were a generous man."

"Then I have you to thank for her trust."

"You do," Emlyn replied, her chin lifted. A slight blush swept across her cheeks.

Richard kissed her hand. "I count on you for your honesty. And I welcome your companionship if only for another day or two." He leaned close to Emlyn, but Henry could hear his whispers. "I have missed you."

She curtsied, a shy smile on her face.

"Go see to Constance," the king said, returning her smile.

Richard had promised Constance he was in quiet negotiations with contacts in Paris. What that meant was he had a plan to spirit Arthur away from Philip. "My spies report on his movements, but I will only send my best men when the time is right," he'd privately told Henry and Stephan. "Robin will be here by Christmastide. We shall talk then."

Henry's sister Bea had written with news of Marian's new daughter. Not surprisingly, Robin was nothing but a ghost, not one word of him, and Henry had wondered if he would return to Normandy. Apparently the king believed he would—his 'best man' would infiltrate Paris, a city familiar to Robin. Henry's heart clenched for his friends. Apart again.

His gaze flicked to Stephan, blue orbs shining, riveted on Henry. Stephan remained motionless, and it was all Henry could do to turn his thoughts back to the king's words.

"In the meantime," Richard continued, "it seems I am become my sister Joanna's delivery boy. Her message made it clear I was to personally hand this letter to you, Lord de Grey." He gave Henry a chastising look and held out a folded, sealed parchment.

Henry recognized Joanna's seal.

Richard tapped the letter. "I would be envious had I not received one myself. I hope her husband Raymond is not the jealous kind, though…" His gaze darted from Henry to Stephan and back. "Does he know?"

"I could not say, sire," Henry said. "That is not the stuff of your lady sister's missives."

Laughing, Richard gestured to him to break the seal. As he read, a smile curled his mouth. "She has given her husband a son, also named Raymond," Henry beamed. "A healthy boy, God bless them. You must be pleased, sire."

A fleeting frown touched Richard's face and then was gone. His wife had not provided an heir, but who was to say if that was as much the king's fault as it was the queen's. They still spent little time together. The king had been as occupied with war and politics then as now and Henry found it hard to forgive him, especially when he'd seen certain *ladies* coming from Richard's chambers.

In mid-October, the king's chancellor successfully negotiated a compromise on ownership of Les Andelys with Walter de Coutance, the archbishop of Rouen. It was hard to tell whether there had been any arm twisting, but Richard seemed pleased with the outcome.

Near Christmas news of the Holy Roman Emperor reached them. The man who had kept the king imprisoned more than thirteen months had died. Richard wanted an ally elected in the Emperor Henry's place and by the end of the year he sent a delegation to champion his nephew Otto for the position. Should he be elected, Philip of France's influence would shrink, his own allies drying up left and right.

Christmas court at Rouen was festive. The great hall was decked in aromatic holly and pine and lit with hundreds of candles, made all the better when Robin arrived. His reunion with Henry and Stephan was jubilant, their embraces ones a mother would love.

Robin couldn't conceal the joys of fatherhood. "Lucy arrived on the first day of August kicking and screaming. Marian says she has her brother's fire."

Alarmed, Henry looked around the room. Count John was at court. If he came in and overheard…

Before Henry could caution his friend, Stephan teased, "I certainly hope the babe looks like Marian." He shifted close to Henry to make room for Robin.

"Marian claims I am quite handsome." Robin threw his leg over the bench and greeted other knights at the table. Two looked away disgusted and three others rose and walked away. The king had exonerated Robin, but many still felt his betrayal. Robin shook his head, swore quietly.

Stephan tried to distract him. "You wouldn't want anyone to call Lucy handsome."

"On the other hand, mayhap it will keep the boys from lusting after her," Henry suggested.

"Good God, I should return to England right away,"

Robin cried. "I'll not have boys at my door and desirous of my little girl." He sighed, and then smiled softly. "She does favor Marian. I can see it in her face. She will be a beauty."

Stephan pounded Robin's back. "It is good to have you back."

"I'd not be here if the king hadn't summoned his barons to meet with Hubert Walter in Oxford. When your brother received his, there was a separate message for me." Seeing Henry nod, Robin grunted. "You knew?"

"Only that the king expected you here. For what, we aren't privy," Henry said. "You attended the council with Gil?"

"Not the council meeting. I met with Walter privately to receive the king's message. I rode on to Portsmouth, sailed into Honfleur two days past." Richard was walking towards him, but not close enough to hear. "Why am I here?" Robin asked. "The king signed a truce with the French."

"Truce?" Stephan laughed. "Name one man who would be shocked if hostilities break out."

Henry added, "Mayhap if it had been until the feast of St. Hillary next month, but until Hillarymass a year hence? This peace will never last."

"Is that so?" Richard's deep voice boomed behind them.

The knights swung around and clambered to stand.

"Sire, we were—"

"Of course you were," Richard said. A moment of tension flickered between the king and Robin, but Robin smiled. "Welcome back, Sir Robin."

"At your command," Robin said.

"I am glad you came, Robin. I wasn't sure you would." Sincere, Richard grasped Robin's arm and held it firmly.

"There are few men I trust more." Richard sat, studied the knights. "All we need is our young friend Allan to gather the bets on the truce." Richard chuckled, and the men raised his drinks to him.

A commotion by the door drove the room to silence.

"Don't let me interrupt the festivities. Eat, drink!" John shouted. He tossed his rich woolen cloak to a squire, grabbed a goblet off one table and strode towards Richard. "We should all enjoy my brother's generosity."

Conversations swelled around them. Robin wouldn't slink into the walls to avoid John, but he must regret that he'd spoken of Marian and his family in the presence of so many.

"Sire." John lowered his head and then tossed it back, his dark hair falling in soft waves to his shoulders. The gold threads on his crimson tunic shimmered from the torchlight.

Robin exhaled sharply and Richard twisted to meet his gaze. "I know there is bad blood between you," he said and glanced up at his brother, "but John knows I will not tolerate any actions against you."

"Your word is law, my king," John said. He smiled at Robin, but his eyes gleamed with darkness. He held his goblet out. "Pour me a drink, Robin."

Stephan sensed Henry's unease and squeezed his knee beneath the table.

"My pleasure, my lord," Robin said stiffly.

"The last time we shared an ale was in a dark tavern in Hull if I recall. There were threats involved—"

"Enough, John," Richard snapped. "I would remind you that your actions were treasonous."

"And Robin's were not?" John snorted. "What of his collusion with the constable at Nottingham? My God, we were on the same side."

Robin handed a goblet of sweet-smelling wine to John. "We were not on the same side," he said and lifted his own cup to the king and to John. "But we are now."

"Robin has always acted in my interest," Richard said. "In the interest of England."

John chuckled and drummed the table. "So you finally admit he has been your spy in my camp?"

Richard looked from John to Robin and back again. "It is true, and I will not explain my motives to anyone, including you."

John snorted. "And FitzHenry, Hal's bastard? I truly would like to know more of his story."

"Not now, John. We shall talk later."

Henry gulped his wine, more relaxed despite the glare John shot Robin.

"I look forward to that, and mayhap Robin and his friends—" John turned black eyes on Henry, "can tell me why I have not heard from Lord Weston."

Henry sucked in a breath, but Richard's laughter distracted John.

"Your little spy, brother?" Richard laughed again. "I heard Lady Nichola tossed him out of Lincoln. Henry can give us that story firsthand."

Henry choked. God's nails. De Camville must have written the king. Did Richard know that Nichola had no plans to marry off her daughter to Henry, and that Henry was part of that plot?

"I'm surprised she did not write you herself," Richard added. "Speaking of collusion…" He let his voice trail. No need to remind John the de Camville's had supported John's attempted coup while Richard was on crusade.

John merely shrugged, his face unreadable. It sent a chill through Henry's bones. He and his friends could never trust John. He would not be done with them. In

John's mind, their involvement in the events that prevented him taking the crown before the siege at Nottingham were revenge-worthy. No matter what the king said, John would not let it lie.

Richard downed his wine. "Henry has made quite the impression on the Lady Nichola. You'll tell us of your wedding plans later. After all, there is plenty of time." He slapped Henry's back, ignoring the frown on Stephan's face. "Lovely girl I hear."

Henry forced a smile, unnerved when John eyed him.

"More wine then," John exclaimed smugly. "Henry must need to drown his sorrows since you've given him a mere child, brother. But mayhap he and Robin can share the court whores." A young page blushed as he poured more drinks for the men. John brought a cup to his nose, sniffed, and looked at Robin. "But no, I don't recall Robin taking a whore to his bed whilst he served me. Does our dear Robin have a special lady?"

Henry clenched his fist beneath the table, felt Stephan's hand wrap round his. Robin breathed slowly, showing no emotion. No one at the table said a word, until one drunken knight piped in, "Robin was just telling us—"

"That if he ever had a wife and girl-child," Stephan interrupted, "he'd pray the babe not have an ugly face like his own." Stephan shoved Robin playfully. "Poor child! What a horrible fate."

The king laughed, but John looked skeptical. He swallowed back his wine and then played with food set out on the trestle. Eyes narrowed, he met Robin's and laughed right before plunging his dagger into the roast pig.

forty-five

MARCH - SEPTEMBER 1198

Spring crept in quietly and to Henry's surprise, the truce held. The king's plans for Robin had not yet taken shape, but Robin would be away for weeks at a time and spoke nothing of his work. He'd meet with the king on his return and not cavort with the men. Henry and Stephan tried to draw him out, but he'd have none of it.

As the months drew past, King Richard won more of Philip's liegemen to his side and the noose tightened around the French. Henry and Stephan spent the better part of the summer patrolling the River Seine and protecting deliveries of supplies. Quartered at Les Andelys at the foot of the Rock, as the men called Castle Gaillard, they woke each morning for months on end to the creak and rumble of heavily-laden wagons. The carpenters, stone cutters, miners, and smiths, young and old, trudged up the steep path to begin their daily work. They joined dozens of others who lived in barracks in the castle baileys. By August the castle was nearing completion, and in only two years, an incredible feat.

Harvest ended. War began anew.

King Philip launched raids in the Norman Vexin torching a score of villages. Richard's full troop had not yet mustered at Les Andelys and he felt his hands tied. His mood was foul, like the atmosphere charged for a storm. He wouldn't risk his sixty knights against the larger French force. Shadowing them was frustrating and distasteful, but that would change soon and he watched and paced, waiting for Mercadier's arrival.

They didn't have to wait long. That evening two hundred knights, and twice that number of foot and mounted soldiers, thundered into Les Andelys. The next morning, scouts reported more than seventy French men-at-arms and knights were looting a village five miles from Castle Gaillard.

"Now we will answer Philip's attacks," Richard said and ordered his troops to mount.

When Lionheart's knights approached, the pall from the smoldering village made it seem like a gray winter's day. The French were scattered. A few had mounted, begun their withdrawal and were retreating across farmland. Stephan offered Henry a tight smile. Shields in one hand, lances seated under their arms, the king's men formed up knee to knee and four across. Charging down the hill, Henry felt the pounding of the horses' hoofs through his bones. Ahead, his first enemy dropped his booty, turned and shouted to others. The man started for his shield and gripped his sword. War cries resonated from the men around Henry, but his throat was dry. He couldn't cry out.

The first lances clanged off shields, some found flesh.

Above the cacophonous noise, the screams came to Henry's ears. He shoved them from his mind as the charge broke around him and the knights found their adversaries. He felt his stallion beneath him, a mass of muscle, listened to his own harsh breaths, and focused on a French knight seating himself in his saddle. Miraculously, the man positioned his shield, but couldn't avoid the collision and wobbled when Henry struck him. Henry's lance splintered, the blow snaking up his arm. Henry swung past, pivoting his horse and drawing his sword. The man had no time to flee. Henry was on him again, his blade arcing down powerfully. The strike caught his arm and his sword clattered to the dirt.

"Yield," Henry bellowed, sword inches from the man's throat. Enemy faces suddenly haunted Henry, and blood roared through his head. His stomach roiled. Such a waste... "Get out," he shouted. The knight looked at him like he was mad. "Now."

The knight dug his spurs to his stallion's flanks. Henry watched him, trembling. The French were retreating, but Richard's knights pursued them, slashing viciously. A head flew. Blood spurted like rain. Trails of booty—pots, candles, cloth, remnants of villagers' lives—littered the field. Men fell to the sword, wounded, writhing. Swords crashed, curses and screams lingered on the air.

Henry's horse pranced, anxious, its neck glistening with sweat. Henry tugged his helmet off and shoved back his mail hood. He watched the last of the retreating French, but felt no solace. There was no order to their withdrawal—every man for himself, seeking safe haven in the wood beyond the battlefield.

Breathing hard, Henry removed his leather gloves. Blood of dead men and horses trickled through the trampled fields and he stared at the streams of crimson.

The air reeked of death and turned earth. The smell struck Henry and he almost retched. There was an eerie calm, yet not. There were wounded—groaning, whimpering, crying. Wounded horses too, flailing on the ground, snorting. They would lift their heads, but then laid them against the warm dirt. They didn't scream, but lay silent.

The captured were rounded up. Some thirty knights and sergeants, more than a hundred horses. A good day for King Richard. A bloody day.

More blood flowed in the days that followed. King Richard took Dangu and soundly defeated the French at Courcelles and Boury. Dangu became command headquarters where the men and their horses could find a moment's peace. Richard was restless, anxious for scouts' reports of King Philip's location. Richard claimed he could smell Gisors only some five miles away. The impressive border castle had been a contentious issue for decades between the French and the Angevins, long in the hands of Richard's father. But Philip had taken it while Richard had been imprisoned after the Crusade. Richard wanted it back.

Philip would come to Gisors' aid. It was only a matter of time.

With a small patrol Henry and Stephan crossed to the eastern bank of the River Epte and turned south to reconnoiter. Two other larger patrols followed nearby.

At midday the air turned thick with dust. Henry and Stephan drew close enough to hear the creak of wagons and clink of mail. Close enough to see the enemy. Hundreds of French troops marched north. Three hundred knights by Henry's count, and at least as many men-at-arms and sergeants. Richard was confident Philip would be accompanying the large troop. Gisors might be their final destination, but the king's garrison at Dangu could be under the sword by day's end.

The knights tracked the French, but the troop didn't turn to ford the river. Dangu was safe for the moment. "Marching to Courcelles?" Henry asked.

Richard grunted, smiled. "They don't know it's already in our hands. Stephan," he said, "return to Dangu and rouse Mercadier and the rest of our men."

Stephan started to protest any herald could deliver that message, but Richard gestured brusquely. He was in no mood to have his orders questioned. Drawing a breath, Stephan tipped his head to the king to acknowledge the order, then spurred his mount back through the thick wood and across the river. Richard sent messengers to warn his patrols to stay concealed along the riverside.

An hour passed, then another. Deep within the wood, Richard rendezvoused with his patrols, strengthening his numbers. They shadowed their enemy, knowing it wouldn't be long before the French would be within sight of Courcelles. Once Philip realized the castle had fallen, he would prepare to take it back.

Henry held his stallion's reins tightly, listening, praying to see Mercadier and his two hundred men.

The king grew impatient. "We cannot let them get to Courcelles."

"We should wait for Captain Mercadier, sire," one of the knights said.

Henry's fist clenched. They had less than a hundred knights to three hundred French, plus their foot soldiers. But Philip's men had been marching since early morn, their formation loosening the further north they advanced. Many straggled behind the main troop. The French had no idea King Richard's mesnie was upon them. The time to attack was now.

"We have surprise on our side," Henry said reluctantly. "They've marched near twenty miles and will be tired. Our mounts are fresh."

"We have the advantage," the king agreed. "And we must take it now."

Henry crossed himself and repeated the battle cry of the English. "*Dex Aie, Dex Aie.*" God aid us.

Richard gave a brisk nod. "God will be with us." He straightened in the saddle and drew his sword. His confidence imbued the men with hope and courage and the sound of four score or more blades being drawn from scabbards was like a magnificent chorus. Every scrape, every ping and *whoosh*, echoed in the wood, God's open-air grand cathedral.

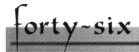orty~six

SEPTEMBER - OCTOBER 1198

At King Richard's signal, the knights charged in a tight wedge from the wood. The unsuspecting French heard the horses' hoofs strike the ground and scrambled to get in fighting positions. French heralds blew their horns. War cries resounded up and down the English line. With lances couched, the knights barreled into the enemy.

The king unhorsed a knight with his first blow. Henry lost his lance, but unseated his opponent. Charging forward, he whipped his sword out, roaring, sighting two men-at-arms crouched behind a wagon. Spurring his horse towards them, he prayed he could get to them before their crossbows were loaded. He slashed down and heard the first man scream. The second aimed his weapon. Pivoting, Henry swung, but not before he felt the swish of the bolt past his head. The soldier dropped the bow and ran. "Fight, you cowards," a harsh voice shouted above the chaos.

At the rearguard sunlight glinted off axes and maces

swung. The clash of swords grew ferocious. Henry plowed down one soldier and stormed into the melee, the fighting so close he could hear the grunts of the men around him as they strained to fend off blades. King Richard batted away a mace with his shield, ever advancing forward. He swept his sword downward driving into men surrounding Philip, leaving dead and wounded in his wake.

Not far behind the king, Henry crossed swords with a knight and brought his shield round to shove the man back. Without warning, his horse screamed. Blood splattered Henry's face and streamed down his hauberk. His horse stumbled and Henry careened into the dirt. The animal writhed beside him as he struggled to stand. Sweat burned his eyes, but spurs clinked at his back and he twisted to avoid another attacker. The soldier came back at him. Henry ducked the swing of his axe, and then beat him off with punishing downward hacks. The man collapsed, his weapon clattering out of reach on the road.

"Do you yield?" Henry shouted, his blade at the man's throat. The Frenchman crossed himself, begged for mercy. Henry acknowledged him and charged off. Advancing towards the king, his sword arced round in ferocious swings. His blade found neck, arm, helmet. Man-to-man combat blurred around him. His arms ached. A sword nicked his face, another sliced into his leather glove. He felt the stings, smelled his blood, but kept moving, unthinking. His lungs hurt, his heart beating so fiercely he swore his chest would crack.

"Retreat," a French voice cried. "Retreat."

The cocoon around Philip surged forward and broke into a gallop. They spurred north towards Gisors, barely two miles away. Philip's knights defended their king, many brave souls remaining in the rear to stop Richard's men. But King Richard and a score of his knights were like mad bulls and blazed through them. And then another hue and cry rang out. Mercadier and his men were charging up the road to join the battle. More soldiers fell to their onslaught.

Henry sheathed his sword and found a riderless horse. He grabbed the reins, but struggled to mount, his body begging to rest, his hauberk too heavy and slick with blood. He exhaled sharply, trying to find the strength to pull himself astride.

A mounted knight reached over the stallion's saddle. "Need a hand?"

Stephan. His spirits lifted and he grabbed Stephan's hand.

Mounted, Henry galloped beside Stephan in King Richard's wake. If they could stop Philip before he reached the safety of his castle—victory!

Philip must have had three score knights surrounding him as he retreated. The ground hadn't been touched by rain for weeks and dust and dirt kicked up by the horses choked the air. Henry couldn't see King Richard though he heard his voice cry out, "*Dex Aie!*"

The sun beat down on them, the wind blasting their faces, and with the dust, it was hard to breathe. From somewhere ahead, Henry heard the vicious clank of swords and drew his own. He exchanged a glance with Stephan and they plunged into the fray. His horse jumped a body on the ground, and there, just ahead, the stone curtain walls of Gisors loomed.

King Richard's troops advanced towards the bridge and the slaughter continued. A dozen men turned to fight, staying back to give King Philip time to enter the city. A hail of arrows sailed from the battlements. The shafts struck French and English alike.

"Sire," Stephan shouted. "Too close!"

"Pull back," Richard ordered. He whipped his stallion round to retreat, curses spewing from his mouth. Philip— almost within his grasp. The bastard had reached the bridge beneath the safety of the defenders' arrows. Richard's voice bled with frustration—almost agony—as he thundered down the road.

Henry started to follow the king, but held back. Bowmen on the battlements had stopped firing and gawked, but not at the fleeing English. "The bridge," someone bellowed.

The bridge swayed and groaned. With a tremendous crack, the wooden beams gave way. French knights and their horses slammed into the river. Cries for help died as men were dragged down by the weight of their armor, drowned unless they managed to grab hold of a horse or floating debris. The noise was deafening.

Sweat poured down Henry's face. His pulse raced. *Stephan*. Memories surfaced—the River Lyon, another bridge. On their way to the Holy Land. Stephan trapped beneath the water. So vivid that Henry gasped for a breath.

A crossbow bolt struck the ground in front of his horse. The animal shied, jerking Henry back, the memories fading beneath the last groans of the bridge.

"Henry, get out of there," Stephan shouted.

A commotion on the opposite riverbank stopped Henry again. "God's blood!" he cried.

Stephan reined in and followed Henry's gaze. Four men dragged a soaked Frenchman from the water while others looked on, shocked and dismayed. Dozens were in the river, but no one else seemed to get the same attention.

"Is that the French king?" Henry asked.

Stephan rose in his stirrups. "It is! Damn you, Philip!" He stabbed the air with his sword.

When they returned to Dangu and King Richard heard he had missed the soaked French rat, there were still drinks all around and cheers and praises to God. Despite Philip's escape, the day's skirmish had been a great blow to the French and to Philip's ego. Richard's troops had captured over one hundred men, many important knights, dozens of men-at-arms, and two hundred horses. "It was not our might, but God's," Richard said, "and the justice for our cause, which triumphed."

Within a few days, Philip mustered his army and attacked and burned Evreux. Incensed, Richard sent Mercadier and savaged Abbeville. The plunder was great that day— French merchants had been gathered for a fair. The routiers came away with leather and gold, stores of goods from the recent harvest, and finely-crafted daggers and blades.

There were victories at Neufmarché and Pacy and after the routs, the king's men gathered at Les Andelys. Wine and tales of valor flowed freely in the hall, the braggadocio inciting more outlandish stories as the evening grew late. They empathized with Earl Robert, distressed he had captured eighteen knights and many men at Pacy, but not recaptured his castle there. William le Queu, the castellan of Lyons-la-Forêt, was in his cups with good reason to celebrate. He had led the raid on Neufmarché at Count John's side, where one hundred twenty French were captured.

At the far end of the trestle, Stephan offered Henry comforting touch, held his eyes. It was enough to be in battle, but to hear the horrors repeated round the table again and again? Henry wasn't certain he could stay any longer.

Stephan grasped Henry's trembling hand and leaned close to whisper, but William's voice rose, suddenly indignant. "A thousand and five hundred knights, Philip says? *And* Mercadier's men. Lying bastard."

"At Neufmarché?" Stephan asked. That was a huge force, one they hadn't seen in four years of fighting. "Philip's French against you and Count John's men?"

"At Gisors," William said and downed the wine in his cup.

Robin looked up. Half-listening, he preferred to ignore any mention of the king's brother. "Where did you hear that?"

"One of the sergeants we captured claims King Philip is spreading word that his men were outnumbered by more than three to one at Gisors."

"He makes excuses for his defeat," Robin scoffed. "His clerks will tell how valiantly he fought. We know the truth. We saw him run and leave his best knights to save his hide. We were there."

The men around them pounded the table with their mugs and raised a toast to King Richard.

"A pity the Capetian bastard did not drown," Stephan said. "Might Archbishop Walter intercede on our behalf and ask God to smite the man from the earth?"

The more sober knights grew wide-eyed. Most knew Stephan had little use for priests, God, and the Church, so his call to the archbishop seemed unnatural.

Henry had to laugh. "Would you go to Mass if he did?" he asked.

Stephan gripped his mug. If he held it any tighter it would crack. "I just might!"

"Go to Mass, then," Count John said. He had come in

unnoticed but now stood behind Stephan. Wind whistled through the open windows, the only sound in a room of thirty men. "Confess your wicked thoughts about asking our Good Lord in heaven to take Philip from us." John glared at Robin, but smiled and slapped Stephan on the back. "Of course, we all have worse sins to confess, eh?"

Henry's skin crawled, but a few others chuckled.

Laughing, John reached over Stephan's shoulder and snatched Robin's wine. He looked pointedly at Robin. "What news from Lincolnshire?"

Robin met John's eyes with mild disinterest, but fire seethed behind his face. He drowned his bread in the thick gravy on his trencher. "None that I've had, my lord," he said and bit into the bread as if taking off John's head.

John gulped down the drink. "I hear that Ringsthorpe is practically deserted. Why did your father leave?"

"His business, not yours or mine, my lord," Robin said coldly.

"Henry's business I would say," John said. "Greyton Manor without its carpenter. A pity. I hear you brag he made the best bows in England."

Robin nodded, his face neutral.

John hammered away, intent on provoking Robin. "My friends tell me Lord Weston is still missing. Didn't you last see him in Nottingham?" Shaking his head, he poured himself more wine. "Such a mystery. That poor dear man must have met some untimely end."

Heat crawled up Henry's neck. Poor dear wife beating, traitorous, blackmailing bastard.

"God's will be done," Robin said and stabbed his eating knife into a chunk of meat.

John frowned, skeptical. "Lord Weston's sister Lady Elle stands to inherit—"

"What are you suggesting?" Henry's voice rose.

"She did not love her brother," John said dryly.

"And that is cause to suggest she might have something to do with Weston's disappearance?" Henry scoffed, aware of the stillness of everyone else around him.

John sniffed at his drink. "Interesting that you defend Lady Elle, Henry. She ignored her brother's wishes when she did not marry you. She chose that landless, penniless squire. Quite the story there, even my own mother involved. So many secrets, plots and intrigue." His eyes grew icy as he brought the wine to his lips and swallowed a swig. He clamped a hand on Henry's shoulder. "But as they say, the truth always outs."

forty-seven

OCTOBER 1198

Quiet descended on the hall after John's departure. A muted conversation wafted from the far end of the room, but most of the knights had bedded down for the night, their loud snores resonating.

Robin stared into the dying embers of the hearth as if watching a ghost. "He knows. Not just about my da, but about Marian and my children." He buried his head in his hands. "I must see the king. I cannot stay here."

Henry nodded reluctantly and Stephan agreed. John hadn't mentioned Marian, but it seemed he knew secrets that could hurt them all—the love Henry and Stephan shared, the foul play in Weston's disappearance.

Henry wondered how Robin would get a private audience with King Richard when Hubert Walter, one of Richard's most trusted advisors and a highly skilled negotiator, arrived the next day. The door to the king's audience chambers remained closed to all while Richard and John met with the archbishop. Stephan and Henry left Robin pacing in the hall, waiting word that Richard would see him, and they had gone to the tiltyard for a practice. Clouds scudded across the sky and rain, now off to the east, had left the ground muddy. Henry ran his lance through the ring and then watched Stephan put spurs to his horse.

An out-of-breath squire ran onto the field as Stephan's lance hooked the ring. Clods of dirt splattered the animal's sleek muscled legs and Stephan's boots and chausses.

"Lord Henry, Sir Stephan," the squire called. "The king wishes to see you."

The knights handed their lances to the young boy and urged the horses towards the bailey. Grooms took their animals near the door and Stephan strode into the hall and up the stone stairs behind Henry.

Robin had been ordered to the king's chamber too and waited—still pacing. Henry couldn't imagine why the king would have all three of them there when only Robin had requested to meet with him. Something was afoot.

The tonsured clerk noted their arrival and hurried into the king's chamber to announce them. Voices carried through the ornate oak door, but when the clerk reappeared he said they must wait. Finally, after Robin must have walked a mile, the door creaked open. A bell was pealing for evening prayers. Henry entered, Robin and Stephan at his heels. The archbishop and Count John were there, and John shot Henry a calculated smile that made him shiver.

The knights greeted the archbishop formally, kissing the flaming red ruby on his extended hand. Hubert, who had seen Robin in Oxford a year earlier, placed his hand on the knight's head. "It is good to see you, my son," he said and offered a blessing before crossing the room to warm himself by the hearth. A large hound there looked up at him, sniffed at his intrusion, and then nestled peacefully on the bearskin rug.

Richard hovered over a map spread on the table. "The Archbishop leaves for Paris on the morrow," he said as the knights drew round. "You will accompany him."

The archbishop seemed taken aback. Robin sucked in a breath. He would jump from the window to escape if he could, Henry thought, glancing from his friend to the others. Henry had little desire to go to the French capital, but might this bring a lasting peace between King Richard and the French?

Archbishop Hubert spoke first, his voice ringing with confidence. "My own men and clerks are sufficient, sire."

"Of course, and they will see to your needs, my lord archbishop," Richard conceded. "I have another task for these three. Have your clerk find them suitable clothing. They should appear to be part of your entourage."

John shifted, his brow furrowed. He seemed as surprised by the king's request as everyone else in the room.

"Sire—" Robin interrupted, but Richard held his hand up and addressed the archbishop.

"I would count on your own men to be discreet about their presence. Thank you, my lord," Richard said, dismissing the man.

Hubert hesitated, but nodded with a bow. "As you wish, sire."

"Richard," John said as Hubert paused by the door, "are you certain I should not accompany Archbishop Hubert? He may be civil but tough with Philip, but I will be blunt." John picked up a wooden figure and tossed it in the air. The dog raised its head, ears perked until John caught the figurine and set it strategically on the map. "Send Mercadier along with us. We will make certain Philip knows we'll be at Paris' gates with an unbeatable force, the likes of which he has never seen."

"The coward is already at my mercy, Johnny," Richard said, "running with his tail between his legs after his embarrassment at Gisors. The Archbishop needs no extra help from you or Mercadier at this time." He gestured towards the door. "Now I must speak with my knights. You and I will talk later."

John wasn't pleased, but hid his displeasure. There was something satisfying about watching John swagger after the archbishop, but Henry could think of little else but being dressed in the archbishop's colors. The king wanted them to slip into Paris unnoticed, and then what?

Robin stood stiffly, his green eyes focused on Richard. The king turned round, met that piercing look. "You do not look pleased, Robin."

"I asked to see you, sire, to tell you that I must return to England."

Richard placed his hands on Robin's shoulders. "You cannot leave now. You must go to Paris to escort Arthur back to Normandy."

Arthur... A deal had been struck then, Henry thought.

"You have the archbishop's men," Robin argued.

"Will King Philip truly release the boy into the archbishop's hands?" Stephan asked. "He might refuse."

Richard agreed. "My faith in you is higher than any other men I know but for Archbishop Hubert himself," Richard said in a tone that spoke of his belief in the knights. This was a king who would trust them with his life. "He alone could not protect the boy, *if* that was his mission. But he will not be escorting Arthur back. You will be infiltrating Paris now. Waiting."

"For what, sire?" Robin asked.

"The Bretons will send their representatives to retrieve Arthur, two of whom will be part of the exchange along with a sizable payment."

"A ransom?" Henry asked. Was it the night air wafting through the open window that sent a chill through his bones? "I didn't think the boy was being held captive."

"As close to captivity as possible with Philip." Richard grunted. "He will give them safe passage, but that will be no guarantee. His own agents, mercenaries, the Bretons themselves, John's men—I would not trust a one of them."

"Philip will claim any attack on Arthur was on your orders," Stephan said.

The muscles in Richard's jaw tightened. "The Bretons would be roused back to war against me. The wound reopened. Others will believe the lies and join them." He wandered to the coffer and poured four cups of wine, offering them to his knights.

"When will the Bretons arrive in Paris?" Henry asked.

Richard raised his drink to the knights. "Just before Christmastide."

"What?" Robin groaned. "You expect us to stay undercover for near two months?"

"I do," Richard said matter-of-factly and tossed back his wine. "If anyone can, it is you."

"I had hoped to be home by Christmas." Robin looked Richard in the eye. "Once Arthur is safely across the border, I *will* return to England. I must protect my family from your brother."

"Truly, Robin, John may be spiteful, but I think you worry too much on his threats." Richard noticed Henry shaking his head. "You agree with Robin?"

"John would have kept you in Philip's dungeons, sire,

bolted the chains round your neck, hands and feet himself." Henry's stomach felt hollow. Speaking so honestly to his liege lord was not easy. "Is he the good, loyal brother now, to stay in your favor? To be heir to the crown?"

Richard sighed, took a gulp of wine. He didn't answer but turned, resting his hand on Robin's shoulder. "Do what you must."

The knights sought haven on the battlements, deserted except for two guards on the opposite tower. Stars blanketed the sky and calmed Henry's concerns about the mission to Paris, but Robin was restless and still unhappy.

"I'll send a message to my brother to keep a closer watch on Marian and your family," Stephan said, offering to ease Robin's fears.

Henry glanced sidelong at Stephan, a smile curling his lip. "Because you are oft in the habit of writing your brother."

Stephan punched Henry playfully. "Then you write to Bea."

Henry considered a moment. "Better yet, through Little John and Elle."

Robin kicked the stone wall, his heart not lightened by his friends' banter. "You could do this on your own."

"You have contacts in Paris." Henry rubbed his hands to warm them. "We need more than the king's spies to get in and out with our lives."

Stephan slid his hand across Henry's back. "The king knows it is likely there will be a threat against Arthur. Three of us stand a better chance than two of surviving this mission and bringing the boy home."

Robin started towards the hall. "We should get some sleep." Looking back he managed a smile and said, "Or whatever it is you two might do."

As Robin's footsteps faded on the stone steps, Henry pressed closer to Stephan. "What might Robin be thinking?"

"I have an idea or two," Stephan said, his hand slipping beneath Henry's tunic. "Did you notice that bearskin rug in the king's chamber?"

Henry turned to face him. "I could imagine being with you there, the fire blazing, but I'm not certain the dog would make room for us." He glanced at a guard silhouetted on the northeast tower. The bailey was quiet. They were alone with only the stars watching. He touched Stephan's cheek, and then brushed his lips with a kiss. A fire would be nice, but not needed tonight. The fire in Stephan's eyes alone would keep him warm.

Henry grew warmer still when Stephan cupped his buttocks, pressed against him, his arousal evident. Henry's blood would boil before the night ended.

Stephan kissed him deeply. His touch was gentle, but hot with desire. Henry's pulse roared in his ears. Stephan's hands roamed his back and buttocks beneath his tunic. His fingers grazed Henry's chest running along every muscle, every scar.

Henry moaned. "I love you," he whispered.

"My heart is yours. Always." Stephan tangled his hands in Henry's hair. Caressing his face, he claimed another kiss that left Henry breathless.

Stephan stepped back, but Henry wrapped his arms round his waist, not willing to let him go. Henry nuzzled against his neck relishing the familiar smell of musk and sweat. His close-cropped beard was scratchy, but that didn't matter. Henry met those blue eyes and stroked Stephan's temple with his thumb. "The times we've been apart—God, I missed you so. The loneliness was unbearable."

Stephan kissed the tip of his nose. "For me as well. Last winter when you went to—"

Henry pressed a finger to Stephan's lips. "Never again. Do you hear me?" His voice cracked. "Never again."

Stephan swung Henry round, pinning him to the stone wall and kissing him urgently, hard. Stephan thrust against him, pressed their braies down. Hard flesh found hard flesh. Trembling in Stephan's arms, Henry's breaths grew ragged, his knees weak. They thrust against each other, moaning into deep kisses to hide the sounds of their lovemaking from anyone but the stars.

forty-eight

OCTOBER - DECEMBER 1198

The French village looked like any one in King Richard's domains. Fields tipped with frost, plowed under until spring planting. The archbishop's retinue trotted down the road under watchful eyes. Peasants held back their young children in the shadows of doorways. They were no different from common folk anywhere Henry had been. These people wanted nothing more than to have a meal to eat and to live peacefully. And they had that in this time of truce, but burnt shells of cottages and a barn and new wooden crosses in the churchyard served to remind them they were at the mercy of their kings.

Henry winced.

"This is not Greyton," Stephan said.

Not wanting to speak about his fear for Greyton, Henry nodded with controlled confidence and gestured at the village. "Another round of negotiations, another chance for peace. For these people and for ours, I pray this one lasts."

If Stephan questioned that response, he didn't say. Ahead, the leading riders had reined in at the gates of an abbey. They'd shelter here, and tomorrow, on to Paris, where the three king's men would slip into the city's underbelly to await the Bretons.

Sleep didn't come easily that night to Henry, but Robin was at ease playing chess with one of the knights. Stephan discovered two of Archbishop Hubert's men had been at Arsuf, the bloodiest battle of the crusade. Henry rolled over to watch the orange and golds of the fire dance in the hearth. He had no desire to relive that war. The nightmares came less often now, the drums and war cries there, but distant. He was finally lulled to sleep by the crackle of the fire.

But a different horror came.

Fire! Greyton consumed by flames.

Henry couldn't breathe. Sweat streamed down his face, burned his eyes.

The hall—nothing but ash. The stone-built part of the house was a blackened shell. Smoke permeated the air. The roof of the chapel burned, the walls collapsing. Wind hurled the fire, the din louder than a raging storm. Henry held his arm up to block the unbearable heat. Backing away, he stumbled over a body—one of his villeins. Another lay nearby. Bodies scattered haphazardly. Tanner's wife, dead. Smith, burned alive. A woman face down in the dirt—dear God—Marian! Blood pooling round her bruised and naked body. A babe on the cobbled stone. Men dressed in black galloped away from Greyton. They wore the crest of John, Count of Mortain.

"NO!" Heart pounding, Henry jerked upright.

"Henry," Stephan cried, pulling him into his arms.

"It's just a dream."

Henry shook uncontrollably. "John…at Greyton. He destroyed it. Killed everyone."

Stephan cradled him, rocking back and forth. "A bad nightmare, love. Nothing more," he whispered and pressed his lips to Henry's forehead. "It will not happen. We won't let it."

"He will never forgive us." Henry choked on his words. "Robin is right. John will never forget."

Henry's cries hadn't woken the archbishop's men, but Robin was watching them. He scrubbed a clenched fist across his forehead, smacked the chess pieces to the floor, and stalked out of the hall.

Gray skies threatened rain, but the archbishop's entourage took to the road and by midday the six- to eight-meter-high walls of Paris loomed. The stone curtain wall was huge and still under construction, but menacing with multiple turrets and gates flanked by towers. Guards scrutinized the crush of people making their way through the gates. Henry was grateful the archbishop's men came in peace today, but glad he wore gambeson and hauberk beneath his cloak.

The knights rode alongside merchants and farmers bringing their wares to sell. They came in mule- and man-drawn carts. Young and old, tired and eager, some so entranced by the formidable walls, the archbishop's men had to tell them to make way. When they saw the mitre atop the archbishop's head and his flowing deep crimson robes, they stepped aside, signed themselves, bowed and gawked.

The crowd thinned as the archbishop's entourage drew closer to the left-bank bridge that crossed to the Île de la Cité on the Seine. The east side of the island was dominated by the cathedral of Notre-Dame, still under construction, its nave lacking a roof. The choir was impressive, dwarfing almost everything in sight. To the west, the great tower of the king's palace soared at least thirty meters high and rivaled it in height. Philip's banner wasn't flying, a sign that he wasn't present. The archbishop would be negotiating with his intermediaries, which was common practice.

The archbishop insisted his attendants visit the cathedral before proceeding to the palace. "We must thank the Heavenly Father for our safe arrival and offer prayers for successful negotiations," he said.

Notre-Dame welcomed them, the scent of incense wafting from the choir. Candlelight flickered beyond the huge pillars that rose to the vaulted ceilings, their majesty undeniable. The holy place reminded Henry of boyhood visits to Lincoln Cathedral. Kneeling, he offered a prayer for Bishop Hugh there and prayed the cathedral's reconstruction thrived under the bishop's guidance.

Stephan and Robin signaled and he crossed himself, then quietly crossed the marble floors to join them in seats at the west end of the choir. Archbishop Hubert and his men departed with little fanfare and without a sideways glance at the three men being left behind who would meld with the crowds after the sun set. Moving about unnoticed would be easier after dark, and they'd find food and shelter with monks of one of the abbeys across the river.

"How do you like our Notre-Dame?" a voice behind them asked.

Robin didn't turn. "Jean, old friend. This place has its merits. But not so impressive as Canterbury." He kept his voice low. "Are you here for the negotiations? Last we met, you were hoping to spirit young Duke Arthur to

Paris."

"And here we are all," Jean said. "Why am I not surprised to see you in our fair city?"

"I have accompanied the archbishop."

"But he just departed for the palace."

"So he did," Robin said with a small smile.

Henry caught Jean de Charny's strong profile from the corner of his eye. It took a moment for Henry to place the man. They had met briefly after the fall of Acre when de Charny served as a trusted advisor to King Philip. The knight's head was bent as in prayer, silvery hair brushing his shoulders. His wrinkled hands rested on the rail behind Robin.

"What of you, Jean?" Robin asked.

"I am here to observe the truce talks. I would prefer to go to my country home, but your king and mine seem determined to hack at each other until one of them leaves this earth. May the archbishop's negotiations bring us long-lasting peace." Jean crossed himself. "As for Arthur, you can imagine King Philip is troubled by the Breton's betrayal."

"Will he let Arthur depart?"

"He will honor that agreement, but may have strong words for the Breton barons who escort the boy. Why the interest in Arthur now, Robin? You came with Archbishop Hubert for the peace talks...ah, never mind." Jean sighed and smiled. "I am far too old for this."

Robin reintroduced Jean to Henry and Stephan. "Seven years since we met in Acre," Jean reminded them. "There are still men here who recall the two English knights who charged across the plain amidst our fleur-de-lis."

Henry would not forget—it was one of his first engagements against the Saracens. He swallowed hard. He killed many infidels that day, but couldn't save one French knight. The image haunted him.

Jean's light voice brought him back. "Why are you still with this rabble?" he asked, cocking his head towards Robin.

"Some of us never learn," Henry said wryly.

"We rather like our rabble," Stephan said.

Robin splayed his hand across his heart. "Me?" he mocked, and chuckled softly.

Jean glanced towards the chancel where two monks knelt on the steps near the altar. The finely carved doors at the other end of cathedral opened and a solemn group of men walked in. A bell began to peal Vespers.

"The abbey of St Bernadette," Jean said.

"Thank you," Robin said, acknowledging the place the men would meet.

Henry took in a deep breath, tried to relax. At least they would have one friend in Paris, he thought. Robin had worked undercover here before, perhaps more times than Henry knew. He was a good judge of men, and he trusted Jean de Charny.

Jean rose, and then disappeared as silently as he'd come.

The negotiations ended less than a week later and from a side street near the abbey of St Bernadette Henry watched Archbishop Hubert's retinue parade out of the city. It was dreadfully cold in Paris for late October, but it was the thought of three of Lionheart's knights against a city of enemies that sent a shiver through his bones.

They passed most days in the shadows of the abbey and ventured to a nearby tavern after dark. Jean appeared once or twice a week, a regular visitor to judge by reactions of those gathered. He would share a few private words with Robin sitting amongst the spirited crowds celebrating another day of peace. French soldiers drank alongside merchants anxious for news of the war, of victories against the English king. There were exaggerated stories of French bravery and no mention of King Philip's spill into the River Epte. Conversation was not for the faint of heart, and the regulars knew of Jean's service in the Holy Land and wanted to know if the fights against the English were as bloody.

Henry gulped down his wine, closing his eyes when Jean described the siege at Acre. Drums and war cries pounded in Henry's head, so loud he could not hear Jean. Stephan pressed a hand to his knee. Startled, he sucked in a breath. Jean had been in the midst of telling the others of an Englishman's bravery that day in Acre, but he paused, looked at Henry with empathy and quickly ended his story.

It was early December when Jean reported the Bretons had arrived. Huddled in a corner of the tavern they had a last drink with the French knight.

"Be cautious on the road west," Jean said.

"That is our plan," Stephan said.

Jean pursed his lips, nodding. "Our patrols report there are robbers attacking travelers."

"French wolves in sheep's clothes?" Robin asked, but Jean only shrugged. "King Philip needs little reason to blame us should any harm come to the boy."

"Reason? Does Philip have any?" Henry scoffed. "Philip wins whether the boy lives or dies. Dead, and King Richard faces a two-front war against the Bretons *and* the French. Alive, Arthur may yet turn his allegiance back to Philip. And Philip pulls the strings on his little puppet."

Jean winced. "You don't mince words, Henry. I do not

know my king's mind, but I should know him well enough not to be surprised by his actions, especially where your lord is concerned." Jean swirled the ale in his cup and brought it to his lips, but then paused and asked, "The Bretons. Do you trust them?"

Robin exchanged glances with Henry and Stephan. "We trust no one."

forty-nine

The young duke left the royal palace two days later accompanied by ten men. Heavy cloaks hid their garb, and someone must have convinced them to keep the ducal crest packed away. Arthur rode a black bay in the middle of the entourage. Despite their numbers, the group drew little attention riding through Paris' streets. Their pace picked up after they crossed the Seine. Stephan and Henry hung back to keep watch while Robin scouted ahead of the party. As far as Henry could tell, the Bretons didn't seem concerned about the potential for danger.

The city walls faded in the distance. Morning dragged into midday and the sky darkened. Temperatures dropped and rain and sleet fell intermittently. More of the same bedeviled them the second day, hounding them like a wolf pack. That night the duke's men settled in the hall of a fortified manor.

"Who wants to sleep with a dozen snoring knights

anyway," Stephan said when Henry led them towards the barn after grooms had tended to the duke's horses. "Two snoring is quite enough." He winked at Henry.

Unpacking, the three knights tossed damp cloaks across the stalls to dry out. They removed their chausses, gambesons, and hauberks, and changed into clean tunics and red and gold surcoats that bore King Richard's lions.

A steward admitted them to the hall. Arthur played chess with one of his knights by the hearth. Conversations were cut short and the men there, including the boy's tutor, looked up. Andre shook his head. "You three are like a bad dream."

Henry rested his hand across his heart. "King Richard sent us to keep watch over Duke Arthur." He turned to the boy and bowed. "My lord."

Arthur's advisors grumbled, but Andre calmed them with a wave of his hand. "We are quite capable of—"

"I need no help from you." Arthur scoffed.

Robin cleared his throat. The boy was as arrogant as the day almost three years earlier when they had saved his life. "We are following orders from the king, my lord. Surely you will not mind if our men watch for assassins."

Henry and Stephan glanced back, implying the world beyond the oaken door was a dangerous place.

Arthur followed their gaze and took the bait. He hadn't forgotten the attack. "Where are your men?"

"Well hidden beyond the gates, my lord," Henry said. "We don't want your enemies to know our strength."

Exhaling sharply, Arthur gave a quick nod. "Eat," he commanded, "and then coordinate your watch of the manor with my men."

✦

Robin bit into a chunk of bread, chewed and swallowed it back with some wine. They were seated at the far end of the trestle, not mingling with Arthur's men. "The duke is growing up," he said softly.

"Still arrogant as hell," Henry said.

Robin nodded. "I need some sleep. One of you take the first watch."

"Can't we have our large force of hidden men keep an eye on the place?" Stephan chuckled.

Wind buffeted the door and rattled the oil cloth on the windows. "It will be a cold night out there," Henry said.

"Which is why I suggest you take first watch." Robin rose and said, "I'll take second and you can come inside and warm each other up."

Heat crept up Henry's neck. He was glad the candle on the trestle guttered, hiding his face burning with the thought of being in Stephan's arms.

Stephan stabbed a piece of fish, dangled it from his dagger, and scowled. "How long until Christmastide?"

"Eat your fish." Henry laughed. "This is better than the salted herring in our packs."

"Aren't travelers allowed a bit of meat? Or soldiers?"

"Just old people, the sick, and young children." Henry jabbed him in the side, took a bite, and wiped his mouth on his sleeve. "It's not so bad."

Stephan stared past the dripping chunk of fish and looked at Robin. He was having none of their banter. "Thinking of Marian?" he asked.

"I hoped to be with her for Christmas." His voice held sadness, but acceptance. "I do this for the king. But after this, no more." He tipped his flask and emptied it. "And that will be the last time I say that."

"Mayhap there will be a letter from Little John when we reach Les Andelys on the morrow," Henry said, hoping for Robin's sake there might be word of his wife and child.

Stephan stood and retrieved his cloak. "Here's to a quiet night." He shielded his face from the cold wind when he opened the door and headed outside.

"You and Stephan should go back to England," Robin said when he and Henry left a few minutes later to spread their blankets in the barn.

"My betrothed's mother would not appreciate that." With Henry and Stephan across the Narrow Sea, Nichola didn't have to think of them. But Greyton would be too close, a constant reminder. He'd thought of York, and though the brothers l'Aigle had put their dislike for each other aside, Stephan wouldn't want to be part of his brother's mesnie. But Nottingham—only five and twenty miles…

Settled in the barn, Henry closed his eyes. Nottingham. He could easily travel there every month, whether on king's business or his own. Check on Allan and Robin's operation. He sighed, curling up beneath his blanket, letting his dreams take him home.

A cold nose nuzzled his neck. He jerked up, but Stephan pulled him back and spooned his body. His cold fingers fisted against Henry's chest. Henry turned and pecked his cheek. He couldn't think of anything but sleep, and Stephan didn't press him. It was enough to be alone together, close like this, Stephan's warm breath on his neck, their hands entwined.

Sleep quickly captured them both. Henry didn't hear a thing until Robin shook him awake in the dead of the night. His watch was quiet and when the household woke, he slipped back into the barn. Robin and Stephan had been forced to rise when two squires stumbled in to saddle the duke's horses. A servant appeared with hot porridge and they ate greedily. With the sun barely up, they were on the road.

Many hours later Arthur held back to let Henry draw up beside him. "Is it as huge as they say? Richard's castle?" he asked, skeptical of rumors that must have surfaced in Paris and bubbled in Philip's palace.

"One of the largest I have every seen," Henry said. "And I have seen quite a few."

Arthur's dark eyes lit. "Philip would grow red in the face if anyone spoke of it."

Henry hid a satisfied smile, threw a sidelong glance at Stephan riding beside him. Philip must have thrown a tantrum when Richard ignored the pope's demand to stop construction.

"You will be impressed, my lord," Henry said. "If not for the trees and hills here, we might see it in the distance by now."

"It would take ten years to build such a place, but the king has seen it completed in just over two," Stephan added. "It sits high above the river on the Rock—well, you will see it soon."

"We will stay only a day to two." Arthur pulled his cloak tighter. The cold wind howled round them, trees swaying menacingly. "Will you accompany us to Dinan?"

Henry dreaded the thought of another week on the road, but Arthur's civil behavior was a welcome change. Would that last or would the spoiled child erupt? "It is what the king has ordered," he said.

"Maman writes she will throw a huge Christmas feast in my honor." Arthur's tutor Andre had brought that news in a letter from the duchess. Anything that arrived solely through French messengers was suspicious. There's hope for the boy, Henry thought.

"Maman said Emlyn will be there," Arthur added. "You remember her? Maman has become quite fond of her as I knew she would. It will be a grand feast, and you must stay, be my guest. Brittany has pledged allegiance to your king—"

"Your uncle," Stephan reminded him.

Arthur nodded. "Maman does not like him." He chuckled. "I may be a child in her eyes and yours, but I am no fool. I learned many things whilst at the French court. Now I would like to have your impressions of King Richard."

Henry dared to hope Arthur would be open to hearing him out. He would share the good with the bad. He was ready to begin that conversation, but Arthur spurred his horse. He forced two men traveling in the opposite direction to separate. Both travelers frowned at the boy's impudence, and Henry shook his head. The riders formed back up on the road and stopped. Henry shifted behind Stephan to get past them, suddenly wary. He scrutinized their powerful mounts and dirty, unkempt cloaks.

Shouts suddenly erupted from the front of the retinue, but instinct kept Henry's focus at their backs. "Behind us," he shouted.

Stephan pivoted in his saddle. "Shields," he cried and whipped out his blade.

Behind them, the two strangers had swords drawn. Assassins? Robbers? To the credit of the Arthur's men, no cries to "Protect the duke" rang out.

Henry and Stephan backed their horses closer to the duke's men to tighten the circle around Arthur.

"Get out of our way," Andre ordered from the front of the line.

Henry looked over his shoulder. He couldn't see Arthur's face, but the boy gripped his shield in one hand, a long blade in the other. Robin was speaking to Andre, his words lost to the wind. Their adversaries stayed stone still, but Henry caught movement from the trees—there were more of them.

Robin must have seen them too and shouted, "What do you want?"

Henry swallowed hard but nudged his horse forward. Assassins would have attacked them already, used the element of surprise. They would be dead. These men couldn't be John's or sent by the French king. Did they know Duke Arthur and mean to ransom him?

"We are on king's business," Henry said. "Be on your way."

Suddenly, angry voices swept through the duke's men. "This is Richard's doing!"

"Angevin devil!"

"Bastard!"

Henry couldn't believe it—the Bretons thought the attackers were king's men.

"No," cried Robin, with Henry and Stephan repeating his chorus. Two Bretons drew swords and held Henry and Stephan at sword point. Another knight launched himself at Robin. They hurtled to the ground, rolling to a stop in front of a broad-chested man who emerged from the wood.

"Fools!" the man bellowed, his sword resting on Robin's cheek. "Silence, all of you. My men grow impatient." The leader gestured, his dark cloak billowing in the breeze. Men with bow, a few with crossbows, stepped into view. "Drop your swords!" he ordered. "Get off your horses. I'd hate to have my men loose their bolts."

There were too many of them to fight their way out, even if the Bretons fought with them.

"Outlaws?" Henry whispered to Stephan as swords clanked to the ground.

Stephan tossed his down. "Let us hope," he said,

jumping down from his horse.

Two score or more bowmen targeted them. There was little they could do but comply. At least they were still alive.

The Bretons surrounded Arthur and Andre rested a trembling hand on his shoulder. *Keep quiet, boy,* Henry thought. Anger simmered in Arthur's eyes, but he exchanged a glance with his tutor and held his tongue.

The outlaw leader let Robin and his Breton attacker stand, gesturing them towards Andre. He waved his own men forward. One, a gaunt man with a dirt streaked face and filthy hands, held out a well-worn leather bag. "Jewels, coin—careful, slow," he croaked at Henry. "We won't take your life, but…" He eyed their fine horses greedily.

Henry untied the silk purse from his belt and emptied it for the outlaw. He wore no jewels unlike some of Arthur's men who grumbled as they removed their gloves. The thieves were happy to slap the gloves into their belts, pluck rings from fingers, and seize brooches, pins, and silver chains from round their necks. The outlaw pointed the tip of his sword at Henry's leather chain. "It's a wooden cross from my mother, God rest her soul," Henry said, holding it out for the man to see.

The man crossed himself. "Keep it."

Stephan had two pennies in his pouch. The outlaw shook his head. "Least your mount is pretty."

"He doesn't like strangers," Stephan said.

"We'll see about that," the man replied and grabbed the reins.

"Men—let's be off!" the outlaw leader cried. His men swept away with all their horses and pack animals.

Andre turned to Robin. "How far to Les Andelys?"

"Half a day's walk," Robin said, brushing the dirt from

his clothes.

No one said a word. The men retrieved their swords where the outlaws had left them. A good thing Henry supposed.

Hours later, Arthur led his entourage up the steep path to Castle Gaillard.

fifty

DECEMBER 1198 - JANUARY 1199

No matter how many times he stood atop one of Castle Gaillard's nine towers, Henry's sense of majesty and awe never diminished. Even the young duke Arthur had been impressed. It was a pity King Richard had not been here the two days of their stop to show it off to Arthur himself. It could have created a strong bond between nephew and uncle.

Daily on the journey west to Dinan, and in what time they had at the palace there during Christmastide, Arthur questioned the knights. Andre had schooled him on Outremer, the siege of Acre, and Breton involvement on the march towards Jerusalem. Arthur could name every Breton knight who had not returned. He was a good listener, interested in Stephan and Robin's views of the crusade. Henry chose to escape those conversations, and two days after the sumptuous Christmas feast, the knights turned back to Castle Gaillard.

But Robin bid them good-bye, turning south on the

second day on the road. He would leave for England soon, but wanted to pay one last visit to Queen Eleanor. She was three years shy of eighty and their paths might never cross again.

"I owe her my life." Robin exhaled, nodding, seemingly deep in thought about the twists and turns that had led him from carpenter's son to one of Richard's trusted knights. Work he had undertaken for the queen would go to the grave with him.

When he secured his saddle pack, Stephan tossed him a flask of wine. "You sacrificed more than you knew—Marian, Robert."

"I would not blame the queen mother for a decision—and my stubbornness—that kept me away from Greyton all those years." He tied the wine to a hook on the saddle and turned round.

"I cannot believe you're leaving for good." Henry embraced Robin, tears in his eyes. "It will not be the same here without you."

"We shall see each other in England." Robin's arms tightened around Henry. "I'm sure of it."

Henry planted a kiss on Robin's cheek, then pulled away.

Stephan grabbed Robin by the arms. "You give my brother the letter I wrote. He will answer to me if he does not offer you a place in his household."

"It is a good thing you and Gil have made amends, else, with words like these he might slay me at his door." One brow arched, Robin offered a lopsided smile.

Stephan gave him a brotherly hug. "Bring my family and yours our greetings."

"And God be with you," Henry added.

Two to three days from Les Andelys, Henry and Stephan

arrived at Falaise. King Richard and his entourage had arrived two days earlier, having spent Christmas at Domfront. He was not so much in a festive mood, but cheered somewhat when he sat with the knights and Henry spoke of their journey with Arthur. "He seems more amenable to being your ward, sire. Who wouldn't be if he had the run of a great castle?"

"He has no choice," Richard said harshly, then rubbed his brow and looked more conciliatory. "You appear to have a rapport with the lad, Henry. When this business with Philip is concluded—soon, I hope—I shall send you two west to retrieve...er, ask him to join me at Castle Gaillard."

"The French king—is he the reason for your foul humors, sire?" Stephan asked.

"The Capetian, the pope, his legate." Richard wrapped his hand around his goblet. His knuckles turned white, his reddening face a sharp contrast as he told of Pope Innocent III's proclamation of a new crusade. The papal legate Peter of Capua had been sent to encourage Richard to end hostilities with the French. Remembering his promise to return to re-take Jerusalem, Richard capitulated, agreeing to terms based on the status quo, each king keeping the castles they currently held. "And then the legate suggested—at the Pope's request—I should release the bishop of Beauvais because he is a servant of God. The Pope! He would intercede on behalf of that bastard after ignoring pleas for my release when the Emperor Henry kept me prisoner?" Richard spat into the floor rushes.

Henry was incredulous. The warrior bishop had been captured, sword-wielding, fully armored and in the midst of a skirmish. He was no innocent by-stander, but his worse offense had been his treatment of Richard while he was a prisoner of the Holy Roman Emperor.

The legate had hastily returned to Paris to arrange a meeting between the two kings, set for the feast of St. Hilary. The legate was fortunate his departure preceded news about Count John. The knights had been in the hall with the king the eve of the Calends of January when another messenger from France arrived.

Richard stared at the seal—Philip's seal. Breaking it, he unfolded the letter. "My brother." He exhaled angrily and then downed his wine.

Conversation in the hall died. Henry exchanged a worried look with Stephan. What had John done now?

The flickering flame of a rush light on the far wall cast a pale sickly glow on the king's face. Richard's hair had faded to a dingy reddish-gold and was peppered with gray, but like his beard, well kempt. He seemed exhausted, not that Henry could blame him after nearly five years of fighting the French.

Richard thumbed the ingrained lion design on his cup. "John has taken up with Philip against us."

"Christ," Henry muttered. "Surely not, sire. This is Philip's doing, to sow suspicion and set you and your brother against each other." To think John would willingly give up all he had earned from Richard these five years made little sense.

Richard wasn't listening. Before anyone else dared speak, he shouted orders that all John's lands on both sides of the Narrow Sea should be seized.

Word traveled quickly throughout Normandy of the king's displeasure, and John stormed through the gates at Les Andelys the day before the Epiphany. He had come with only two men, both detained, their weapons seized by guards just inside the bailey. John tossed off his sword belt and strode ahead with grim determination, his boots pounding the stone cobbles.

In the hall, many men had just returned from mid-afternoon prayer at the chapel. Spying John, knights surrounded the king, swords drawn, but Richard waved them to his side. John drew down to his knees before his brother.

"My king, my brother—Philip lies! He will do anything to tear us apart." John met his brother's calculating eyes. "I have not pledged my fealty to him. I swear to you on everything that is good and holy."

Richard grunted. "Holy? Do you know the meaning of the word?"

"So it is not one of my virtues." John spread his palms up and cast his eyes at the floor.

Nervous laughter whirled through the room, but not from Henry. He couldn't think of any good qualities John might possess. Next to him Stephan frowned, echoing Henry's thoughts, mirroring Richard's whose breaths were slow and resolute. The laughter died quickly.

"What must I do to prove my loyalty, sire?" John asked.

Richard inclined his head, studied his brother, letting the silence dig at John as he knew it would. Henry chastised himself for thoughts of John being chained in a dungeon, but he couldn't forget John's cruelty and his orders to Robin to murder young Arthur. *He cannot be trusted.*

Finally, Richard bellowed, "Do you deny that Philip has a charter with your name on it?"

"I do. I swear on Maman's soul, Richard! I have sent two of my knights to the French court to protest, to demand the Capetian bastard show this charter he claims to have. Trust me, sire. No one at the French court will produce this document. You must believe me."

Richard's green eyes flicked around the room while the quiet lingered. "Get up, Johnny," he finally said.

John was forgiven, though the king ordered him to stay at Les Andelys until his own spies could verify John's assertion. Henry tried to avoid the count, but when John saw him, it was like a moth drawn to a flame.

"Hello love-birds," John said.

Henry ignored him and the poke from Stephan against his thigh under the table. He stuffed a gravy-soaked chunk of bread in his mouth.

Leaning forward John set his goblet on the trestle. "Where is your little Robin bird?" He forced his way on to the bench between them. "In Paris? Spreading rumors about me? Hm?"

"You imagine things, my lord," Stephan said.

Incensed, Henry couldn't hold his tongue. "Robin is an honorable man and would not speak ill of any man, unless it was a truth."

In the middle of gulping his wine, John choked. Coughing, he wiped his mouth on his sleeve. "You're right, of course." He picked at the platter of roasted chicken near Stephan. "I hear he plans to return to Lincolnshire. Taking up carpentry with his da?"

Henry heard treachery in John's voice, but Stephan laughed. "Can you imagine Robin as a carpenter?"

That thought made Henry chuckle, but John kept niggling away. "Or will he be checking up on FitzHenry...Allan, isn't it? I do think my brother is too trusting leaving a boy with access to the treasury there in Nottingham. Such temptation. But wait—another honorable man. Ha! Am I right?" John filled a trencher with chicken, studying Henry and Stephan. "I can be pleasant. On occasion." Standing, he tossed meat from the table to the dog and her pup hanging at his heels, and then wandered towards the knights sitting with the Earl of Chester.

Five days later, the papal legate sent word—Philip had agreed to the terms of a truce. Richard sailed up the Seine to their designated meeting place not far from Philip's castle at Vernon. English and French knights faced off on opposite sides of the river, banners billowing like sails on the sea.

On the riverbank, Henry rested easily when the king's boat dropped anchor mid-river. Richard had sworn he would not dock and leave himself vulnerable to the French. The presence of the pope's representative, Peter of Capua, did nothing to inspire his trust in Philip. Astride a sleek black destrier on the shore, Philip sat stiff-backed and surly and wrapped in a jewel-trimmed ermine cloak. Underestimating his treachery, even under a flag of truce, would be a mistake.

From the far bank the legate greeted King Richard, his voice muffled by the rustle of tree branches and the banners snapping in the wind. Henry shifted on his horse, his scabbard scraping against his mail chausses.

Richard stood in the boat in the bright January sunlight. His silver helm had a golden crown encrusted with emeralds and rubies. His deep crimson cloak billowed revealing the lions on his surcoat. "Come aboard," he called to Philip and waved towards food and drink spread beneath the canopy.

Henry watched the French closely as Philip declined the offer. Peter of Capua shouted the terms of the five year truce to conclude their business and Richard's boat sailed back towards Les Andelys.

fifty-one

MARCH 1199
Châlus-Chabrol, Limousin

The truce of St. Hillary's day halted hostilities with the French in Normandy, but rebellious barons in the Limousin gave King Richard no rest. Mercadier and his men, sent south to deal with the insurrection, were attacked by a large force and suffered great losses. To no one's surprise, the attack had been led by four French counts. King Philip denied any involvement.

Within days of that crushing blow, Richard's spies discovered Philip was building a castle on the Seine between Gaillon and Boutavant. "What of our accord? You see what a snake he is," Richard said. He summoned his chancellor to deliver word to Philip—demolish the castle immediately or the truce was ended and he would attack. Tired of Philip's games, Richard urged the chancellor to suggest terms for a new treaty that might lead to a more lasting peace.

By the Calends of March, Count John had been exonerated of charges that he had switched his allegiance to King Philip. No one in Paris could produce a charter showing John's seal and granted by the French king. Philip's accusations against Count John were indeed false. Exhilarated, Richard ordered a celebration and his servants prepared a lavish feast despite the Lenten season. It was a huge gathering, with more bishops, earls, chaplains, barons, and knights together than at court in Rouen two Christmases past.

Stephan settled in for a game of chess with Will Marshal, but Henry left the feast early, weary of talk of war and of John's voice. He was almost asleep when Stephan entered the small room they shared.

"Awake?" Stephan whispered.

Henry grunted and rolled over, watching Stephan undress.

"Will told me we leave day after the morrow to join Mercadier's forces," Stephan said as he sat on the bed and tugged off his boots.

That decision didn't surprise Henry. Despite the loss of men from the earlier French attack, Mercadier was besieging the castle at Châlus but King Richard's presence would send a message to the viscount of Limoges and his friends.

"What of John?" Henry asked. "Will he accompany the king?"

Stephan brushed Henry's hair away from his eyes. "Forget him."

"Make me," Henry said, his voice lusty.

Stephan's hand slid beneath the blanket and moved down to stroke Henry's hardening flesh. "I will." He smiled.

Henry moaned, his fingers combing through Stephan's

hair. He pulled Stephan closer, tilting his chin up, caressing his face. Stephan threw off the blanket and goose bumps spread across Henry's skin. Leaning in, Stephan teased him with kisses and writhed as Henry's hands slid into his braies.

"Yes," Henry gasped, grasping Stephan's hips, "you will."

Stephan's touches, gentle or rough...slow...fast...filled Henry with fiery desires. Not lust, but joy with words of love. Their kisses became urgent, deep. Henry buried himself deep in his lover. And later when Stephan took him, love spilled from their tongues. They pledged to let no one tear them apart.

"Until death, I am yours," Stephan said.

Henry kissed him. "And you are mine."

The castle at Châlus-Chabrol dominated the landscape overlooking a valley flecked with small villages. Mercadier's troop had ravaged fields and farms when they'd moved in. Richard's men added to the devastation, taking what they needed from grain stores and smoke houses. The locals had fled, knowing there would be no relief, and the castle garrison had only two score defenders.

Châlus-Chabrol was bleak and cold that twenty-sixth day of March. Days of nasty weather and the recalcitrant traitors inside the castle were trying the king's patience. Hammers beat steadily throughout the day, and siege machines loosed one barrage after another. While the sappers dug ever closer to the walls, messengers from the garrison finally ventured out with a white flag, wishing to offer terms to end the siege.

"Get out of my sight!" Richard's voice resounded from the command pavilion.

Outside the king's tent, Henry and Stephan had been warming themselves by the fire. Both knights shot to their feet, hands on the hilts of their swords. Richard's visitors practically tripped over each other backing out of the pavilion. A squire pitched them the reins of their horses and the two hastily retreated to the castle.

Richard shoved back the flap of the tent to watch them, shaking his head. "Idiots," he muttered, and then shouted, "Idiots!" A squire handed him a cup of wine which he downed. "Don't come begging for me to bend. Surrender, else you will all hang."

The men couldn't have heard the king's final shouts, but Henry imagined Richard had not minced words with them. The besieged do not suggest terms to their king. Fight to the death or surrender—those were the only options when faced with the Lionheart. Surrender, and then Richard would show mercy.

"Won't be long now, sire," a bent old man called. His cart was piled high with dirt from the tunnel.

"God's will," Richard replied.

A rain of bolts and arrows from the battlements began, just a brief show of defiance, but enough that the thumps and pings of strikes against the sappers' tunnel made Henry cringe. The defenders were spare with shots. There was little to be gained from firing at those who worked safely beneath the wooden tunnel to undermine the castle walls.

Richard signaled one of his commanders up the line and a siege machine groaned. A huge boulder sailed across field and ditch, its shadow like a menacing wraith. It darkened the tower and crashed against it, the noise reverberating through the camp. Shards of rock flew into the air, the choking dust forcing the defenders back from the ramparts. The sounds of rock settling on the ground were buried beneath the cheers of Richard's men.

The king shouted, "Again!"

The stone thrower's crew cranked the windlass bending back the beam. Richard watched them, their sweat-streaked faces gleaming with pride. The sergeant checked the firing position and nodded to the king. Richard snapped his head and the siege machine whipped the boulder in the sling towards its target.

Richard paced away from the tent with Mercadier alongside him. Henry and Stephan quickened their steps, shields raised towards the garrison to provide cover for the king. Richard, as was often his habit, left his own shield in his tent and wore only his helm. Mercadier, fully armored, pointed out the sappers' progress as they walked. "A matter of days," the captain said. That wall would come tumbling down.

"Then we shall move on the viscount's castles at Nontron and Montagut," Richard said with a satisfied smile. "Aimar of Limoges will have nothing when we finish with him." The viscount had been a thorn in Richard's side for more than twenty years, and while the Norman borders were quiet, Richard would crush the rebellious baron and his friends.

A bolt slammed into Stephan's shield and he staggered, pitching into Henry. The other knights and squires scrambled to cover Richard. Henry remained upright eyeing the bolt that sliced into Stephan's shield, its tip inches from flesh. Heart thudding, he was comforted by Stephan's crooked smile and helped him find steady legs.

"Stephan?" Richard pressed shields aside despite the best efforts of his men to protect him.

"I am fine, sire," Stephan said.

Mercadier gaped at the battlements. He chuckled, and

Richard and everyone surrounding him followed his gaze. Waving a frying pan in the air, one lone defender blocked bolts fired from the king's crossbowmen.

"Is he a soldier or a cook?" Richard laughed and gestured for his own crossbow. He took aim and the bolt soared, smacking the iron pan. The soldier dropped his makeshift shield and took aim at the king. Shaking his head, Richard said, "Courageous little sod."

The words were barely out of his mouth when Richard grunted and lurched backwards. Henry and Mercadier caught him, the others round him oblivious. Henry's breath caught. The crossbowman's bolt lodged in the king's shoulder. "Sire!" Henry cried. It looked deep. A hand's width away, and Richard might have been killed. Henry's worst nightmare…

Richard grabbed Henry's arm to steady himself. "God's nails," he muttered angrily.

Sweat broke out on Stephan's forehead and he blinked rapidly, gaping at the king. William de Braose, another of the king's barons, realized what had happened and guided Richard back to his tent. Mercadier hurried Henry and Stephan along, ushered them inside to keep them quiet. There was no need for word of the king's injury to spread. No one need know…yet.

Sitting down hard on a stool, Richard took the cup of wine de Braose offered. He was breathing hard, obviously in pain. Mercadier sliced his tunic open to reveal the entry point. Richard growled at the shaft protruding from his left shoulder. "All night, do you hear?" He met de Braose's eyes. "Keep the mangonels pounding that tower all night, all day, until the bastards surrender." He smashed his fist against the trestle, his voice unflustered.

Henry swallowed hard. He couldn't take his gaze from the king. Surely the others in the tent felt as helpless as he did. Stephan saw his concern and leaned close to whisper. "It's the Lionheart—he's not like other men. He'll be fine."

Richard grabbed the shaft and winced. "Any of you ever extracted…?" He didn't finish the question, didn't give the men a chance to answer, just started to yank on the bolt.

"No, sire, don't—" Mercadier shouted too late.

The shaft broke. Not a piece of it visible, the iron head remained buried deep in Richard's shoulder.

"Get a surgeon." Richard scowled. "I do not make it easy for him."

Mercadier raced away while de Braose and Henry helped the king to the cot and Stephan lit every oil lamp and candle. The surgeon would need good light to do his work. Richard took a long draught of wine. "I am one ahead of you, Stephan."

At first Henry thought the king was talking about the drink. He always figured Richard's size allowed more tolerance for wine. Henry had seen him drink twice as much as most men and not be in his cups.

"I wish it were not so, sire," Stephan said.

Not drinks, Henry thought, but one more wound by crossbow. Only those two would keep count. Richard's last had been at Gaillon; Stephan's at Nottingham when the king's men took the outer bailey.

"And this one not even in the midst of battle. Christ," Richard said angrily and groaned. "This one," he paused, wincing, "hurts like shite."

"What can I get you, sire?" Henry asked.

"Mayhap a priest."

Henry must have paled because Richard laughed, then uttered another loud groan.

Within minutes Mercadier and his surgeon arrived.

The man cleansed the king's shoulder at the entry point to soak up excess blood and probed the wound with deft hands. He exhaled sharply several times, wiped his brow, called for linens and water, and unrolled his tools and herbs.

"I must dig it out, sire," the surgeon said.

"Get to it." Richard bit into the hilt of long dagger as the physician began his work. His eyes bulged, then closed as the pain increased from the man's cutting into his flesh. Sweat glistened on his skin, and a tear slid from beneath his eyelids. He began to thrash and the knights held him down. A moment later, he blacked out from the pain.

Greyton in flames flashed through Henry's mind. *No!*

"Henry?"

The voice sounded distant. It called again softly, but Henry could only look from Richard's face to his own hands. They were pale, white, drenched with sweat. His arms felt weak and ached from the effort to keep them from trembling.

"You can let go," Stephan said laying a gentle hand on his arm.

Henry's breath rasped, but he nodded and let Stephan lead him away. He had been in battlefield hospitals more times than he liked, including at Stephan's side. He had seen healers treat wounds from swords and daggers, seen bolts and arrows extracted, limbs lost. But none like this, deep and lodged in bone and muscle. The surgeon looked up worriedly at Mercadier and de Braose. Intent, the man focused on his work, the life of the king in his hands.

Outside, the sun had set, but the camp was lit by bonfires. Henry and Stephan guarded the entryway into the tent, turning away those who sought an audience with the king. The siege machine loosed round after round of missiles at the castle. The crash of stone against stone shook the command tent and the surgeon uttered a "Thank God" lifting the iron bolt for all to see. Henry shifted to look at the king who lay still, covered in blood.

"Is he alive?" de Braose croaked.

"He lives," the surgeon said and doused the wound with wine. He mixed herbs to make a paste that would aid healing and fight infection, and then wrapped the king's shoulder with clean linens. He was still at the bedside when Richard woke late that night and asked for food and drink.

Relief washed over Henry, and from his pallet near the door he whispered a prayer and drifted back to sleep. The next day the king was stiff and in pain, but seemed in good spirits. He spoke lucidly of the surgery with Mercadier and the surgeon, but spent most of the time drifting from wake to sleep.

Two days after surgery, the king moved easier and enjoyed more waking hours. The surgeon had confined him to bed, but Mercadier and de Braose delivered reports on the engineers' progress on the tunnel and Richard followed with orders. Stephan or Henry brought his meals. "You'll be back on your horse in no time," Stephan told him when he complained about what he called his incarceration. No one else was allowed to see him, his injury still withheld from the troops.

The ground shook beneath Henry's cot on the twenty-ninth day of March. The din of the siege engine teased him from a deep sleep, but it was the crash of a wine jug and cups onto the ground that startled him. Henry sat up, thinking the king had tipped them trying to grasp his drink.

Sunlight filtered into the tent. Richard sat on the edge of bed, the light illuminating his contorted face. His gaze drifted from his sweat-drenched bare chest to his arm. Henry would have cried out, but his mouth was dry, his heart racing. He stared at the king's inflamed flesh.

"Jesu, Jesu," Richard muttered, "I am dead."

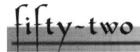fifty-two

MARCH - APRIL 1199

Stephan and Henry hurried to Richard's side. Richard sucked in a breath. "Stephan, get the surgeon and Mercadier. Hurry."

"And my clerk," he called before Stephan bolted through the tent flaps.

Richard's face was sheathed in sweat, his cheeks blistering with heat. A jagged red streak jutted down his arm just below the bandage. A second scored his chest. Henry recognized the signs, had seen them on wounded soldiers. Infection had set in.

Henry took a cloth dipped in water and sat beside the king. He wiped Richard's face with shaking hands, his mind numb. *God, dear God... My king is dying.*

"Twelve miles," Richard said.

Distraught, it took Henry a moment to understand the king's reference. More than ten thousand men had marched east from Jaffa through the worst winter storm. Their food was rotting, their mail rusting, and they were forced to turn back. Six months later, Richard led them a second time within reach of the Holy City. "The night was so clear we saw the lights of Jerusalem," Henry said. "I will never forget that sight."

The crusader army didn't draw closer that night, or on any other in the months they remained in Outremer. Advised by his council that he didn't have the men or resources to besiege the Holy City, that even if Jerusalem fell he would not be able to hold it without many more troops, Richard ordered the army back to the coast. They left the Holy Land a few months later. Henry had never questioned the king's decision. It was the right thing…at that time.

"Why do you suppose God has killed me, Henry?" Richard's eyes were watery and a dull gray-green. "I swore I would return to the Holy Land, take Jerusalem back."

With the surgeon and Richard's clerk behind him, Mercadier bulled into the tent and hovered over Richard. The surgeon approached the bed, but the clerk stopped by the door, his mouth agape.

The surgeon removed the linen wrapped poultice. "Forgive me, sire," he said.

"Henry, bring my chaplain," Richard said. "Tell no one."

Henry hurried out into the cool early spring morning. He had stopped trying to understand God's ways when he was twenty summers and on his way to Outremer. He had taken the Cross and expected God would take them to Jerusalem. God's will be done. But why was it God's will that innocents die? That King Richard—God's champion in the Holy Land—would not lead the Christian army into Jerusalem?

The surgeon tried to make Richard comfortable, but his

pain deepened. Skin near the wound swelled, the red-webbed lines lengthened, and the first signs of blackened, rotted flesh appeared. The stench was masked with scented candles and strong incense. Richard remained lucid. He prayed with the Abbot Milo, spoke with Mercadier and Will de Braose, one of his barons, and dictated letters to his clerk.

Henry watched the candles shrink—like Richard's life ebbing away. All the years he fought for this king, even when he disagreed with his actions, he still believed in him. *What happens now?*

Richard broke his thoughts, calling Henry and Stephan to his side. He gestured to sealed parchments on the table. "You will take these to my mother at Fontevrault. I have written my wishes in them, have messages she must see sent to my wife and to Joanna. Others will deliver word to Will Marshal and Archbishop Hubert in Rouen." He listed off castellans at a number of his castles who would be informed. "Philip will attack us as soon as he hears…" He left the rest unspoken.

Henry felt the veins in his neck bulge. He held back tears, unwilling to accept that Richard would be dead in a matter of days.

"Why did John go to Brittany?" Richard's voice cracked. "Of all the bad timing."

John had been there for weeks, extending an olive branch or so the king had told them. The thought of John being anywhere near the young duke chilled Henry to the bone. Perhaps the king had seen it as a test now that Duchess Constance had agreed to send Arthur as ward to Richard when he returned to Castle Gaillard. Now there would be no *when*.

"My mother must get word to John," Richard said.

The hair on Henry's neck prickled.

"If the Bretons learn I have named John as my successor, he will not leave Arthur's court alive."

Exhaling sharply, Stephan nodded and shot a painful glance at Henry. Richard was right about the Bretons, but John? King? Henry thought of Greyton again, wondering if his worst fears would come to pass.

"My brother..." Richard pressed his eyes closed a moment, held his breath to ward off pain. When he spoke, his voice was strong. "I reminded John he will never find men more loyal than you and Robin. He will need you, Mercadier, and the Marshal, to defeat Philip."

"You are my king." Henry clenched his fists at his side. He couldn't say more. *I cannot...swear loyalty to John.*

Stephan knelt by Richard. "You took me into your household when I was barely eighteen summers, sire," he said. "I would not have followed any other to Outremer. My life has little meaning without you." He choked back tears.

Richard smiled, but turned his eyes to Henry. His voice turned raspy and low. "Without me, Stephan says? I think he has found more meaning with you than most men will find in a lifetime." His palm found Henry's knee. "My last order for you—bring my lady mother to me ere I pass from this earth."

Henry grasped Stephan's hand and placed theirs atop the king's. Siege engines pounded the walls of Châlus-Chabrol, the world around them oblivious to the dying king.

"Hold on, sire," Henry said forcing thoughts of Greyton to the back of his mind. "We leave for Fontevrault as soon as our horses are saddled."

In Austria, Richard and his knights had traveled almost fifty miles a day for three days straight. Henry and

Stephan managed to cover the distance to Fontevrault Abbey—some one hundred forty miles—in just under three days.

When Eleanor saw their ragged state, she sat down, her mother's sense telling her they brought bad news. She gripped the arms of the chair, her hands growing white. "What has happened?"

"The king, your son, is grievously wounded." Henry held the letters out.

She closed her eyes, pursed her mouth, and when she finally looked at the seal she released a long ragged breath. "Live by the sword..." She let the rest of the verse trail and broke the wax to read, her hands trembling. Her eyes grew misty as she looked past Henry to Stephan to her servant. "Find Sir Robin and Abbot Luke. Tell the abbot we must leave for Châlus-Chabrol as soon as I pen a message for Berengaria. And the Abbess—I must speak with her. Bid them all come to me."

"Robin?" Henry asked, surprised.

"He left for England months ago," Stephan said.

Eleanor managed a smile that said she knew better. "Robin made the mistake of visiting me ere he left. I had...things for him to do...in Paris." She looked at another servant. "Get these men food and drink and set up a warm bath."

"There's little time, at least not for the soak, madam."

"Food, then," she replied, and gestured to the servant. Instructions were sent to the grooms to saddle the fastest horses, for she could not afford the luxury of a journey by cart or litter. She left to change from her simple light gray habit to something more suited to riding.

Platters of food arrived just as Robin sprinted into the room, his face lit and bursting with energy. He embraced

Henry and Stephan, but their happy reunion was short-lived. When Henry told him about the king he slumped in a chair, his fist clenched.

Abbess Matilda and Abbot Luke joined the knights before Robin could explain the queen's work that had kept him away from England. Any questions they had would remain unanswered for now. Queen Eleanor returned, composed, and if she had wept privately, there were no signs of misty eyes now. The circle of close friends gave her strength to do what must be done. Within the hour she sent the Abbess on her way to take the news to Richard's wife at Beaufort.

"Robin," Eleanor said, "I know you were to leave for England on the morrow. I have rarely asked more of any man, but I have one more request."

"When is a request from you not an order, madam?" Robin teased.

Eleanor didn't smile. "John is at the Breton court."

Robin's face fell, but he said nothing. Henry's blood throbbed through his veins—he knew Eleanor's next words—but could not speak.

"You must get to him." Eleanor's words came haltingly. "Before they learn Richard is not long for this world. You must get him safely away—"

"Me?" Robin protested. "John wants my head."

"And Arthur will have his if the Bretons get news of Richard." Eleanor's hands shook. "You have infiltrated Paris and more strongholds than I could name. You can get to John unnoticed where no others could." She looked apologetically from Henry to Stephan. "I trust few men. John will see what faith I place in you. You must get him out of Brittany. For me, Robin. For the crown."

The room was quiet except for the fire crackling in the hearth.

Robin nodded. "I will cross the border with him, but then turn north to the Narrow Sea."

"Thank you," she said and handed him Richard's message.

"Madam, Henry can accompany you," Stephan said. "I will go with Robin."

"No," Eleanor and Robin commanded.

Henry was taken aback by the vehemence in their voices. Stephan's expression said the same, but Robin was quick to explain. "One man alone has a better chance of succeeding than two or more. We all should do what we must. The queen mother needs your protection."

Eleanor grimaced. "I may be old, but I can take care of myself, Robin Carpenter," she said, getting half-smiles from all the men in the room. "You seem to forget I went on crusade with Louis of France. I crossed the Alps in the dead of winter with Richard's future bride at an age when most are dead and buried. And I endured Henry's house arrest for fifteen years."

And she had buried so many of her children, Henry thought. Of ten, only John and her daughters Joanna and Eleanor still lived. And Richard... God willing, he would be able to say his goodbyes to Eleanor.

Robin kissed Eleanor's hand, but she stood and held him in her arms. "See John safely from Brittany. Don't let me lose another child." She kissed his cheeks and watched him leave, her hands clasped to her heart. The huge oak door started to close behind him, but a servant entered and announced their horses were saddled, packs ready with dried meat and skins with wine.

In the courtyard, Henry's bones ached just thinking of beginning the journey back to Châlus-Chabrol immediately, but he knew they could not risk waiting until the morrow. Though Eleanor would be astride a fast horse, he didn't believe they would get to the Limousin in less than four days.

He stared at the horses. There were four fine animals, but he had expected to see eight, four to lead on rein so they could quickly change out without stopping to get new mounts after a half day ride.

"I told you I need no other protection," Eleanor said. "Go enjoy a soak, rest overnight, and plan for the morrow."

"The king will hang us if we leave you on your own, madam," Stephan said.

"Richard certainly will not. And John will never bother to ask the details of my journey." She grasped Henry's hand. "My youngest child has never liked you, and trust? You know him. My words, Richard's? Those will make little difference to John once he wears the crown. You must decide—if you swear fealty to John do you still lose everything?"

Henry had always admired Queen Eleanor, and found himself respecting her that much more for her bluntness and honesty. "Whether I stay or leave, I will lose Greyton. John will see to that," he said. "But if I—" he looked at Stephan, "if *we* leave, we can live somewhere... anywhere...together."

He helped Eleanor mount. "God keep you in these difficult times, madam."

"Give my best wishes to Sir John and Lady Elle, and to Allan." She ran her thumb along Henry's cheek, lifting his chin. Her eyes burned with emotion as she looked at Stephan, then back to Henry. "Take care of each other."

Henry lowered his eyes, felt a blush creep across his face.

Stephan took Eleanor's hand and said, "We will, madam."

Eleanor spurred her horse away from the courtyard of the abbey with the Abbot Luke at her side. Henry turned to the groomsman. "Saddle two fast horses and put ours on leads."

Stephan sighed and massaged his sore buttocks. "That soak sounds so tempting. It might be months before we have a chance for another."

Henry planted his hands at his hips.

With a mischievous wink, Stephan said, "After Robin?"

"Robin." Henry nodded and flashed a smile at Stephan. "And then home. England."

fifty-three

APRIL 1199

Robin approached the royal palace from the southwest, recalling a postern gate that was not well guarded. The keep rose in the opposite corner and there were apartments for guests leading off the hall. Business would have been concluded after the midday meal, and it was early for an evening gathering. Robin glanced at the apartments, doubting John would be there when the day was so fine. The gardens skirting the chapel offered a quiet place for walking and reflection...and other pursuits that a man like John enjoyed.

Robin hugged the shadows of the wall near the chapel. He heard the familiar voice. John. He was embracing a woman—one of the duchess' ladies Robin suspected. John always seemed drawn to married ladies or those with good prospects—and they fell into his lure. Sleeping with the brother of the king, being his mistress—there was something dangerous, yet tempting. Robin wasn't certain what they saw in John. He was short, hardly a soldier. A dog compared to King Richard. Perhaps his dark eyes captured them, had some power over young women.

Certainly the lady he had pressed against the wall was enraptured. He kissed her neck, her mouth, and she moaned, arching toward him as he plied her breast. His hand trailed to her waist, along her hip, and then he wasted no time pulling her gown up. Within moments he was swiving her, and little gasps escaped her throat. He grunted, grinding against her, thrusting, faster and deeper. She whimpered, called out his name and he stiffened, climaxing with a great groan. For a minute they hung against the wall unmoving. He finally pecked her cheek, pinched her buttocks, and pulled away, tucking his flaccid cock into his braies and adjusting his hose.

"Hawise," he said.

"My name is Millesant."

"I was thinking of Hawise, one of the court whores at Rouen."

Millesant slapped John. "Bastard."

He rubbed his cheek. "She was a much better garden fuck than you, dear lady."

Her hand shot out again, but John seized it. His fingers hooked Millesant's neck and he dragged her close, forcing his tongue into her mouth. She wrenched away from him and stalked off.

"Bitch," John muttered. Retreating to the stone bench, he retrieved the goblet he'd left there and sat, fanning himself and gulping back the drink.

Robin looked round the deserted garden. He would be able to whisk John away. No one would look for him until morning. By then, they would be safely across the Norman border. His job would be done.

He approached John, his footsteps unnoticed on the

soft green sward. "My lord," he said quietly.

Startled, John whirled round. "What are you doing here?"

"Please, my lord, quiet." Robin held out the crinkled parchment. "I have letters from the king and your mother. Read them at haste, and then we must leave."

John frowned, but the skepticism on his face disappeared when he saw the seals. "What is it?" He took them, slid his thumb beneath the wax to open Richard's.

"The king, your brother..." Robin didn't need to finish his message.

John read the words, swallowed hard, the veins in his neck rippling. He tore open the second message and stood, hands trembling, when he grasped that his life was about to change. "Let me get my pack—"

"There is no time, my lord. No one must see you leaving," Robin said. "I've horses for us outside the walls. Come with me now. Your mother made me promise she would not be burying two sons this week."

John didn't argue. He followed Robin out through the narrow passage and beyond the postern gate. Neither man said a word as John swung astride his horse. Robin's saddle pack was askew, the leather strap unbound. A thief? The beggar had left his flask, and would have found what was left of some salt pork and dried biscuits. He tapped the bag—far from being near empty, it was overflowing. Robin looked around, saw a flicker of movement in the wood.

"What are you waiting for?" John asked and started away.

Robin caught Stephan's eye and tipped his head.

A woman's shrill voice from the garden knifed through Robin. It struck his gut, sent it roiling with fear.

"Out that gate!" It was Millesant. Boots sounded on

the path—she had company. Two swords were unsheathed. "He gave the Lord John a letter," she shouted. "He said they must leave."

No! What else had the woman heard? John was already out of sight as Robin leapt on his horse. The gate swung open, and two guards charged him. Millesant was screaming. God help us, Robin thought. So close to turning for England, for Marian—he couldn't get caught now.

Robin's horse reared and the guards panicked, falling over themselves to get out of the way. Henry and Stephan plunged from the wood, the last of the sunlight glinting off their blades. Curses flew from their lips. Swords hammered the guards' shields. Outnumbered, the two Bretons retreated behind the gated wall.

"Out of here," Robin shouted, his breath ragged.

The three king's men raced off in John's wake. After a mile at a hard gallop, Henry and Stephan held back to watch for anyone tracking them. Robin caught up to John and with a few more miles at their backs, they finally slowed to give the horses a rest. The roads fell into darkness and curled through a deep forest.

"You of all people," John said. "Were you with Richard?"

"I was at Fontevrault with Queen Eleanor when word came from Châlus-Chabrol."

John glanced at him, but didn't ask what business Robin had with his mother. The shock of the news had dimmed and was now buried behind a cold façade. "The great warrior struck down—not in the midst of battle, but whilst walking through his own camp. God can be spiteful I would say. Did he find the Roman coins buried there?"

Was it surprising the first thing John considered was

coin? Not hardly. "I heard nothing about such a find, my lord," Robin said, knowing there had been rumors a buried treasure was King Richard's only reason for being in the Limousin.

John rubbed his jaw. "He could never stop, could he? If he wasn't fighting Philip Capet, he had to make an example of those rebellious southern barons of his. And look where it got him. Richard must be as angry as a bear about it all. But he loves me. I am his heir. I am the king," John said wistfully and then cleared his throat. "As it should be."

Robin chose not to remind John that Richard might not yet be dead, though he knew from his own battle experience that gangrene could kill a man in two days.

"Richard wants to be buried at our father's feet at Fontevrault. Ironic, isn't it? He drove the man to his death, fighting him until the end." John scoffed, shook his head, conveniently forgetting how he had abandoned his father as he lay dying.

"It tells me that as flawed as their relationship was, King Richard has great respect for your father," Robin said.

John sneered. "I can't say Richard ever felt that way about me. Pompous golden-boy. It's no wonder Philip hates him." His eyes narrowed. "What of your father, Robin?"

"We had our disagreements. Is any father-son relationship without them? But it's good to know those are behind us." It was more than Robin wanted to say. Any mention of his family kept them in John's mind.

But John was thinking of his own family. "Richard, dead. Maman must have taken it hard."

"What would you expect, my lord?" *Her favorite child...gone.* Robin couldn't imagine what it was like to lose a child. Thinking of Robert and Lucy sent ripples of longing through his heart and soul. To be home…with Marian. To watch his children grow.

"No tears," John said, "at least not in front of others."

Robin nodded. "Her concern was for you."

"A first for Maman," John said cynically. "We must get to Chinon to secure the treasury, and from there to Rouen."

Robin cleared his throat, his hands tightening on the reins. "I will see you safely across the Norman border, my lord, and as far as St James de Beuvron. The Earl of Chester and his men can accompany you south."

John reined in, forcing Robin to hold up. "Does my mother know you would desert me in this hour of need?"

Robin kept his eyes focused on the road ahead. "You will want a large retinue—for your own protection as well as for the coin you secure." He listened for the drum of galloping horses, but Henry and Stephan—and the Bretons, if they'd saddled up to pursue John—were far behind.

John studied him with deep interest. "Should we make a peace, Robin?"

Robin wanted to laugh in John's face, but he must play along. "I am nothing but a household knight now."

"Is it land you want again? A title?" John's lip curled.

"I have served my time." Robin couldn't help the hostility creeping into his voice. "And I do not want to watch you lose everything King Richard took back."

"Ouch," John groaned, his eyes wide. "You have no faith in me!"

"You have done well the last few years, but the tide is shifting. You'll be at war with the Bretons when they learn Richard did not name Arthur to succeed him. And who, besides the French, will line up behind the Bretons?

Maine? Anjou?"

"But most of the barons will support me, here and in England," John said, reaching for the wineskin hooked on his saddle.

"Support, yes—mayhap for a brief while. But trust? They still remember your actions against the king whilst he was on crusade and during his imprisonment. You have their support because they would not have a boy crowned who sits in Philip Capet's lap."

John uncorked the wine and took a deep swallow. "And you feel the same way."

"You have repeatedly threatened me and my family." Robin's gut lurched. "I know I am only alive because of King Richard's grip on you, my lord."

A shadow fell across John's face. "You kept me from the crown!" He sounded like a petulant child.

"It was my duty for my king and country."

John laughed harshly. "And now you must take me to that crown. Funny, life. My mother and brother Richard say I should be grateful, but why should I listen to them? She never had much use for me, and I was always in his shadow." John sneered. "Richard's time is over, Robin. I will not forget...any of it."

John spurred his horse. Robin wanted to leave him on his own, but it would be many hours travel to the Norman border in the dark. Outlaws might lurk in the wood, ready to pounce on a lone traveler. He glanced over his shoulder. He could leave John with Henry and Stephan, but he knew they were there for him, not John.

God's bones, my lady, he cried out to Eleanor. *Why did you ask this of me?*

It was well past midnight when Robin left John at Ranulf's castle at St James and rendezvoused with Henry and Stephan just north of the village.

Two days later the three knights sailed from Barfleur. It was the sixth day of April, the year of our Lord one thousand one hundred ninety-nine. They did not know it as their galley shoved away from the docks, but Richard Plantagenet, who wore the crown less than ten years, ended his reign at seven that evening.

fifty-four

APRIL 1199
England

Robin arrived in Nottingham on the eleventh day of April. Guards on the barbican tower watched the trickle of people and carts in and out of the middle bailey. Children played games in the streets. Chickens and goats ran free and merchants went about their business. The news of the king's death—for certainly the gangrene must have taken him by now—had not come this far north.

Guards in the upper bailey recognized his name, but the hostility Robin encountered on his last visit to Nottingham was nonexistent. A clerk admitted him to the hall and scurried away. Robin walked the length of the room, admiring the gold-threaded designs on the linen cloth on the table. Equally impressive gilded candle holders, crimson-cushioned benches, and a sideboard replete with silver platters and cups and embossed flagons for wine lent the room an air of opulence. Robin smiled.

Allan had done well. Too bad it must end.

Surprisingly, his palms began to sweat. *Get me away from this place.* Outside, bells pealed midday and he was finally admitted to a solar off the hall.

"You don't do your business in the keep?" Robin asked, teasing his former squire.

Allan grinned and pounded Robin's back. "I am closer to the secret passages here. Easier to escape." Pouring cups of wine, the clerk Baldwin chuckled, shaking his head. "That will be all," Allan told the servant. "My God, Robin, it is good to have a friendly face nearby. Does the king's business bring you?"

The clerk left them to their reunion. Robin waited for the man's footsteps to fade. Allan grabbed a piece of cheese and dried apple from the platter on the edge of his desk and studied Robin's face while he chewed. "What has happened?"

"London may know by now, and heralds will be here, Leicester, Lincoln, and north within a few days." Robin swallowed hard, still torn. "King Richard is dead. Mortally wounded at a place called Châlus-Chabrol." He provided what details he knew.

Stunned, Allan stared past Robin. "He named John to be king?"

"There was little choice." Robin gulped down his wine. He noticed Allan looked harder, definitely older. "But you could choose to serve John."

Allan's green eyes narrowed. "You cannot possibly believe John will allow me to retain this office."

Robin chuckled. "You know me—and John—well. In his words, 'I will not forget'. You should leave Nottingham, the sooner the better."

"I've had a pack ready for four years." Allan studied the fine oak of his desk, the magnificent tapestries draped on the walls, and the warm fire in the brazier. "Even hid some stores in the undercroft that Tuck and the boys might grab for old time's sake. I'll meet up with them in Sherwood, tell them your news. What of you?"

"I leave for York on the morrow to join Marian. My daughter is near two now. I want to see her grow, to be a husband to Marian, a father to my child. To watch and wait, to see what King John will do."

Allan rubbed his fingers together. "Never been to York," he said.

"Join us there. Bring Tuck along."

"Tuck? He'll not leave. He does God's work here, feeding Nottingham's poor." Allan's eyes sparkled. "You remember our motto, 'Rob from the rich, give to the poor'."

Smiling, Robin said, "I do like that turn of the phrase. And the cause is a good one, but Marian will want me to find a way to help that doesn't involve anything illegal."

Robin stood, extending his hand to Allan. The younger man shoved it aside and wrapped him in a brotherly embrace. "May we find peace and joy in our new lives. God be with you, Robin."

When Allan finally released him, Robin strode to the door. He stopped, glancing back. "See you in York," he said and then hurried to retrieve his horse. In the middle bailey he tipped his head to pretty girls, young and old, and to the men he passed. He stopped to fill his pack with dried meat, cheese, and a pasty warm from the bakehouse ovens. "Goodbye, Nottingham," he said as he rode beneath the iron gate of the barbican. "May our paths never cross again."

It had been winter when Henry last visited Cartholme, so spring looked glorious on it. Trees were budding, lambs at their mothers' teats, villeins in the fields. A ploughman and his team of oxen worked the fallow field where barley or oats would be sown. Two men mending a fence looked up from their work and one, a big man who Henry would recognize a half mile away, began to wave.

Little John took long strides towards them, shouting, "Lord Henry! Stephan."

Women gathered at the washtubs in the yard turned to the ruckus, their conversations fading fast. Children interrupted their games and chores and a young maid took hold of one fair-haired little girl to keep her back from the approaching horses. A moment later Elle rushed into the sward, her skirts rippling in the breeze. The little girl wiggled away from her maid to tag behind Elle.

Despite having been in the saddle for hours, Henry and Stephan jumped from their horses and into Little John's arms. "Bless you both," Little John said. "Why didn't you send word? We'd have a feast spread."

Elle kissed both knights. "Baby John is sleeping, but you remember Eleanor?" she said, whisking the child from behind her skirts.

The little girl looked so much like her mother that Henry was taken aback. And she was tall for five summers he thought as he leaned down to kiss her hand. Her smile was like Elle's, her nose scrunched up until she giggled, and then curtsied when Elle prompted her.

"The queen mother asked that we bring greetings to her namesake," Henry said.

"How is Queen Eleanor?" Elle sensed something wrong and reached for Little John.

"Not well…" Henry took a long breath, felt Stephan's arm slip round his waist.

Elle looked at Stephan then back to Henry. She paled, their joyful reunion stolen away in a breath. "Is she ill?"

"The king," Henry said. "He suffered a mortal wound. He was dying when we left to deliver word to the queen mother."

Elle crossed herself and threaded her fingers through Little John's. "God be with him," she said.

Bringing her hand to his heart, Little John closed his eyes, shaking his head in disbelief. Lost for words he turned away a moment, and then said, "We've heard nothing."

"The news will come across the Narrow Sea any day now." Henry's stomach clenched. "Count John will be…is king."

Stephan's horse stomped the ground to protest.

"He doesn't like it either," Elle said as Stephan stroked the bay's neck. "Do you think John will—"

"Come," Little John said, interrupting his wife. "Let's talk inside."

Settled in the solar Henry told the story. Little John paced, shocked Queen Eleanor had asked Robin to find John. "What a heart-splitting, terrible chore for him."

Henry could hear the children's nurse in the hall entertaining Eleanor and three-year-old John, who had woken from his nap. "Our new king doesn't despise you, so you may have nothing to fear as long as you swear fealty to him and do his bidding."

"And you?" Little John looked between the two knights. "You won't—can't—serve John, and cannot stay at Greyton, so how will you live? In Yorkshire?"

"I will not be a burden to my sister and Gil," Henry started.

Stephan wrapped his hand around Henry's. "They will keep our secrets," he said. "The forests are deep bounding l'Aigle. We can have a small cottage—ours alone—and live there, far from anyone's eyes."

"John will learn nothing from us except that you stopped here on your way to Greyton," Little John said.

"Will you go to Lincoln?" Elle asked.

"You should not," Little John said before Henry could respond. "Fewer people to see you, follow you."

"I will get word to Lady Nichola for you," Elle said.

Henry conceded Little John was right and knew Nichola would understand, but he didn't want her to lie for him. "It's best she know nothing, Elle. I will write, telling her I'll come to Lincoln after I see my sister."

"But you cannot—"

"If she asks you, your story will be the same as hers should any of John's spies come snooping. They will know we went to Yorkshire to see Bea and Gil." Henry tugged at his collar. "After that visit, we leave for Greyton...and never arrive."

Elle had a gleam in her eye. "If John believes you are dead..."

"And how do you suggest we arrange our deaths?" Stephan asked.

"Both of you?" Little John argued. "John would be sure to suspect."

"It could be they drowned when a river barge capsized," Elle said. "Don't you remember the story of the man who tried to rescue his wife? Both died."

Stephan drummed his fingers on the table. "That almost happened to us near Lyon."

"And what chance is there it would happen a second time? And who's boat will go down with you?" Little John asked. "Where are the bodies?" He scoffed. "I know! The current was swift, the bodies dragged out to sea."

"You've another idea?" Elle folded her hands in her lap. "Who needs a body? We assume my brother met an untimely accident, or outlaws. Why not that same fate for Henry and Stephan?"

Henry bowed his head. He couldn't meet Elle's eyes, not when he had lured Edric to his death. Struck the killing blow. *God forgive me for keeping that from you, Elle.*

"Do John's men still ask about Edric?" Stephan asked.

Little John exhaled sharply, still unsure of Henry's plan. "We saw them two or three times that first year. None last year."

"No one will look for you after a while," Elle said.

Grief nearly overcame Henry. "I could never know your children, or be an uncle to Bea's." He met Stephan's eyes. "Is that what we want, Stephan?"

"I hate it. But while John is king, I don't think we have a choice. For now, we live. We visit Greyton, and then l'Aigle. By that time, England will know King Richard is dead and we must disappear."

Little John grunted. He raised his cup, his expression sour. "Long live the king."

Elle left them in the hall to give instructions to cook and chamberlain. Soon the table was spread with food and drink, and servants carted one bucket of hot water after another up the stone stairs of the keep. The food was tasty, but Henry could only think how good a soak would feel after days riding a sweaty beast and living off the road. Elle encouraged the knights to take advantage while the bath water was hot and they excused themselves as soon as they'd devoured the herbed fish in almond milk. There would be time for more talk later or on the morrow. Bath, sleep, Stephan, but maybe not in that order.

Henry hadn't expected the bank of candles, or the dried roses and lavender on the floor. The oversized tub brought a smile to his face. He was sure Elle had it built specially to accommodate Little John. A brazier warmed the room and thick woolen blankets and overstuffed pillows looked enticing on the bed. Stephan's pallet was laid out for the servants' sake, with at least as many accouterments as the bed. It would look well slept in before the sun rose.

Stephan slid the door bolt in place. Henry was behind him, lifting his tunic over his head and pressing him against the door. He smothered him with kisses as Stephan turned to help him remove his clothing. Boots came off, hose and braies tracked across the floor, and they climbed into the tub. Stephan leaned back, running a finger up and down Henry's arm, with Henry settled between his legs.

Stephan yawned. "I did not realize how much my bones ache. I think I could fall asleep here."

"We cannot have that." Henry forced his arm from beneath the water. He grabbed the soap cake from the bench by the tub, and lathered his arms and face. Stephan grabbed the cake and gently scrubbed the muscles of his torso. Henry sighed. "You may be right about sleep."

He closed his eyes as Stephan traced an old scar and dragged the soap to his groin. Henry gasped, the long, slow strokes sending fire through his veins. He didn't care that they had all night and days and nights together to come. He wanted this moment to last.

Turning, Henry straddled his lover. "I am not so sleepy now." He grinned and thrust against Stephan, his hands fondling their hardening cocks.

"I see that," Stephan said and moaned.

Henry took the soap and washed Stephan's chest, face, and neck. He kissed him hungrily. "Bed?" he said breathlessly.

They dried off quickly and fell into an embrace on the bed. Touches, kisses, and whispered words of love and longing led to their becoming one. The dying embers of the fire crackled and they finally slept tangled in each other's arms.

Dawn came too soon and Henry woke, watching how peaceful and handsome Stephan looked. His cheek was warm against Henry's chest. *Every day can be like this now.*

He drifted back to sleep until a cart rumbling into the courtyard woke him again. Sunlight the color of Stephan's hair streamed through the shutters. Stephan shifted, a smile on his lips, but he showed no inclination to rise. Henry was more than content to stay in bed. There would be plenty of time to inspect Cartholme, and Greyton could wait a few days. But the scent of bread baking curled up the stairwell and made his stomach growl.

"Hungry?" Stephan asked, their eyes meeting.

"For you," he said and leaned close to brush his lips against Stephan's forehead. "Food can wait."

Stephan's hand slid behind Henry's neck and he crawled atop him until they were chest to chest, groins pressed together. Upstairs, a child squealed and they both laughed and listened to the nurse urging little Geoffrey to quiet down. Eleanor's footfalls sounded lightly on the stairs. Geoffrey and the nurse followed her down more slowly. "Wait, E'nor," Geoffrey shouted.

Henry kissed the tip of Stephan's nose. "Tonight," he said and winked.

Stephan rolled off Henry and stretched. He threw his arms behind his head watching as Henry dragged himself from the bed and dressed. "Promises…"

Henry and Little John spent the morning reviewing the accounts for Cartholme and Greyton. After the midday meal Stephan accompanied Henry to inspect the outbuildings, including the stables, rebuilt after the fire that had been the work of Edric Weston's henchman. The mill and the chapel, the hedges and stone fences were well kept. The fields were newly turned, and beans, barley and oats would be planted soon.

Dusk was still an hour away when they settled in the hall. Little John and Stephan played a game of chess by the window splay, and Henry sat with his legs stretched out near the hearth.

Seated near Henry, Elle huffed and placed her embroidery on the side table. "It is a good thing Eleanor's maid has patience for this, because I would not be able to teach the child."

"You will teach her to ride."

"We have already begun those lessons. She is more skilled than boys twice her age."

"I am not surprised," Henry said, "not with you as her mother."

Little John chuckled and looked up from the chess board. "She has already frightened off two potential suitors." He cleared his throat. "Suits me just fine—I won't have any talk of marrying my Eleanor off until she's of an age. And mayhap not even then!"

They spent the evening sharing gossip and facts, news of the campaigns in Normandy, and speculating what King Philip would do with John on the throne. On that depressing note, Henry bid them goodnight. Stephan stayed a short while longer to finish a second game with Little John and then sprinted up the stairwell.

"I won," Stephan said, closing the door to the bedchamber.

"Get over here." Henry tossed off the blanket revealing his naked body. "I made a promise to you this morn."

Stephan undressed as he crossed the room, nearly tripping over his hose. A horse's hoofs sounded in the cobbled courtyard before he climbed on to the bed.

"Sir John!" The frantic voice cried out from the yard. "Dear God, Sir John…"

Stephan looked outside as Little John and Elle met the rider. He didn't need to hear the conversation. Elle crossed herself and Little John glanced at the tower, unaware Stephan was standing there.

"Henry," Stephan said. "England knows."

fifty-five

APRIL 1199
Greyton, Lincolnshire

The messenger had come from Lincoln telling that the bells tolled and the heralds cried, "The king is dead. Long live the king."

Within an hour Henry and Stephan galloped towards Greyton. Elle tried to convince Henry there was no need to rush. John—King John—still had to consolidate his power and win support from his barons. It might be a month or more before he was crowned at Westminster. Still, for Henry there was a sense of urgency. His nightmares about Greyton had been all too real.

Moonlight sliced through the tree canopy like the blades of hundreds of swords. Shadows enveloped the knights forcing them to slow. When they turned off the old Roman road towards Greyton the moon laid a path for them. Moonlight glittered on the Witham where they crossed the old stone bridge. The forest gave way to pastures, newly green from early spring rains.

Henry stared intently to the west where the skies darkened, clouds blotting out the stars. His hands tightened on the reins. Birds stirred in the trees and a flock took flight, startling him. Weaving back and forth, diving, rising, the creatures turned as one. They glided on a gust of wind, silhouetted against an eerie glow. Henry reined in, his heart thudding. That glow—he'd seen it the Holy Land where Saracen campfires speckled the hillsides, when villages burned in the distance. The familiar smell suddenly struck his nose.

"Oh, God!" He spurred his horse to a gallop.

Not clouds, but acrid smoke rose over Greyton. His home was burning.

Stephan cried out for him to stop, but raced behind him.

It was mad to rush into the village—Henry knew it. Whoever had done this might be there still. *John's men.* Henry's stomach roiled.

At the village well, both men leapt from their horses. Frightened, the animals bolted back down the road. Stephan filled a bucket, but looked around hopelessly. The fires were too far gone. He tossed the pail to the ground angrily. Henry stepped towards the manor house, hesitant. Wind whipped through the village fanning the flames. Every cottage, every shop—gone. The air smelled of blackened timbers and burning wood. The chapel where Queen Eleanor attended Elle and Little John's wedding smoldered, red-hot timbers spitting sparks in the air. The manor hall was engulfed in flames. Showers of oranges and reds shot skyward to lash the heavens, the air black with ash.

Henry reached for Stephan, sliding his fingers into Stephan's hand.

"What can I do?" Stephan asked.

Henry choked back a sob and rested his head against Stephan's. "Hold me."

The thatched roof of the hall caved in. With groans and creaks, the timber walls collapsed. The stone built part of the manor might stand, a blackened hull. There would be little left should John give his home—his birthright—to another. *King John.* Bitter words Henry would never forget.

"John has decided our fate," Henry said. He hadn't expected anything less. He had never planned to live at Greyton without Stephan. His villagers had been settled at Cartholme or in Yorkshire. It was just a manor house. A village. His village…his home.

Here—he had been born and raised. His father too, and Bea. This land had been granted to his great-grandpere by the Conqueror's son Henry I.

Henry's eyes grew hot with tears, but he blinked them back and whirled round to stare towards the river remembering how he and Bea raced along the road.

Almost ten years earlier he left this home to serve his king, his country, his God. And serve them well he did, though there were times he questioned 'why'? He served with good men. Allan and Little John, Tuck, and Will Scaflock. Robin, with Marian. God would keep his friends safe. King Richard—God rest his soul—a great warrior, a king who might have had a more powerful kingdom than any other had it not been for greedy enemies.

Now you have made your brother king. I will never understand how you could forgive him.

Henry looked from one end of Greyton Manor to the other. From the mill pond to the cart path disappearing into the wood and tracing north to Ringsthorpe. If he had ever believed for one moment that he and Stephan could serve King John—and he did not think he had—he had an answer now from John himself.

"Has John beaten us?" Henry asked.

"He will believe he has." Stephan took Henry into his arms and whispered, his voice firm, "But he hasn't won if we don't let him."

Henry took a rasping breath, watched the smoke and cinders soak the air, the blaze consuming everything. Would John look for them, or was his revenge satisfied?

The land would be here, but Henry did not expect to see it ever again. His memories would have to hold him to it. His sister would have claim, though knowing John, Bea would pay a heavy price to keep it.

Henry took Stephan's hand and pressed a kiss to his palm, twined their fingers together and placed them over his heart. Their eyes met, their souls were one. Henry needed no land, no home. He loved Stephan and felt loved by him. His home was with Stephan.

He kissed his lover gently, laid his forehead to Stephan's. "We have the forest."

"We do," Stephan said with a smile.

Henry felt the curl of Stephan's lip, their breaths warm against each other. They walked away, Greyton at their backs. Smoke didn't obscure the rising moon or the stars in the east. If it was possible, the stars seemed brighter.

They were forever, those stars. Henry glanced sidelong at Stephan. *Like us.* Now and for always.

EPILOGUE

Richard was buried at Fontevrault on the eleventh day of April 1199 at the feet of his father Henry II, as he had requested. Richard's heart was buried in the cathedral at Rouen; his entrails and brain at Charroux, an abbey founded by Charlemagne.

As soon as King Philip heard that Richard was dead, he invaded Normandy. The Bretons took up arms and by Easter, the twenty-fifth of April, Anjou, Maine and Touraine swore fealty to Arthur.

John was invested as Duke of Normandy on that same day in Rouen. He sailed for England and was crowned King of England at Westminster on the twenty-seventh day of May 1199.

Arthur was captured by King John's forces in August 1202. In 1203, he was imprisoned in Rouen and disappeared from the historical record that April. Historians speculate John ordered Arthur's murder, or may have killed the sixteen-year old himself.

Thank You

Thank you for reading *Swords of the King*. If you enjoyed this book, please consider posting a review wherever you typically share your opinions about books. It is impossible to overstate the importance of reviews. Also, sign up for my newsletter, https://charlenenewcomb.com/mailing-list/subscribe-to-my-newsletter/, for exclusive content, giveaways, and announcements about sales and more. Get a taste of a forthcoming Stephan l'Aigle short story at the back of this book.

Charlene Newcomb
May 2018

AUTHOR'S NOTE

Richard the Lionheart is one of the most famous—or infamous—of the kings of England. My fascination with his reign began with episodes of a television show that placed him in the Holy Land during the Third Crusade. My world history history classes barely touched on the crusades, and at university, my concentration was on U.S. History. The history major in me wanted to know more about Richard I, so I delved into the man and the legend. And that's where the idea of knowing Richard and the Third Crusade through the eyes of fictional characters Henry de Grey and Stephan l'Aigle took hold. By the time I was writing the last chapters of Book I, plot arcs for Book II were taking shape in my head. And I couldn't leave readers with Henry and Stephan riding off into the sunset, er, into Sherwood Forest for a happily ever after, and poor Robin banished—sort of—by King Richard. What would happen to the lovers when the king returned to Normandy where Philip of France was running rampant over the Angevin Empire? The difficult part was choosing the 'inciting incident' that would set the events of Book III in motion. For me, that surrounded the kidnapping of Constance of Brittany and subsequent spiriting away of her son to Philip of France's court.

So—what is fact and where have I embellished the story?

The Duchess Constance was abducted by her husband Ranulf de Blondeville, Earl of Chester. I found conflicting information about Arthur's presence during the kidnapping incident in March 1196. Chester's biographer, Iain Soden, indicates that both Constance and Arthur were summoned to meet with King Richard. Other biographies and the chroniclers do not mention

Arthur. J.A. Everard analyzed a number of accounts of the events written by Constance's contemporaries in her book *Brittany and the Angevins: Province and Empire, 1158-1203* and offers a chronology which helped frame my fictional characters' roles. In April 1196, King Richard does go to Rennes, but Arthur is not present. Everard notes Arthur and his advisors were in St Malo de Beignon in August, but when Richard failed to have Constance released, the Bretons swore fealty to Arthur. When did Arthur turn up in Paris? Again, there are sparse details, with at least one source noting his presence there in the Fall of 1196. Everard indicates the bishop of Vannes delivered Arthur to the Capetian court and suggests that happened after the August gathering.

Did John plot to murder Arthur in 1196? No, but my interpretation there and later in the book when Arthur leaves Paris, provides a nice bit of foreshadowing. In 1203—approximately four years after *Swords* ends—Arthur is at war with King John. The sixteen-year-old is captured and held at Rouen Castle where he disappears from the historical record. John is suspected of ordering Arthur's murder, or murdering him by his own hand.

Everard also notes that John was in Brittany at Constance's court when news reached him about Richard's fatal injury at Châlus-Chabrol. Some historians speculate that John's fallout with Richard in early 1199 may be evidence that he was in cahoots with Philip of France and seeking alliance with the Bretons; others dismiss the idea but have no plausible explanation for his presence there in April 1199. Neither Everard nor Marc Morris, who also reports John's visit to Brittany in his King John biography, provide us with the name of the man (or men) who secreted John away.

Who told Eleanor, Richard's mother, that he was

dying? Her biographer, Alison Weir, writes that, on his deathbed, Richard "sends a messenger to Fontevrault, calling upon her to come to him without delay."

Richard's meeting with the old hermit who warned him "Be thou mindful of the destruction of Sodom, and abstain from what is unlawful, for if thou dost not, a vengeance worthy of God shall overtake thee" is reflected in Roger de Hoveden's *Annals*, but to accommodate the plot, I placed that incident at Les Andelys in 1196 rather than in 1195. In my author's note for Book I, I mentioned historians' accusations who cite this to suggest King Richard was homosexual, something I don't refer to in my series. Read more on my take on this in "Medieval man, sex, and mortal sin in *Men of the Cross*," https://charlenenewcomb.com/2014/11/17/medieval-man-sex-and-mortal-sin-in-men-of-the-cross/, a post on medieval sexuality on my blog.

Nichola de la Haye's daughter Adela is fictional. Nichola, hereditary castellan of Lincoln Castle, did have at least three children, possibly four, with her second husband Gerard de Camville. I wrote about their lives for the *English Historical Fiction Authors* blog - https://englishhistoryauthors.blogspot.com/2015/10/johns-man-in-lincoln-gerard-de-camville.html. In *Swords*, I went with four children *plus* Adela. Nichola, like her contemporary Queen Eleanor of Aquitaine, is a fascinating woman. She and Gerard did support John while Richard was on crusade and during his subsequent imprisonment by the Holy Roman Emperor. Nichola led the defense of the castle in 1191 in a forty day siege against royalist troops, and in 1216, she averted a siege of rebellious barons supporting the French invasion against King John. If I could invite any historical figures for cream tea, Nichola and Eleanor would be at my table.

The Itinerary of King Richard I by Lionel Landon was invaluable, allowing me to know Richard's precise location at certain times. John's whereabouts are occasionally referenced in the *Itinerary* and in *The Annals of Roger de Hoveden* and in biographies, but there are plenty of gaps that gave me some creative freedom. My go-to biography was John Gillingham's *Richard I*, with Marc Morris' *King John: Treachery and Tyranny in Medieval England* coming in second. You can see a more thorough list of my references resources on my blog, https://charlenenewcomb.com/reference-resources-more/reference-resources.

On a final note: I have been criticized for Robin's use of bow and arrow as English knights used lance, mace, ax, and sword when on horseback. Some readers immediately think of the famous English longbows, which at over six feet in length would have been quite unwieldy in a cavalry charge. I agree! (But no sooner do I write this than I see the longbow used on horseback by Robin in the film *Robin and Marian*!) That aside, Robin's bow is more in line with the size of ones used by the Saracens, who were quite skilled with loosing arrows during a charge. In my *Battle Scars* series, Robin's path to knighthood was not a traditional one. He developed his expertise with bow long before he met Richard, and even after he was knighted this was part of his character, vital to the man who will become known as Robin Hood.

ACKNOWLEDGEMENTS

This writer cannot say 'thank-you' enough to friends and other writers who have provided moral support through the solitary writing process. On weekends I spend many hours at the local coffee shop, and the regulars know me and ask 'what chapter are you on now?' We joke that they should watch their conversations—they may end up in a future story.

Beta readers Sarah, Nelda, Julie, Mary, and Jody provided feedback and spotted typos, but any remaining errors—or ones I created while fixing the typos—are mine. My writers group cronies are tireless cheerleaders. Thank you to Mark, Marie, Ryan, and Cathy. I wouldn't be writing if it wasn't for their encouragement.

ABOUT THE AUTHOR

Charlene Newcomb lives, works, and writes in Kansas. She is an academic librarian by trade, a former U.S. Navy veteran, and has three grown children. When not working at the library, she is still surrounded by books and trying to fill her head with all things medieval. She loves to travel and enjoys quiet places in the mountains or on rocky coasts. But even in Kansas she can let her imagination soar.

Website: http://charlenenewcomb.com

Facebook:
https://www.facebook.com/CharleneNewcombAuthor/

Twitter: http://twitter.com/charnewcomb

Subscribe to Charlene's newsletter for occasional updates and exclusives
https://charlenenewcomb.com/mailing-list/subscribe-to-my-newsletter/

ALSO BY CHARLENE NEWCOMB

Battle Scars series
Men of the Cross
For King and Country

Other novels and short stories

Keeping the Family Peace

"A Certain Point of View" in
Star Wars: Tales from the Empire

"Shades of Gray: from the
Adventures of Alex Winger"
free online (linked from the author's website)

And numerous short stories in the
Star Wars Adventure Journal

COMING SOON

"A Knight's Tale (Passages)"
a short story featuring Stephan l'Aigle

Praise for Battle Scars

MEN OF THE CROSS
IndieB.R.A.G. Medallion Honoree

"The author draws a vivid picture of the Third Crusade... filled with excitement, passion, and plenty of action." *–Andrew Latham, author of The Holy Lance*

"It takes guts to approach such myths as Richard Lionheart and the events of the Third Crusade. It takes considerable skill and imagination to twist the story somewhat, thereby bringing something new to the table. Ms Newcomb does just that..." *–Anna Belfrage, award-winning author of The Graham Saga and The King's Greatest Enemy*

"...a wide-sweeping historical novel, full of vivid detail, action and an intricate plot combined with an M/M romance with all the emotional tug-o-war needed." *–Mark at Sinfully Gay Romance Book Reviews*

FOR KING AND COUNTRY
IndieB.R.A.G. Medallion
Finalist, Chaucer Award for pre-1750 Historical Fiction
Editor's Choice, Historical Novel Society

"A breathtaking gallop through Richard the Lionheart's England." *–Sharon Bennett Connolly, author of Heroines of the Medieval World*

"The history is sharp, the action appropriately bloody, the passion undeniable."*–Christopher Monk, historical consultant, medieval manuscript specialist at Rochester Cathedral*

Coming soon

A KNIGHT'S TALE (PASSAGES)

APRIL 1185
Near the Breton-Normandy border

Stephan l'Aigle had every intention of celebrating his eighteenth birthday. His adversary had no such plans for him.

Sunlight glinted off the sword arcing towards Stephan's neck. He angled his shield to catch the blow. "Bastard!" he cried. "Hell waits for us both!"

Stephan didn't believe there was a Heaven, and men like him surely would never get there. But if his kind all ended up in Hell, then more the merrier.

Sweat stung Stephan's eyes and he blinked, almost missing the knight's second swing. Their blades collided mid-air. Arms trembling, Stephan beat back the Breton with his shield. This would not be his first and last stand on the battlefield.

Battle was like tournaments, except this enemy intended to run him through. And the highs of thrust, plunge, parry, and hammer was almost like sex. Adrenaline pumped through Stephan's blood. Foreplay building, heart racing, focused solely on the immediate surroundings, not seeing or hearing anything but this one man. Stephan could almost smell him. Musk and sweat.

The knight cursed. His stallion's breaths came hard. Blood speckled his hauberk and the coppery scent struck Stephan's nose, the daydream gone in an instant. This man wanted to kill him! Battle, then, not sex.

Stephan would have smiled if there had been time, but every second meant life or death. He pressed knees to his horse and urged him closer to the enemy. The man swung his blade and grunted, straining to get the upper hand.

"Swine," Stephan shouted. He bashed the knight with his shield, sent him swaying in the saddle. Once, twice, Stephan's sword hacked down. The knight lost his grip on his shield and Stephan's sword pierced flesh. Blood spurted from the neck wound and splattered Stephan's face. Screaming, the man toppled to the ground and lay still.

Stephan's gut roiled. *I killed him.* His first kill. He choked back the urge to retch, heard the din howling around him, blurred and unreal. The sickening feeling dimmed in an eye blink. The strike of swords diminished to nothing, but a charging knight came at him, blade swinging wildly as Breton cries to withdraw echoed across the field.

"Retreat! Retreat!" The order resounded on the thick afternoon air.

The knight's sword glanced off Stephan's shield and the man stole away.

Stephan cast his gaze round the muddied field at the bodies, the trodden banners, and writhing stallions. He was drenched in sweat, but a chill struck him bone-deep. Tournaments hadn't prepared him for the blood of battle.

Hoofs pounded behind him. His horse skittered as he glanced back, relieved to see a knight in Duke Richard's colors. Stephan steadied his dark bay, mesmerized. The knight brandished his sword in victory as he drew next to Stephan. Blood rained down on them both and dribbled from the knight's blade to his glove and gauntlet.

The Duke of Brittany's troop fled into the woods, their banners whipping like a galley's sails on the Narrow Sea. "Shall we follow?" Stephan asked, looking after the retreating Bretons.

"Not so quick." The knight was a giant of a man. He wore confidence like a badge, and had a powerful presence that turned all eyes on him. His magnificent gray-dappled horse was lathered in sweat and as bloodied as the knight himself, but it pranced and sidled, then pawed the ground. "Round up the prisoners. See to our wounded," he shouted, pivoted the Spanish destrier, and spurred towards friendly lines.

Stephan gaped after him. Was that the duke himself?

Shouts of victory nearly buried orders flying across the field. Bile crept up Stephan's throat. He had to harden himself against the death. This was his life now. He needed a good fuck...

But the only thing getting skewered back in camp was chicken roasting on spits. Fragrant with garlic and onions, the chicken and a stew bubbling in a large pot on the fire would quell the growl in Stephan's stomach but would do little to ease the ache in his groin. Bold tales and laughter fueled by free-flowing ale might be his only company tonight.

"I saw you at a tourney in Paris last year with Huntingdon's mesnie." The knight next to Stephan at the trough splashed himself with water. It glistened on his muscled torso before he wiped it dry and pulled a clean tunic over his head. "L'Aigle, am I right?"

Stephan nodded. "I captured three knights that day," he bragged, wringing out his washing cloth. He scrubbed the blood from his cheeks and forehead.

"Watch the boasting. They'll accuse you of being too much like me." The knight grinned and dried his face on his sleeve. "I am Robin du Louviers, with Lord Richard's men."

"Sir Robin," Stephan said, studying Robin to gauge his interest in more than friendly conversation. Robin had light brown hair with flecks of gold, where his own was golden like the sun. Like Stephan, he was tall, but not quite as big as Stephan. He was broad through the chest, but Robin's shoulders were wider than most, his right arm like a small log. This was the knight whose skills with bow were compared to Richard's Welsh mercenaries, a man who could loose three arrows in a charge before seating his lance! Stephan wanted to know more about the handsome rogue. Those arms would feel good wrapped round him, but Robin gave no hint he was inclined to bed men.

Robin gestured towards the manor house commandeered by the duke. "Lord Richard saw you fighting today. Join us. He wants to meet you."

I hope you enjoyed this excerpt from *A Knight's Tale*, a short story about Sir Stephan l'Aigle's early years serving Richard before he became King of England. This tale will be free to my newsletter subscribers later in 2018.

Sign up now to get notified when the story is available: https://charlenenewcomb.com/mailing-list/subscribe-to-my-newsletter/.

Printed in Great Britain
by Amazon